PASSION'S WILDCAT

"It's going to be a long night," he remarked somberly, looking down at the angry young woman whose every breath drove him to distraction. He resisted the temptation to smooth the tangled curls from her forehead. "You may as well relax and get some sleep."

"Sleep? But I thought we were supposed to—to—" She blushed fiercely as her voice trailed away.

"How is it one woman can ask so many questions?" Ben growled. "You've the face of an angel and the temper of a wildcat, Jessamyn Clare," he said, encircling her waist and pulling her against him. "But I'll not be the one to tame you. No, by damn, I will *not*."

"Then let me go," she commanded.

"I think not," he disagreed. His gaze was smoldering with passion's fire. His head lowered relentlessly toward hers. "Damn it, it makes us come alive," he whispered as his lips descended upon hers in a fiery, demanding kiss.

As she clung to him, all thought of resistance fled from her mind, leaving her sweetly pliant for his pleasure— and hers.

CIMARRON BRIDE

CATHERINE CREEL

ZEBRA BOOKS
KENSINGTON PUBLISHING CORP.

ZEBRA BOOKS

are published by

Kensington Publishing Corp.
475 Park Avenue South
New York, NY 10016

First Printing: March, 1989

Printed in the United States of America

*For my children, Caleb and Caitlin.
These two little "Texas Tornadoes"
fill my heart with love—
and keep my head spinning.*

One

Cimarron, New Mexico . . . 1876

"Hell, Mooney, that ain't the way to do it!" The rangy, squint-eyed dissenter shot to his feet and pointed an emphatic if somewhat unsteady finger at the podium. "That ain't the way to do it at all!"

"And just what *is?*" demanded Horace Mooney, his bearded face reddening in anger. All eyes in the crowded, smoke-filled meeting room darted his way before shifting back to the foolhardy citizen who had dared to openly criticize the self-proclaimed most important man in town.

"If'n you'd get off your high horse long enough to take note of what all's been said," Jeb Poole provided smugly, "you'd be able to see there's only one way to get her back."

He paused for effect, his bloodshot eyes gleaming with a mixture of certain knowledge and characteristic devilment while the others waited impatiently for him to provide justification for his bold words. Finally, his mouth curved into a smile of pure satisfaction. He hooked his thumbs in the front pockets of his worn denim trousers and rocked back a bit on the heels of his boots.

"Ben Chandler," he stated simply. It was clear he believed the name itself said it all, for he did not choose to elaborate any further.

"What in tarnation has Chandler got to do with any of this?" Mooney ground out with a furious scowl. "If he gave so much as a tinker's damn about the woman, he'd be here with the rest of us right now!" There was a rumble of agreement from the others.

"Could be he ain't got word yet," Jeb countered with an eloquent shrug of his bony, flannel-clad shoulders. "Could be he—"

"Yeah, well, it *could* be a lot of things, but the fact is our new schoolmarm's gone and gotten herself carried off by those thieving, murdering savages, and we've damned well got to figure out a way to get her back before it's too late!"

Horace Mooney's gaze made a hasty but thorough sweep of the room as he finished this rousing statement. Encouraged to see as well as to hear the expressions of approval from his fellow Cimarronites, he puffed out his chest in a familiar gesture of superiority and declared, "It took us nigh on to a year to find a qualified teacher to fill the position, and I sure as hell don't want to listen to the womenfolk yammering on about it for another year while we try to hook ourselves a replacement!"

"Qualified?" a young cowpoke standing near the doorway challenged with a crooked grin. "You mean *gullible,* don't you?" His insolent remark earned him a glare from the older man, but he was spared any further censure when someone else unexpectedly intervened.

"Seems to me, Mooney, you care a far sight more about the inconvenience of the 'situation' than you do about the woman," observed Will Grant. A kindly faced man in his middle forties, he drew himself to his feet and met Horace Mooney's acrimonious gaze without flinching.

8

"There's not a man here who'd argue that it's our Christian duty to do whatever it takes to get Miss Clare back," Grant went on to say. "Though it's true none of us have ever set eyes on the woman, it still falls to us to take responsibility for her predicament. It's because of us she was on that stage in the first place; it's because of us she's in the hands of those renegades now." He paused for a moment, allowing his eyes to travel across the faces of the men around him before proclaiming firmly, "I agree with Jeb that Ben Chandler's the one to do the job."

"Damn it, man, we can't wait for Chandler!" thundered Mooney, his fist pounding the top of the rough-hewn podium. "It'll be dark soon! We—"

"Hold on, Mooney!" a bespectacled man at the back of the room suddenly piped up. He stood and jerked his head toward Will Grant. "Will's right! No one knows them Apaches like Chandler does!"

"No, and no one knows the high country better, neither!" another member of the group opined with a decisive nod as he, too, rose from his seat. "Hell, there ain't a man in the whole of the Territory who'd stand as much of a chance against them bastards!"

His words were greeted by a loud chorus of harmony, and the air of excitement in the crowded room increased tenfold. Horace Mooney, grinding out a curse, made an angrily desperate attempt to bring the meeting to order once more.

"Sit down and shut up, all of you! I'm in charge here, damn it, and I say—"

"I say we call this dangblasted meetin' to an end and ride on out to Chandler's place!" the young cowpoke suggested with a curt slap of his hat against his leg. Another roar of agreement rose from the men as chairs scraped noisily on the wooden floor and the crowd began surging toward the door.

"*No!*" bellowed Mooney, his features positively livid. "If we're set on asking for help, then we'll ride to Fort

9

Union and—"

"This ain't no matter for the military!" Jeb Poole pronounced with a grimace of disgust. He had made no move to leave with the others. At the sound of his voice, the men grew silent and turned to stare expectantly at both him and Mooney again.

"Soon as they get the news," predicted Jeb, "they'll go chargin' up into the foothills hell-bent for leather, only those redskins'll be long gone afore them pissant pony soldiers get within a mile of their camp! No sir, if you ever want to see that schoolmarm of yours alive, someone'll have to go in after her alone. Someone who—like it's been said—knows the Apache *and* the high country better'n all the rest of us put together." His eyes gleamed with satisfaction once more as the discussion came full circle back to the man he was proud to count as his friend. "Ben Chandler's your only choice."

The crowd erupted into a din of approval again, leaving Horace Mooney to bellow for order and pound uselessly on the podium with his clenched, white-knuckled fist.

Suddenly, the door was flung open. A blast of cool air rushed into the smoky confines of the room as a tall, dark-haired man stood framed in the doorway with the late afternoon sunlight at his back. His fateful appearance was greeted by a quiet roar from the crowd, his name falling from more than two dozen pairs of lips.

The newcomer said nothing while his fathomless cobalt-blue gaze made a deceptively casual sweep of the room. Sizing up the situation in that one brief instant, he gave the ghost of a frown and negligently tugged the hat from his head.

"Heard you'd called an emergency meeting of the board," he declared in a low, deep-timbred voice that was as thoroughly masculine as the rest of him. "What's the emergency?"

The question had been directed at Horace Mooney,

10

whose eyes became mere slits in his bearded, hotly flushed face. He had never liked Ben Chandler, not in all the years he'd known him. As a matter of fact, he'd always found himself unaccountably riled whenever the other man was around. Whether it was because Chandler's superior size and attractiveness made him feel downright puny and homely, or because Chandler seemed to be damned near perfect at everything he set out to do, Horace didn't know. But whatever the reason, he couldn't look the handsome young rancher in the eye without feeling the familiar anger well up deep inside him. It had become a habit—and habits are not easily broken.

"You're late, Chandler!" he snapped. "I sent word out to your place more than two hours ago!"

"I was hard to find." It was offered as a simple statement of fact, not as either excuse or apology, and several of the onlookers smiled briefly in appreciation before Jeb Poole spoke up again.

"The noon stage was attacked," Jeb told the man who had been both steady friend and sometime employer throughout the past five years. "Apaches." He added this last with a terse nod, his gaze locking with Ben's in silent understanding.

"Anyone killed?" Ben asked quietly, his sun-bronzed features tightening while his eyes gleamed with a dangerously fierce light.

"Nope. But the poor sonofabitch driver's laid up over at the line office with an arrow stuck in his ribs. There weren't nothin' left of the coach but ashes by the time he was found." Jeb took one of his infamous pauses before relating the most important detail of all. "The new schoolmarm was on that stage."

"Schoolmarm?" Ben Chandler's brow creased into a scowl as realization dawned on him. *Damn it, he'd forgotten all about the woman!*

11

"Yes—schoolmarm!" Mooney interjected harshly. "You were there when I read her letter of acceptance to the board, remember? It's been known for more than a month she was due to arrive today! Only she won't *be* arriving! She was carried off by those same yellow-bellied, bloodthirsty heathens you're on such damned good terms with, and now we—"

"How do you know it was Gray Wolf's band?" demanded Ben. His voice held an undeniable edge, his gaze taking on the look of cold steel.

"Because the driver recognized the leader of the bastards, that's how!"

"It was Gray Wolf all right," Jeb reluctantly confirmed. "There weren't no mistakin' the description." An ironic little smile touched his lips. "Hell no, there ain't many Apache bucks standin' more'n six feet tall and wearin' a fancy silver belt buckle with a wolf on it."

Although the rugged perfection of Ben's features remained inscrutable, his eyes clouded with the sudden pain of remembrance. He had given his Apache "brother" the buckle as a token of friendship some years back. That had been only a short time before he had brought his pretty new bride to the same wild, strangely enchanting country where a raw young recruit had become a man—and where fate had made him a part of the Territory's turbulent future.

Emily. For one brief moment, the time-blurred image of her face rose in his mind. . . .

"Mooney there wants to call in the troops," he became dimly aware of a gray-haired man near the podium informing him. "But most of us think you're our best hope. You're the only one who has any real chance of coming back alive, Chandler. You know it and so do we. That's why we're asking you to go after her."

There was a rumble of renewed agreement amongst

the crowd. The sense of urgency and excitement increased to a fever pitch once more, leaving Horace Mooney to growl low in his throat and appear on the verge of apoplexy.

"No, damn you, *no!* As president of the school board, I insist we—"

"This ain't the sole concern of the school board, Mooney!" the young cowpoke exclaimed as he tugged the front brim of his hat lower on his head. "I ain't got no young'uns of my own, but that don't mean I aim to stand by and let them damned redskins make off with a white woman! Now let's quit all this yammerin' about the cavalry and get on with what's got to be done! Either Chandler agrees to go up after her alone, or else the rest of us'll damn well ride to it!" he vowed with all the reckless courage of his youth and inexperience.

Every eye in the room once again fastened on the man in question, a strong and resolute man who towered nearly a full head above those around him—a man clearly destined to carry out the task before him.

"Will you do it, Ben?" Will Grant was the one to finally put it in the form of a request. His pale green gaze was full of somber entreaty. "There's no denying you'll be risking your own life, but—"

"You already know the answer, Will," Ben quietly cut him off. His movements were steady and unhurried as he replaced the hat atop his head and moved his steely gaze back to Horace Mooney. There was no need for words between them. They understood one another perfectly as their gazes locked in silent combat.

"I knew he'd do it!" one of the onlookers proclaimed, his broad smile holding both triumph and relief.

"Ben Chandler's never been one to shy away from trouble, that's for damn sure!" another man heartily opined.

The room was thereupon filled with a loud refrain of

13

male voices as others in the crowd joined in to add their own enthusiastic votes of confidence. Following the natural progression of things, there came a round of well wishes and unsolicited advice for the only man in town with enough skill and experience—and enough courage —to venture into the midst of the Indians with essentially nothing more than his wits to protect him.

To say that there was a single soul envious of Ben Chandler at that particular moment would be a lie; indeed, there were some present who, if truth be known, seriously doubted the likelihood of his safe return. But they wanted the schoolteacher they'd paid for, they wanted swift justice, and above all else, they wanted to see "that snake-livered sonofabitch Gray Wolf" bested by one of their own. The clever Apache warrior and his small band of renegades had eluded capture for years, a fact that had become an increasingly sore point with both the soldiers at Fort Union and the good citizens of Cimarron.

Ben Chandler, trailed by the still excitedly buzzing crowd, strode silently back outside into the fading sunlight. He unlooped the reins from the hitching post and swung up onto his mount. His bronzed, chiseled features betrayed nothing of his feelings, while his deep blue eyes remained equally unfathomable. Sitting tall in the saddle, he looked every inch the virile, fiercely independent rancher he was—a far cry from the callow young soldier he had once been.

"Take care and watch your scalp," cautioned Jeb Poole, flashing him a gap-toothed grin.

"Get word to Martha for me."

It was more of a command than a request, but Jeb was by now thoroughly accustomed to the other man's way of ordering others about. He'd always put it down to the fact that Ben had never quite left his years of military training behind him. *Yes, sir, once a blue back always a blue back,* he mused, his eyes full of mingled affection and

14

admiration for his friend.

"If you've not returned by sunrise tomorrow," Will Grant said as Ben prepared to rein about, "we'll have no choice but to notify the Army."

"Army, hell!" disagreed the same cowpoke who had urged the crowd on with such youthful fervor a few moments ago. Still feeling brave, he folded his arms across his chest and struck a decidedly cocksure pose. "If he ain't back by then, *we'll* come lookin' for him!"

"Give me two days," Ben decreed quietly, the merest suggestion of a smile playing about his lips in response to the younger man's brashness.

Will, who knew better than to argue with Ben Chandler once he'd made up his mind, nodded in mute agreement and watched as Ben gave an almost imperceptible tug on the reins. The sleek, magnificently formed Appaloosa beneath him snorted softly and tossed its head in a show of spirit before obeying the unspoken command.

The two dozen men standing on the boardwalk watched in thoughtful silence as their "best hope" rode away. When he was almost out of sight they began to disperse, the majority of them wisely calling it a day and returning home to their families, while the remainder turned their steps toward the familiar bastion of Lambert's Saloon.

Horace Mooney waited until everyone was gone, then stepped outside and looked southward. He squinted his eyes, just able to make out the solitary horse and rider growing smaller in the wind-swept distance.

"Damn you, Chandler, you're a dead man for sure this time!" he prophesied in a seething undertone.

The thought, surprisingly enough, gave him little comfort. He cursed again and set off for his brand-new mercantile at the other end of the street, unable to shake the unpleasant memory of other battles with the damnably perfect Ben Chandler.

The object of Horace Mooney's inexplicable wrath, meanwhile, tossed a quick glance overhead at the brilliant blue sky. With any luck, Ben mused as his sun-kissed brow creased into a pensive frown, he'd make it to Gray Wolf's camp before nightfall. And if his luck held, he'd not only be able to strike a bargain with the Apaches for the woman's release, but would also be on his way back to town with her before news of the renegades' attack even reached Fort Union.

He shifted in the saddle and pulled his hat lower on his dark head, his thoughts returning to the meeting he had interrupted a short time earlier. If a long-standing tradition of the frontier had been followed, the military would have been called in without delay. But, he reflected while his eyes took on a particularly hard glint once again, tradition had more and more of late been put aside in favor of vigilante justice.

At least when a man took matters into his own hands, he had a pretty good idea of what the outcome would be.

It wasn't so much a question of the soldiers being unwilling, or even incapable, of doing what was needed, but rather one of stupid political wrangling. The cavalry could not effectively patrol the Territory when its troops were engaged in performing duties that held little or no significance for the beleaguered settlers.

But in this particular case, Ben Chandler told himself as his piercing blue gaze was now drawn across the broad pasturelands to the beckoning peaks of the Sangre de Cristo Mountains, it didn't matter. Just as Jeb Poole and the others had concluded, the only way to get the schoolteacher back was for him to ride into Gray Wolf's camp alone, unarmed, and pray like hell that the friendship he and the Apache had once shared still counted for something. . . .

*   *   *

16

Jessamyn Clare, striving valiantly to gather her fleeting courage about her, huddled in one dark corner of the wickiup and kept her wide emerald-green eyes fastened on the opposite side of the circular skin tent. The opening was covered by a loose flap of hide, through which periodically one of the older squaws would duck inside in yet another futile attempt to coax the beautiful golden-haired captive into eating.

Another wave of revulsion shook her as she glanced down at the small wooden bowl on the dirt floor beside her. The dwindling firelight revealed a chunk of meat—the likes of which she could not readily identify—surrounded by a corn mush flavored with a dark, strong-smelling grease. There were no utensils with which to eat the food, but their lack did not bother Jessie. Even had she been the least bit hungry, her churning stomach would never have allowed her to keep the meal down.

Accompanying the bowl of food was a second one filled with a liquid, which was not water but rather a fermented drink called *tiz-win*. It was this unclarified, highly potent liquor, made from corn, that both male and female members of the band had been drinking since the warriors' return from the day's successful raid. As a result, the Indians had grown increasingly boisterous in their celebration, their laughter and song and cries of triumph echoing stridently throughout the moonlit mountain camp.

"Dear God, I cannot bear it!" Jessie whispered brokenly. She fought back a fresh onslaught of tears and covered her ears in a desperate attempt to shut out the awful sound of her captors' revelry.

Now, now, Jessie girl, you can bear anything you have to. The memory of those words, spoken often yet so very long ago by her beloved grandmother, returned now in her hour of need to comfort her and give her strength. *You can bear anything you have to. . . .*

Relaxing her tensed muscles a bit, she unwound her arms from about her knees and climbed shakily to her feet. The skirts of her blue silk traveling suit, once so stylish and immaculate—as befitting a new school-teacher on her way to her first post—fell in dirty, tattered folds about her legs.

She was grateful for the warmth and protection of her jacket; only that morning she had buttoned it primly over her white linen, lace-collared blouse, but it was now entirely buttonless and ripped at the sleeves. The pins had fallen from her hair during the violent struggle she had set up against her raucously laughing abductors, so that the long, golden brown curls hung down about her face and shoulders in a wild cascade tangled with twigs and leaves.

Other than the damage to her appearance, the only real injuries she had suffered thus far as a result of her terrifying ordeal were a few minor scratches and bruises—nothing at all when compared to what she had seen happen to the poor driver. She shuddered anew at the memory of the way he had screamed with pain as the arrow ripped through his body. The last she had seen of him, he had been slumped on the ground beside the burning stagecoach, his face contorted in agony. She had never witnessed such suffering before, nor had she felt anything to compare with what she had felt upon being seized by a half-naked savage and thrown across his horse.

Fervently wishing there were someone else to share her captivity—and cursing herself for the selfishness of her wish—she once again bemoaned the absence of fellow passengers. The young couple who had ridden with her as far as Raton had stayed behind at the station to wait for a different stage, while the man who usually rode shotgun had been called away from the Clifton House at first light. That had left only the driver to provide her with both company and protection as they set off through the very heart of some of the fiercest Indian country ever traveled by white men.

It had been utter folly for the stagecoach to make its run without benefit of an armed escort. There had been no real defense against the dozen or more Apache braves who had appeared out of nowhere and thundered down upon them. No, Jessie recalled as a sob of anguished defeat welled up in her throat, fighting back had proven useless. . . .

No doubt Lillian will be pleased to learn that her worst predictions came true after all, she suddenly found herself musing, a twist of grim humor creeping into the midst of her fear and despair.

"Lillian," she repeated the name of her stepmother aloud, her voice tremulous and edged with the same contradictory mixture of resentment and tolerance she had always felt for the woman who had sought to take her mother's place.

The thought evoked painfully vivid images of home and family. St. Louis seemed a world away. Was it possible she had been gone only a few weeks? she asked herself as she began to pace about the dimly lit confines of the small frame hut. Why, oh *why* hadn't she listened to her father's and everyone else's objections? Why had she been so blindly, so recklessly determined?

A glorious calling, she had termed it, this burning desire of hers to bring truth and knowledge to the children in the wilderness. She could remember all too well the day she had told her family of her shocking, ultimately disastrous plans. . . .

"You're going to do *what?*" demanded Richard Clare in stunned disbelief, looking at his daughter as if she had just been struck with insanity.

"I am going to teach school. In New Mexico Territory. A place called Cimarron," Jessie calmly reiterated.

She faced her father and stepmother in the parlor, where the three of them had retired after their usual quiet Sunday dinner at home. The only member of the family missing from the familiar domestic scene was Jessie's younger brother, Andrew, who had already given her plan his wholly enthusiastic blessing before taking himself off to engage in a secret round of baseball. Richard Clare, it seemed, did not approve of any physical activity other than a good brisk walk in the park.

"Surely you cannot be serious," Lillian protested with an indulgent little smile. She carefully arranged her London-smoke skirts about her on the silk brocade settee and smiled again. A handsome woman with dark red hair and a flawless complexion, she was nearly a decade younger than her distinguished gray-haired husband. "Young ladies of your beauty and breeding should not be entertaining such absurdly fanciful notions. No indeed, my dear Jessamyn, you should instead concern yourself with making an advantageous marriage before you find yourself in the unenviable position of being too old to do so."

"It is *not* a ridiculous notion, Lillian, and I am perfectly serious!" insisted Jessie, her green eyes flashing as she abruptly stood and moved to take a defiant stance before the fireplace. As always, it was difficult for her to control her temper whenever the other woman introduced the subject of marriage. It had been a source of controversy between them for longer than she cared to remember. "And since I have already reached the advanced age of two and twenty, then perhaps you had best resign yourself to the truth once and for all. I have no desire to remain here and become a—a *parlor decoration* for some man while there is a need for my particular talents elsewhere!"

"And what are these *particular talents* of which you speak?" Lillian challenged after exchanging a knowing look with her husband.

His wife's refusal to lend any credence to Jessie's startling announcement helped to make Richard Clare's worried brow clear somewhat. Since his marriage to the attractive widow some eight years ago, it had suited him to leave the raising of his headstrong daughter almost entirely in her hands. He considered Lillian an eminently wise and capable woman; it had never really occurred to him that what Jessie needed most was *his* attention.

"In the event you have forgotten," she answered, her voice full of mingled pride and resentment, "I received my teaching certificate several months ago. You have known of my intention to teach school for some time now. The academy was more than willing to help me find a post here in St. Louis, but I happened upon an advertisement in the newspaper recently and I . . . well, I offered a response."

"The devil you say!" exclaimed her father. His face had suddenly become flushed with anger, prompting Lillian to rise and cross swiftly to his side. She placed a soothing hand upon his arm, her gaze cold and full of reproach as she looked across at her stepdaughter.

"You should not have done such a thing, Jessamyn," she admonished sternly. "Good heavens, think of the scandal should anyone find out you were so lost to propriety that you—"

"I don't care a fig about any scandal! My actions achieved the exact results I had hoped for! The board in Cimarron wrote back without delay to let me know that I have been engaged as their new schoolteacher on the basis of my impressive credentials alone. They not only sent me an advance against my first year's salary, but they have also made all the necessary arrangements for my journey there!"

21

"This has gone far enough, young lady!" snapped Richard Clare. He pulled free of Lillian's restraining hand and stalked across the room to confront his wayward daughter. "You will write another letter, *this* time informing the good people of Cimarron that you will be unable to accept the post they have so generously granted you! By damn, I will not have any daughter of mine going to that godforsaken country to teach a bunch of wild, heathenish—"

"I am no longer a child, Father!" Jessie vehemently cut him off. Her eyes glistened with hot tears as her own temper flared to a dangerous level. "I have every right to do whatever I please in this matter—and it pleases me to accept the post!"

"But, my dear," Lillian came rustling forward to intervene with a conciliatory smile at her, "what about Franklin? Have you told him of your plans?"

"Franklin Barringer has nothing to do with this!" denied Jessie, her eyes ablaze with emerald fire now.

"Doesn't he? Why, the poor boy has been in love with you for years! And the Barringers have made no secret of the fact that they desire you as a daughter-in-law. Come now, isn't the prospect of marriage to Franklin much more appealing than this impulsive madness of teaching school amidst a horde of savages?"

"As I have told you time and again, I do not love Franklin! Nothing would ever compel me to marry without love, whether the marriage was to my *advantage* or not!"

"Nevertheless, I will not allow you to proceed with this foolhardy scheme!" proclaimed her father, his hands closing tightly about her upper arms. He shook her a bit for emphasis as he said, in a low voice edged with paternal fury, "You are a Clare, and the Clares do not abandon their duty to family and society! You will do as I say, Jessamyn, do you understand? You will forget all about

22

Cimarron and turn your mind completely to fulfilling your duties here!" His fingers clenched upon her soft, unprotected flesh until she was forced to stifle a cry.

"I knew I should never have allowed you to attend that blasted academy!" he continued to rage. "I believed it to be a passing whim of yours, all this foolish talk of teaching and independence and making your own way in the world! Your head has become filled with utter nonsense; what you need is a husband to keep you under control!"

"No, Father, what I *need* is a life of my own!" she countered defiantly. Finally allowing her heart to rule her head, she found herself pouring forth all the pent-up anguish of the past eight years. "Ever since Mother died, I have been doing my absolute best to please you, to make you proud of me, to make you love me! Well, no more, do you hear? No more!"

She jerked away from him and took a step backward, the tears spilling over from her lashes to stream unheeded down her face. When she spoke again, her voice was fairly choked with emotion.

"I am tired of trying to live up to your expectations, tired of playing the dutiful daughter and feeling increasingly useless! I have betrayed my own instincts too long!"

Her heart twisted at the spasm of pain that crossed her father's face. They had engaged in a battle of wills all too frequently over the years, but this was of far more significance than their other skirmishes. For Jessie, the teaching job in Cimarron represented a chance to meet her destiny, to escape the stifling, orderly existence she had always known. *It was now or never.* She took a deep breath and attempted to explain more calmly.

"For more than two years, I have recognized in myself the desire to educate. Long before I attended the academy, I was aware of it. I am sorry if you believed it a

23

passing whim; for me, it is a calling. The moment I set eyes on the advertisement, I knew I had to go to Cimarron. Don't you see? I'll be going where I am needed, where a great deal more will be required of me than merely gracing my father's house and stitching a fancy seam!"

"No, Jessamyn, I do not see!" he responded. "If you think for one moment I am going to allow one of my own flesh and blood—"

"It is not up to you to *allow* me anything! I love you, Father, but I—I must follow my own counsel. I will be leaving in one week's time."

"If you go through with this," Richard Clare warned stonily, his manner devoid of any warmth, "you may rest assured you will never find an ounce of forgiveness in me!"

"Richard!" gasped Lillian in horror. "You cannot mean that!"

"But I do," he insisted, his aristocratic features growing coldly impassive. "I mean every word of it. If Jessamyn defies me in this, I will force myself to forget I ever had a daughter. As she has so aptly pointed out, I am powerless to stop her. And she stubbornly refuses to listen to reason." His eyes, full of a harsh light, flickered briefly to his wife before returning to fasten upon his unrepentant daughter. "She refuses to consider my feelings—or yours—and therefore must reap the consequences of her actions."

"Oh, Father, will you not at least *try* and understand. . . ." Jessie implored him.

"There is nothing more to be said between us," he brusquely cut her off. "I can only pray that you will come to your senses before it is too late."

With that, he walked stiffly from the room. The front door opened and closed an instant later, giving evidence of the fact that he had gone off to be alone with his anger and disappointment.

Staring after him, Jessie became lost in her own troubled thoughts. Several long moments had passed before she remembered her stepmother. She glanced up, surprised to find Lillian suffering from an uncharacteristic loss for words. The gazes of the two women met and locked, while a highly charged silence rose up between them.

"Don't worry, my dear," Lillian finally said by way of solace, though her words were noticeably lacking in conviction. "I'm quite sure that, after he's had time to think things over a bit, he will relent."

"Will he?" murmured Jessie. Her mouth curved into a faint smile of bitter irony before she turned to stare down into the wide, freshly scrubbed marble fireplace. "Will he indeed?"

"But then," added Lillian thoughtfully, "it is to be hoped you will reconsider before too much damage is done."

"Damage?"

"To your reputation of course. Surely, my dear, you must see that this *situation* of yours will soon become the talk of the town. Why, it certainly isn't every day that the daughter of Richard Clare, one of the wealthiest and most influential men in St. Louis, runs away to teach school in the wild West! Have you given any thought to what will happen should you decide you wish to return home?" She sighed for effect and drifted over to idly finger the lace curtains at the window. "I daresay even Franklin Barringer will not have you then. No man wants a wife who is so publicly willful and impulsive."

"I don't care what any man wants!" cried Jessie in exasperation. She opened her mouth to say more, but thought better of it and instead whirled about to leave. Lillian's voice momentarily halted her flight.

"You may very well find yourself carried off by

Indians, who will scalp you—or worse. If you will not think of your family, Jessamyn, then think of yourself! I beg of you, my dear, for your own sake, consider the terrible dangers you will be facing. Of what use will you be to the world if you are dead?"

"Of what use am I now?" she retorted, then smiled briefly at the other woman to soften the effect. "For better or worse, Lillian, I have made my decision. I am going to Cimarron."

In the end, of course, that is what she had done, in spite of the desperate, last-minute attempts of both her father and stepmother to dissuade her. As the train pulled away from the station that bright summer day in St. Louis, Andrew had grinned broadly and waved, Lillian had gently dabbed at her eyes with a silk handkerchief, and Richard Clare had stood tall and straight on the platform while fighting the urge to call after the daughter he loved with all his heart but had never been able to reach. . . .

Jessie heaved a long, ragged sigh and smoothed a trembling hand across the tear-streaked smoothness of her cheeks. Thinking of home and loved ones made her heart ache unbearably and made her predicament seem all the more horrible.

Although she tried not to speculate upon what the Indians meant to do with her, she could not help wondering if this night would be her last. She had read graphic, sickeningly gruesome stories of the terrible fates suffered by captives like herself. Unaware of the fact that the Jicarilla Apaches did not commit the same barbarous atrocities upon their victims as did other tribes—unless revenge was involved, that is—and abhorred any mutilation such as scalping, she naturally feared that this manner of torture might be visited upon her.

You can bear anything you have to. She repeated the words over and over to herself, dismayed to feel panic gripping her once more.

"Dear God, what am I to do?" she pleaded aloud. The sounds of the ongoing celebration burned in her ears, the pounding cadence of the drums beating the terrible, paralyzing anticipation ever farther into her brain.

"Ink-tah!"

Jessie started in alarm at the voice and spun about to discover that the same old woman who had brought her the food had ducked inside again. The squaw was wearing a loosely belted garment of deerskin, with her gray-streaked black hair hanging in braids on either side of her round, weathered brown face. Her expression was one of stern impatience.

"Ink-tah!" she repeated.

While Jessie could only stand and stare at her blankly, the woman muttered something beneath her breath and ambled forward across the dimly lit hut. She offered no warning of her intentions before she seized Jessie's arms in a suprisingly strong grip and jerked her down upon her knees.

"Let go of me!" cried Jessie angrily, her indignation bringing a spark of courage to the fore. She was tempted to rise again but sensed correctly that her defiance would only serve to bring even rougher treatment.

The squaw said nothing in response. Instead, she snatched up the bowl of food and thrust it into the younger woman's hands, punctuating her actions with a guttural command that clearly meant *eat.* Jessie shook her head.

"No! No, I—I am not hungry!" she insisted. Without pausing to consider the wisdom of her actions, she tossed the bowl aside. It landed upended, its unappetizing contents spilling onto the dirt.

At that point, the old woman evidently lost all patience

with her charge. Her features grew ugly, and she compressed her lips into a thin line of anger as she raised her hand to deliver a stinging blow to the rebellious prisoner's cheek.

A shocked Jessie had no time to react. A breathless cry broke from her lips when she was hit. She felt herself tumbling backward to lie sprawled upon the hard earth, where she lay stunned for several moments. Then, hurriedly pushing herself back up into a sitting position, she swept the wildly streaming hair away from her face. Her eyes narrowed in vengeful outrage when they fell upon her tormentor, who was already escaping outside again.

"Damn you!" muttered Jessie, the rarely spoken malediction falling from her lips with remarkable ease. Bringing a hand up to her swollen cheek, she climbed to her feet and crossed to the opening. She cautiously drew aside one edge of the flap and peered outward.

She found that twilight had by now deepened into the cool, clear darkness of a late summer night. Her wide, anxious gaze flew to the huge fire in the center of the camp, where the flames danced toward the sky and cast eerie shadows over the faces of the Apaches who ringed the crackling blaze. Men, women, and children alike were gathered to give thanks for their good fortune; in truth, the six horses captured by their braves were valued far above the single human captive.

Blissfully unaware of the fact that Gray Wolf had decided to keep her for himself, Jessie's frightened eyes sought out the face of the tall, solidly built warrior who was obviously the leader of the renegades. A shiver ran the length of her spine when she caught sight of him, for he was without a doubt the most fearsome-looking man she had ever seen.

He stood a full head above his comrades, the firelight playing across his broad, harshly chiseled features. Like the other men, he wore his course black hair in two long braids, while his muscular body was encased in a pair of tight breeches, a fringed deerskin jacket, and a pair of beaded moccasins with high buckskin tops. He was not yet thirty, Jessie surmised dazedly, her eyes drawn back up to his face. There was an undeniably cruel set to his mouth, and the fierce light in his dark eyes made her breath catch in her throat. She was about to tear her gaze away when she noticed the silver belt buckle gleaming at his waist.

In the center of the buckle was etched a wolf. Jessie thought it strange that an Indian should be wearing something that so clearly belonged to the white man's world. She gave it no further thought, however, for at that moment her attention was suddenly and quite effectively forced elsewhere.

Without warning, the old woman returned. The squaw pushed her unceremoniously away from the opening while ranting at her in the Apache tongue. Jessie drew herself rigidly upright and glared down at the woman.

"Keep your hands off me, you evil-tempered savage! If I am to die, then I will at least do so with dignity!" she declared with a great deal more bravado than she actually felt.

Her words, or rather the boldly defiant manner in which she uttered them, achieved a startling effect. The old woman suddenly fell silent and grinned from ear to ear. She said something else, chuckled quietly, then left.

Jessie stared after her in complete bewilderment. She sank wearily down beside the dying blaze and tried without success to bring order to the chaos that was her mind. Her nerves felt raw and strained to the outermost limit, and she was dismayed to feel hysterical laughter rising up within her. Covering her face with her hands, she found herself unable to hold back the flow of tears. She was almost beyond caring what happened to her, almost beyond caring about anything. In that moment, she would gladly have chosen eternal sleep over the merciless uncertainty that was tearing her apart.

How long she remained like that she could not say. The next thing she knew, the old squaw was ducking inside again with a much younger and prettier woman at her side. The two of them urged the exhausted captive to her feet and led her quickly outside.

Emerging into the cool fragrance of the mountain air, Jessie numbly realized that the drums had stopped. In fact, all noise had stopped. She looked up to find nearly fifty pairs of eyes fastened upon her in the silence of the moonlit night. Her heart leapt in alarm while her face paled. Trembling violently from head to toe, she was afraid her legs would give way beneath her.

Dear God, please help me! her mind screamed. *Please don't let me die!*

If not for the supporting arm of the younger squaw about her shoulders, she would of a certainty have crumpled to the ground. She could do nothing more than gaze helplessly across at the sea of solemn, bronzed faces before her.

Then, the miracle Jessamyn Clare had been praying for stepped forward.

Two

Jessie's eyes grew very wide. *It was a white man!*

She bit at her lower lip to stifle a sob of joy. The most profound relief she had ever known washed over her, setting her head to spinning and her heart to pounding within her breast. Although she could scarcely make out the face of the man who was emerging from the shadows into the fire's revealing glow, she never doubted for a moment that he had come to save her.

"This woman is the one?" Gray Wolf asked of the tall stranger. The young Apache chief stood only a short distance away from Jessie, his dark, hawkish eyes darting suspiciously back and forth between the golden-haired captive and the man who had once been his friend.

"She is the one," Ben Chandler confirmed quietly. There was nothing in his deep, resonant voice to betray the half-truth, nor did he allow any trace of emotion to cross his face. His steady gaze, while taking on the appearance of cold steel, narrowed imperceptibly as it raked over Jessie.

Damn! he swore inwardly. Instead of the sour, pinch-featured old maid he had expected to find, he saw instead a girl with the face of an angel. Her beauty was clearly discernible in spite of her pitifully bedraggled appear-

31

ance, he thought, his eyes drawn to the alluring curves evident beneath the torn and dirty blue silk. The fact that she was both young and comely would make his task even more difficult, for it was unlikely Gray Wolf would surrender such a captive without a great deal of resistance.

She looked to be little more than a child, Ben mused to himself, the vengeful fury inside him blazing stronger with each passing second. His blood boiled at the sight of the dark purplish bruise on her face. In that moment, he would have gladly killed the person who had caused her pain.

Finally, his unfathomable blue gaze met the round, luminous green depths of hers. Her terror-stricken eyes pleaded silently with him to help her, while she trembled visibly in the tight, restraining grasp of the squaws.

Ben Chandler was surprised to feel a sharp twinge in his heart, surprised to discover he could be so affected by a woman who was nothing more than a stranger to him. It both confused and annoyed him to realize that the iron control he usually maintained over his emotions had given way. *What was there about the girl that stirred his heart, that prompted him to feel this fierce protectiveness toward her?*

"You are certain?" probed Gray Wolf, referring again to the disputed identity of the captive. It was obvious he was far from convinced of the other man's claim.

"I am certain," Ben reiterated firmly.

He had as yet to remove the hat from his head, so that all Jessie could see in the golden firelight were the shadowy planes of his face. Her bright, anxious gaze fastened on the strong, chiseled mouth and chin of her rescuer, and she found herself wondering if he had perhaps been among the men she had glimpsed working at the station earlier that day. It never occurred to her that he was anything other than an employee of the

32

stagecoach line, nor that he had come alone. She assumed there were others waiting nearby, and she wondered dazedly why they did not come forward as well.

In spite of the fear that held her in its grip, she had immediately been struck by the way the tall cowboy carried himself, for it was with an easy masculine grace that bespoke unwavering confidence. *He did not seem afraid.* Gaining strength from his courage, she unconsciously squared her shoulders and held her head higher.

The stranger's next words brought a hot, telltale flush to her cheeks and a gasp of startlement from her lips.

"The woman is mine," declared Ben, his voice strong and clear above the crackling of the fire and gentle rustling of the leaves. He met Gray Wolf's dark, penetrating gaze squarely and uttered the lie once more. "She is mine."

Jessie had the good sense to say nothing. Her eyes, round as saucers in the delicate oval of her face, flew to the Apache leader, then back to the other man. *Good heavens, why had he said such a thing?*

"Our white brother has no woman!" contended one of the young braves standing beside Gray Wolf. He grunted in disdain and jerked his head toward Ben. "There is none but the old one in his house. . . . I myself have seen this and know it to be true!"

"He is not our brother!" hissed Gray Wolf. It was a pointed reminder that the good will that had once existed between the Apache and Blue Eagle, as Ben had been called, was no more. The bond had been broken by not one thing, but many, and could never be healed.

"Still, you have allowed him to come into our *go-tah* unharmed," an old man interjected with a faint, wryly indulgent smile at Gray Wolf. He, too, had once possessed the young chief's hatred of the white invaders. But now that he was passing into the winter of his life, he no longer fought against the inevitable. There was, after all, he had consoled

33

himself, honor to be found in the wisdom of acceptance. "He has come in peace; let him speak and deny Standing Bear's charge if he can."

Gray Wolf, although visibly angered by the old man's interference, held his tongue and sliced his burning gaze back to Ben. Everyone else did the same, waiting for the white man's response. A baby cried and was quickly hushed by its mother. The solemn group assembled about the dancing flames looked vastly different from the one that only minutes earlier, had been laughing and singing with such gleeful abandon.

Jessie's pulses leapt in renewed alarm. Her frightened gaze traveled swiftly over the faces of the Indians before coming to rest on Ben. *Please God, help him!* she prayed silently, holding her breath. He had to say the right thing. . . . He had to!

If she had been closer to him, she would have been able to glimpse the almost savage light of determination in his eyes. There had been only one other time in Ben Chandler's life that he had been forced to lie to the proud, fiercely independent people who had befriended him—and that occasion had resulted in disaster. He would not fail again, he vowed, his brain already choosing the words.

"Standing Bear speaks the truth," he readily admitted to Gray Wolf. His handsome features remained impassive, and his manner was deceptively nonchalant. "Until now, there has been only the old woman—a kinswoman—at my house. But that has changed." He paused for a moment and allowed his eyes to wander toward Jessie again. Giving a curt nod in her direction, he proclaimed, "The woman you hold captive is my bride. She was on her way to join me when you attacked the stage today."

Bride? Jessie's mind echoed in astonished silence. Taken aback by the man's bold falsehood, she hurried to regain her composure. She immediately realized that she had to play along with the lie, and she groaned inwardly in dismay at the thought, for she had never been any good at lying. Even as a child, she had been unable to deceive anyone for more than a few minutes time. Still, she told herself as she swallowed hard and lifted her chin in an unconscious gesture of proud defiance, this was a matter of life and death—*and she meant to live!*

"Thank God you have come!" she finally breathed, her words no lie but the wholehearted truth. She struggled against the hands that held her and dramatically exclaimed to the tall stranger, "Oh, my love, I—I feared I would never see you again!"

Mingled satisfaction and amusement lit Ben's eyes for only an instant before he turned back to Gray Wolf and scowled darkly, "Tell them to let her go." It was a command, not a request.

For a moment, it appeared the Apache leader would refuse. If the menacing look in his eyes was any indication, he was battling the urge to react with violence. For too long now, he had been master of his own fate; it enraged him that a white man, even one who was a former friend, would order him about as though he were a squaw. Still, he forced himself to control his bitter indignation. He was of a mind to toy with Chandler and the woman; it would be amusing to watch them try and outsmart him.

Gray Wolf uttered a terse command to the two squaws holding the captive. They obeyed without hesitation, their hands dropping to their sides. Stumbling a bit as she was released, Jessie hastily gathered up her skirts and flew across the clearing to Ben.

Without a word, he reached out and drew her close, his strong arm slipping about her waist in what appeared to be a familiar embrace. Her eyes swept closed while she leaned gratefully against his hard warmth. As if by

35

instinct, her own arms lifted to him, her fingers curling tightly about the corded muscles of his neck. She choked back a sob and turned her face to the broad, powerfully muscled expanse of his chest in a desperate attempt to shut out, if for only a moment, the horrifying danger that still threatened her.

"Courage, Miss Clare," Ben murmured in an undertone close to her ear, as though he were whispering an endearment instead of a stern exhortation. "No hysterics—not yet."

Jessie, brought back to reality by his words, opened her eyes and tilted her head back to look up at him. She inhaled upon a soft gasp when she beheld the solemn, remarkably handsome visage beneath the hat. Able to see his face clearly for the first time, she was immediately struck by the fact that he was much younger than she had thought. But it was the rugged perfection of his sunbronzed features that caused her eyes to widen in stunned astonishment.

Never in her life had she seen a man to compare with the one who clasped her trembling curves against the length of his virile, muscular body. He was so thoroughly, undeniably masculine—not at all like the young men she had known back in St. Louis.

There is not even a trace of softness about him, Jessie mused light-headedly, unaware that she was still holding her breath. She felt incredibly safe and secure in his possessive embrace. In spite of the fact that the two of them were standing in the midst of an Indian camp, her confidence in his ability to save her burned even brighter in her heart. *This man will let nothing stop him,* she told herself in wonderment, though she could not say why she knew it to be true.

Raising her startled eyes to his at last, she felt a sharp tremor course through her body. The tall, handsome stranger was staring intently down at her, the golden firelight reflected in his magnificent blue eyes while his arm tightened about her slender waist. His gaze, so deep and unfathomable, seemed to bore through to her very soul. . . .

"Why is it you have taken another woman to wife *now*, Chandler?" Gray Wolf suddenly demanded, his lips curling into a sneer. "Many moons have passed since—"

"It was time," Ben cut him off tersely.

Jessie could feel the way his entire body tensed, and her eyes anxiously searched his face for any sign of what was wrong. She was thrown into further confusion when he finally elaborated.

"A man grows weary of life alone," he told Gray Wolf in a quiet, deep-timbred voice that was nonetheless clearly audible above the fire's roar. "It was time to bury the past."

Bury the past? Jessie echoed silently. *Chandler*, she then repeated his name in her mind. Her wide, luminous green eyes lifted to Ben's face again before flying to Gray Wolf. She felt a sudden pang of alarm when she noticed the foreboding devilment gleaming in the Apache's dark gaze.

"The words you speak are true enough, Chandler," allowed the renegade leader smoothly, "but how is it you have taken a wife without leaving your home?" His question brought a snicker of scornful amusement from several of the other men, as well as knowing smiles from the women.

"It is a white man's custom to choose a wife from the land of his birth when he cannot be troubled to leave his home. My bride and I have known one another many years. I wrote to her and asked her to join me."

"Ah," replied Gray Wolf. He paused and allowed his gaze, full of malevolent humor, to encompass his people. When he turned back to Ben, his eyes narrowed and his mouth curved into a faint smile of unmistakable

37

challenge. "Then you and your 'bride' have not yet been joined as husband and wife?"

"Not yet," admitted Ben, telling himself that a little truth always made a lie more believable. He glanced down at the beautiful young woman he was holding and declared, in a voice laced with steel, "But she is mine. And I will keep what is mine."

Something in the way he said it drew Jessie's gaze swiftly back up to his again. She had relaxed her grip on his neck by this time and now stood pressed close to him, with her arms loosely encircling his waist. Her eyes met his for only an instant, but it was long enough for her to catch a glimpse of the fierce light glowing in those cobalt-blue orbs, a light that both disturbed and thrilled her.

"Will you?" retorted Gray Wolf. The smile on his face broadened with malicious intent before disappearing entirely, to be replaced by an ugly, menacing snarl. "Your words hold no power here, Chandler! It is I who say what will be done!"

"Let us kill them both!" cried one of the other braves, his thirst for blood made even stronger by the intoxicating effects of the *tiz-win* he had been drinking.

His merciless suggestion brought a clamor of agreement from most of the young men, while the band's elders sadly shook their heads at this renewed, inevitably pointless desire to kill. Mothers gathered their babies close, older children suddenly began to whoop and scamper about in mock warfare, and several of the young squaws tossed more logs on the fire so that the flames crackled and danced even more riotously than before.

Jessie, her face paling and her eyes filling with terror as a savage din rose in waves over the camp, clung frantically to Ben.

"Dear God, Mr. Chandler, why don't the other men come to help us?" she strained upward to ask him, her voice rising almost hysterically above the savage din.

"There are no others." His reply was surprisingly calm.

"No others?" she echoed in shocked disbelief. Reading the truth in his eyes, she shook her head numbly and returned her horror-stricken gaze to the threatening melee that surrounded them.

What will happen to us now? she thought, dread twisting at her heart. She was only dimly aware of Ben's hand moving to draw her head back down upon his chest, of his strong arms clasping her protectively against him while he waited for the uproar to end. His words of comfort seemed to come to her from a great distance away.

"Don't worry," he bid her. "It's the Apache way to make a show of hatred against their enemies. They won't kill us." *He hoped to God he was right.*

Within a matter of minutes, the wild outburst was over. It ended as abruptly as it had broken out, when Gray Wolf jerked his arm up in a signal for quiet. No one dared to disobey the leader's unspoken command, though some did comply with obvious reluctance.

"I have decided to let my old friend and his woman live!" proclaimed Gray Wolf, his gruff, authoritative voice resounding throughout the firelit clearing. "We have sworn to kill only for revenge, we will not break our vow!" There was a rumble of disapproval over his decision, but none of the men was either brave or foolhardy enough to press the matter further.

For the second time that night, Jessie grew faint with relief. She closed her eyes and collapsed weakly against Ben, too exhausted for the moment to do anything more than rest within the warm safety of his arms. His gaze once again smoldered in vengeful fury for what she had suffered, but he would not allow his emotions to rule his head.

"You will let us go in peace?" he asked Gray Wolf in a low and level tone. He was not surprised when the

39

Apache refused; he had not expected to achieve success so easily.

"No."

"Then name your price for her." He was all too familiar with the Indian custom of trading horses for captives, and he had come prepared to offer whatever it took to secure the schoolteacher's release. He was not prepared, however, for the way in which Gray Wolf suddenly threw back his head and laughed.

Others joined in to share his inexplicable mirth, and Jessie's eyes shone with bewilderment as she raised her head to stare at them. Strangely enough, their laughter frightened her more than their previous clamor for her death.

"Is your price so high you think I cannot meet it?" Ben queried with deceptive nonchalance. *Damn!* he swore inwardly, not at all pleased with the way things were going. In all his years of dealing with the Apaches, he had encountered few surprises. No, if there was one thing he had learned, it was to be on his guard against being lulled into a fatal belief that there *would* be a surprise. An Indian wanted you to think he was waiting with one more trick up his sleeve. Any man who lost sight of the present and looked ahead to the next would find himself with no more future.

"I will name no price," Gray Wolf finally answered, sobering again. His eyes still glittered with some dark amusement as they flickered contemptuously over the two "lovers" before him. "The woman is yours, Chandler. You have said so."

"She is mine. Yet you have said you will not let us go," Ben pointed out. *What is the bastard up to now?* he asked himself. He sensed danger of a different kind, a danger he did not recognize. It was not like Gray Wolf to behave in such a secretive manner, nor was it in keeping with his nature to display this sort of childlike playfulness. Usually, a man knew right away where he stood with the fierce Apache chief—alive or dead.

"I will let you go when the sun rises," Gray Wolf generously relented. A ghost of a smile touched his lips. "But first you will be the honored guests in our *go-tah* for this night. We were as brothers once, Chandler; I will keep my word and let you go in peace. The freedom of your woman will be my gift. But you will also take with you the memory of this night."

Jessie gazed up at Ben in utter confusion. He was as much in the dark as she. Realizing it would do him no good to ask Gray Wolf for an explanation, he waited for the question in his mind to be answered.

He did not have to wait for long. In the next moment, Gray Wolf issued a command in the Apache language. Half a dozen giggling young squaws came forward and seized hold of Jessie.

"No!" she screamed in wide-eyed resistance.

"Go with them," Ben directed her quietly. "They won't hurt you."

Unbeknownst to her, he now understood what Gray Wolf intended. He had witnessed a similar "punishment" once before, when a member of another band had made the mistake of insulting a young woman who loved him. As it turned out, the girl was the daughter of a chief, and her father claimed the right to avenge her honor.

The miscreant, a loose-tongued brave who had in truth committed no more serious a crime than foolishly commenting on the young woman's unattractiveness, had found himself imprisoned alone with the chief's daughter for an entire night. Not only that, but he had been threatened with a suitable—and highly painful—revenge if he did not perform his "duties" as her new husband. The threat had apparently worked. The following morning, upon being presented with undeniable evidence that the man had fulfilled his obligations,

41

the chief declared himself to be satisfied and welcomed his new son-in-law into the family with open arms. The marriage had reportedly become a happy one, in spite of its inauspicious beginning.

Ben Chandler, on the other hand, had no intention of making Jessamyn Clare his wife. While he could not deny that the prospect of a night alone with such a beautiful young woman filled him with wholly masculine pleasure, he was not about to let either himself or Cimarron's new schoolteacher be railroaded into disaster. *No, by damn,* he vowed while his eyes kindled with grim determination, *the final victory would not belong to Gray Wolf.*

Jessie, meanwhile, fought the women as best she could, but they wrested her away from a surprisingly complacent Ben and spirited her back across the clearing to the same wickiup where she had spent the majority of the evening. They pulled her purposefully inside and began stripping the torn and dirty garments from her body.

"Stop it! Stop it at once!" she cried in shocked, breathless outrage. The squaws paid no heed to her protests or struggles, instead merely continuing with their swift and methodical efforts to render her naked.

Once they had succeeded, they gathered up all her clothing and took it away with them, leaving Jessie with nothing but a blanket to cover herself. The same old woman who had struck her earlier returned to tend the fire. She stole several furtive, wickedly amused glances in Jessie's direction while she worked. Then she, too, left.

Jessie clutched the blanket about her and hurried to the far corner of the wickiup. Although she did not know for certain what was in store for her, she was greatly dismayed at the thought that she had to face it—whatever *it* was—without benefit of clothing. She felt excruciatingly vulnerable, and she wondered if it was an Apache custom to strip a captive naked before setting her free.

"Oh, Mr. Chandler, what do they mean to do with us?" she murmured aloud, not at all expecting that he would soon be there to answer her question in the flesh.

In the flesh turned out to be an accurate description of his sudden appearance in the wickiup. Without warning, he was thrust inside by the four strongest of Gray Wolf's braves. Like Jessie, he was almost entirely naked.

A loud gasp of startlement broke from her lips when she looked up to see him standing before her, clad in nothing but a breechclout. Whatever she had imagined would happen to her that night, she had not imagined finding herself alone with a handsome stranger who was as naked as she.

"Mr. Chandler?" she breathed in stunned disbelief, her green eyes very round and full of acute perplexity. Jessie instinctively pulled the blanket more securely about her as she felt hot, embarrassed color creep over her. Hastily averting her gaze, she stammered out, "Wha—what in heaven's name is going on?"

"The Apaches are having a bit of fun with us, Miss Clare." There was a faint smile of irony playing about his lips as he sauntered closer to the fire's warmth. He appeared not the least bit discomfited by his lack of clothing; in fact, he wore the breechclout as though it were his everyday attire. "We've been officially declared husband and wife."

"What?" gasped Jessie, her eyes flying back up to his face. "Why, that—that cannot be!"

"It can and is," he insisted calmly. His deep, resonant voice filled the small hut as completely as his tall, powerfully built frame seemed to. Jessie swallowed hard and tried, unsuccessfully, to prevent her gaze from straying downward to his bronzed nakedness.

"But *why?* Why have they—"

"To test us. Gray Wolf wants to see how far I'll let this

thing go." His eyes once again gleamed with wry, appreciative humor for the absurdity of the situation.

"Are you saying he does not believe your story?" she questioned in renewed alarm.

"I don't think he's made up his mind yet," Ben drawled almost lazily. "But it doesn't matter. As long as we play along, he'll let us go. He may be a rascally son of a bitch, but he won't break his word once it's been given."

They stood facing one another across the softly dancing flames, while the smoke curled up to fly heavenward through the hole in the domed roof of the shelter. For the space of several long seconds, neither partner in the "marriage" spoke, their thoughts racing along a remarkably similar course.

Jessie, although still in shock by what she had just heard, could not help noticing that the man before her was even more striking without his hat. *And without his clothes,* a tiny voice inside her brain added, much to her dismay. She could feel her face burning as her eyes traveled with a will of their own over his splendid, compellingly virile form.

His thick chestnut hair, streaked golden by the sun, was cut short and waved rakishly across his forehead. His shoulders were incredibly broad and lean-muscled, his sinewy arms looked entirely capable of performing whatever task he set his mind to, while the magnificent breadth of his chest, covered with only a light matting of dark brown hair, tapered downward into a trim waist and lean, perfectly formed hips. His thighs were smooth and granite-hard, his legs long and muscular.

He was without a doubt the most thoroughly *manly* man she had ever seen—and he was certainly the first to be revealed to her in such proud, unashamed masculine glory. She was aghast to find herself wondering what it would feel like to be caught up within the powerful circle of his bare arms; she was even more unsettled to find herself wanting to smooth a hand across the gleaming hardness of his naked chest, to trail her fingers along the intriguing line of dark curls that beckoned downward. . . .

As Jessie had reflected earlier, there was nothing soft about Ben Chandler. He was a man toughened not only by years of physical labor but also by life itself. He had fought long and hard to carve a home for himself out of the wilderness; he had paid for everything with the sweat of his brow. *And the sacrifice of his heart.*

While he was being subjected to a thorough, wide-eyed appraisal by his "bride," Ben's own gaze traveled with a slow, intimate boldness over her appealingly disheveled form. The knowledge that she wore nothing beneath the blanket sent liquid fire coursing through his veins, in spite of his resolve otherwise. He mentally cursed the sudden tightening of his loins, but his eyes nonetheless smoldered with desire before he forced himself to look away.

"Please, Mr. Chandler," Jessie broke the silence at a sudden thought, "I—" Her voice quavering, she gently cleared her throat and inquired apprehensively, "What did you mean when you said 'as long as we play along'? That is, what *exactly* is expected of us?"

Trepidation shot through her when she observed the soft, ironic smile that touched his lips.

"I knew you'd get around to asking me that sooner or later."

Ben told himself there was no use in postponing the inevitable any longer. If the prim-and-proper little schoolmarm was going to fly into a rage of indignation, dissolve into a storm of hysterical weeping, or faint dead away, then so be it. The Apaches would no doubt enjoy any type of scene she created, he mused, his eyes darkening at the prospect. Yes, by damn, he could imagine their derisive, triumphant laughter at hearing

45

their beautiful young captive screaming her head off.

"There's a condition to our release, Miss Clare," he revealed at last. There was a grimly determined look on his handsome face as he began advancing slowly upon her.

"A condition?" she echoed breathlessly, her emerald gaze becoming very round and anxious once more. She instinctively tightened her grip on the blanket and backed farther into the corner of the wickiup. "What do you mean?" A shiver ran the length of her spine when she viewed the intense, purposeful light in his deep blue eyes.

"According to Apache custom, we're man and wife now, remember?"

"Yes, but we are not actually married!" she protested in growing alarm and disbelief. Her hands shook, causing the heavy woolen blanket to slip downward upon her shoulders.

"We are for tonight," he decreed, his voice low and authoritative. He stood towering above her now, his tall powerful frame making her feel both incredibly small and alarmingly light-headed.

"Surely, Mr. Chandler, you are not suggesting—"

"I'm not *suggesting* anything, Miss Clare."

His rugged features grew quite solemn as he suddenly took her arms in a firm grip. Jessie gasped when she felt his warm fingers closing about her bare skin. She tried to pull free, but he held tight.

"Let me go!" she cried in rising panic. *Dear God, had she merely traded one form of torture for another?* "If you have any shred of decency, sir, you will not—"

"Keep your voice down!" he commanded tersely.

"No!" Squirming wildly within his grasp while at the same time striving to keep her nakedness covered, she brought her foot up and delivered a forceful kick to Ben's unprotected shin. He swore beneath his breath, and his

46

fingers tightened with almost punishing force upon her soft flesh as his eyes burned down into the stormy depths of hers.

"Blast it, woman," he ground out, "I don't want to be here any more than you do, but we have very little choice! Gray Wolf has made it clear he'll not release us unless we offer up a convincing portrayal of 'connubial bliss,' so that's damned well what we're going to do!"

"And just how *convincing* do we have to be, Mr. Chandler?" demanded Jessie, her voice lowered but still tinged with mistrust. Hot, bitter tears stung her eyes as she searched his face, and her arms were beginning to ache beneath his forceful grasp. She was painfully aware of the way she was imprisoned against the bronzed, immovable hardness of her "rescuer's" naked chest; the warmth emanating from his body made her skin tingle and her pulses race.

It occurred to her that he could be lying to her, that he could have concocted the story of their so-called marriage for his own benefit, yet she knew in her heart it was the truth. She had not failed to notice the leering, amused glances of the braves, nor the wickedly meaningful looks cast her way by the squaws. Heaven help her, *this* was why she had been stripped of her clothing . . . and why she now found herself alone with a half-naked, devilishly handsome stranger whose gaze seemed to scorch her from head to toe.

"Convincing enough to save our necks," he replied evasively. He found himself thinking that she had the most captivating green eyes he'd ever seen and that her face was far too enchanting for her own good. *Miss Jessamyn Clare,* he silently repeated her name, wondering idly how the devil such a beautiful, refined young lady had come to accept the job of teaching school in a rough-and-ready town like Cimarron.

With secret reluctance, he finally released her arms

47

and turned away. Jessie, her thoughts and emotions in utter turmoil, watched as he dropped down on one knee beside the fire and negligently rearranged the blazing logs with a stick lying on the ground for that purpose.

In fascination, her gaze was drawn to the sight of his naked back, where the muscles rippled beneath the gleaming smoothness. The short, narrow square of the breechclout was all that covered his buttocks, so that his lean hips and long legs were freely caressed by the soft, flickering radiance of the flames.

Jessie felt an unaccountable but decidedly pleasurable warmth spreading upward from somewhere in the vicinity of her lower abdomen. Shocked and confused by her body's reaction to the obvious perfection of her companion's masculine form, she abruptly spun about and brought the blanket up higher about her bare, trembling shoulders.

"I—I don't suppose there's any use in trying to persuade the Indians that we should *not* be together, is there?" she wondered aloud, though without much hope.

"None at all," came the expected answer from Ben.

"Very well then," she murmured, releasing an audible sigh as she absently scrutinized the shadows cavorting with what appeared to be mocking abandon on the wall. "It seems we must resign ourselves to our fate, Mr. Chandler, at least for this one night." She took a deep, steadying breath and added, in a nervous rush, "But first we must come to an understanding! Apaches or no Apaches, I will not willingly subject to being—being *ill-used* by you or any other man! Circumstances may dictate our actions for the present, but I have no intention of allowing myself to be forever trapped by the capricious schemings of a cruel, maniacal savage! In other words, Mr. Chandler, I—"

"In other words, Miss Clare, you want to make sure I don't do any more than *pretend* to rob you of your

48

innocence," he finished for her. She could have sworn she detected a note of unholy amusement in his voice, and it was this suspicion that prompted her to whirl about to face him again.

"I fail to find anything humorous in this situation!" she snapped, her green eyes flashing with indignation.

"Do you?" he retorted in a low, deceptively mellow tone.

He stood to his full height once more and favored her with a long, hard look that made her face flame anew. His eyes, glinting like cold steel, seemed to be taunting her, and she dazedly wondered why he should be so annoyed with her. After all, what in heaven's name had she ever done to him? *She* was the one who had suffered these long, agonizing hours of terror and uncertainty—not *him*.

"I find it funny as hell," Ben went on to confide. "It isn't every day I have the pleasure of being offered my life in return for a single night of marriage to a woman—no, damn it, a *girl*—who hasn't got brains enough to stay where she belongs."

"Why, you—you have no right to speak to me like that!" Jessie sputtered in outrage. Eyes splendidly ablaze, she lifted her chin to a proud, defiant angle and told him, "You can lay claim to nothing but half an hour's acquaintance with me, Mr. Chandler—a paltry foundation indeed upon which to base your unsolicited and woefully inaccurate opinion!"

She had no idea how much her anger heightened her beauty, and she was equally oblivious to the fact that the blanket had once again slipped perilously low upon her body. The graceful silken curves of her shoulders and upper arms shone pale in the firelight, while a tantalizing hint of her full young bosom swelled above the frayed edge of the brightly colored wool. To Ben Chandler, she represented the kind of danger he had taken great care to avoid all these years; he was bound and determined to avoid it still.

"You should never have come here," he pronounced curtly, his dark brows knitting into a frown. "And once we're out of this, I'm going to see to it that you get back to St. Louis—even if I have to take you there myself."

"*You*, sir, have neither the privilege nor the authority to see that I go anywhere! What in heaven's name business is it of yours whether I—"

"I'm one of the men who hired you, Miss Clare. And if I'd had any idea you were so damned young and inexperienced, I'd have cast the deciding vote against you and spared the both of us this trouble!"

"How on earth would that have changed anything?" She momentarily forgot the embarrassing intimacy of the situation and marched forward to confront him. Tilting her head back, she met his penetrating blue gaze without flinching and argued quite feelingly, "If I had been old and vastly experienced, would that have made any difference to Gray Wolf and his men? I think not, Mr. Chandler! The Indians would still have attacked that stagecoach without provocation, and I would still have been taken captive, and you would still be standing here in the midst of this *trouble!*"

"Maybe," he allowed with the ghost of a smile as he once again cursed the wild leaping of his heart. His gaze smoldered anew with wholly masculine longing while it raked over the upturned loveliness of her face and the alluring shapeliness of her blanket-clad curves. He was, after all, flesh and blood, and there was no denying she was a desirable young woman. "But if you had turned out to be what I had expected," he pointed out, "I doubt if Gray Wolf would have put up even a token fight over letting you go. And I wouldn't have to worry about protecting your reputation should word of this *honey-*

moon of ours get out."

"You needn't concern yourself about my reputation!" Jessie assured him with a spirited toss of her head. The luxuriant, tangled mass of burnished gold locks danced riotously about her face and shoulders. "As a matter of fact, Mr. Chandler, you needn't—"

Suddenly, and quite without warning, his strong arms shot out and caught her up against him. Before she could utter a single protest, he brought his lips crashing down upon the parted softness of hers.

Jessie felt her head spin alarmingly. Although she was at first rigid and unyielding within the powerful circle of his arms, she soon found herself surrendering to the mastery of his warm embrace. Her fingers threatened to relax their grip on the blanket, and she clutched weakly at the only barrier between her naked curves and Ben's hardness as his mouth captured hers in a kiss that made her grow faint. She had never been kissed before—at least, not in the boldly demanding manner in which she was now being kissed—and she was certain she would never have been kissed like that in the entirety of her life if fate had not thrown Mr. Chandler into her path.

A low moan rose in her throat as his arms tightened possessively about her pliant, beguilingly formed body. She began to kiss him back with all the innocent fire he was awakening within her, her lips moving sweetly beneath his and thereby unknowingly causing his reluctant desire to flare to an even more dangerous level.

Ben groaned inwardly and sought to maintain control over his raging, long-dormant passions. Opening one eye, he glanced toward the opening and saw that the squaw who had been sent to check on the "progress" of the newlyweds had now retreated in apparent satisfaction. It was with an iron will that he forced himself to put an end to the delectable torment.

Jessie was left breathless and becomingly flushed—

and not a little disappointed—when the kiss ended as abruptly as it had begun. She could only stare up at Ben in wide-eyed bewilderment when he released her and set her firmly away from him.

"Sorry if I frightened you," he murmured by way of apology, though he displayed no visible sign of remorse. He stood gazing down at her with a strangely unfathomable expression on his handsome face, and his deep, wonderfully resonant voice seemed to hold an underlying warmth as he explained, "We were being watched."

"Watched?" she repeated stupidly. Coming back to earth at last, she shifted her bright, troubled gaze hastily toward the doorway. "Good heavens, you mean to say they intend to—to *spy* on us this entire night?" The thought filled her with horror, for more than one reason.

"It looks like it. The Apaches are usually modest when it comes to such things, but they'll put aside their own rules and traditions whenever it suits them. . . . And there's no doubt it suits them tonight."

He muttered a curse and frowned down into Jessie's beautiful, stricken countenance. Recalling all too vividly the feel of her soft body in his arms, the way her sweet mouth had surrendered to the hard pressure of his, he found himself thinking that the man who would someday initiate her into the earthly delights of passion was a lucky bastard indeed. Strangely enough, the thought of another man touching her provoked a wealth of emotion—none of it pleasant—within his breast.

How the hell are you going to make it through the night? his mind's inner voice knowingly challenged.

Jessie's eyes fell before the disturbing intensity of Ben's. She felt a great deal more uncomfortable with him than before; she was acutely conscious of his proximity, of his virile nakedness, and most of all, of his complete power over her. Although she was loath to admit it, it stung her to realize that his impetuous, wickedly enchanting embrace had been prompted by nothing more than the necessity to provide a show of marital harmony to their captors.

"Come on," he said quietly. His hand closed about her arm, and the contact sent an invisible current through them both.

"Where are we going?" she asked in a weak, tremulous voice.

"To bed."

"To bed?" she gasped, the color draining from her face. She hung back when he tried to lead her toward the far corner of the wickiup. Her gaze was full of emerald fire as she vehemently declared, "You may have taken the liberty of one kiss, Mr. Chandler, but do not make the mistake of thinking I have any intention whatsoever of allowing—"

"Enough!" he ground out, scowling fiercely down at her. "You're not in a position to *allow* anything, Miss Clare. Hell, woman, we're not sitting in your parlor back in St. Louis, and I'm not some dewy-eyed boy asking for the honor of kissing your hand! No, damn it, you'll have to forget all those things you were taught to say and do when you were alone with a man. For this one night, you'll have to pretend you're one of those other women you and your friends knew about but didn't dare speak of. I've told you what's got to be done," he finished, his hand tightening on her arm, "so let's get to it!"

Without further preamble, he hauled her unceremoniously over to the dimly lit corner and pulled her down to the ground with him. Jessie, shocked into speechlessness by his rough treatment of her, fought back tears and sought desperately to prevent the blanket from revealing her naked limbs. Almost before she knew what had happened, she was lying on the cool ground with Ben's tall, muscular frame stretched beside her. Her head was resting on his shoulder, and his arm was clamped across her waist to hold her securely against him.

Still wrapped in the blanket, she lay stiff and indignant, her breasts heaving beneath the wool. She could hear the strong pounding of Ben's heart beneath her cheek, and she watched the steady rise and fall of his chest through eyes still glistening with tears. *How could a man be both savior and tormentor at the same time?* she asked herself in resentful silence.

"It's going to be a long night," he remarked somberly, glancing down at the angry young woman whose every breath drove him to distraction. He resisted the temptation to smooth the tangled curls from her forehead. "You may as well relax and try to get some sleep."

"Sleep? But I thought we were supposed to—to—" She blushed fierily as her voice trailed away.

"We are. But even an Apache bridegroom has to rest now and then."

Something in his voice made Jessie's color deepen. She dared not ask him to elaborate. Releasing a faint sigh, she took his advice and allowed her tense muscles to relax a bit. The emotional and physical exhaustion that had plagued her earlier had been replaced by a certain inexplicable renewal of energy. She was surprised to realize that she was wide-awake and not the least bit tired. Just as when Ben had held her close during those terrifying moments outside, she began to feel safe and warm once more.

"Why did you come here, Mr. Chandler?" she suddenly asked, staring toward the fire. Her voice was soft and tinged with a slight endearing hoarseness, causing Ben's pulses to leap damnably. "Why did you risk your life to save a woman you did not even know?"

"You were in trouble," he answered simply. He shifted a bit on the hard ground and placed his other hand

54

beneath his head. His gaze followed the direction of Jessie's, his eyes mirroring the blaze that hissed in the quiet warmth of the hut. Outside, the celebration had resumed. "Besides, I knew what I was getting into. Gray Wolf and I are old friends."

"Indeed? Well, then, I shall pray that I am never gifted with such *friendship!*" she murmured. He said nothing in response, but merely transferred his vigilant blue gaze to the flap at the opening of the wickiup. She sensed his watchfulness, and she sighed again while letting her thoughts wander.

Pressed closely against the naked bronzed length of his body as she was, she could not keep her eyes from straying downward to where the breechclout rested low on his hips. There was a discernible bulge beneath the square of soft hide. Her cheeks flamed guiltily, and she silently berated herself for the immodest curiosity that urged her to think about what lay hidden from her fascinated gaze. She was not entirely ignorant when it came to male anatomy, but there was no denying she had gained her knowlege from books alone.

"Give the devil his due, Miss Clare," Ben suddenly whispered.

Before Jessie had time to ask him what he meant, he gathered her close with both arms and rolled so that she was atop him. Her breathless cry of surprise was silenced when he captured her lips with his own once more. This time, however, she was startled to feel his hot velvety tongue plunging within her mouth to explore the virgin softness therein. She inhaled sharply and attempted to put an end to the shockingly intimate kiss, but he brought a hand up to the back of her head, his strong fingers entangling within the silken thickness of her hair to hold her captive for his pleasure—and hers.

She was powerless to resist the sweet abandon calling her. Returning his thoroughly convincing passion with an answering, boldly enthusiastic deception, she felt as though she were being swept away by a flood tide of vibrant, exquisite sensations and emotions she had never known existed. She completely forgot that the rapturous embrace she and Ben were sharing was motivated by necessity. . . . She forgot everything but the man who was kissing her with a sensuous, demanding expertise that sent wildfire coursing through her.

Long after he knew the witness to the night's second performance had departed, Ben Chandler ignored the voice of reason. Though he knew himself damned, he refused to relinquish possession of the innocently seductive angel in his arms, even going so far as to move a hand down to where the firm roundness of her bottom curved alluringly upward against the blanket.

He molded her to his hardness with an ever-increasing fervor, while masterfully swallowing her soft gasps and moans. His other hand swept the shimmering curtain of golden tresses aside so that his warm lips could roam hungrily downward to brand the hollow of her throat before returning to claim her mouth in a kiss, which made her alternately long to beg for mercy and plead for more.

Luckily for them both, fate intervened.

The pyramid of logs burning in the center of the wickiup collapsed noisily, sending forth a shower of embers across the ground—perilously near to the very spot where the "newlyweds" lay entwined. The flash of light and movement caught Ben's eye. In one swift motion, he rolled Jessie to her back and came up on his knees beside her to smother the glowing coals with dirt. Then, without a word, he climbed to his feet and went to tend the fire.

"Is—is the woman gone?" stammered Jessie, sitting up at last. She struggled to regain control of her dangerously erratic breathing, and it was with unsteady fingers that she rearranged the folds of the blanket about her still-tingling curves.

"Yes," Ben answered in a low, husky voice. His back was turned toward her, so that she could not see the way his features tightened as if in either pain or fury—or both. His deep blue gaze was suffused with a dull glow as he scowled down at the accursed blaze.

It's going to be a long night.

His own prophetic words came back to taunt him. With an inward savage oath, he jabbed viciously at the fire and told himself that Gray Wolf would never know just how much of a punishment the next few hours were going to be. . . .

Three

Jessie sighed in contentment and stretched her arms lazily above her head as she awakened to the dawn. Her eyelids fluttered open, and she smiled to herself while her sleep-drugged gaze slowly focused on the column of soft light filtering down through the hole in the roof of the wickiup.

Morning had come, and freedom would not be far behind, she reflected happily. With a sigh, she brought her arms downward . . . and touched warm, hard flesh.

The smile froze on her face. Her eyes grew round as saucers as she turned her head to look at the man who still slept beside her. His ruggedly handsome features appeared younger and more vulnerable in slumber, and she found herself wondering dreamily what his first name was. It seemed strange to continue calling him Mr. Chandler, especially after all the two of them had shared. . . .

The shocking memories of the night came flooding back, causing her to blush to the very roots of her golden brown hair. *Good heavens, how could she have behaved so wantonly?*

With agonizing clarity, she recalled the way she had responded to his kisses, the way she had played her part with such shameful willingness and enthusiasm. Never in her life had she allowed a man to do what he had done. What was even more unforgivable was the fact that she could not conjure up any feeling of disgust for what he had done. No indeed, though she hated to admit it, she had actually *enjoyed* the ordeal!

"Jessamyn Clare, how could you?" she whispered in self-recrimination. She heaved a disconsolate sigh and raised up on one elbow, her eyes darting instinctively back to the chiseled planes of Ben's face. The memory of his wildly compelling embraces made her tremble and crimson anew.

Mortification turned to incredulity as it then dawned on her that the blanket was no longer wrapped about her body alone, but instead was spread across his tall frame as well. She drew in her breath upon a sharp gasp and hastily lifted the top edge of the cover to peer beneath its concealing folds. Her eyes filled with dismay as her worst fears were confirmed: *She was lying next to him entirely naked.*

A soft, strangled cry broke from her lips. Acting solely on impulse, she jerked the blanket away from him with a vengeance and scrambled furiously up to her knees on the ground. She was in the process of trying to wrap the rough woven fabric about herself again when Ben awoke with a start. He was on his feet like a shot, poised in defensive readiness, when his searching gaze lit upon Jessie.

Wide-eyed and breathless, she stared up at him as though transfixed. The blanket, clutched protectively to her naked breasts like a shield, hung down the front of her body to trail in the dirt; she had not been granted sufficient time to secure it about her. Thus, it hid very little from Ben's appreciative eyes.

The tantalizing glimpse of her pale, satiny curves sent liquid fire racing through his veins. His burning gaze raked over the slender roundness of her naked hips and thighs on either side of the blanket's woefully inadequate drape, then traveled back up to the wild mane of hair framing her beautiful face and tumbling down over the bare smoothness of her shoulders. Her eyes glistened like two fiery emerald pools, while her lips, soft and parted with innocent seductiveness, seemed to be inviting the hard pressure of his.

Damn you, Miss Jessamyn Clare, Ben swore inwardly, reason and desire waging a fierce battle within him. He was tempted; God knew he was tempted. But the events of the previous night were still fresh in his mind. For his own sake as well as hers, he forced himself to turn away.

"Cover yourself," he commanded in a quiet, controlled voice. "They'll be here soon."

Jessie gazed up at the bronzed tenseness of his naked back and swallowed hard. Somehow, the light of day made his splendid lean-muscled masculinity seem even more overpowering—and even more indecently captivating.

Feeling alternately as though she had been granted a reprieve and suffered an unknown disappointment, she hastened to do as he said. A sudden horrifying thought flew into her mind while she wrestled with the blanket's folds, causing her to blush hotly and ask in a voice that was tremulous and full of dread, "Did anything—did anything *happen* after I fell asleep, Mr. Chandler?"

"No."

"But when I awakened this morning, I discovered the blanket—" She broke off in embarrassment, searching for words that would not only convey her meaning, but would also save her further distress. *I beg your pardon, sir, but do you perchance recall having taken advantage of me in my sleep?* Groaning inwardly when the preposterous question popped into her mind, she rose to her feet and demanded, with a valiant attempt at composure, "Why did you see fit to cover yourself with *my* blanket?"

"I must have gotten cold." He did not add that he had remained awake for an endless, damnably torturous period of time after she had drifted off in his arms, nor did he make mention of the fact that the feel of her warm, soft body lying next to his had made him curse a thousand times over the man responsible for the delectable torment. He had no memory of stealing her blanket; the mere thought of her naked curves pressing against him made his loins tighten. There was a particularly grim set to his jaw when he turned back to her at last.

"Do you suppose they will return our clothing?" she asked in a tumble of words before he could speak. Even though she held the blanket securely about her once more, she was plaqued by the disturbing sensation that he could see right through it.

"Probably." His eyes still smoldered when he frowned down at her and decreed, in a low, tight voice, "From here on out, Miss Clare, we're going to forget about what happened last night. The truth of the matter is, there'd be hell to pay if anyone found out the new schoolmarm had spent the night alone with a man—especially if the man was me."

"Why especially you, Mr. Chandler?"

"Because there are some in Cimarron who—" He broke off abruptly, as though he had discovered himself on the verge of revealing too much. When he spoke again, it was only to reinforce his warning. "Do as I say and keep quiet about it. No harm was done. Nothing of any significance took place between us—nothing but a few kisses we'll soon forget—so there's no reason to stir up trouble." It was as if he were trying to convince himself as well as her.

Nothing of any significance, Jessie echoed in dazed silence, then wondered why his words brought a sharp

61

twinge of pain to her heart.

"We did what we had to do," he added coldly. "There'll be no need to speak of it again."

"Very well, Mr. Chandler," she agreed, lifting her head to a proud, defensive angle while at the same time trying to quell the sense of betrayal she felt. *He owes you nothing,* she told herself sternly. *Don't be a fool. . . . He was only playing a part. . . . He would have done the same for any other woman under the circumstances.* "We shall do as you suggest and forget about last night!"

With that, she swept past him to the opening and lifted the flap to peer angrily outside. She was dismayed to feel sudden tears stinging her eyes, and she resolutely blinked them back while trying to focus on the awakening camp. The clearing, bathed in the soft, gathering light of the dawn, appeared deserted.

Ben's piercing blue gaze followed Jessie's every movement. In spite of what he had just said, he knew he would never be able to erase the memory of what they had shared. He tried to tell himself that it had been only his lust stirring and not his heart; both had been held in check for so long that he had almost forgotten what it was like to feel his whole body come alive the way it had done last night.

Don't lose your head, Chandler, an inner voice of caution spoke up. *She's young. . . . She's a complete innocent. . . . Damn it, she's the sort of woman men either marry or forget.*

He knew he had no business wanting her the way he had last night—the way he still did, if he were honest with himself. But the practice of self-scrutiny was something Ben Chandler had abandoned long ago. There was only more confusion, more pain when a person looked inward. No, it was better not to examine one's thoughts too much, especially when they involved a member of the opposite sex.

With a sudden, sharp intake of breath, Jessie released her grip on the hide flap and took a hasty step backward. The old squaw entered and silently thrust an armload of clothing at her, then turned to Ben.

"Ish-tia-nay?" she asked him, a wide grin splitting her lined and weathered face as she gestured toward the younger woman.

"Ish-tai-nay," Ben confirmed with a solemn nod.

The old woman cackled in delight and swung an arm about, landing a hard smack with the palm of her hand on Jessie's backside.

"Schlanh-go para-ah-dee-ah-tran!" the squaw proclaimed with another broad laugh of satisfaction. She ducked out of the wickiup, leaving an indignant Jessie.

"What did she say?" Jessie demanded.

"She wanted to know if you were a woman now."

"If I was a wo— Oh, I—I see." Her face flamed as a wave of embarrassment washed over her, but she stiffened and asked coolly, "And what else did she say?"

"Are you sure you want to know?" His eyes gleamed with some secret amusement, while the merest hint of a smile played about his lips.

"Yes, Mr. Chandler, I do!"

He did not immediately answer, but instead moved forward to stand towering above her. She stared up at him, her eyes wide and luminous, her entire body tingling with expectation. Without a word, he reached out to take the bundle of clothing from her. She gasped and clutched at the edges of the blanket to prevent it from slipping lower.

"It was her opinion that you must be very contented," he finally disclosed, his deep voice brimming with wry humor.

Jessie's mouth formed a silent O as she blushed fierily once more. Quickly looking away, she was all too aware of the way Ben's penetrating gaze remained fastened on her.

"Get dressed," he commanded. He held her traveling suit and undergarments out to her, and she virtually snatched them from his grasp with an unintelligible word of thanks.

She escaped into the far corner of the wickiup. Casting frequent worried glances over her shoulder to where Ben had turned his back in order to draw on his trousers, she struggled to keep the blanket modestly about her while at the same time donning her fine linen chemise and ruffled white cotton drawers. That accomplished, she bent down to look for her corset, only to make the unhappy discovery of its absence from the pile. It seemed the lace-trimmed "Primrose Path" had been confiscated by one of the Apache women for future use as a personal adornment.

Jessie frowned in puzzlement, then hurriedly stepped into her petticoat. Fashioned of muslin, it featured a deep kilted flounce all around and wheels of embroidery on the outside of each plait. Her lingerie was without a doubt of the highest quality; the greater majority of the women in New Mexico would have counted themselves fortunate to possess so much as a single outer garment of such elegance.

The blanket was discarded at last, freeing her hands for the task of fastening the buttons of her skirt and blouse. Once she had pulled on the jacket as well, she turned hesitantly about to face Ben again. Having finished dressing long ago, he stood waiting with obvious impatience near the opening.

"I wish I did not have to face the citizens of Cimarron looking like this," Jessie remarked with a faint disconsolate sigh. She attempted to drag her fingers through the tangled golden locks, only to abandon the effort as hopeless in the next instant.

"They won't care what you look like," he said,

knowing it was a lie. In truth, he mused irritably, every blasted man in town would be falling all over themselves once they'd caught a glimpse of the beautiful new schoolteacher. Yes, by damn, even that bastard Horace Mooney would probably find an excuse to drop by the schoolhouse on a regular basis. The thought of the uproar she was sure to cause made his eyes darken with inexplicable fury.

"Perhaps not, Mr. Chandler, but I will!" retorted Jessie.

Now that the two of them were fully clothed and facing one another in the light of day, she began to feel like herself again. After all, she was Miss Jessamyn Clare of St. Louis, a paragon of virtue and good breeding and intellectual pursuits. How could she have forgotten everything she had been taught? It seemed almost as though the previous night had been nothing but a dream. . . . A dream that was both heaven and hell . . . A dream inhabited by a woman who could not possibly be akin to the one standing so rigidly erect with her emerald gaze so cold it could chill a man to the bone.

"Since you have already made it quite clear you regret casting *your* vote in favor of my employment," she went on to clarify with another proud lift of her head, "I naturally hope to make a favorable impression upon the other members of the board!"

"You will," Ben assured her with a scowl. He took a firm grip on her arm and pulled her none too gently forward. She gasped in startlement, her eyes reproaching him even before she had opened her mouth to utter an indignant protest against such unwarranted roughness.

"Why, how dare you—"

"Listen to me, damn it!" His hand tightened with near bruising force about her outraged flesh. "We're not in the clear yet. The Apaches will be expecting a pair of lovebirds to emerge from this wickiup. It's all part of the

65

game, Miss Clare, and we've no choice but to play along for a little while longer." He released her arm and demanded more evenly, "No matter what Gray Wolf says, you keep your mouth shut, understand?"

"No, Mr. Chandler, I most certainly do *not!*" Her eyes blazed vehemently up at him, while two bright spots of color rode high on her cheeks. "It may have been necessary for me to affect a subservient attitude last night, but not this morning! While I fully realize the importance of continuing our charade, I fail to see why I should have to feign complete imbecility! Do you truly think me incapable of—"

"My opinion of you doesn't matter!" His voice was whipcord sharp. "I know a hell of a lot more about these people than you do, so you'll just have to trust me when I tell you to keep quiet!" His eyes, more than ever the color of molten steel, flickered angrily over her stormy, upturned countenance. Tempted to either kiss her or shake her, he wisely resisted both. "It's the custom for new wives among these people to display a certain amount of embarrassment after the honeymoon. And by damn, *Mrs. Chandler*, the honeymoon's over!"

Another loud gasp was forced from her lips as she was hauled unceremoniously outside. Ben propelled her forward, away from the wickiup and into the center of the cool, fragrant clearing where the flames had roared heavenward the night before. Nearly the entire camp had gathered by this time to await the arrival of the "newlyweds." Gray Wolf himself stood watching the approaching couple beneath a canopy of massive pines. A faint telltale glimmer of humor lurked in his dark eyes while his old friend drew closer with the woman he had claimed as his own.

Jessie did not find it in the least bit difficult to pretend embarrassment—she *was* embarrassed, and greatly so. Painfully aware of the fact that she was the subject of much ribald speculation and commentary, she tried without success to ignore what was going on about her.

Several men nudged one another and exchanged grunts of ear-burning laughter while their gazes traveled lewdly over her. The women were not much better, for they giggled like schoolgirls while making all-too-comprehensible gestures toward her. Clearly enjoying themselves at her expense, they made no effort to conceal their mingled satisfaction and amusement at her obvious maidenly discomfiture. Even the children joined in on the fun, racing gleefully about and chanting something she could not understand but that was clearly not intended to be complimentary.

Ben drew her up beside him as he finally paused before Gray Wolf. The tall Apache eyed the two of them narrowly for a moment before giving a curt nod of his head.

"The night has passed," he remarked to Ben with deceptive nonchalance. Then, turning to Jessie, he studied her in somber, nerve-racking silence for a moment before asking bluntly, "You are Chandler's woman now?"

Startled by the question, Jessie felt hot color flood her face. Her eyes, very wide and full of alarmed confusion, flew instinctively up to Ben's face for help. His steady gaze warned her to follow his instruction and keep quiet.

"She is mine," he answered for her.

"I ask it of the woman, Chandler!" Gray Wolf pointed out harshly, his eyes bridling with fury.

"She is mine," Ben repeated in a deep voice laced with steel. "The game is played out, Gray Wolf. Keep your word and let us go."

As had happened the previous night, his gaze locked with his former friend's in silent combat. There was no longer any true feeling of brotherhood between them, only anger and the natural mistrust of one enemy for another.

"Let her speak!" growled the Apache leader. He shifted his dark, hotly glittering gaze to Jessie again and demanded once more, "You are Chandler's woman now?" The whole thing might have started out as the game Ben termed it, but it was obvious that it had become much more than that to Gray Wolf.

Jessie cast another hasty glance up at Ben. Then, gathering her courage about her again, she looked the fierce Indian warrior squarely in the eye and gave him the answer he sought.

"I am his."

Strangely enough, the words seemed to ring true. It was as though they had originated in the very depths of her heart, as though—as though she had actually become Ben Chandler's woman during the long night of mingled fear and ecstasy. *Dear God, how was it possible for her to feel this way?*

"You do not lie," proclaimed Gray Wolf, apparently satisfied with what he saw reflected in her eyes. He nodded an unspoken command, and the circle of Apaches became two long lines instead, offering a clear path to freedom for the captives. Ben's gaze locked with his former comrade's one last time.

"Take your bride and go, Chandler," the young Apache chief commanded him stonily. "Do not come back. The next time, I will show no mercy."

"Neither will I," promised Ben, his own features forebodingly grim. He seized Jessie's arm in a possessive grip before adding, "A word of warning, Gray Wolf, from one old friend to another. The owners of the stage line won't stand for what happened yesterday. Attack one of their coaches again, and they'll hunt you and your people down like animals."

"And the hunters will become the hunted!" Gray Wolf vowed, the savage light burning brighter than ever in his dark eyes. *"Go!"* His face was a mask of barely controlled fury, and Jessie shuddered involuntarily beneath Ben's hand.

Without another word, he led her toward the spot where one of the older boys stood waiting with his horse. She forced herself to refrain from looking back over her shoulder as she matched her stride to Ben's, for she knew instinctively that they were not yet out of danger. Given what she had learned thus far of Gray Wolf's volatile nature, it was still possible that he would change his mind and prevent them from leaving. Her entire body remained tensed, and she literally held her breath as Ben clasped her about the waist and lifted her up to the stallion's broad back. He mounted behind her, one sinewy arm slipping about her slender waist while he took hold of the reins with his other hand.

"Remember what I said," he cautioned Gray Wolf, his eyes narrowing imperceptibly as they fastened on the Indian's stoic contenance. "What was once between us may be dead, but I'd hate to see your women and children reduced to begging."

"Why?" the Apache challenged bitterly. "It is what the white men want, is it not, to make us beg for what is ours? No, Chandler, your words are twisted, for it is *your* women and children who will one day beg. For their very lives!" His prophecy, just short of a declaration of war, was punctuated by an eruption of shouts and cries from the other braves.

Their loud, stridently voiced accordance with their leader's warning struck renewed terror in Jessie's heart. She grew faint with relief when her "husband" finally urged the horse away from the camp. Ben's arm was clamped so tightly about her that she could scarcely breathe, but she offered no complaint, for his strong embrace once again provided her with a desperately needed sense of security.

She could feel the heat of his hard body against hers. Like her corset, his saddle had been confiscated by their captors, so that his long booted legs rested on either side of her white stockinged limbs while he guided the animal unhurriedly down the mountainside. The curve of her hips was molded intimately by the enveloping tautness of his denim-clad thighs, and her back was pressing against his broad chest in such a way that she was aware of every beat of his heart. Strong and steady, his pulse seemed to demand a like response from hers, urging her to put the horrors of the past twenty-four hours behind her.

The sunlight sparkled down through the trees as they rode, setting the earth ablaze with color. The cool, fragrant air of the forest was alive with the sounds and smells of an early morning in late summer. Birds, insects, and other wildlife greeted the new day in their usual bustling manner, while the ever-present wind, stilled to a whisper during the night, now gathered strength to set the leaves rustling and branches swaying anew.

To Jessie, nature's awakening glories seemed almost otherworldly. *Safe,* she repeated silently. *Ben Chandler is taking me to safety.* Why then did she have this nagging sense of further danger? There was an old saying about jumping from the frying pan into the fire. . . . Was it possible she was doing just that?

"Bear up a while longer, schoolmarm," he admonished softly, his deep voice startling her from her turbulent reverie. "If our luck holds, we should be in Cimarron in time for breakfast."

"Do you think the Indians will come after us?" Raising a hand, she swept aside the limb of an aspen tree and stole a quick look back at Ben. His handsome features tightened momentarily as she shifted her weight forward a bit.

"No. Gray Wolf will keep his word."

"How can you be sure?"

"Because I know him. Whatever else he is, he's no liar."

"You were his friend, weren't you, Mr. Chandler?" she asked with a puzzled frown. "What happened to—"

"It was all a long time ago," he cut her off. His eyes darkened with unwanted remembrance, and his arm tensed about her waist.

Jessie lapsed into pensive silence again. Her fingers entwined in the horse's thick mane while her emerald gaze traveled over the surrounding beauty of the high country. She watched as a lone chipmunk scampered across a heavy carpet of dried pine needles on the ground, only to disappear, chattering angrily, into the dense foliage as the stallion's hooves pressed into the soft earth nearby. From the branches of one of the tall pines came the laughing call of a family of piñon jays; overhead, two bald eagles soared upon the warming air currents, their wings spread majestically outward as they climbed higher and higher in the cloudless blue sky.

"After you've rested up a couple of days," said Ben, keeping a watchful and experienced eye on the sloping land as he guided his mount homeward, "you can take the eastbound stage out of Cimarron. I'll see that you're reimbursed for your passage back to St. Louis."

"But I'm not going back to St. Louis!" Jessie protested. Her eyes flashed resentfully up into his when she twisted about to face him, unaware that the abruptness of her movements caused him to curse inwardly at the sudden contact of her backside against his masculinity. "I told you, Mr. Chandler, I am not going to abandon my post as schoolteacher here! In spite of all that has happened—or perhaps *because* of it—I am more determined than ever to remain and fulfill my duties!"

"You're too young for the job, Miss Clare, and too damned—" Breaking off, he clenched his teeth and forced his smoldering blue gaze away from her beautiful,

71

stormy countenance. He had been about to say *too damned pretty* but had thought better of it. The feel of her soft curves against him made him burn with another surge of desire, a desire that was so sharp and intense it was all he could do to keep his hands off her. He was sorely tempted to drag her off the horse and take her right there on the forest floor—but he did not. He hated himself for his weakness, for wanting her so badly it hurt, just as he hated *her* for making him feel things he had sworn never to feel again.

"Too inexperienced?" Jessie finished for him with a smile of bitter sarcasm. She twisted back around and lifted her chin in an angrily defensive gesture. "What I lack in experience I shall make up for with diligence and enthusiasm. And you needn't concern yourself on my account any longer, Mr. Chandler. Once we reach Cimarron, your responsibility for me will be at an end, will it not?" she challenged defiantly, sliding foward again to escape his disturbing closeness. A loud gasp escaped her lips when his powerful arm suddenly brought her forcibly back against his hard body.

"No, by damn, it will not!" he ground out. "We're not talking about some Sunday school picnic, you little fool. This country is hell on any woman, especially one who's been brought up to do nothing more than pour tea and stitch samplers! You don't have any idea what you're taking on here, Miss Jessamyn Clare, which is why I'm going to save you from yourself and send you back where you belong! If I were your father, I'd take a switch to your bottom and make you forget this damned nonsense, then I'd marry you off to the first suitable young man who—"

"But you are *not* my father," she pointed out icily, her tone one of righteous indignation, "a circumstance for which I am profoundly grateful! And even if you were, there would be nothing you could do to make me change my mind! I am a grown woman, Ben Chandler, and as such am free to follow the course of my own choosing!"

She struggled against the near-bruising pressure of his arm, using both her hands to try and force him to ease his hold. He did not relent, however, at least not right away, instead maintaining his steely grip until they came upon a stream a short distance ahead. Once there, he dismounted and dragged Jessie down as well. She pushed vehemently away from him, only to gasp when his hands shot out to close about her arms.

"Enough, damn it!" he snapped. His gaze scorched down into hers, his mouth a tight, thin line of displeasure. "Cool your temper, Miss Clare. You're a schoolteacher, remember?" he added with a sardonic half smile.

"What in heaven's name are you doing?" she demanded, her own anger overriding any fear she might normally have felt. "Why have we stopped?"

"Breakfast." He released her, albeit reluctantly, and turned away to lead the horse to the water's edge. Jessie stared after him in wrathful bemusement, wondering what there could possibly be for them to eat. Now that she had time to think about it, she realized that she was indeed quite hungry, and her mouth felt uncomfortably dry.

She gathered up her dirty tattered skirts and picked her way carefully through the greenery to the snow-fed mountain stream. Kneeling on the ground, she cupped her hands together and bent to scoop up some of the water. It was cold and clear, and she drank deeply before finally climbing to her feet again.

Ben, having already quenched his own thirst, ran a soothing hand along the stallion's sleek neck while murmuring a quiet word of encouragement to the animal. With only a passing glance in Jessie's direction, he negligently tugged the hat from his head and began

73

stripping berries from a plant beside the stream.

"What are those?" she queried as she watched him. She patted at her forehead with a damp lace-edged handkerchief before expertly twisting her tangled mane of burnished gold hair into a knot.

"I told you—breakfast" was all he would say.

Her eyes bridled with irritation, but she wisely held her tongue. It occurred to her for the first time that she was entirely alone with a stranger—well, *almost* a stranger—in the midst of a forest high in the mountains. There was not a single soul around, at least not a human one, and hence no one to see or hear what took place between them.

He could ravish her there and then; she was completely defenseless. Remembering the bold embraces they had shared, she felt a warm flush stealing over her. She told herself it was utterly ridiculous to think he would force himself upon her, when throughout the long night he had been presented with the perfect opportunity to do so and had not seized advantage of it. For heaven's sake, she mused scornfully, it was as though she actually *wanted* him to sweep her into his arms and carry her off into the woods. The thought provoked a torrent of conflicting emotions within her breast. And though she scoffed inwardly at her overactive imagination, she could not banish the disturbing image of her conquest at his hands.

"Here."

Coloring guiltily, she looked up to see that Ben was offering her a handful of the berries. She hesitated at first, then took them and lifted one cautiously to her lips. Tasting it, she was pleasantly surprised at its sweetness.

"Why, they're good!"

"The Apaches can live on them indefinitely," he remarked, his eyes meeting hers. "So can a white man— if he can keep his scalp long enough."

"You know a good deal about the Indians, don't you,

74

Mr. Chandler?" she asked, her gaze falling beneath the piercing blue intensity of his. When he did not answer, she turned her back on him and wandered over to the stream again. "I—I suppose you've spent your entire life here in New Mexico, haven't you?"

"Not all of it."

She could hear the soft crunch of his boots upon the leaves as he moved past her to the horse, contentedly grazing at a patch of thick grass. He gathered up the reins and led the animal forward.

"It's time we moved on," he decreed with a slight frown in her direction. "I'd advise you to do whatever you have to do now. The call of nature will have to wait once we leave the trees behind."

Her cheeks flaming in embarrassment, Jessie whirled to face him, only to find that he was already sauntering away to give her a moment of much needed privacy. Her mortification increased when, several minutes later, she emerged into the small clearing where he waited and saw that his eyes were alight with what appeared to be knowing amusement. She drew herself up proudly, her own fiery gaze daring him to offer a comment.

"Shall we be on our way, Mr. Chandler?" she suggested stiffly.

"Whatever you say, Miss Clare," he answered with only the ghost of a smile.

His strong fingers encircled her waist and lifted her effortlessly up to the horse's back. Although she behaved as though the contact repulsed her, she was in truth rendered wonderfully light-headed by the feel of his hands upon her. She told herself it was beyond comprehension, the way she became all warm and dizzy every time he touched her. *Dear God, what was the matter with her?*

Ben swung up behind her, his arm slipping masterfully about her slender, uncorseted waist once more while he

75

reined about and set them on a course that would, barring disaster, take them down the mountain and across the plains to Cimarron in a few hours time. Unbeknownst to Jessie, her arrival was being eagerly anticipated by literally hundreds of people, for it wasn't every day that a schoolteacher—much less one that was young, pretty, and of the female persuasion—came to town. As a matter of fact, she would be the first.

"I—I owe you a debt of gratitude for saving me from the Indians, Mr. Chandler," declared Jessie after they had ridden in silence for a while. She didn't know whether to be disappointed or relieved by the fact that he had removed his arm from about her at last. Her hips were still molded to intimate perfection by his hard thighs, but she tried not to give in to the temptation to lean back against his chest. "When I think about what might have happened if you had not come—"

"Don't think about it," he spoke close to her ear. His voice, low and resonant and unmistakably commanding, sent a delicious tremor coursing through her. He kept an easy, practiced hold upon the reins while the stallion followed an instinctive path through the forest. "They wouldn't have killed you," he relented enough to disclose. "The Apaches don't kill women." He did not add that her life, while spared, would have been the harsh and physically difficult existence of a slave's.

"Perhaps not, but they would have held me captive for whatever length of time it suited them, wouldn't they?" she argued correctly. "So you see, I am indeed obliged to you for rescuing me. I don't know how I can ever repay you for risking your life for me, but rest assured that I will find a way."

Ben's gaze darkened while his grip on the reins tightened. *Damn it, he could think of a way. A way that would land them both in a hell of a lot more trouble than they were already in . . .*

76

"The best thing you can do for me, schoolmarm, is to light out for home and never come back," he ungallantly declared.

"You've made your feelings on that particular matter all too clear, Mr. Chandler!" she retorted with a flash of spirit. Jessie would have shot him a speaking glare as well, but she did not want to risk bringing about closer contact between them again. Tossing her head in unspoken defiance, she purposefully changed the subject. "The letter I received made no mention of the number of pupils I will be teaching. Have you any idea how many there will be?"

"A dozen. Maybe two," he revealed with an ill grace.

"One or two dozen?" She frowned and released a long dissatisfied sigh. "Since you are a member of the school board, Mr. Chandler, I should think you would be able to offer a more accurate accounting!"

"There's no way to know for sure until school starts." Although it was on the tip of his tongue to tell her the number of students in Cimarron wouldn't matter once she was safely back in St. Louis, he clamped his mouth shut and instead mentally consigned her to the devil.

"I see. Then what you are saying is that there has been no recent survey of school-age children."

"No. What I'm saying is that a survey would do no good," he replied enigmatically, then said nothing more.

"Why not?" Jessie demanded in growing exasperation. She had never met such an obstinate, close-mouthed man in her life! In that respect, too, she mused, he was vastly different from the men she had known back home.

"Because there are some who won't send their children to school. Life here consists of endless hard work, Miss Clare. It's not at all unusual for a boy to be kept at home to help with the chores. The girls might have to cook and clean and tend stock instead of learning

77

how to read and write. Schooling sometimes has to wait until a family can afford the loss of extra hands."

"But surely the parents must realize how crucial an education is to their children's future!"

"Most do. That's why you were sent for." He smiled faintly and cast a brief speculative look overhead at the sky. "But knowledge doesn't help put food on the table or keep a man from losing his ranch."

"And do you yourself advocate placing work above learning, Mr. Chandler?" she challenged.

"It's different for me."

"Indeed? And why is that?"

"Because I'm not in a position where I have to make a choice."

"You mean you don't have any children of your own?"

"I have two," he revealed quietly.

"You—you do?" Strangely enough, she had never thought of him as having children. But of course, she chided herself, it made perfect sense that he would have at least one of his own, serving on the school board as he did. Still, it was difficult for her to envision him as a father to anyone.

"Twins. A boy and a girl, seven years old."

"*Twins?*" she echoed, her eyes widening in surprise as she impulsively swung around to look at him.

"What's the matter, schoolmarm?" he asked in a tone brimming with wry humor. "Don't they have twins back in St. Louis?"

"Of course they do!" Hot color stained her cheeks, and she hastily averted her gaze from his before confessing, "It's simply that I would never have imagined *you* as a father—that is, as raising two children without the help of a wife." That he had no wife, she already knew, thanks to Gray Wolf.

"I'm entirely capable of doing both, Miss Clare—

fathering children as well as raising them." Observing the way her color deepened, he was dismayed to find himself thinking she was adorable when she blushed.

"Yes, but what about a mother for them? After all, children need a woman's care. . . ."

"They have a woman's care."

Jessie waited for him to elaborate, but he did not. She twisted abruptly about again, her thoughts and emotions in chaos over what he had said. Was it possible that Gray Wolf was mistaken and that his former friend had already taken a new bride? Or could it be that Ben Chandler was referring to a woman who lived in his house without benefit of marriage? She had heard that such shamelessly immoral behavior was all too common in the West.

Good heavens, she then wondered, *was that why he had not taken full advantage of last night's circumstances? . . . Because he was in love with another woman?* She felt inexplicably heartsore at the thought.

They rode in silence for the space of nearly half an hour. Jessie was the first to speak again, which she did after spotting a deer bounding gracefully across the rocky sloping trail just ahead. The movement startled her at first, prompting her to gasp and clutch instinctively at Ben's arm.

"Oh, I—I thought it might have been the Apaches!" she breathed in relief, her pulses racing.

"They won't come after us," he reassured her. She would have been surprised to learn of the effort it cost him to refrain from wrapping his arms about her and pulling her close. The urge to protect her was greater than ever, and he muttered an oath underneath his breath at the thought of the many dangers she would face if she chose to stay on in the Territory. He had already lost one woman. . . .

He caught himself just in time. *Jessamyn Clare was not his and never would be.*

"Are there other Indians in this part of the country?" queried Jessie, her eyes darting apprehensively about in spite of her resolve to be brave. She moved her hand back to the horse's mane but could not completely still the trembling of her fingers.

"Not any longer. These mountains used to be the hunting grounds for both the Jiccarilla and Utes, but most of them are scattered across the plains now. There's a government agency at Cimarron; they get their rations there." His rugged features became grim, his eyes suffused with a dull light. "Some say it's a case of too little too late."

"But what about Gray Wolf and his band? Why isn't something done about them? How is it they are allowed to go freely about attacking innocent people and—"

"They're not *allowed* to do anything, Miss Clare," he informed her tersely. "No one can catch an Apache in the mountains."

"How did you know where to find them last night?" she persisted.

"I've been to their camp before."

"Then why don't you lead the authorities to—"

"A man doesn't betray the trust of others," he insisted in a tight, almost angry tone of voice. "And even if I didn't give a damn about that, there's no way we'd reach the Apaches alive. Either they decide to let you find them—or they kill you before you set foot anywhere near their women and children."

"How is it you know them so well, Mr. Chandler?" she asked, her curiosity aroused to such an extent that she didn't mind probing a trifle more than was considered polite.

"How is it one woman can ask so many questions?" Ben countered in mingled amusement and irritation.

Jessie's eyes flashed at that, but she battled the temptation to offer him a suitably scathing retort. She compressed her lips into a thin line of resentment and settled angrily forward. But he merely encircled her waist with his arm again and pulled her back against him, as though to prove she could never escape him unless he decided to let her.

"You've the face of an angel and the temper of a wildcat, Jessamyn Clare," he murmured half to himself. "But I'll not be the one to tame you. No, by damn, I will *not!*"

Stunned into speechlessness by this raw, bluntly worded declaration, Jessie closed her mouth and swallowed hard. Outrage, coupled with something else she dared not name, set her heart to pounding fiercely within her breast. For the moment, she was unable to do anything more than rest complacently back against Ben Chandler's broad chest and stare, wide-eyed and breathless, into the surrounding depths of the forest.

Four

"Cimarron."

The sound of Ben's deep voice roused Jessie from unconsciousness. She had fallen asleep only a short time earlier, exhaustion having overtaken her at last. Unaccustomed to remaining astride a horse for so long, she had begun to feel that the journey would never end. Her legs and backside were numb after so many hours on horseback; the pain would come later.

"Cimarron?" she repeated drowsily, stirring in Ben's arms. The noonday sun beat down mercilessly upon the two riders as they approached the outskirts of town.

"Straight ahead," he confirmed. He felt a sharp sense of loss when she drew away and sat upright before him.

Jessie blinked hard to clear her sleep-blurred gaze as she looked at the settlement in the nearing distance. Surrounded by high rimrocked desert mesas, gently rolling mountain foothills, and gama-grass-covered plains dotted with buttes and old volcanoes, the town appeared to be some wild, earthly paradise cradled in a bowl of rich prairie country in order to beckon travelers to its midst.

Paradise indeed, thought Jessie with a soft smile of irony. *Satan's Paradise.* That's what Cimarron had been termed in the newspaper she had scanned while waiting for the stagecoach yesterday at the Clifton House. She could just imagine what her father's reaction would be if he knew his only daughter was about to set foot in a town whose very name meant "wild" and "unruly."

Her eyes shone with increasing excitement, and she hastened to try and bring at least some semblance of order to her woefully bedraggled appearance. Ben's handsome features tightened as he watched her adjust her long tattered skirts about her shapely limbs. When she turned slightly and raised her hands to her hair, his eyes were irrevocably drawn to the alluring curve of her bosom. The buttonless edges of her jacket gaped open, so that he was treated to the damnably tantalizing sight of her full young breasts swelling upward against the thin cotton of her shirtwaist.

He cursed the fire in his blood but could not force his burning gaze away. Suddenly, he was assaulted by a vivid recollection of what it had felt like to hold her body close to his, to feel her breasts pressing against his naked chest while her lips moved so sweetly beneath his. . . .

Groaning inwardly, he didn't know whether to be grateful or sorry when she lowered her arms. He stared at the back of her head, noting the way her thick golden hair glistened in the sunlight. Now that the moment had finally come, he was seized by the startling impulse to rein about and ride off with her to the mountains again. *What the hell was the matter with him?* He was behaving like some callow, lovesick son of a bitch with his brains between his legs.

"How many people live in Cimarron, Mr. Chandler?" questioned Jessie. She had twisted her hair into a knot again and now settled her skirts about her for the third or fourth time. Her anticipation over their arrival had driven all thought of the previous day's horrors from her mind. Reflecting that she was about to begin a new life— one that would in no way resemble her boring, too restrictive one back in St. Louis—she felt her whole body come alive with a sense of adventure.

"Maybe two hundred in the town itself," Ben answered in a voice that sounded distant to his own ears. He forced his arm from about her waist and took hold of the reins with both hands. "And at least that many more in the county."

She said nothing else for the moment, staring as if transfixed toward the odd collection of adobe buildings and frame structures with false fronts lining the wide, dusty main street. The town was not at all what she had expected; if anything, it was larger and a bit more prosperous-looking than the image she had carried with her since reading the advertisement. Little did she know that Cimarron, which certainly appeared peaceful enough at present, had come by its violent reputation honestly.

"Is it true that one man used to own all the land for miles around?" she asked, recalling something she had read on the train westward.

"It's true."

His maddening reticence earned him a sharp sideways look of reproach from Jessie. She wanted to ask him a good deal more but was prevented from doing so when she spied a group of horsemen thundering out to meet them. Following a momentary attack of nerves while Ben slowed his own mount to a halt, she raised her head and squared her shoulders, determined to make a favorable first impression upon everyone she encountered.

"Well I'll be damned!" cried one of the approaching riders. "You done it, Chandler!"

"We didn't think you'd make it back alive!" another admitted with a broad grin. "Hell, we was just sittin' around jawin' over which one of us was gonna be the unlucky bastard to tell Martha!"

"Damn! Is *that* the schoolteacher?" a thatch-haired

young cowhand blurted out, his eyes wide and incredulous as they lit upon Jessie.

The other four members of the group, drawing up in front of Ben and the beautiful young woman he had rescued, displayed much the same reaction. A combination of disbelief and admiration was written on their faces, and it was obvious from the way their astonished gazes fastened upon Jessie that they, like Ben, had been expecting someone more along the lines of a pinch-featured old maid.

"Are you all right, ma'am?" the first speaker inquired with heartfelt sincerity, sweeping the hat from his head while the others hastily followed suit. Jessie flushed beneath their solemn stares.

"I am quite all right, thank you," she replied, her mouth curving into a brief but warm smile. She felt Ben stiffen behind her.

"Beggin' your pardon, Miss Clare," the thatch-haired fellow spoke in contrition, "but we . . . well, we was—were, I mean—just so glad to see ole Ben here . . ." His voice trailed away in embarrassment.

"Welcome to Cimarron, Miss Clare. We're mighty thankful you didn't come to harm," the oldest of the group announced quietly, holding his hat over his heart and giving her a polite nod of his head.

"Let's get on with it," muttered Ben. Impatiently urging the stallion forward, he seemed oblivious to the fact that the self-appointed welcoming committee was forced to move abruptly out of the way. The cowboys, who had been so brash and exuberantly vocal moments earlier, followed in almost reverent silence.

A crowd was already gathering by the time Ben and Jessie reached the outlying buildings of the town. Men, women, and children stood along the boardwalk, eager to catch a glimpse of the unfortunate woman who, for all they knew, had suffered every manner of ill treatment while a prisoner among the Indians. There were some whose speculations about her captivity bordered on the vulgar and extreme—after all, wasn't it well known what those hot-blooded savages *did* to young white women— but the majority of the citizens were genuinely concerned about the welfare of the new schoolmarm and would gladly offer a word of solace.

Jessie felt a knot of anxiety tightening in her stomach as she gazed upon the sea of faces in the near distance. To her wide and sparkling green eyes, it looked as though the town's entire population of two hundred had turned out to greet her. She was acutely conscious of the buzz of excitement rising upward from the assembly, and her trepidation only increased when Ben remarked, in a low voice edged with unaccountable displeasure, "They just want to get a look at you. You're the first schoolteacher in Cimarron who wore skirts."

"Oh? And what did the others wear?" she impulsively tossed back at him over her shoulder. Instead of rising to the bait as she was sure he would do, he chose to repeat a word of caution.

"Remember. . . . Say nothing about last night."

"You may rest assured, Mr. Chandler, that I will make no mention of it!" Dismayed to feel another sharp twinge of pain, she silently berated herself for such sentimental foolishness and tried, with only partial success, to focus her attention on the passing sights of Cimarron.

The first thing to draw her troubled gaze was a four-story stone building, apparently a mill of some sort, towering above the street near the center of town. The Cimarron River—in actuality an unpretentious little stream that in all likelihood would have been called a creek anywhere but in this land of scant rainfall—flowed a short distance away. Nestled beneath the trees along its bank was a magnificent, sprawling adobe mansion divided into a pair of two-story sections by an inner courtyard and surrounded by massive walls to exclude unwelcome visitors. A great many smaller adobe buildings encircled the main house, giving it the appearance of some peculiar medieval kingdom adapted to New Mexico's climate and culture.

To Jessie, the grand estate seemed absurdly out-of-keeping with the modest structures that made up the rest of the town. Her curiosity piqued, she forgot about her annoyance with Ben and made a futile attempt to question him about it.

"Mr. Chandler, what is—?"

"The next eastbound stage will be through here in a couple of days," he interrupted brusquely. "I intend to make sure you're on it."

"Indeed? Then your intention shall most definitely be thwarted!" she vowed in a simmering undertone. She would have said more but did not get the chance; their journey together had finally come to an end.

The horse, following his owner's silently communicated wishes, halted in front of a two-storied adobe building whose weathered but professionally lettered sign declared it to be the St. James Hotel. There was another sign hanging just below that one, which read "Lambert's Saloon." Jessie frowned in puzzlement, wondering why they had stopped at a place of such dubious distinction. She had rather expected him to take her directly to the offices of the stagecoach line, in order to tender her statement regarding yesterday's attack, or perhaps to a respectable boardinghouse where she could secure a room and find rest after her ordeal.

She would have given voice to her confusion, but the crowd surged forward now, surrounding the two of them as Ben dismounted and pulled her, almost roughly, down as well. The hushed tones of the citizenry became an outright roar, with everyone talking at once and striving to get a closer look at the beautiful young schoolmarm.

Her eyes clouding with consternation, Jessie could not help but be a trifle overwhelmed, and her gaze moved instinctively to Ben in a silent plea for help. But he had already turned away, subjected to a barrage of questions from the men while the large group of women took charge of "poor Miss Clare" and spirited her inside the hotel. Children traipsed along after their mothers, as curious as anyone to discover what their new teacher was like.

The next thing Jessie knew, she was seated on a red velvet sofa in the center of the hotel's small but comfortable lobby. The furnishings, whose predominant colors were red and gold, appeared surprisingly elegant, and the pleasant aroma of cinnamon and nutmeg wafted throughout the brightly lit confines of the room.

Their maternal attentions intensifying to an almost suffocating level, the women were perilously near to driving an exhausted Jessie to tears. She tried in vain to answer each of the dozens of questions thrown her way, and she did not protest when two of her benefactresses plopped down beside her and proceeded to take her hands in a grasp of intended comfort.

"Were they terribly cruel to you, my dear?"

"Merciful heavens, child, what were you thinking to travel all this way alone?"

"Is it true that Gray Wolf was the one who attacked the stage?"

"You must be weary to the bone. How about a cup of tea and something to eat?"

"You're not injured, are you?"

"Would you like us to send for the doctor?"

Into the midst of this solicitous chaos came a desperately needed purveyor of sanity. Jessie heard a feminine voice booming authoritatively above the others, and she moved her wide, luminous emerald gaze upward to see a tall woman with flaming red hair parting the crowd to stand before her. The woman's features, though attractive enough, appeared quite severe at the moment. Her light blue eyes, however, were full of kindness as they fell upon Jessie.

"Come with me, Miss Clare," she directed in a firm tone, at the same time extending her hand in a decidedly no-nonsense fashion.

Jessie was only too happy to comply. She rose to her feet and smiled weakly up at the woman who was perhaps ten years older than herself. The attire of her newfound ally was very similar to that worn by the other women. She was dressed in a simple gown of printed calico, with her bright red hair pinned low on her neck and a coarse muslin sunbonnet hanging down her back as a result of an interrupted trip to the general store. A white cotton apron and a pair of sturdy brown leather high-top boots completed the ensemble, which had been fashioned for practicality rather than aesthetic value.

"And just what do you think you're doing, Lissa Boone?" a raven-haired young matron demanded angrily. A dozen others voiced their objections as well, but none so vigorously as the buxom older woman who had been seated to Jessie's right.

"You're not needed here, *Miss* Boone"—a pointed reference to the redhead's spinsterhood—"so kindly take yourself back over to the front desk where you belong and leave this poor girl to those of us who know how to handle such things!"

"I might consider doing just that, Abigail Higgins, if not for the fact that your *handling* is the last thing Miss Clare needs at this particular moment!" countered Lissa Boone. With a look of sharp rebuke clearly intended for the entire group, she took a gentle hold upon Jessie's arm and charged, "For heaven's sake, can't you see she's been through enough without having to sit here and listen to your silly prattle?"

"We were only trying to help!" one woman protested.

89

Lissa said nothing more, instead leading a profoundly grateful Jessie across the lobby and through a set of wide double doors. An angry murmur followed them as they went, but they paid little attention to it. The two of them climbed the narrow carpeted staircase to the second floor of the hotel, whereupon Lissa threw open the first door they came to and propelled the younger woman inside.

"It's not much to look at, I'm afraid, but it's clean and you'll not be bothered," she declared earnestly.

"Thank you," Jessie replied with a warm, slightly watery smile. "I—I don't know what I would have done if you had not come along!"

"Oh, they meant well, I suppose," allowed Lissa begrudgingly. "But anyone can see you're ready to collapse. Now you get undressed and into bed. I'll be back up with some hot water and a bite to eat in a few minutes."

She left without waiting for a response, closing the door softly behind her. Alone at last, Jessie heaved a ragged sigh and turned her gaze upon the room.

It was, contrary to what Lissa Boone had said, a perfectly charming room. A big brass bed took up most of the space, its thick, downy mattress covered with a patchwork quilt and pillows featuring insets of ribbon-trimmed lace. A washstand sat in one corner, a small chest of drawers in another, while the single window featured beautiful white lace curtains. A luxurious carpet of crimson-patterned wool stretched across the gleaming wooden floor. The room smelled comfortingly of lemon oil and soap, reminding Jessie of home.

Home. Cimarron was home now, she mused dazedly, her head still spinning from all the commotion downstairs.

Ben Chandler's handsome face swam before her eyes, and she suddenly realized that she had not even been given the chance to bid him good-bye. She wondered if he lived in town, if she would see him again soon, if the woman called Martha was counting the moments until *she* would see him again. . . .

The questions ran together in her mind, causing her to press her fingers to her temples. She made her way across the room to the washstand. Staring at her reflection in the framed mirror hanging on the wall, she gasped in horror at the woman who stared back at her.

"Dear Lord!" she whispered brokenly. It was the first time she had viewed the ravages of her ordeal, and she was appalled by the sight. Dirty and bedraggled and looking not at all like the properly bred young lady she was, she felt hot tears of utter dismay start at her eyes. It made her groan inwardly to realize that the entire town had seen her looking so awful, but what upset her the most was the thought that Ben Chandler had seen her thus from the very first.

Battling the tears, she began pulling her tattered clothing off with a vengeance. She tossed the offending garments into a heap on the floor, then sank down dispiritedly onto the bed, clad only in her chemise. A knock at the door startled her from her turbulent reverie a short time later.

"Miss Clare?" It was Lissa's voice.

Jessie, glancing down hastily at her scantily clad form, hesitated a moment before opening the door. She could feel herself blushing when the other woman's eyes flickered briefly over her.

"We'll need to see about getting you something to wear" was all Lissa said as she swept inside with a kettle of hot water in one hand and a tray of food balanced on her hip with the other. "I know you'll be wanting a bath, but I thought you could at least wash up a bit for now. I'll bring water for the tub later, after you've rested. There's hot coffee and sandwiches on the tray; I've got the cook standing by ready to fix whatever else you might want."

91

"This will be fine, thank you, Miss Boone. You—you've been very kind," Jessie remarked with a telltale catch in her voice.

"It's nothing." The tall redhead returned to the door and paused to send her a look full of compassion and understanding. "I won't ask you what you've been through—God knows you'll have to explain enough later on. But I want you to know that if you need anything—anything at all—I'm here. I know a little of what you're feeling, Miss Clare. That's why I know you need to be alone right now." With those enigmatic words, she was gone again, leaving her weary guest to stare after her in mingled bemusement and relief.

Soon Jessie was fast asleep, the pillow dampened by a few tears of emotional release and the warm summer breeze stealing quietly through the half-open window to stir the air around. The noise drifting up from the street below did not disturb her slumber, nor did the sounds coming from inside the hotel itself. She was young and healthy and vibrantly alive, and a few hours of deep, dreamless sleep did much to revive her sorely tested spirits.

Upon awakening at last, she was delighted to find one of her own gowns, cleaned and freshly ironed, draped across the foot of the bed. She had thought never to see her baggage again, since she herself had witnessed the burning of the stagecoach. Miraculously, however, her trunk had survived, having been retrieved by someone, and now rested beside the washstand. Her eyes shone with happiness at its presence, for she had brought a great deal more than clothing with her from St. Louis. There were books and other supplies to aid her in her new endeavors, photographs of her family, and a few cherished mementos from her childhood. She offered up a silent prayer of thanksgiving for their return and released a soft sigh as she took a seat on the bed again.

Her silken brow creased into a frown when her gaze shifted downward to her chemise-clad body. She had washed as best she could with the kettleful of hot water, but the bath Lissa had mentioned seemed more than ever imperative. Musing that she couldn't very well go in search of the woman while wearing nothing but a thin cotton shift, she reluctantly stood to don the clean gown. Fate, however, as if having decided it must now make at least a minimal degree of reparation for all it had forced her to endure, intervened in the person of Lissa Boone.

"Miss Clare?" the tall redhead called out in a hushed voice on the other side of the door. Certain she had detected the faint creaking of the bedsprings inside the room, she raised her hand and knocked lightly. Her face lit with a smile when Jessie opened the door. "I thought I heard you stirring. I expect you'll be wanting that bath now, won't you?"

"More than anything in the world!" Jessie confirmed with a soft laugh. She cast a brief glance back toward the bed before declaring earnestly, "I want to thank you for bringing my trunk up and for the gown as well."

"You were sleeping so soundly it seemed as though you were dead to the world," said Lissa, her lips curving into another smile. "I can accept your thanks for the gown but not the trunk. Ben Chandler's the one who hauled it over from the stage office."

"Mr. Chandler was here?" She could feel the warm color flying to her cheeks, and she looked away in confusion as her pulses took to leaping crazily.

"He was." If Lissa noticed anything unusual about Jessie's reaction, she chose to keep quiet about it. "He said to tell you he'll stop by tomorrow to see how you're getting along."

"He . . . Does he live nearby?"

"No. Didn't he tell you?" asked the other woman with a slight frown of bemusement. "He has a ranch about ten miles south of here. Ben doesn't get into town much. But Martha brings the twins in at least once a week."

"Oh, I see," murmured Jessie, her gaze falling again. She tried desperately to ignore the renewed twinge of pain deep in her heart.

"Martha is Ben's cousin."

"His cousin?" She looked up in time to glimpse a sparkle of knowing amusement in Lissa's light blue eyes.

"His older cousin," the redhead went on to reveal while a grin tugged at her mouth. She leaned against the door frame and folded her arms across her chest. "Let's see . . . Martha must be fifty if she's a day. She came out here from back East three or four years ago. Those kids were getting to be regular little hellions by then; I guess Ben figured they needed some good old Yankee discipline. Consuela—she's the housekeeper out at the Chapparosa—had looked after them since they were babies, but she always had her hands full enough cooking and running the house."

Jessie listened in fascination, her heart inexplicably soaring at the news that Martha was neither wife nor sweetheart to Ben Chandler. She waited anxiously for Lissa to continue, but the woman apparently decided she had said enough.

"Well, we'd better see about that bath of yours," announced Lissa, uncrossing her arms and drawing herself up to her full height of nearly six feet. "The bathroom's just down the hall to your right. I'll get one of the girls to help me carry up the hot water while you get yourself ready. I've already laid out clean towels and there's plenty of soap, but you might want to bring along some of your own if you've got any. What they use here isn't exactly what you'd call kind to the skin."

Lissa went on her way, leaving Jessie to follow the older woman's advice and rummage through the trunk for one of the cakes of lavender-scented soap Andrew had given her as a going-away present. She drew out a pale yellow wrapper as well, which she hurriedly donned before traveling down the hall to the bathroom.

An hour later found her bathed and dressed, her skin radiantly aglow from her efforts and her damp golden tresses arranged in a loose style that allowed several escaping tendrils to curl in a soft, becoming manner about her face. She wore the fitted, properly corseted and bustled gown of robin's-egg-blue silk Lissa had prepared for her, a crisp linen chemise and lacy ruffled drawers underneath it, stockings of fine white cotton, and a pair of polished black kid boots with fashionably pointed toes and high leather-covered heels.

Wondering idly what she should do now that she was ready to face the world again, she gathered her courage about her and set forth from the security of the sunlit room. She then ventured downstairs in search of her only friend and acquaintance in Cimarron.

Lissa was at her post at the hotel's front desk, and she beamed a smile of welcome at Jessie when she caught sight of her. The lobby was momentarily deserted, a fact for which both women were grateful.

"I must say, Miss Clare, you don't look anything like the person I took upstairs a few short hours ago!"

"I'm happy to report I don't feel like her, either, Miss Boone," Jessie confided, an ironic little smile touching her lips.

"Enough of this Miss Boone nonsense," Lissa scolded amiably. "The name's Lissa."

"And mine is Jessie." Her silken skirts rustled softly as she moved forward. "Am I the only guest at present?" she asked, puzzled by the fact that she had seen no one else since her arrival.

"For the time being," Lissa confirmed with a nod. "But the place won't look so empty come Friday. We've only got four rooms, you see. Even then, the only time we have a full house is when the stage has to make a stopover in Cimarron for the night. And that usually only happens on Friday."

"Your hotel is quite lovely, Lissa," remarked Jessie, her emerald gaze sweeping the elegantly furnished lobby once more.

Draperies of rich red velvet, tied back with gold satin cord, hung at the windows. The floors were covered with a larger version of the carpet in Jessie's room upstairs, and adorning the walls were several large gilt-framed paintings. Of particular note was that of a bearded, fierce-looking man dressed in a suit of armor, and alongside it one of a gentle-faced man clothed in the garb of a monk. She did not know that, in adherence with an old Spanish custom, it was required to hang the likeness of a man of war beside one depicting a man of peace.

"I'm afraid it isn't mine," said Lissa, referring to Jessie's comment about the hotel. "A couple by the name of Lambert own it, but I run it for them. Mr. Lambert himself does most of the cooking. He's a famous chef, you know, who used to cook for the President. We have quite a few dignitaries traveling through our town," she added, obviously proud to make the claim. "Lately, though, things have been pretty quiet. Until you came along, that is." She strolled from around the desk and ushered Jessie companionably over to the sofa. "Yes indeed, Jessie Clare, you being taken prisoner by Gray Wolf and his band, and then rescued by none other than Ben Chandler, has done a lot to stir things up around here!"

"I suppose you're right," murmured Jessie. She recalled all too well the sensation her arrival in town with Ben had created. She took a seat beside the kindly redhead and gave a passing worried glance toward the doorway. Lissa, taking note of the concern written on her face, hastened to set her mind at ease.

"I told everyone to keep clear while you were resting. It turns out I didn't have to. Ben had already given strict orders you were to be left undisturbed until tonight. And when Ben Chandler talks, people tend to listen."

"He—he did that?" Jessie stammered in surprise, more touched than she cared to admit by this unexpected solicitude of his. *He's only doing his Christian duty by you, you little fool,* a tiny voice inside her brain insisted sagely.

"Indeed he did." Lissa smiled wryly. "It must have worked, too, seeing as how no one's been around. But then, they all know they'll have a chance to get a good look at you tonight."

"Tonight?"

"There's a town meeting planned for eight o'clock. You're to be the guest of honor."

"Good heavens!" she breathed, her eyes widening in mingled disquiet and determination. "I honestly believed myself prepared to face everyone, but . . . do you suppose I shall be called upon to address the gathering?"

"They'll be expecting a speech of some sort," admitted Lissa. "But you've no need to trouble yourself on that score. All they really want is to see what you're like and hear a little bit about what happened yesterday. I'd be lying if I didn't say that was foremost in their minds. But they'll also be wanting to hear what you've got planned for the school."

"Do you know when school is scheduled to begin?" Jessie's green eyes sparkled with the light of enthusiasm now, for she was eager to begin her duties.

"I don't know, at least not exactly. Some time around the last of the month, I expect. Nothing's ever definite around these parts, Jessie," Lissa observed with a faint, disconsolate sigh. "Life has a way of changing things, and life here is . . . well, I'm sure it's not what you're used to." She forced a cheerful expression to her face, rising to her feet to say, "You'll be the first real live schoolteacher Cimarron's had in more than two years. The last one lit out for the border before he'd been here three months!"

"Three months?" echoed Jessie, standing as well. A warning bell sounded in her brain, but she stubbornly ignored it. "What on earth could have happened to make him leave without finishing out the year?" Another feeling of uneasiness crept over her as she watched the way the other woman's eyes took on a strangely guarded look. As her grandmother had always said, you could tell a lot by a person's eyes. . . .

"There was some difficulty with one of the students," Lissa disclosed evasively. She was hesitant to reveal more. The last thing she wanted to do was scare away the new schoolmarm, especially when there was every reason to hope a repeat of the unpleasant episode would never take place.

Jessie wanted to probe further, but when the tall redhead pointedly changed the subject, she had to settle for what she had already heard.

"Would you like a hot meal now?" suggested Lissa. "If so, I can take you on out to the kitchen and introduce you to Mr. Lambert."

"I'm not very hungry," she declined with a brief smile. "But I should be happy to meet Mr. Lambert." At a sudden thought, she inquired, "Will I be staying here at the hotel for the duration of the school year?"

"No." Lissa shook her head and explained, "You'll be boarding around."

"Boarding around?"

"That means your meals and lodging will be provided by different families—those who have children in school, that is. In the past, teachers here have moved from one home to another every two weeks, but I expect you can work out whatever arrangement you like with the school board."

The first thought that flew into Jessie's mind was if she would perhaps board at Ben Chandler's home first. She was both excited and apprehensive at the prospect. Suddenly recalling what he had said about making certain she left town on the next eastbound stage, she lifted her chin to a proud, defiant angle and vowed to show him she had a good deal more backbone than he had given her credit for.

Yes indeed, Mr. Chandler, she promised him silently, *you shall soon be made to realize that no one, least of all you, can engage Jessamyn Clare in a battle of wills and hope to win!*

Her beautiful green eyes flashing with the force of her determination, she accompanied Lissa from the lobby and into the kitchen.

After being introduced to Henry Lambert—a charming Frenchman who had served as the White House chef under President Lincoln—and his pretty young wife, Mary, Jessie set off by herself to explore the town. She could not help but be aware of the curious stares and whispered comments directed her way as she proceeded down the main street. The afternoon had already given way to evening, which meant that most of the townfolk were at home with their supper. But there were still a few people going about their business or simply relaxing in the shade, and it was they who turned to gaze at the beautiful, stylish young woman traveling purposefully along the boardwalk.

Jessie made a mental note of the names of all the establishments she either passed or glimpsed nearby: Delaney's General Merchandise Store, The National Hotel, Swink's Gambling Hall, Dahl Brothers Trading Post and Warehouse, The Yellow Front Saloon, Hunt's General Store, The Cimarron News and Press, Meagers & Sanderson Stagecoach Line Office, Colfax County Jail, and at least half a dozen others. She discovered that the town had grown up around a plaza, in the center of which sat an old white well-house with a red roof.

Two young horsemen tipped their hats respectfully to her as they rode past, while a few of the old-timers, occupying their usual places on benches in front of the general stores, called out a jovial, raspy greeting to her after she had crossèd to the other side of the street. The only women she encountered either smiled timidly at her or fixed her with a long, critically scrutinizing stare that made her bristle inwardly with annoyance. She remained as silent as they, however, and merely nodded in their direction while passing by.

Finally, she concluded that Cimarron was a quaint, orderly, and peaceful town, not at all unlike those she had seen depicted in thick scholarly books about the frontier. It certainly did not look as though the place deserved to be labeled as wild and unruly, she mused, only to be reminded once again of Ben Chandler's caution about its roughness. He was clearly mistaken and had probably only issued such a dire warning in an attempt to make her go running back to St. Louis as he wished!

But why does he wish it? she wondered resentfully. It was a complete mystery to her, his being so dead set against her teaching school there in Cimarron. Was it simply because he considered her too young and untried, or did his fierce, thoroughly overbearing disapproval owe its origins to something else?

Telling herself, without much conviction, that his opinion did not matter, she realized that she had come full circle back to the St. James. She went inside and turned her steps toward the small but elegant dining room, remembering how Lissa had earlier advised her supper would be served no later than seven that night. Her appetite had improved considerably during her walk, and she soon delighted Henry Lambert by ordering the

100

complete five-course meal that was his specialty.

The town meeting commenced shortly after the appointed hour of eight o'clock. Jessie was grateful of Lissa's supportive presence at her side as she marched down the street to the meeting hall—in actuality, a former saloon located next to Hunt's General Store—and made her way inside the crowded, noisy smoke-filled room. A hush fell over the assembly when she moved resolutely to the front to take her place upon the wooden platform. Her beautiful face was faintly flushed and her insides were a veritable mass of nerves, but her eyes shone with a fiery spirit that would see her through whatever life held in store for her.

"Sit here, if you please, Miss Clare," said Horace Mooney, obviously relishing his position of power at the night's affair. He indicated a ladder-back chair resting beside the podium where he stood, then gallantly held it while Jessie did as he bid. "Allow me to introduce myself, Miss Clare. I am Horace Mooney, the chairman of the Cimarron School Board," he told her in his usual pompous manner.

"How do you do, Mr. Mooney," she responded politely. Her bright gaze moved past him to the seemingly infinite number of faces before her, and she knew a moment's secret panic. Suddenly, she wanted more than anything for Ben Chandler to be beside her up there on the platform. She yearned desperately to be able to draw upon his solid strength once more, to hear his splendidly deep-timbred voice exhorting her to conquer her fears the way he had done inside the firelit wickiup last night. . . .

"This meeting will come to order!" bellowed Horace, pounding on the top of the podium with the brass-handled gavel presented to him by his own loving family.

101

It was only fitting, his wife had insisted loftily, that the head of the school board have in his possession the symbolic instrument of his importance to the community.

"We don't want to listen to you, Mooney! We want to hear what the little schoolmarm there's got to say!" a man hollered from the back of the room. There was an immediate outbreak of laughter, followed closely by the sound of wives hushing their errant spouses.

"*Order!*" Horace, his face red with anger as he scowled murderously out at the rows of people seated on rough-hewn benches, pounded three more times before he was satisfied with the degree of silence. "I know you're all anxious to hear from our guest of honor. Well, damn it, so am I!" He turned to cast a brief, significant look from beneath his thick eyebrows at Jessie. "Miss Clare has been restored to us safe and sound," he pronounced as dramatically as any politician running for office. "For that, I'm sure we're all eternally grateful."

"Hell yes!" came from somewhere in the crowd.

"Someone throw that man out!" ordered Horace with a furious stab of the gavel into the smoke-clouded air above the podium.

"Take it easy, Mooney!" someone else adjured. "Let's get on with things!" His words were roundly seconded by many, prompting Horace Mooney to start pounding again with a vengeance.

"Order, I say!"

Jessie suppressed a smile, for the absurdity of the proceedings did not escape her. She gazed at the men and women before her and reflected that they were not so very different from their counterparts back East. But their mode of dress certainly was. Instead of the dark suits and starched white linen shirts affected by the men of St. Louis, the men here wore denim trousers, long-sleeved cotton shirts in solids or stripes or plaids, leather boots with fancy stitching and pointed toes, and wide-brimmed cowboy hats that were at the moment either being held by one hand upon the knee or tilted negligently back upon the head.

The attire of the women, as she had noted earlier, was rather plain and simple, with the most popular fabrics being those suited equally to the climate as well as to life on the frontier. Calicoes, ginghams, and muslins in every conceivable pattern and color were fashioned into dresses and bonnets and aprons. There was a noticeable absence of less practical flourishes such as bustles or flounces.

Jessie, who had always been strictly admonished never to go anywhere without benefit of a corset, was amazed to see that the ladies of Cimarron apparently did not mind *their* figures being publicly displayed in a more natural state. Seized by the sudden shocking temptation to follow suit, she was forced to hide another smile.

"Miss Clare has traveled a great distance, has been subjected to danger and deprivation," Horace went on to proclaim. "And I say we show our gratitude for her presence here tonight in the best way possible, by welcoming her with a warm round of applause. Ladies and gentlemen, I give you Cimarron's new school-teacher, Miss Jessamyn Clare!"

His words brought the desired result. The crowd erupted into applause that was loud and enthusiastic, and there were even a few cheers and whistles added for effect. Jessie rose to her feet in acknowledgment of the thunderous clapping. She smiled and gave a polite inclination of her head, then stepped to the podium at Horace Mooney's insistence. The crowd grew quiet when she opened her mouth to speak.

"Thank you very much for your welcome," she began, her voice quavering a bit. Clearing her throat gently, she took a deep, steadying breath and continued. "I am very

103

happy to be here tonight. As Mr. Mooney said, I have come from far away and have—have indeed faced a certain measure of peril."

Her heart pounded fiercely beneath the tight heart-shaped bodice of her silk gown, and her green eyes flickered downward for a moment. She thought of all that had happened the day before. The image of Ben Chandler's handsome face forced its way masterfully into her mind, bringing a rush of guilty color to her cheeks. Disturbingly vivid memories of their night together would not be banished, no matter how hard she tried. But she was determined to present no outward evidence of the tempest raging within her.

"You are no doubt curious about my brief captivity among the Apaches," she said, raising her head with deceptive composure. "So I will tell you what you wish to know. Early yesterday afternoon, the stagecoach on which I was a passenger was attacked by Gray Wolf and his men. The driver—who, I was relieved to learn, will recover from his wounds—was injured and left for dead, the coach was set aflame, and I was taken prisoner. The Indians took me to their camp in the mountains, where I was found by Mr. Chandler."

"Ben's the only one who could've done it!" the irrepressible Jeb Poole called out.

"Shut your trap, Poole, or you'll find your backside out in the street!" threatened Horace.

"Are you gonna be the one to put it there?" Jeb shot back with a taunting grin, earning him a venomous glare from Mooney and another burst of raucous laughter from several of the men in the room.

When the noise had died down again, Jessie continued. She chose her words carefully now, for she knew that whatever she said would affect her new life in Cimarron, both socially and professionally. Drat it all, she had never been any good at deception!

"Mr. Chandler was able to bargain with the Indians for my release," she recited with remarkable ease. Her troubled widening emerald gaze and slightly trembling shoulders were the only clues that betrayed her inner struggle. If anyone in the room had been familiar with the beautiful young schoolmarm, they would have recognized the signs and known she was hiding something. "The Apaches did not threaten to kill me," she added, "as I had naturally feared they might do. And I—I suffered no ill treatment at their hands."

Unless one counts a night of feigned connubial bliss with a perfect stranger, she added inwardly, then was dismayed to feel herself blushing before more than a hundred pairs of watchful eyes. She hastened toward the conclusion of her story.

"I'm afraid there is nothing more to tell," she lied. "Mr. Chandler and I were allowed to go free this morning, whereupon we traveled with all due haste here to Cimarron." Certain she had carried it off, she felt her tensed muscles relaxing. Her mouth curved into a faint smile of relief. "And now, if you don't mind, I should like to—"

"You mean to say them red-skinned bastards didn't do nothin' to you? *Nothin' at all?*" a man near the front demanded in obvious disbelief. It had been on the minds of nearly everyone to ask the same thing, but it seemed no one else possessed the courage—or lacked the sensitivity—to do so.

"If you please, sir," Jessie responded in a voice edged with annoyance as well as renewed consternation, "I have already said quite enough upon the subject and now wish to focus on my duties as your new schoolteacher."

"Tell me, my dear," directed Abigail Higgins in a ringing tone from her seat in the third row, "exactly what did the savages accept in return for your release? That is, you mentioned a bargain Ben Chandler made with them.

105

What exactly did he bargain *with?*" Her expression was smugly challenging, and it struck Jessie that the woman was even more arrogant and unpleasant than she had first believed.

"I don't know. I was inside one of the huts when he arrived at the camp." That, at least, was the truth. "He was standing beside Gray Wolf when I was brought out."

"Well then," Abigail doggedly persisted, "what happened after that?" A murmur rose from the crowd, increasing in volume while Horace Mooney made only a halfhearted attempt to bring about silence again.

Jessie's eyes flashed their brilliant deep green fire as she sought to control her rising temper. She drew herself proudly erect and met the other woman's gaze squarely.

"I have already said, Mrs. Higgins, that I prefer to move on to the mat—"

"Yes, Miss Clare, we know what you've said." The buxom matron clad in an unbecoming shade of mauve smiled cattily and declared, "It's what you haven't said we want to hear!" Heads nodded and all manner of remarks flew freely about the room at that.

Jessie began to feel as though she were facing an inquisition rather than a group of people who considered themselves decent, God-fearing folk. Most of them were precisely that, but it was the handful of agitators in the crowd who were stirring things up to such an extent that the talk was straying farther and farther away from the relevant issues.

Unaware of the fact that emotions in Cimarron always ran high when it came to the subject of Indians, Jessie stood on the platform and watched helplessly as near pandemonium broke out among the crowd. Tempers flared, arguments waged, and in the midst of it all a few brave souls attempted to restore order to the proceedings.

After several long moments of such chaos, Horace

106

Mooney broke off his own voluble "discussion" with some of the other men and stepped back up to the podium. That fancy brass-handled gavel of his beat out a sharp command that echoed about the room. The commotion died down to a rumble, and a feminine voice that had not previously been raised in comment now took the opportunity to do so.

"I thought we all came here tonight to listen to Miss Clare!" Lissa Boone pointed out with a stern frown of reproach for her fellow Cimarronites. "And yet here you are, treating her as if she's done something wrong by living to tell about her misfortune! For heaven's sake, it isn't right to—"

"We might have expected *you* would be the one to take up her cause, Lissa Boone!" Abigail rudely interrupted. "Why, everyone knows you were once the woman of one of those murdering heathens!"

Jessie gasped in startlement, her eyes growing very round as she looked from the spiteful Abigail to the pale and furious Lissa. Strangely enough, no one else in the room appeared to be surprised by the older woman's cruel accusation. *Was it true?* she wondered dazedly. Her heart filled with compassion at the thought of what Lissa must be feeling either way. Prompted to intervene, she moved back to Horace Mooney's side and entreated the crowd,

"Please, may we not continue with the meeting? I know many of you are concerned about the education your children will receive under my care. Indeed, is not your concern for their welfare the very reason you advertised for a teacher as far away as St. Louis? So please, ladies and gentlemen," she suggested with a winning conciliatory smile, "let us put aside all other questions or indifferences and give the matter of your children's future the attention it deserves."

She was satisfied to see approval evident on the faces

of many as her gaze traveled anxiously about the former saloon. It seemed that even Abigail Higgins could not argue with what she said, for that particular lady fell silent and begrudgingly settled back upon the bench.

Thus, the good people of Cimarron resumed their seats, the highly charged tension in the room subsided, and Jessie sensed that she had won the first battle— *without Ben Chandler's help.*

Five

With a soft smile of contentment upon her lips, Jessie snuggled down beneath the covers and closed her eyes. The night had been difficult, she mused with a sigh, but she had persevered and been rewarded with an outpouring of support for her efforts.

The meeting had lasted a good deal longer than anyone had anticipated. When it had finally broken up at half past ten, she and Lissa had walked the short distance back to the St. James in almost total silence. In spite of Jessie's attempts to draw her new friend into conversation—a conversation far removed from any mention of Abigail Higgins's insults—the strangely preoccupied redhead had offered only a token response. And after they had climbed the stairs to retire for the night, Lissa had left her with a scarcely audible "good night."

Jessie's happiness momentarily clouded at the thought of her friend's subdued behavior. It required little imagination to guess the source of Lissa's obvious disquiet. Her green eyes kindled with renewed anger as she recalled Abigail's unwarranted attack. That the woman would cause further trouble, she was certain. She would have to remember to be on her guard around Abigail Higgins.

Her thoughts drifted back to the meeting again. A glimmer of wry amusement sparkled in her gaze when it occurred to her that she had probably transposed the names of some of the men and women she had met that night. At least she was good at remembering faces, she consoled herself with an inward smile. It was just that there had been so many people crowded around her at the conclusion of her speech, and it seemed that everyone had some particular wisdom to impart about either their beloved offspring or Cimarron itself. Horace Mooney, making no secret of the fact that *he* was impressed with her—a sentiment apparently not shared by his wife, if her sour expression was any indication—had promised to call another meeting before the beginning of school next week.

"Next week," Jessie whispered aloud, her pulses racing at the thought. She was going to be a teacher. In spite of her father and Lillian, in spite of Franklin Barringer and his repressive, highly unromantic notions of marriage, *in spite of Ben Chandler*, she was going to be a teacher!

Excitement making her restless, she turned swiftly upon her side and repositioned the pillow beneath her head. Her mind was far too active to grant sleep at the moment, so she heaved another sigh and opened her eyes to stare into the moonlit darkness of the room.

The faint sounds of music and laughter drifted up from the crowded saloon. Housed on the first floor of the same building, it had existed even before the hotel. Lissa had warned her about the noise, saying things could get pretty boisterous along about midnight. But she had also hastened to assure her that she was perfectly safe, so long as she remained in her room.

"The bartender usually chases the last customers out around two in the morning," Lissa had added with a crooked smile. "After tonight, Jessie Clare, you'll be glad for the fact you'll soon be boarding around."

Realizing she had not yet been told where she would be staying first, Jessie lay perfectly still and listened. She could not help but be curious about the drunken revelry taking place immediately below her. Like nearly everyone back East, she had either read or heard colorful stories relating what went on in such "dens of iniquity" out in the wild West. She wondered if it were true that half-naked women—"fallen angels" as it were—paraded themselves boldly about and danced atop the bar while men shot it out over a game of cards. Musing that it was difficult to imagine such wicked happenings in a peaceful hamlet like Cimarron, she laughed softly and rolled to her back again. She folded her arms beneath her head while her gaze absently scrutinized the shadows on the ceiling.

The tinkling strains of piano music swelled to a crescendo now, and Jessie was certain she detected at least one woman's voice raised in song. It suddenly occurred to her to wonder if Ben Chandler ever frequented the saloons in town. If so, did he enjoy the company of any of those women with painted faces and exposed bosoms? The possibility that he *did* made her eyes blaze with inexplicable fire.

"It's no concern of yours what he does, Jessie Clare!" she muttered aloud, her beautiful countenance stormy and a dull ache in the pit of her stomach. After all, she told herself, he's a grown man. He can do whatever he pleases. And if it pleases him to—to *socialize* with females of easy virtue, then so be it!

But her heart remained unconvinced. Before she knew it, her mind had once again returned to the delectably shocking events of their enforced intimacy inside the wickiup. Her face crimsoned while her traitorous body tingled anew at the memory of Ben's sweetly masterful embrace. Dear Lord, she agonized as her head whirled in

111

confusion, would she never be free of last night's deviltry?

Striving valiantly to purge all thought of the bold, devastatingly handsome rancher from her brain, she closed her eyes and raked the covers up to her chin. The unbidden recollection of her naked body lying next to Ben's plagued her with merciless glee. An involuntary shiver ran the length of her spine, but she refused to admit that it had been caused by anything other than a sudden burst of cool night air coming through the window.

It dawned on her that the music and laughter below had given way to an abrupt silence. Her eyes flew open and she frowned in puzzlement, wondering if perhaps the bartender had decided to close early out of respect to the hotel's lone guest.

Far from it. In the next instant, the sharp report of gunfire rent the silence. Jessie gasped and sat bolt upright in bed, her throat constricted with alarm.

"What in the—?" she breathed shakily, her widened gaze dropping to the floor.

Another shot rang out, followed by still another. A strangled cry broke from Jessie's lips as a bullet suddenly came tearing up through the carpet. In a split second, it had ricocheted off one post of the brass bed and shattered the window. An explosion of broken glass showered the room, jagged pieces of it falling on the floor and covers and embedding in the lace curtains.

Stunned, Jessie could only sit and stare dazedly at the destruction for several long moments. She came to life again when the door was thrown open to reveal an obviously worried Lissa. The redhead held aloft the coal-oil lamp clutched in her right hand.

"Jessie! Lord have mercy, are you all right?" Clad in a high-necked white nightgown and with her flaming hair streaming down her back, she flew to Jessie's side. "Are

112

you all right?" she demanded anxiously once more. Tiny pieces of glass crunched beneath her shoes.

"I—I think so!" Jessie faltered weakly. She glanced down at the bed, only to see that the lamp's glow revealed a multitude of sparkling glass strewn atop the quilt.

"It's a wonder you weren't killed!"

"I heard shots being fired below and then *this* happened!" explained Jessie in a breathless rush. She eased herself carefully from the bed and stepped into the velvet slippers Lissa fetched for her from the trunk. Tossing a wrapper about her shoulders, she belted it on over her thin white gauze nightgown. "Do you suppose anyone was—was killed down there?" she wondered tremulously, her wide, apprehensive gaze dropping significantly to the floor again.

"I don't know, but I'm sure we'll hear about it soon enough," replied Lissa in her usual pragmatic manner. "Let's get you out of here and down to my room." She placed a supportive arm about Jessie's shoulders and led her forward into the dimly lit hallway.

The Lamberts, their faces portraying no small measure of concern, came scurrying up the stairs from their own quarters at the rear of the hotel. They, too, were dressed only in their nightclothes, having been jolted rudely awake by the sound of the gunshots.

"Dear God in heaven, Miss Boone, did you or Miss Clare come to any harm?" the attractive Frenchman asked, much distressed at the thought.

"No, Mr. Lambert," Lissa calmly assured him. "We're both of us fine, though Miss Clare suffered a close call when her window was shot out."

"Oh, Henry, you must do something about that place!" his young wife insisted, her eyes glistening with tears of righteous anger. "Once and for all, you must put an end to this violent conduct! Our guests are being endangered at every turn, and I—"

113

"Yes, my love," he solemnly agreed, giving her hand a soothing pat. "I will do what I can."

After offering profuse apologies to Jessie for the terrifying misadventure she had suffered, the Lamberts returned downstairs to investigate the matter. Lissa led Jessie down the hall and into her own room. The two of them passed the remainder of the night without further disturbance, though Jessie lay awake for a long time.

Her thoughts returning to what Ben Chandler had said about Cimarron's wildness, she told herself it would be absurd to pass judgment after one unfortunate incident. Nevertheless, the nagging possibility that his warning had been truth and not fiction continued to plague her until she fell asleep, whereupon her dreams were invaded by visions of a tall, ruggedly handsome man who spirited her away on his horse while bullets flew about them.

The following morning, Jessie was horrified to discover that a man had actually been killed in the saloon.

"Good heavens, Lissa, what happened?" she asked, sinking down upon the bed. She had been in the process of brushing her hair when Lissa, whose duties began with the dawn, returned upstairs to relate what she had learned from Mr. Lambert.

"The same thing that usually happens," the redhead disclosed with a heavy sigh. She frowned and slowly shook her head. "Some poor puncher got drunk, sat in on a few rounds of poker, then decided he was getting tired of losing. He pulled a gun and started blasting away at the table. One of the soldiers from the fort shot him when he decided to aim at the dealer."

"You mean to say a human life was taken as a result of nothing more important than a *game?*" Jessie asked in wide-eyed disbelief. Aghast at what she had just heard, she shuddered and found herself wondering if the poor man had a family somewhere.

114

"I'm afraid so. Mr. Lambert has tried to lessen the violence by posting a sign requesting that all men leave their guns at the door, but not too many comply."

"But surely something could be done about—"

"I wish it could. But this isn't St. Louis, Jessie. For men here, strapping on a holster is as natural as pulling on their pants. And to tell the truth, it has to be that way."

"Why?" demanded Jessie. "Why does it have to be that way, when men use those same guns to murder one another?"

"You don't understand," Lissa observed with a faint smile of indulgence. "But you will once you've been here a while. You will," she reiterated on her way out the door.

Jessie stared after the other woman, her brow creasing into a perplexed frown as she contemplated everything she had just heard. It troubled her greatly to realize that a man had died in the room immediately below hers. She was certainly not unfamiliar with death; the loss of her mother had turned her own world upside down when she was only twelve. But the senseless violence of a stranger's death made her feel sick inside, and she felt seeds of doubt springing to life in her mind once more.

"I have done the right thing in coming here. I *have!*" she insisted aloud, as if trying to convince herself. Her sparkling emerald gaze, still full of uncertainty, traveled with a will of its own to the floor below.

Later, armed with a renewed spirit of determination and dressed in a stylish but practical suit of sphinx-gray muslin, Jessie set off to procure a horse and buggy. She had inquired about the location of the schoolhouse at the previous night's meeting, only to learn that it wasn't in town at all but a distance of some five miles west. Anxious to see the building where she would soon begin her duties, she planned to drive out and take a look at it.

115

Lissa had gravely cautioned her against going alone, offering to accompany her after the noon meal, but she was reluctant to postpone the excursion. There was nothing else to occupy her for the day, which made her plans all the more attractive. She did not tell the other woman of her final decision, however, and thus left the hotel feeling a trifle guilty but nonetheless excited.

Marching purposefully toward the livery stable behind the St. James, she passed the saloon on her way. Her gaze was instinctively drawn to its swinging double doors. To prevent the general public—most especially ladies and children—from looking in, the windows were shielded by heavy grates, a double advantage in that horses had a way of backing into the glass panes and breaking them.

"It's shocking what goes on in that place!" a woman spoke behind her. Jessie turned to face one of the young matrons she had met the night before. "Did you know, Miss Clare, that another man was gunned down in there last night?" the woman asked, her hand tightening about the smaller one belonging to a pixie-faced girl of three or four.

"Yes," answered Jessie, her mind racing to remember the pretty brunette's name. She smiled down at the child before remarking to the mother, "I was very sorry to learn of it." It was best, she told herself, to make no mention of her own involvement in the tragic affair.

"It happens far too often, you know. We have a sheriff who is paid good money to uphold the peace, but he's usually home in bed whenever the shooting starts!" She eyed Jessie narrowly for a moment, then added with another disapproving glance at the saloon, "There's a roulette wheel in there. And a piano. And even, so I've heard tell, a big painting of a woman, naked as the day she was born, lying on a sofa with her—" She broke off abruptly when it occurred to her that her daughter was listening to every word. "Little pitchers have big ears," she leaned forward to whisper conspiratorially to Jessie, giving a meaningful nod down at the plump, fair-haired child.

"Indeed they do," agreed Jessie, doing her best not to smile.

"Where are you going?" the young woman suddenly demanded. Her eyes flickered up and down Jessie's impeccably attired form, and she did not wait for an answer. "I'm afraid, Miss Clare," she pronounced with a stern frown, "that you'll have to adapt your wardrobe more appropriately to our weather. The heat can become almost unbearable at times. All of us have learned to wear only the minimum amount of undergarments; women have been known to collapse out here as a result of lacing themselves into corsets. And under *no* circumstances should you wear silk as you did last night. Not only does it prevent the skin from breathing properly"—this statement Jessie knew with a certainty to be in error—"but we don't go in for such showy finery here in Cimarron. You don't want to set yourself above us, Miss Clare," she advised with an affronted air, leaving little doubt that she thought the beautiful new schoolmarm had done precisely that.

"I shall keep that in mind," promised Jessie, her green eyes bridling with an equal amount of irritation and ironic amusement.

"Well, little Faith and I had best be on our way for now," the talkative young matron concluded at last. "But you'll be seeing a good deal more of us starting day after tomorrow."

"The day after tomorrow?" echoed Jessie in bewilderment.

"Didn't you know?" She gave a sigh of exasperation and reached up to adjust her blue calico bonnet. "Horace Mooney promised to send word to you first thing this morning! You're to board with us first. I might as well tell

117

you right now, so you can't say you weren't given fair warning, things are going to be a bit crowded. Aside from my husband and myself and the four girls, my younger brother is staying with us for a while. You'll have to share a room with the children. I am sure, however, that we will all manage somehow. That's why I was the very first to volunteer," she revealed smugly.

Jessie found herself at a sudden loss for words. Not for the life of her could she remember the woman's name, nor could she even begin to imagine what residing under the same roof with so many strangers was going to be like. *Good heavens,* she mused with an inward groan of dismay, *to think of having to listen to this woman's voice every morning and evening . . .*

Although it occurred to her that she might very well prefer being awakened by a nightly outbreak of gunfire at the hotel, she scolded herself for such uncharitable thoughts and forced a polite smile to her lips. She wondered what her reaction would have been had she discovered it was under Ben Chandler's roof she was to spend the next two weeks.

"Day after tomorrow, Miss Clare!" her future hostess called out as she headed on down the boardwalk, impatiently tugging the little girl along with her. "My husband will drive you on out when the time comes!"

Jessie managed another smile and raised her hand in a gracious acknowledgment of this last bit of information. The smile faded as soon as the woman was out of sight.

"Oh, fiddlesticks," she murmured, repeating a silly phrase she had often heard her brother Andrew use. Shaking her head at this latest disaster—albeit a relatively minor one—to befall her, she released a long sigh and once again turned her steps in the direction of the livery stable. Her optimism had waned somewhat by now, but she refused to give up on the idea of viewing the schoolhouse.

The wide double doors of the livery stable were standing open when Jessie got there. She hesitated for a moment as she peered inside the ramshackle wooden building, then gathered up her skirts and marched forward to speak to the large gray-haired man she spied leading a horse from one of the stalls at the back.

"I should like to hire a horse and buggy for a few hours, please," she told him.

He started in alarm, as if the sound of a feminine voice was entirely foreign to his ears. Dressed in a sweat-soaked work shirt and dirty trousers, he smelled strongly of horses and whiskey. Jessie tried not to wrinkle her nose in disgust. His gaze raked insolently over her, while his craggy features twisted into an almost hostile scowl.

"We don't rent to no women!" he growled.

"You don't—" she repeated in disbelief. "Well, why not?" she demanded in the next instant, her eyes shooting sparks of indignation.

"Because we don't!" he maintained stubbornly. "It's the policy."

"Then I suggest it is time to adopt a new policy," Jessie countered with a proud, angry lift of her head. "One that does not discriminate against customers on the basis of their sex!"

"Hell, I never said nothin' about—about *that!*" the fellow rasped in embarrassment, his face red as a beet. "You got no call to say I was talkin' indecent to you, woman!" It was Jessie's turn to color when the reason for his sudden distress finally dawned on her.

"What I meant, sir," she clarified, her tone one of sorely tried patience, "was quite simply that it is not fair for you to exclude women as customers of this establishment. Now, as I said in the beginning, I need a horse and buggy. This *is* a livery stable, is it not?"

"Damn right it is, but—"

"Then please be so kind as to tell me how much it will

cost to rent what I require for . . . say . . . three or four hours' time."

"The usual fee's a dollar a day, but I still don't—"

"Of course you don't." Stepping briskly forward, she produced the correct amount from her small beaded and tasseled bag. She held it out to the incredulous man, saying, "I suppose it is the custom to pay in advance, so here you are. I shall wait out front while you bring the horse and buggy around."

For a moment, she feared the man would not take the money. But remarkably, he did—though with an ill grace—and she heaved an inward sigh of relief when he spun about to do her bidding. He muttered something under his breath as he went, something Jessie could have sworn contained the words *female* and *Yankee*. Her eyes glistened with triumph while she watched him stalk to the open wagon yard at the rear of the building.

Soon she was on her way out of town, the buggy's wheels bouncing and jolting over a rough road that would scarcely be called a path back home. She passed several people in wagons and on horseback before she left Cimarron behind. Offering a smile and friendly nod in response to their greetings, she did not realize that the sight of a woman traveling alone was a rare one in the Territory. Lissa had pointed out the dangers to her; so, oddly enough, had the man at the livery stable. But she was convinced there could be no harm in driving a few short miles over the narrow road that wound its way across the rolling, sunlit prairie.

She breathed deeply of the fresh air, enjoying the feel of the warm wildflower-scented breeze against her face. Her fascinated gaze traveled over the spellbinding beauty of the New Mexico countryside, and she smiled to herself when she tossed a glance overhead at the clear, brilliant sky. It wasn't long before she spotted a large herd of cattle grazing peacefully on a hillside. The sight of them made her think of Ben Chandler. Her mind's accursed preoccupation with him only deepened when she looked across the broad pasturelands to where the towering peaks and deep canyons of the Sangre de Cristo Mountains loomed upon the horizon.

"Why must I keep thinking about that night?" she lamented, her brows pulling together in a troubled frown. It didn't make sense. Of far more significance was the attack upon the stagecoach and those subsequent terrifying hours she had spent as a prisoner among the Apaches, and yet something within her chose to make the most frequent and inescapable memory the one of Ben Chandler's strong arms about her, of his hard, smooth-muscled body pressed against her soft curves, of his warm lips moving over hers with slow, demanding expertise. . . .

Stop it! she cried inwardly, ashamed of the way her whole disloyal body burned. Until now, she had always managed to suppress any real stirrings of passion. Not that there had been much occasion to do so, she mused with a soft, rueful smile. She had been mildly attracted to a few young men, had found them to be charming and pleasant company, to be sure, but she hadn't wanted any of them to kiss her a second time. Never, *ever* had she felt the way Ben Chandler had made her feel—the way he still made her feel. It was downright wicked, she told herself, her beautiful green eyes ablaze with emotion. Wicked and wrong and heavenly . . .

"That's quite enough!" she decreed aloud. Shifting angrily upon the padded leather seat, she gave a brisk slap of the reins. Her enjoyment in the wild, enchanting landscape about her was diminished now, so that she became increasingly impatient to reach her destination.

It took longer than she had expected. Horace Mooney had put forth a brief description of the spot to her—"a fork in the road immediately past an old tumbledown

121

barn to your left"—but he had said nothing about what the schoolhouse itself looked like.

The sun was blazing almost directly overhead by the time Jessie drew the horse and buggy to a halt. She turned her head to stare at a log building standing amidst an overgrown tangle of brush and grass and trees several hundred yards from the road.

"Good heavens, that can't be it!" she murmured in disbelief, hoping in vain that she had somehow either overshot the distance or not yet traveled far enough. However, she knew she had not been mistaken when her searching gaze lit upon a big iron bell hanging outside the door.

The sight of the building, little more than a cabin really, caused her spirits to plummet. Looping the reins and setting the buggy's brake, she climbed down from the leather seat and frowned disconsolately toward the rough, neglected-looking structure while shading her eyes against the sun with her hand. The schoolhouse she had imagined was a neat, well-built frame building painted white, with large windows and with its yard enclosed by a tall whitewashed picket fence. What she saw instead was . . . well, it was *not* the sort of place to invoke dreams of educational greatness!

Perhaps the interior looks more promising, she mused in an attempt to console herself. She lifted her skirts as high as her booted ankles and began making her way through the dense, undulating sea of grass. Moments later, she was forced to an abrupt halt when the ruffled hem of her petticoat became caught by a prickly stand of cactus growing close to the ground. She gave a brisk tug on the white lawn petticoat, only to hear the unmistakable sound of the fabric tearing.

"That was a perfectly witless thing to do!" she told herself severely. Muttering a most unladylike oath beneath her breath, she bent and hastily gathered her full

122

muslin skirts high upon her shapely stockinged limbs in order to survey the damage.

"Now that's what I call a hell of a pretty sight," a man's voice drawled from the doorway of the nearby schoolhouse.

Jessie started in alarm, a loud gasp escaping her lips as she frantically smoothed her clothing back down into place and whirled to face the voice's owner. Her cheeks flamed crimson at the thought that someone had seen her with her skirts up about her knees. Lifting her head in a proud, angry gesture that belied the fear in her eyes, she gazed at the man standing with one hand braced negligently against the door frame.

"Who are you, sir?" she demanded in her best schoolteacher voice. "And what are you doing here?"

"I might ask you the same thing," he retorted with a low chuckle. Tilting his hat back upon his head, he straightened and moved at a leisurely pace down the front steps, the splintered wood creaking softly beneath his high-heeled cowboy boots. A slow taunting smile spread across his darkly attractive features as he advanced upon Jessie. "This is public property. So I guess we've both got a right to be here."

Wide-eyed and breathless, she stared across at the raven-haired young man. He looked much the same as any other young puncher she had seen around Cimarron, but there was one notable difference. Whereas the others had displayed a charming gallantry and reverence toward her, this one was virtually undressing her with his eyes. His gaze raked over her with insolent boldness as he approached, and the look on his face left little doubt that he liked what he saw.

Battling the temptation to spin about and run back to the buggy as fast as her legs would carry her, Jessie determinedly stood her ground.

"I am the new schoolteacher," she announced in cold,

crisp tones, her voice quaking only a little at the end. "I don't know who *you* are, but I suggest that you leave at once!"

"Well now, *schoolmarm*," he replied, his smile broadening into a predatory grin, "if you're who you say you are, then how about taking me on as your first pupil?" He didn't stop advancing until he was only a few inches away, his eyes glittering hotly down into Jessie's and his left hand moving up to tug the hat from his head. "It's just the two of us here, so what do you say we go on inside and get down to the learning?" There was no mistaking the derisive laughter in his voice, nor the lustful darkening of his gaze as it lingered caressingly upon her full young bosom.

"I will not dignify such—such insulting nonsense with an answer!" she countered, her eyes flashing in outrage and more than a touch of very real alarm. "If you don't mind, I've business to attend to and should like to get on with it!" She attempted to step around him, but he quickly moved to block her path.

"What's the hurry, schoolmarm?" he challenged lazily. "Like I said, we're alone out here. I think we ought to get to know one another, seeing as how we're both new to these parts."

"Let me pass, sir!"

"No."

Jessie's wide, startled eyes flew back up to his face, and her heart leapt in her throat when she saw that his playfulness had given way to a deadly serious intent. A warning bell sounded in her brain, telling her that the danger presented by the brash stranger was growing stronger with each passing second.

Get out of here! her instincts warned. *Get out of here before—*

But it was already too late. The stranger's hands shot out to grab her arms and yank her close. His arms tightened about her like a vise, forcing the breath from her lungs and threatening to crush her ribs. A scream welled up deep in her throat, but it was silenced by the cruel pressure of his mouth slanting down upon hers.

Shuddering with both fury and revulsion, Jessie immediately set up a struggle to be free. She twisted and writhed violently in the man's ruthless grasp, but her arms were imprisoned at her sides and the kicks she aimed at his legs appeared to have little effect. His lips assaulted hers with such force that she tasted blood, his tough, wiry body grinding into her soft curves so hard that she felt violated even through her clothing.

Desperation drove her to try another tactic, one that was admittedly risky but, if successful, would serve to grant her some time to think of something else. Acting purely on instinct, she suddenly made her whole body go limp.

The ploy worked. The stranger raised his head from hers, gritting a savage curse while supporting the unexpected burden of her entire weight. He glared murderously down into her face, his narrow, fury-laced gaze full of suspicion. Jessie feigned unconsciousness, forcing her eyes to remain closed as she was lowered roughly to the ground.

"Stupid little bitch!" her would-be conqueror ground out. Releasing her with painful abruptness, he straightened, then loomed indecisively above her while several opposing urges warred within him.

He hadn't meant to get mixed up with a woman just yet—especially not the local schoolmarm. Not only was it dangerous, but he couldn't afford the distraction right now. Besides, he mused contemptuously, women like her were usually too damned prissy and skittish for his taste, and this one, though she had shown enough fire at first, had in the end proven herself no different.

You're losing your touch, Cole Hagan, you randy

bastard, he told himself, his eyes gleaming with iniquitous humor. Still, he thought as he stared down at the golden-haired young beauty lying helpless in the grass at his feet, there was something about her . . .

His head shot up at the sound of hoofbeats in the near distance. Damn it, someone was coming! The last thing he needed was to be found standing over a woman who had fainted dead away at his kiss.

With a muttered oath, Cole Hagan sprang into action. He spun about and raced for the horse he had left tied behind the schoolhouse. By the time the approaching rider had reached the spot where Jessie's buggy waited, Cole was galloping away in the opposite direction, his flight concealed by the trees.

We'll meet again, schoolmarm, he vowed silently, his eyes glittering hotly at the thought. *And next time, I'll see about finding me more of that fire. Yes, ma'am, you can count on that,* he promised. It had struck him that the danger was worth it after all. His loins burning with the memory of her soft, delectable body against his, he pulled the hat lower on his dark head and gave his horse full rein.

Jessie scrambled to her feet at last. Her thick golden locks tumbling down out of their pins, she hurriedly raked the hair away from her face and whirled to face the man who was at that moment drawing his mount to an abrupt halt a few feet from where she stood. Pale and shaken, she gazed incredulously up into the grim, handsome features of Ben Chandler.

"Damn it, woman, what the bloody hell do you think you're doing out here?" he thundered. He flung down from the saddle and crossed the distance between them in long, angry strides. "I wouldn't have thought even *you* would be so damned brainless—"

He broke off when he suddenly glimpsed the lingering pain and terror in her eyes. His smoldering blue gaze made a quick sweep up and down the length of her disheveled form, and his features visibly tightened at the sight of her bloodied lip. "What happened?" he demanded, his tone deceptively low and level.

Jessie gazed mutely up at him, her face displaying a mixture of relief and confusion and surprise. Oddly enough, she was reluctant to tell him about the stranger's attack. Either because of a sense of shame or because of a fear that he would do something drastic, she did not know. All she knew was that she could not bring herself to speak the truth.

"Tell me, Jessamyn . . . what happened?" Ben repeated, his hands closing with a firm but gentle grip about her arms.

Jessamyn. The sound of her name upon his lips made her heart leap alarmingly and her body tremble from head to toe.

"I—I fell," she lied, hastily averting her gaze from the penetrating intensity of his.

"You fell?" he echoed in disbelief. He did not fail to notice the rush of guilty color staining her cheeks.

"Yes, I was walking to the schoolhouse and I—I must have tripped on something."

"How did you cut your lip?"

"Oh . . . that," she murmured breathlessly, raising a hand to the tender spot and small trickle of blood near the corner of her mouth. She stole a quick, uneasy glance up at him before offering, with as much composure as she could muster, "I injured it when I fell. The ground here is very rocky and uneven, and I was so anxious to see the schoolhouse that I . . . well, I suppose I was a trifle careless." Her eyes flew back up to his face when he let go of her arms.

"You were careless all right," Ben readily agreed, his eyes darkening with inexplicable rage again. "Careless and just plain stupid!"

127

"I beg your pardon!" she gasped, her own gaze becoming very round.

"Beg it all you like!" he shot back. "You little idiot, I ought to tan your hide good and proper!"

Indignantly reflecting that such action on his part would be anything but good *or* proper, Jessie raised her head to a proud, rebellious angle and folded her arms tightly across her full, angrily heaving breasts. Her eyes kindled and blazed with defensive wrath.

"Am I perhaps entitled to know what I have done to provoke such violent impulses in you, Mr. Chandler?" she queried with biting sarcasm.

"You were warned against coming out here alone, weren't you?"

"Yes, I suppose I was, but—"

"No buts, damn it! The next time Lissa or anyone else tells you not to do something, you'd better listen! You might have gotten yourself lost or hurt or even carried off by Indians again!"

The light in his eyes grew even more savage when he recalled how he had felt upon discovering she was out on the range alone. He had ridden into town as soon as he could get away, heading straightaway to the hotel to check on the woman who had haunted his dreams and made him curse every waking thought.

Lissa had met him with the news of her young friend's absence and with her suspicions about where Jessie had gone. A visit to the livery stable had confirmed those suspicions; it was unlikely the hapless man there would ever again make the same mistake he'd made that morning.

"Why, that—that's ridiculous!" sputtered Jessie. "For your information, Mr. Chandler, I never strayed from the road and I fail to see what was so dangerous about driving a few miles outside of town to the very location where I will begin teaching next week!" She thought of the recent horrifying incident his arrival had interrupted, but she determinedly pushed it to the back of her mind. "If I am to carry out my duties as Cimarron's new schoolteacher, then it is entirely necessary for me to—"

"So you're still planning to go through with it?" he broke in to demand, the tone of his deep, resonant voice leaving little doubt as to his continued disapproval.

"I most certainly am!" A sudden gust of wind sent her rumpled, grass-stained skirts flapping about her legs and her errant tresses fanning in front of her face. She raised her arms and angrily gathered up her long hair, then held it secure with one hand while smoothing down her skirts with the other.

Ben studied her every move. His fathomless blue gaze traveled over the stormy beauty of her upturned countenance, down across the provocative swell of her breasts, and lower to where she was having trouble keeping her skirts in order about her slender, well-rounded hips and shapely limbs. He cursed the fire in his blood, a long-dormant fire that always blazed to life now whenever he so much as looked at the stubborn, infuriating, damnably bewitching young woman before him.

"You cannot make me change my mind, Mr. Chandler," Jessie told him, growing increasingly unsettled as a result of his scrutiny. "In spite of your efforts to dissuade me, I shall be here at the schoolhouse on Monday morning, ringing the bell for my young charges and doing my absolute best to make certain none of the other members of the school board regret the decision to hire me!"

He said nothing in response, though the grim set of his jaw and fierce glow in his eyes spoke volumes. Jessie felt a sudden overwhelming need to escape. Casting him one last defiantly purposeful look, she turned her back on him and began making her way through the overgrown tangle of greenery once more. She had already reached the front steps of the schoolhouse—acutely conscious of Ben's searing gaze on her the whole time—before she gathered enough courage to steal a glance back at him. She suffered a sharp intake of breath when she discovered him towering above her.

"Come on," he commanded quietly. Taking a firm grip on her elbow, he startled her by leading her up the steps to the door. "We'll see how long you last once you find out what's in store for you."

She frowned in annoyance but bit back the retort that rose to her lips as he swung wide the door and sent it crashing back against the rough unpainted log wall. The rank and musty smell inside the building came forth to greet them full force. Jessie could not help wrinkling her nose in disgust.

"Good heavens, what is—?"

"Skunk," supplied Ben, a faint smile lurking at the corners of his mouth. "And no telling what else."

Peering inside the single dimly lit room, Jessie suppressed a groan of dismay. It was far worse than even the outside had led her to suspect. She shot a speaking glare up at Ben before turning her attention back to the disheartening sight before her.

A thick coating of dust and leaves and other debris covered everything. The floors were splintered and bare, the two windows on either side of the room were broken, and there were a number of large cracks in the walls where light shone through. Five double rows of handmade wooden benches faced the front, where the teacher's desk, once probably quite sufficient for its purpose, had been sawed in half by someone as a not-very-funny prank. There was a blackboard of sorts—three wooden planks that had been painted black and nailed up on the wall behind the desk. To complete the dismal picture, a hugh black potbellied iron stove sat in one corner, the floor around it covered with a thick, hardened crusting of soot and ashes.

"It needs some work," observed Ben. Jessie's mouth twitched at the understatement.

"Indeed it does, Mr. Chandler." She frowned at the thought of just how much work it would take to transform it into the schoolroom of her dreams. But she had never been one to admit defeat easily. She would not turn tail and run merely because of a little dirt and disrepair!

"Now maybe you'll admit I was right. You don't belong here. This isn't the sort of place for someone like you."

"On the contrary," she disagreed, her eyes filling with a renewed light of determination as she contemplated the task before her. "It is *exactly* the sort of place for someone like me!"

"What do you mean?" demanded Ben, his eyes narrowing imperceptibly.

"I mean, Mr. Chandler, that I have a great many things to do before Monday comes!" She gathered up her skirts and moved forward to make a closer inspection, leaving Ben to frown after her in bemusement. The frown deepened into a scowl when she charged accusingly from the front of the room, "How did you and the other members of the board expect the children to learn anything amidst this squalor?"

"We didn't."

"You didn't? But—"

"We were planning to have the place cleaned up before school started."

"Then why did you want me to see it like this?"

"Because I hoped it would help convince you to leave," he confessed without any trace of repentance.

"Why, of all the sneaky, underhanded—" she stormed

131

indignantly, only to be cut off by the sound of his deep voice, whipcord sharp, resounding throughout the sparsely furnished room.

"Damn it, Jessamyn Clare, why don't you open your eyes and look around you? Women like you don't last out here. You're not meant for this kind of life!"

"How do you know what I'm meant for?" she countered. She gave an angry toss of her head, which sent the luxuriant mass of golden curls bouncing riotously about her face and shoulders. "What makes you think I don't have what it takes to last?"

"I've known women like you before." His impassive features belied the sudden pain of remembrance clouding his gaze.

"Perhaps you have, but that is no reason to anticipate *my* failure!" she feelingly insisted. "What gives you the right to judge me? Oh, I will most certainly allow that I owe you my very life," she said with a bitter little smile, "but that life is nonetheless still mine to do with as I please!"

"Is it?" he challenged in a low tone scarcely above a whisper. His eyes held a disturbing warmth as they moved over her face before returning to capture her wide, luminous gaze. "Is it?"

Jessie wanted to ask him what he meant, but she was suddenly afraid. A long, highly charged silence rose up between them as they faced one another. She dared not speak or move . . . or do anything to break the spell. *What does it mean?*

Without a word, Ben moved slowly toward her. He did not stop until they were mere inches apart, so close that their breaths mingled and their hearts stirred in unison at one another's nearness.

Jessie could literally feel the heat emanating from his hard masculine body. The faint scent of leather and soap hung about him, and the front of his blue cotton shirt was unbuttoned into a small V, which allowed her a glimpse of the dark, softly curling hair that covered his chest and tapered down into the waistband of the denim trousers molding his lithely muscled lower body to perfection.

His superior size and strength made her feel incredibly small and feminine—and reminded her of things she had promised herself to forget. She remembered all too well the unfamiliar, shockingly pleasurable sensations she experienced while being held within the powerful circle of his arms. Her lips parted a bit while she stared expectantly, breathlessly up into the rugged handsomeness of his face. She felt positively scorched by his gaze as it caught and held hers, felt as though he could somehow peer into her very soul and see that her senses reeled at the very thought of being touched by him. . . .

"Get away, Jessamyn," he whispered huskily. "Get away before it's too late."

"Too—too late?" she faltered in bewilderment. She swayed weakly toward him, only to give a soft gasp when his hands came up to close about her shoulders and hold her steady.

"You're playing with fire, Miss Clare," he cautioned, his voice still low. His face was inscrutable, but his eyes smoldered with barely controlled passion. "And, by damn, you *will* get burned if you don't have a care!"

"What are you talking about?" she asked, her whole body growing warm while in the back of her mind she wondered if he was going to kiss her.

"I think you know" was all he would say. A strange, ultimately perplexing half smile played about his lips as he suddenly released her and reached up to tug the front brim of his hat lower. "Let's get you back to town."

"But I don't want to go back to town just yet!" she protested, feeling perilously close to tears and not knowing why.

"Let's go," he repeated as if she had not spoken.

133

Disregarding the mutinous look on her beautiful face, he took hold of her arm and propelled her back outside into the welcoming sunshine.

Jessie was tempted to jerk her arm free, but she wisely quelled the urge. A fiery blush rose to her face when she reluctantly admitted to herself just how much she had wanted Ben Chandler to kiss her back there in the middle of the schoolroom. She had wanted it so much it hurt. *Dear God, what is the matter with me?* she lamented, hoping for divine guidance in dealing with her own confusing desires and emotions.

Her thoughts were drawn involuntarily back to the cruel merciless kiss the dark-haired cowboy had forced upon her only a short time ago. There could be no comparison. Whereas the stranger's intent had been to brutally conquer, she remembered the sweet mastery of Ben's embraces, the way he had sought to tenderly initiate. Even though fate had provided him with the perfect opportunity to take her and damn the consequences, he had not.

Would you prefer that he had? that mischievous inner voice of hers taunted. *Would you prefer that you really had become his woman that night?* Heaven help her, but she could not answer.

Engrossed with her turbulent thoughts, she was surprised to discover that she and Ben had reached the buggy. He handed her silently up into it, then tied the reins of his horse to the back. Jessie, arranging her skirts about her, did her best to avoid meeting his gaze when he returned a moment later to take a seat beside her.

"Lissa said there was some trouble at the saloon last night," he remarked quietly, gathering up the reins. His features tensed again at the thought that she might have been hurt.

"Yes," she murmured with eyes still downcast.

"I want you on that stage tomorrow."

134

"*What?*" she gasped in disbelief, twisting abruptly about to face him now. "Haven't you heard a word I've said?"

"I heard." He gave a brief flick of the reins and set the buggy on a course back to Cimarron.

Jessie waited for him to say more, but he did not. She caught her lower lip pensively between her teeth, then winced a bit when she was reminded of the small cut there. Although it was the only visible sign of the stranger's attack, she knew she would never forget how frightened she had been. She shuddered to think of what might have happened if Ben had not come along. Once more, he had rescued her from certain danger.

For a brief moment, her thoughts turned from Ben to the other man. She prayed fervently that their paths would never cross again. The memory of his eyes, dark and predatory, burned in her mind, and she felt a shiver of dread run the length of her spine.

"Something wrong?" Ben asked with a frown.

"No," she hastily denied. "No, nothing's wrong."

"Are you sure?" His voice was full of genuine concern.

"Of course." She stole a sideways glance at him, only to feel a dull flush rise to her face. In spite of all they had been through together, she still knew so very little about him.

"You won't be staying st the St. James tonight."

"I—I won't?"

"No."

"Then where am I going to stay?" she inquired dazedly.

"Out at the Chapparosa."

"The Chapparosa?" She had heard the name the day before, when Lissa had spoken of Ben's cousin. Her eyes grew enormous within the delicate oval of her face as realization set in. "But that's *your* place!"

"I know," he replied with a brief smile of irony. "I've

135

decided it's the only way to keep an eye on you. If you're not going to listen to reason, then I can at least make sure you don't go gallivanting off on your own again."

"Don't I have anything to say about this?" she demanded stiffly, not at all certain she liked having her life put into order by someone else—especially Ben Chandler.

"Nope."

"But what about the people in Cimarron? I mean, how is it going to look if I board with you? You were the one who warned me about the possible damage to my reputation, were you not?"

"Has anyone said anything?"

"Well, yes, as a matter of fact, they have!"

"When?" he demanded sharply, his eyes taking on the look of molten steel.

"At the meeting last night. There were no specific accusations, but—"

"What the hell are you talking about? *What* meeting?"

"The town meeting, of course," she replied, frowning at him in bemusement. "Mr. Mooney arranged it." She was surprised at the way his mouth suddenly compressed into a tight, thin line of anger.

"That son of a bitch!" muttered Ben. He turned his smoldering gaze on Jessie and explained, "Mooney didn't tell me about the meeting. He must have set it up after I left town. Damn it, I wouldn't have let you face the wolves alone if I'd known."

"The wolves?" She felt her stomach do a strange flip-flop when his lips curved into a brief, crooked smile of wry amusement.

"The good people of Cimarron," he clarified for her. All traces of humor vanished when he demanded, "What happened?"

"Nothing, really," she was glad to answer truthfully.

Her green eyes sparkled with a renewed sense of triumph. "Things were a trifle *uncomfortable* in the beginning, to be sure, but it didn't take long for the tide to turn."

"In other words, Miss Clare," he offered dryly, "you charmed the devil out of them." The thought made his gaze darken. His hands clenched upon the reins, and a muscle twitched in the bronzed ruggedness of his cheek.

"Returning to the subject of where I am to board, Mr. Chandler," said Jessie, "I think you should be aware that arrangements have already been made for me to stay with someone else."

"I'll take care of that." *Hell yes,* he added silently, *I'll be more than happy to have a talk with Horace Mooney about that—among other things.*

Jessie, perplexed by the telltale signs of anger about him, sat back against the leather cushion. She was painfully aware of his closeness to her on the seat. Shifting as far away as possible, she clasped her hands tightly together in her lap and turned her bright, troubled gaze outward.

God help her, she was going to live in Ben Chandler's house. . . .

Six

"There's someone downstairs to see you, Jessie," announced Lissa, smiling rather slyly across at her while framed in the open doorway.

"Who is it?" Jessie glanced up from where she sat perched on the edge of the bed, making a list of supplies for the school. She had already decided to purchase whatever was required with her own funds and worry about reimbursement later. "I wasn't expecting anyone," she told Lissa. No, she recalled with a slight frown and a telltale flush, Ben had said he would not return for her until quite late that afternoon.

"It's Martha Rosedale," disclosed the tall redhead, her opal eyes twinkling. "Ben Chandler's cousin."

"Oh!" She scrambled off the bed and flew to the mirror, vigorously shaking the creases from her striped grenadine skirts. Her reflection offered confirmation that her hair was pinned securely in place and her white lawn shirtwaist buttoned smoothly across the swell of her bosom. "I wonder why she has come to call?" she mused aloud, turning to face Lissa again. "Do you suppose when Be—Mr. Chandler told her I was going to stay at the Chapparosa she decided to see for herself if I will make a suitable guest?"

"Maybe," Lissa responded with a quiet laugh. "Then again, maybe Martha doesn't even know about that yet. Whatever the case, you're not likely to find out if you stay up here!"

Beaming a warmly lit smile at Lissa, Jessie swept from the room, her steps quickening as she moved down the staircase. She forced herself to slow down a bit before she reached the lobby, where she saw a petite, dark-haired woman sitting on the red velvet chaise. The woman rose to her feet when she caught sight of Jessie.

"Miss Clare?" Her voice was as soft and cultured as her appearance, which wasn't at all what Jessie had expected. As Lissa had told her, the woman was perhaps fifty years of age, but her chestnut hair was untouched by gray and her skin was only faintly lined. She was dressed in a simple but elegant gown of pale green poplin, while her small straw hat was trimmed with a double ruffle of lace.

"Yes, I am Miss Clare," Jessie answered with a nod. "I take it you are Miss Rosedale?"

"Yes, my dear, but I should like it very much if you would call me Martha," the older woman insisted in a warm, friendly manner. "Everyone else does."

"And I am Jessie." She liked this cousin of Ben Chandler's, liked her very much indeed. The realization surprised her somewhat, perhaps because she had expected someone as strong and domineering as he. Martha Rosedale was certainly neither of those.

"Very well then, Jessie, would you mind if we talked a few minutes?" Martha resumed her seat on the chaise, smiling at Jessie as the younger woman sank down beside her. "You must think it very odd to receive a visitor you've never even met."

"Well, to tell the truth, I did wonder about it," admitted Jessie, her own mouth curving into an answering smile. "Does the reason for your visit have anything to do with the fact that I am coming to stay at the ranch? If so, I can assure you I—"

"I beg your pardon, my dear, but what are you talking about?"

"Didn't Mr. Chandler tell you?" She had caught herself before calling him Ben that time.

"Tell me what?" Martha asked in obvious bewilderment.

"Oh I—I see," murmured Jessie. *So his decision had been made on the spur of the moment after all,* she reflected, curious to know what had prompted it. "I'm sorry, but it seems your cousin has insisted that I board at his home first. I hope it won't cause you any inconvenience," she added sincerely.

"Inconvenience? Why, quite the contrary!" Martha assured her with a smile of genuine pleasure. "I am perfectly delighted to hear Ben had the good sense to make such an arrangement. We shall be most happy to welcome you to the Chapparosa, Jessie. James and Hannah—those are the twins—will no doubt consider it quite an honor to have the new schoolteacher living with us!"

"I certainly hope so." She released a faint sigh, and her brow creased into a frown of puzzlement again. "But, if not for that reason, why *did* you come to call on me?" she blurted out, then mentally chided herself for asking.

"Because, my dear, I thought you might be needing an ally! I, too, was once a young woman in a strange town, with no friends or family," the older woman revealed, her eyes full of kindness and understanding. "Though I was not a teacher, I remember all too well what it felt like to have the prospect of a first day's duties looming before me. I was apprenticed to a milliner, you see, and when the time came for me to open my own shop, I found it necessary to do so in another town. To make a long story mercifully short, there were times I despaired of ever finding happiness, times when I was sorely tempted to toss aside my independence and run back home to the loving bosom of my family. But I did not. And that is why I have come, Jessie, not to presume to tell you what to do with your own life, but to let you know there is someone who understands."

"Thank you, Martha," Jessie responded with heartfelt gratitude. Her eyes glistened with tears, for she was greatly touched by the other woman's gesture of caring. "I *have* depaired, you know, and wondered if my dreams of teaching in the West were indeed leading me to disaster." She thought of what she had already endured. Martha, as if reading her mind, reached over to take her hand.

"Ben has told me about your imprisonment by the Apaches. I thank God he was able to find you in time!" She peered at Jessie with compassion for a moment, then probed gently, "You are all right now, aren't you, my dear? Ben said you did not suffer harm, but sometimes the greatest injuries are the ones we cannot see."

"No, I—I suffered no real harm," Jessie assured her, faltering a bit as she wondered just how much Ben had told his cousin.

"I am glad to hear it." Martha patted Jessie's hand one last time, then stood and smiled brightly down at her. "I'm afraid I must be on my way. Consuela, who is our highly beloved and invaluable housekeeper, will begin to worry if I do not return soon with the things she asked for. That was the reason I gave for coming, you see!" she confessed with a soft laugh.

Jessie rose to her feet as well. Hesitating only briefly, she embraced the older woman. A sad, tremulous smile lit her face as, just for a moment, she was reminded of the mother she had lost so long ago.

"I suppose Ben will be bringing you home with him today?" asked Martha while the two of them strolled

141

toward the door.

"Yes," Jessie confirmed with a nod. *Home*, her mind repeated. Ben Chandler's home would be hers for the next two weeks.

"Good. Then I shall warn the twins to be on their best behavior this evening!" With that, she smiled again and was gone.

Jessie, her eyes aglow with the knowledge that she had indeed found a new friend and ally, hurried back upstairs. She had a great many things to do before Ben came for her.

Jessie's first glimpse of the Chapparosa was from the top of a low hill, half a mile away from the ranch's headquarters. Her pulses quickened as she rode beside Ben in the buckboard, and her gaze widened with both astonishment and delight at the sight laid out before her.

The main house was a large ten-room log structure, sitting beneath a canopy of tall cottonwoods, a blue plume of smoke going up from its rock chimney. On the roof were hand-hewn cedar shingles, weathered to a soft gray. The boards that covered the ends of the logs were painted white, as was the rest of the woodwork—the doors, window frames, and veranda pillars. In spite of the fact that the logs themselves had not been painted, the overall effect was a charming lightness that was unique among such buildings.

Jessie's fascinated gaze traveled farther. She saw three corrals, two barns, a bunkhouse, and a number of other outbuildings scattered around the yard. The ranch was surrounded by orchards and gardens, for there was plentiful water and the soil was rich. It was all set against a backdrop of lush green meadows and the towering majesty of the mountains in the near distance.

"Why, it's absolutely beautiful!" she pronounced,

half to herself.

"I'm glad it meets with your approval," drawled Ben, his mouth twitching. In truth, he *was* glad. More glad than he cared to admit. His eyes gleamed with pride when he told her, "It didn't look like much in the beginning. The first few years were spent trying to keep it from going wild again."

"How long have you lived here?"

"I bought the land a couple of years after the war."

"The war?" echoed Jessie, then realized what he meant. "Did—did you serve with the Confederate forces, Mr. Chandler?"

"No." For a moment, it appeared he would follow his usual line of reticence, but he surprised her by disclosing, "I was in the cavalry, stationed at Fort Union. We were so busy fighting Indians, we never even thought about the war until Glorieta."

"Glorieta?" She turned to look at him while he drove the buckboard down the last stretch of road leading up to the house. With a will of their own, her eyes strayed downward to linger upon the firm, chiseled mouth that had claimed hers with such beguiling passion.

"The Battle of Glorieta Pass."

"I've heard of that," murmured Jessie, her brows knitting together in a frown as she tried to remember. "The Union troops were victorious there, were they not?"

"You might say that," he replied with only the ghost of a smile. "As a teacher, Miss Clare, you should know that the fate of the entire western territories may very well have been determined by the outcome of that one battle."

"Perhaps I should have you come and address the class on the subject, Mr. Chandler!" she suggested with a flash of spirit.

"You don't like finding out you're less than perfect, do

143

you, schoolmarm?" he challenged, his eyes alight with roguish humor.

"No more than you, sir!" she retorted.

Ben gave a low chuckle. Pulling the buckboard to a halt in front of the house, he set the brake and swung down. A gigantic black dog came bounding out of nowhere to hurl himself joyfully at his master, who rewarded him with a hearty pat before moving around to help Jessie down. She felt a delicious tremor course through her when he clasped her about the waist and lowered her to the ground. With her face coloring, she looked away in confusion as he reluctantly let her go.

"Welcome to the Chapparosa, Jessie!" proclaimed Martha from the doorway. Her kindly features wreathed in smiles, she was flanked by a boy and a girl, both of whom resembled their father to a small extent and one another almost entirely.

"Thank you, Martha," replied Jessie. She was determined not to let anyone know how nervous she was. Gathering up her skirts, she swept forward with a smile of her own and extended her hand to the little girl. "You must be Hannah Chandler. I am Miss Clare, and I am very pleased to meet you." She was relieved when Ben's daughter accepted her hand and smiled shyly up at her.

"How do you do, Miss Clare," Hannah recited with a slight lisp. She was a pretty child, with long blond pigtails hanging on either side of her head and big blue eyes that sparkled with intelligence. Dressed in what looked suspiciously like her Sunday best, she reminded Jessie of a doll she once owned.

"I'm James," Hannah's brother spoke up boldly. He stepped forward and took Jessie's hand in a surprisingly firm grip for such a small, slender fellow. His hair, a little darker than his twin's, was cut short above his ears, and he, too, had been forced into clothing usually reserved for church services, weddings, and funerals. His gaze

144

literally danced while he grinned up at Jessie with irresistible charm.

"How do you do, James," she said with an answering smile. "I know you and Hannah are going to be a great help to me when school starts next week."

"We've never been to school before!" declared Hannah.

"You haven't? Well, then, I shall do my best to make sure the experience is a happy one for you," Jessie promised solemnly.

"Is it true you were captured by Indians?" James demanded with all the natural curiosity of a seven-year-old boy.

"James Chandler, you're not to mention that again, do you hear?" Martha admonished with a stern frown of reproval.

"It's all right," Jessie hastened to assure her. She nodded at the little boy and told him, "Yes, as a matter of fact, I *was* their prisoner, but only for a day."

"Father saved you, didn't he?" This came from Hannah, who cast an adoring glance toward Ben.

"Yes, he did."

Ben came up behind her now, setting her trunk on the front porch without a word before turning back to see to the horse. Jessie stole a quick look at him. A shadow crossed her face when it occurred to her that he might already regret his decision to have her there.

"Come along, Jessie," Martha cheerfully bid her. "We'll get you settled in your room, and then I'll take you out to the kitchen to meet Consuela. I do hope you won't mind my giving you the bedroom next to Ben's. All of the others are in another wing of the house. I know in some circles it would not be considered entirely proper for you to share quarters so close to his, but the room happens to be the only one which is unoccupied at present and it is, I assure you, the nicest one in the house."

145

"No, I—I don't mind at all," murmured Jessie, though she was in truth uncertain about her feelings on the matter. *The bedroom next to Ben's* . . . Those ominous words struck a chord of alarm within her.

"I am so glad." Martha drew her through the doorway, while Hannah and James, who would much rather have taken themselves off to help their father with the horse but had been given strict orders to remain inside, followed closely behind.

The interior of the house was every bit as attractive and comfortable as Jessie had imagined. The walls were papered in cream and pastel florals, the polished wooden floors featured carpets of thick wool, and the furniture was an intriguing mixture of styles, with the greater majority of it being large, expensive pieces of walnut and rosewood. Lamps with crystal flourishes, curtains of lace alternating with draperies of velvet, and a highly varied assortment of paintings, with classical themes as well as a frontier motif, helped to complete the image of a real home.

Jessie, her eyes moving over everything with a great deal of interest, reflected that the furnishings were an unusual but engaging collection of styles. Nevertheless, it flashed through her mind that she would make a few changes if she were the mistress of Chapparosa. The thought made her flush guiltily.

Wafting throughout the sprawling one-story ranch house was the decidedly appetizing aroma of beef simmered in a rich chili sauce, baked pinto beans, freshly made white flour tortillas, hot coffee and cocoa, and a dessert of *biscochitos,* which were light sugar cookies with a hint of anise and a sprinkling of cinnamon. Jessie inhaled deeply of the mingling scents, which prompted Martha to smile and explain.

"I thought you might enjoy a meal of traditional dishes this evening. Consuela is a true magician and can prepare whatever we want, but she is without a doubt in her element when the menu consists of New Mexican cuisine. You'll perhaps find it a bit spicier than what you're accustomed to," she cautioned. Leading the way down a wide hallway, she paused before the first door on the right and turned back to the twins. "Children, you may retire to your rooms for the present. Miss Clare will no doubt be grateful for some time alone before supper."

"But Aunt Martha," protested James. Both children had addressed her as Aunt from the very beginning. "We want to show her—"

"Later, dear boy," Martha insisted firmly, though she softened her words with an affectionate hand upon his small shoulder. He and his sister reluctantly obeyed, leaving Jessie to smile after them as they disappeared around the corner.

"I certainly hope my other students prove to be as well behaved," she told the older woman. "You have reason to be proud of them, as I know you must be."

"Frankly, my dear, I cannot take full credit," confessed Martha. "Their father has never neglected them as so many fathers do. Quite the contrary!" She opened the door and remarked with an unmistakable note of pride in her voice, "This will be your room, Jessie."

It was, as Martha had claimed earlier, a perfectly lovely room. Tiny scarlet roses danced upon the wallpaper, while ruffled curtains of red gingham trimmed in lace hung at the window. Brightly colored rugs, woven by local craftsmen, were placed at strategic points upon the floor. The furniture, noted Jessie, was different from that in the rest of the house; carved from rich golden oak, it had been brought by wagon across the Santa Fe Trail many years ago.

Her eyes were now drawn to the bed. It was a beautiful four-poster, with a canopy of crocheted white cotton and a pieced coverlet of red calico and bleached muslin. An embroidered bedskirt reached all the way to the floor, which was of such a considerable distance that a footstool sat beside the bed to aid its occupants in climbing up or down.

"I hope you like red," remarked Martha, her eyes sparkling with a touch of wry humor. "It was Emily's favorite color, you see. She insisted upon at least one room devoted to her marked preference for it."

"Emily?" echoed Jessie with a faint frown of bewilderment.

"Ben's wife." Martha heaved a soft sigh, her features sobering and her gaze filling with sadness. "She died shortly after the twins were born. She was such a lovely, delicate creature. James and Hannah look remarkably like her."

"Then she must have been beautiful indeed," Jessie offered in a low tone. She was unprepared for the way her heart twisted painfully at the thought of another woman sharing Ben Chandler's life. *You knew about his marriage,* she told herself. *You've known about it all along.* And yet it had not seemed real to her until now, until this very moment when she stood in the room filled with Emily's things and decorated in Emily's favorite color. Even the children had not served to remind her of that long-ago bride as vividly as this room did.

"Yes, she was considered quite a beauty," Martha affirmed. "And such a kind, sweet-natured little thing. She was not at all the sort of woman you would expect to find on a ranch in this wild land. I did not know her well, but I don't think she was suited to life here. Still, I suppose she loved Ben very much to leave her family and go with him. He adored her, you know. I think he still grieves, even after all these years."

"I—I suppose he does," murmured Jessie, her emerald gaze clouded with confusion. Why should it hurt her to learn that Ben had loved his own wife?

"Well, one can never really tell with Ben. As you have no doubt noticed, he can be incredibly enigmatic at times!" Martha opined with a pleasant trill of laughter. Then, as if suddenly realizing she had said a good deal more than she had intended, she frowned to herself and crossed to the door again. "You'll no doubt want to rest a bit now, my dear. I'll send one of the children to fetch you for supper. If there's anything you need, please don't hesitate to let me know."

"I won't," promised Jessie with a weak smile. As soon as the other woman was gone, she released a long disconsolate sigh and wandered over to the window.

He adored her, you know, Martha had said. Those words burned in her mind as she stared toward the mountains. She wondered if Emily had once stood in this very spot and yearned for the life she had left behind. Or had her life with Ben turned out to be all she had hoped it would be? Had his strength carried her through the dark times? Had his love filled her with such joy and contentment that she had longed for nothing else?

"Why should it matter to *me*?" demanded Jessie, her voice nothing but a hoarse whisper in the silence of the room.

She was startled by a knock on the door behind her. Spinning about, she paused briefly to regain her composure before moving forward to answer it. Hot color rose to her cheeks when she opened the door and found herself gazing up into Ben's solemn, damnably handsome features.

"I brought your trunk."

"Oh, I . . . so you did," faltered Jessie, her eyes falling before the piercing steadiness of his. "Thank you. Please put it over there beside the bed."

Swinging the door wider, she stepped aside and watched while he strode into the room to follow her bidding. Everything about his physical appearance

149

bespoke a powerful, innate masculinity toughened even further by the many years he had spent on the frontier. But it didn't end there, thought Jessie, her pulses quickening as he straightened to his full height once more. His character was every bit as strong, every bit as noble and masterful, and—*God help her*—every bit as compellingly magnetic. Like a moth drawn to the flame it knows is dangerous but cannot resist, she felt drawn to this man. . . .

"I take it the room is to your liking?" he inquired with a faint, mocking smile. His gaze made a quick encompassing sweep of the room before locking with hers again.

"Of course. How could it not be?"

"Women have ways of finding fault where none is due." There was devilment lurking in his deep blue eyes, but Jessie was in no mood to be teased.

"Oh, do they indeed?" she countered, rising to the challenge. She folded her arms beneath her breasts while her eyes flashed up at him. "I take great exception to that remark, Mr. Chandler, particularly since I have offered little or no complaint about anything throughtout the duration of our—"

"Easy, Miss Clare," he drawled lazily. He found himself thinking she was even more beautiful when riled. *Or when sleeping naked in your arms,* a voice deep inside reminded him. The memory sent desire shooting through his veins like liquid fire. Doing his best to ignore it, he returned to the subject at hand. "You don't want everyone at the Chapparosa to know what a wildcat you really are, do you?" he taunted in a low, resonant voice.

"Why, you . . . how dare you!"

"You can fall back on that prim and proper indignation of yours every time, schoolmarm, but I know better."

His gaze traveled over her with bold intimacy, causing her to draw in her breath upon a sharp gasp. In spite of his resolve to keep a safe distance between himself and

150

the fiery, golden-haired angel who drove him to distraction, he took a step closer.

"I know better," he repeated softly, his eyes glowing with such warmth that Jessie felt positively branded. There was little doubt in her mind as to what was in his.

"I thought we had agreed to forget about what transpired that night, Mr. Chandler," she declared with an admirable display of calm.

Inwardly, she was anything but calm. *Damn him!* she thought. *Why is he doing this?* His nearness, as always, made her legs feel perilously weak. She told herself it had been a mistake to come here, a mistake she would regret down to her soul if she did not fight this wild, sweet madness calling her.

"It is, I believe," she went on to insist a trifle breathlessly, "in our best mutual interest to do so, is it not?"

"It is." Ben's mouth curved into another disturbing half smile. "Without a doubt. But do you always do what's best, Jessamyn?" he asked in a quiet voice tinged with underlying passion and sardonic amusement. "Did you ever allow any of those young men back in St. Louis a glimpse of that fire smoldering just beneath the surface?" All traces of amusement vanished when he moved ever closer and demanded, "Was there one among *them* who made you come alive in his arms like I did?"

Once again, the mere thought of her in another man's embrace sent a torrent of jealous rage blazing through him. He knew then that he had gone too far—too far for them both.

"You have no right to ask me such things!" charged Jessie, her eyes sparking with renewed anger while she blushed hotly. Glaring up at him, she could not tell by the look on his face whether he meant to hurt her with such remarks or simply bait her. She was stung by his words, stung by the possibility that he considered her deserving

151

of his contempt for the shameless way she had behaved that night in the Apaches' camp. "You have no right!"

"True," he surprised her by admitting firmly. "I have no right at all." His own eyes glowed dully now, while his jaw tensed. He cursed himself for being a damned fool, then cursed the young woman before him for being so spirited and desirable that he had to fight his own worst impulses at every turn. "My apologies, Miss Clare," he offered her coldly.

She could only stand and stare mutely after him as he left her alone again. Finally, she made her way over to the bed and sank down weakly upon its canopied softness. She took a deep, shuddering breath and raised her hands to the flushed smoothness of her cheeks.

"Why must I be such an idiot?" she murmured, her silken brow creasing into a severe frown of self-recrimination.

The question remained unanswered, for she suddenly rose to her feet and threw open the trunk Ben had just delivered. Following a brief, impatiently conducted search, she brought forth a small velvet box and opened it. Inside, gleaming in the waning sunlight that filled the room, was a small heart-shaped locket dangling from a delicate gold chain.

With loving hands, she lifted the locket from the box and sat down on the floor. A gentle push upon the clasp revealed the tiny likeness of a woman, a young woman with light brown hair and laughing blue eyes.

"Oh, Mother," whispered Jessie. "What am I going to do?"

She stared at the faded portrait for a long time. But her confusion was not lessened by her intense scrutiny of it. And when James came to tell her supper was ready, she had still not discovered what it was within herself that made Ben Chandler capable of eliciting such a strong reaction from her every time they were together. In truth, she blamed herself more than she blamed him.

Her first meal at the Chapparosa proved to be a surprisingly tranquil experience. Not at all surprising because of the food, which was—as Martha had warned—a bit spicy but nonetheless absolutely delicious. No, the surprise came as a result of Ben's altered behavior toward her. Though he held himself far too aloof for her taste, he treated her with all the courtesy and respect he would have shown any other guest in his house.

She was certain she could feel his eyes on her several times as she sat opposite him, between Martha and Hannah, but he was always looking elsewhere whenever she glanced his way. There was no doubt he was avoiding her; except for the barest civilities demanded by his role as a host, he did not address her at all. Relief and disappointment warred within her breast as a result of his sudden indifference, but she endeavored to keep her own behavior toward him on an equal level.

Martha and the twins made up for his lack of warmth, however, and set about entertaining her with colorful stories of their life on the ranch. Jessie could not help but smile at the two young Chandlers' enthusiasm as they talked. No longer feeling shy, Hannah was as animated as her brother, who punctuated his tales with a number of gestures and sound effects. The twins' father regarded them with an indulgent but watchful eye throughout the course of the meal, and his paternal vigilance was noted by the young woman he was trying so damned hard to keep at arm's length—literally *and* figuratively.

Afterward, Consuela came to take the children off to bed. Jessie, who had met the cook/housekeeper before supper, had immediately warmed to her. She was a plump, jovial woman near Martha's age, with graying black hair and lively wide-set brown eyes. Her Mexican heritage was evident in her speech, which was laced at frequent intervals with Spanish words and phrases. It was obvious that she doted on the twins, who responded to her unconvincingly stern looks with a tumble of merry giggles as she ambled from the room in their exuberant wake.

"I thought we might enjoy our coffee in the parlor tonight," said Martha, linking her arm through Jessie's. "I'm afraid we make an early night of things here at the Chapparosa. Life begins with the dawn."

"I am accustomed to retiring early," Jessie told her. "My father insisted upon it when we were young, and we never abandoned the habit as we got older." Of course, she recalled silently, there were many nights during her childhood when she had hidden beneath the covers with a lamp, losing herself in the pages of a book of high adventure, stirring romance, or faraway places. Her eyes twinkled at the memory. "Andrew and I were ever obedient, at least in my father's eyes."

"Andrew?" Martha led her into the other room, while Ben took himself off with the announced purpose of having a word with the hands. Jessie's gaze instinctively followed him as he went, then she forced her attention back to the woman drawing her down onto a cushiony blue chintz sofa.

"My younger brother," she explained with a preoccupied smile.

"Does your family still live in St. Louis?" asked Martha, curious to know more about her.

"Yes. My father and stepmother live in the same house where I grew up. I suppose I would have gone on living there, too, if I had not decided to come to Cimarron and teach." A shadow crossed her face when she thought of her last week at home and of the difficult farewells said at the train station.

"They did not approve of your coming here," remarked Martha, her words more of a statement than

154

a question.

"No. Except for Andrew. He alone understood. Ever since my mother died, he and I have made a habit of supporting one another's schemes, however disastrous!" she declared, a soft, rueful laugh escaping her lips. She grew serious again in the next moment, for painful memories of home always seemed to follow on the heels of happy ones.

"Were you very young when you lost your mother?" Martha asked, her expression one of compassion. She handed Jessie a cup of coffee from the tray Consuela had just brought in.

"I was twelve. Andrew was only seven." *Seven.* The same age as Ben's children now, she realized.

"I was scarcely three when my mother died. And, of course, James and Hannah were much too young to remember Emily. I've often wondered which is the most difficult to endure—the clear and inescapable memory of a mother known and lost, or the lifelong curiosity that can never be satisfied with other people's memories of a woman you carry in your heart but not your mind." She cast a brief, searching glance in Jessie's direction while she stirred fresh cream and a spoonful of sugar into her own coffee. "You mentioned that you have a stepmother. Is your relationship a close one?"

"No, not exactly," Jessie admitted with a sigh. "Lillian always means well, but . . . we're very different."

"And she is also very different from your mother," added Martha with a faint, knowing smile.

"Very. But in all honesty, I don't think any woman could have measured up to the mother I lost. I certainly cannot blame my father for remarrying," she proclaimed thoughtfully. "Now that I am grown, I better understand his need for companionship." *Loneliness is a cold bedfellow,* she remembered hearing long ago. Her eyes filled with a troubled light when she thought of her

155

own bed.

"I have never been married, but I, too, understand. I suppose there will come a time when Ben finally takes another wife," his cousin observed offhandedly.

Jessie very nearly choked on the hot liquid she was sipping. Coughing, she raised an embroidered linen napkin to her lips and sought to regain her breath. The petite brunette beside her, once satisfied that she would recover, offered a consoling pat upon her back.

"Are you all right, my dear? Forgive me if I said anything to distress you!"

"I—I am not the least bit distressed!" Jessie assured her. She hastily returned the cup to the tray, dismayed to feel the telltale color staining her cheeks. As always, she was a poor liar, so that her voice lacked the necessary conviction when she forced a smile to her face and told Martha, "I'm afraid I can be so regrettably careless at times. But I'm perfectly all right now."

"I am relieved to hear it. I should hate to think what my cousin would say if he returned to find Cimarron's new teacher murdered by his coffee!"

Both women laughed at that, and it was while they were in the throes of amusement that Ben entered the room. He frowned with wholly masculine disbelief at the sight of them, their heads together while they giggled like two schoolgirls. Martha was the first to look up and see him, and she quickly sobered while he crossed to pour himself some of the fragrant, near-homicidal brew.

"Oh, Ben, we did not know you had returned," she said with an affectionate smile.

"I gathered that," he murmured dryly. He bent his tall frame into a leather wing chair. Immediately opposite sat Jessie, trying not to look at him and meeting with little success.

"Would you care for cream or sugar, my dear?" Martha offered him.

"You know I take it black," he declined with a slight frown.

"Oh, yes, of course you do. One would think I would remember that after all these years, wouldn't one? By the way, Jessie was telling me that she has a younger brother back in St, Louis."

"Does she?" His penetrating blue gaze shifted to Jessie for only the fraction of an instant before returning to fix, with unaccountable fascination, upon the cup of coffee in his hand.

"Haven't I just said so?" Martha playfully retorted, drawing on the ease of a lifetime acquaintance. She turned back to Jessie. "Hannah would be lost without James. The two of them are almost completely inseparable. Some of the other children in town take pleasure in teasing them about their resemblance to one another, but they rarely take offense. Considering the fact that they are Ben's children, they are remarkably even-tempered," she added with an arch look at her cousin.

"What the devil is that supposed to mean?" he challenged, a mock scowl creasing his sun-kissed brow.

"You know perfectly well what it means, my dear boy. Why, heaven forbid Jessie should ever discover what you are really like!"

"I'm afraid I already have," Jessie murmured without thinking.

Her face flamed when two pairs of eyes, one of them a smoldering cobalt-blue, fastened upon her. Martha looked at her quizzically, while Ben looked at her as though he would dearly love to strike her. Perplexed by his unwarranted antagonism, she tried to cover her embarrassment by trying to explain—which only made matters worse.

"What I meant to say was that Mr. Chandler's true nature was revealed to me when he rescued me from the Indians," she told Martha, measuring her words carefully. If she had allowed herself to meet Ben's eyes, she would have seen them gleaming now with a mixture of ironic humor and irrevocable passion. "Under such difficult circumstances, you see, it—it was impossible for us to pretend to be anything other than what we truly are."

"I'm sure it was," Martha replied softly, reaching over to take her hand in a comforting gesture.

"What Miss Clare neglected to say, cousin," Ben remarked with only the ghost of a smile, "is that our *true selves* became even better acquainted than we had any reason to expect." He was satisfied to watch the hot color fly to Jessie's cheeks once more. "Isn't that so, Miss Clare?"

"I would prefer not to speak of it, Mr. Chandler!" she insisted, her eyes blazing their brilliant emerald fire as she finally met his gaze.

"Wouldn't you?"

"No, I would *not!*"

"Then why the hell did you bring it up?" he demanded.

"Ben!" gasped Martha. Her wide, startled gaze shifted back and forth between the two young people, and her bewilderment only increased when Jessie abruptly stood and Ben did the same.

"I didn't bring it up! I merely—"

"You merely forgot yourself for a moment, is that it?" he obligingly provided. All traces of amusement had vanished now, to be replaced by what seemed to both Martha and Jessie to be an inordinate amount of reproachable anger. "Damn it, woman," he ground out in a low voice simmering with raw emotion, "make up your mind. I'll not have any more of these blasted games between us!"

"Games?" echoed Jessie, her own voice quavering with mingled fury and confusion. "I don't know what you're talking about!"

Before Ben could respond, his cousin hastened to intervene. She rose to her feet and cast him an imploring look.

"Please, Ben, Miss Clare is a guest in your house!" she reminded him uneasily. "While I don't have the faintest idea what could have prompted this—this disagreement between the two of you, could you not at least sit down and discuss it in a more calm and rational manner?"

"Calm and rational?" He gave a short, humorless laugh. "You're right, of course—as always." It wasn't like him to lose his head as he had just done. He knew it, and Martha knew it. Once again, the feisty young schoolmarm had penetrated his iron control, had made him throw caution to the winds and be damned for it.

Jessie, her breasts rising and falling rapidly beneath her bodice, watched the emotions playing across the rugged handsomeness of his face. She was ashamed of her own tempestuous behavior. She felt particularly mortified by the fact that Martha had witnessed the wild, unforgivable outburst.

Things cannot go on this way! she told herself in rising panic. Her knees trembling, she resumed her seat on the sofa and stared miserably downward at the hands she clenched together in her lap. She was only dimly aware of Ben crossing to the window.

Outside, twilight settled upon the mountains and valleys and pasturelands, while the first stars of the late summer night twinkled faintly in the heavens above. The master of the Chapparosa was too engrossed with his thoughts to appreciate the panoramic, multi-hued beauty of the land he loved. His features remained tensed, his gaze full of a dangerously intense light as he stood with his back to the woman who had stirred his well-guarded heart and roused his long-denied passions the first moment he set eyes on her.

"Well, now, that's much better," proclaimed Martha, smiling with a forced lightness of spirit as she reached over to pat the younger woman's hand again. "I suggest we place this incident behind us and get on with our conversation. We've yet to speak of your plans for the school, you know."

"I know, and I'm sorry, Martha, but I—I think it best if I retire now," Jessie stammered, feeling a sudden and desperate need to escape. She did not wait for a response, but stood to her feet and managed a weak smile. "Thank you for your kind efforts to make me feel at home."

"This *is* your home, Jessie, for as long as you are here," the older woman told her sincerely. She wanted to say more, but a worried glance at Ben prompted her to do nothing more than return Jessie's smile and bid her good night.

"Good night, Mr. Chandler," Jessie forced herself to offer him, though her voice quavered toward the end. She fled the room in such haste that she did not hear the words he spoke in a low, deep-timbreed voice, which held a promise of things to come.

"Good night, Miss Clare. Good night . . . *and God help you.*"

Seven

Jessie awoke with a start.

"Good heavens, what was that?" she whispered in alarm. She sat bolt upright in the bed, wide-eyed and breathless, her heart pounding in her ears while she listened for the sound again.

It did not come, even after several long moments of waiting. She told herself it must have been a dream, that whatever she had heard existed only in the realm of her overactive imagination. But she remained unconvinced, even though she lay back down and resolutely closed her eyes once more.

Suddenly, she heard the noise again. It was no dream! It sounded suspiciously like someone beating on the wall—and it was coming from the direction of the room next to hers. *Ben's room.*

Her eyes flew open in earnest now. Swiftly tossing back the covers, she slid from the bed, flinging her wrapper about her shoulders as she hurried from the room and out into the darkened hallway. She moved to stand before the door at the very end. Leaning closer, she held her breath and listened intently.

She did not know what she expected to discover, nor what she would do with the discovery once she made it.

Standing there in her bare feet, with her unbound tresses streaming down about her in glorious disarray and her soft curves clad only in a thin white cotton nightgown over which was draped, quite ineffectually, a robe of tucked and ruffled lavender silk, she did not pause to contemplate the wisdom of her actions. As she did much too often for her own good, she was acting solely on impulse.

It might have been curiosity that drove her out into the hallway to press her ear against Ben Chandler's door, but it was Ben Chandler himself who flung the door open without warning and in so doing caused her to tumble forward into his arms.

"*Jessamyn?*" He frowned, hauling her upright before him. "What the hell were you doing out there?" he demanded harshly, his eyes burning down into the very round, luminous depths of hers.

She turned beet-red from head to toe and made a valiant effort to regain her composure. Lifting her head in a gesture of proud defiance, she tried not to think of the fact that he was holding her prisoner, at least temporarily, in the lamplit privacy of his bedroom. It was a difficult task she had set herself, however, especially since it was the middle of the night and she was in a shocking state of undress and he—*heaven help her*—was wearing nothing but a pair of trousers! She swallowed hard and raised her face to his once more.

"I—I was on my way to the kitchen!" she declared, her eyes blazing defensively up at him. "For a drink of water! I was thirsty!"

"The kitchen's the other way," he pointed out with a faint, undeniably mocking smile.

"Is it?" she retorted with a flash of spirit. "Well, then, I suppose I must have gotten turned about!"

The look in her eyes dared him to say more, just as her adorably disheveled appearance dared him to pull her

162

close and kiss her until she begged for mercy. He groaned inwardly, white-hot desire coursing through him like wildfire. His smoldering gaze raked hurriedly over her soft, damnably enticing curves, which were protected by nothing but a flimsy barrier of clothing that revealed every bit as much as it hid. His eyes traveled back up to the flushed, wide-eyed loveliness of her countenance, and his fingers suddenly tightened about the silk-covered flesh of her arms.

"Let go of me, Mr. Chandler!" gasped Jessie, her pulses leaping with both fear and excitement.

"Tell me the truth, damn you, Jessamyn!" he commanded. "Why did you come to my room?"

"Because I heard a noise! I was awakened by a noise, and I thought I would see if anything was wrong!" she finally confessed. For a moment, she thought he meant to sweep her up into his arms and carry her over to the big brass bed she glimpsed behind him.

But he did not. Still hoping to forestall the inevitable, he released her and turned away.

"It was the windmill you heard," he informed her in a cold, distant voice that belied the turmoil raging within him. "There's a storm brewing."

As if to prove him right, the bothersome sound echoed throughout the room again. Jessie realized that it was not coming from inside the house at all, but from a spot near the barn. A wave of embarrassment washed over her. With trembling hands, she pulled the edges of the wrapper more securely about her and shifted her troubled gaze down to the floor.

"Oh, I see," she murmured. "I thought—" She did not finish the sentence, for the simple reason that she did not know how.

"Get out of here, Jessamyn," he warned her, his voice tinged with a disturbing huskiness that sent a shiver dancing down her spine. "Go back to your own room before I forget I'm an honorable man." He was still facing away from her, so she could not see the smile of bitter sarcasm that touched his lips, nor the hot savage gleam in his eyes.

His words threw Jessie into utter chaos. She stared at him in openmouthed surprise for a moment, unable to speak or move or do anything but wonder if he could possibly have meant what he had just said. As it turned out, she had her own battle to fight, for part of her wanted to stay and brave the danger, while another part of her frantically implored her to leave before she forgot she was a well-bred young lady who wasn't supposed to feel the sort of things Ben Chandler made her feel.

The longer she hesitated, the closer to certain disaster she came. By the time her conscience triumphed over her wicked desires, it was too late.

He had given her the chance, thought Ben. God knows he had given her the chance. But he was only flesh and blood. Just as she was . . . Just as he remembered all too well. Damn it all to hell, but he wanted her more than he had ever wanted anything or anyone! He literally burned for her, ached to hold her in his arms again and mold her sweet body to the searing hardness of his.

He knew he was lost when she did not turn and run as he had expected her to do. No, damn them both, she had stayed and would now face the consequences. . . .

Jessie got no farther than the doorway. A soft, breathless cry escaped her lips when her belated flight was cut short from behind. Without warning, Ben's hand shot out to seize her arm, and he forced her roughly around to face him. Before she could protest, he had caught her about the waist and yanked her close.

"Mr. Chandler!" she breathed, her eyes wide and sparkling with alarm as she tried to push free. "Wha— what on earth are you doing? Let go of me!"

"It's Ben, damn you!" he ground out. Disregarding

her vehement struggles, he imprisoned her with both his arms and kicked the door shut with his foot. "You're mine, Jessamyn. I should have claimed you that night in Gray Wolf's camp!"

"*No!*" She pushed against his bare granite-hard chest with all her might, but to no avail. Tears of helpless rage and defeat welled up in her eyes. "This is wrong! This is wrong and you know it!"

"Wrong or right, you want it every damned bit as much as I do!"

He scooped her up in his arms now and carried her to the big brass bed just as she had envisioned him doing earlier. But the reality was far more frightening—in more ways than one. *Dear God, she feared herself every bit as much as she feared him!* Recalling how he had so masterfully conquered her inhibitions once before, she intensified her struggles and threatened, in growing desperation, "If you don't put me down at once, I will scream and bring the whole house—"

Her words were lost against his mouth as his lips captured hers in a fiercely demanding kiss, which left little doubt he meant to put an end to the tormenting anticipation at last. He lowered her to the bed, then swiftly covered her body with his own, pressing her down into the feather mattress and molding her silken curves to intimate perfection with the length of his bronzed, muscular hardness.

Her head spinning wildly, Jessie pushed against him once more, only to have him seize her wrists in a firm grip and force her arms above her head. He imprisoned them there with one of his hands, while his other hand tangled within her thick, luxuriant mass of dark golden hair to hold her steady for his deepening kiss. Her lips parted beneath the ardently compelling warmth of his, and she suffered a sharp intake of breath when his velvety tongue began a bold exploration of the moist, sweet cavern of

165

her mouth.

Jessie knew herself thoroughly conquered, knew that she would eventually surrender herself, heart and soul, to the man who had first introduced her to the pleasures of the flesh. Although she did not yet understand why she was so willing to risk a lifetime of damnation for a few moments in his arms, she could not deny that her feelings for him ran far deeper than she would ever have believed possible. Little more than a stranger he might be, but his touch set her afire.

God forgive her, but she did want it as much as he did! She hated to admit, even now, that she had wanted it since the night alone with him in the firelit darkness of the Apache wickiup, since he had held her close and kissed her and made her forget the rest of the world just as he was doing at this very moment. . . .

With her own secret passions escalating to meet his, she became much more than a meekly consenting participant. She kissed him back with all the answering fire of her newly awakened desires, her body straining instinctively upward against his. Her tongue followed the provocative dance taught by his, and her lips moved with ever-increasing skill beneath his as she gave herself up completely to the mastery of his embrace.

Ben, driven to near madness by her innocently seductive response, gave a low groan and moved his hand to her breasts. Since the lavender silk wrapper lay unheeded on the floor near the doorway, there was only the thin, delicate fabric of her nightgown between the possessive warmth of his hand and the satiny rose-tipped fullness he sought.

Jessie moaned low in her throat when his strong fingers offered a gentle yet impassioned caress to both her breasts before closing boldly upon one of them. He released her wrists, and she brought her hands down to clutch almost convulsively at the bare, powerfully

166

muscled smoothness of his shoulders. Her soft gasps were swallowed by his mouth as he gently stroked and squeezed her breast, his thumb flicking across the seductive peak until she thought she could bear no more of the exquisite torture.

He soon transferred his highly provocative attentions to her other breast, then finally relinquished the sweetness of her mouth. His lips scorched a fiery path downward until closing about the delectable roundness of her breast, his tongue lightly encircling her nipple, which seemed to beckon his fiery touch through the near transparency of the white cotton.

The sensations wrought by his hot, teasing tongue and possessive mouth sent Jessie's passions soaring heavenward. Her fingers threaded within the sun-streaked thickness of his dark hair, and she bit at her lip in an effort to stifle the soft gasps and moans elicited by his moist, shockingly intimate caress.

She knew there was more to come, but she was not entirely certain what to expect. The unspoken question on her mind was answered in a startling, highly satisfactory manner when Ben grasped the folds of her nightgown and tugged the fabric impatiently upward. The feel of the cool air upon her bare, feverish skin caused her to shiver. Her eyes flew open when she realized that her nightgown was bunched up about her thighs, but she could offer only a token murmur of protest, for Ben immediately set about making her ready for the final blending of their bodies.

"Ben!" she gasped, surprised when his hand trailed purposefully upward along the silken smoothness of her inner thigh. He wasted precious little time before claiming the prize he sought; his strong fingers moved to the triangle of downy curls at the apex of her pale, quivering thighs, then gently parted the soft folds of flesh to touch her at the very core of her womanhood.

167

Jessie stiffened, another small, breathless cry escaping her lips before his mouth came up to capture hers once more. Within seconds, she felt her tensed muscles relaxing, felt her thighs opening wider of their own accord. In that small part of her brain still capable of rational thought, she was aghast at what she was doing, but she could not seem to help it. She was being swept forcibly, completely away by a flood tide of passion and longing and almost unbearable ecstasy. . . .

Without warning, she came crashing back to earth.

It was nothing more than the sight of a picture on the wall that did it. Her eyelids had fluttered open for only a moment, but it had been long enough for her to catch a brief glimpse of the framed likeness of Ben, a much younger Ben, standing beside a pretty, delicate woman dressed in a white satin bridal gown. Illuminated by the lamp's soft golden glow, the portrait had provided Jessie with a sudden, painfully vivid reminder of the young wife Ben had loved and lost, of that other woman who had shared his bed just as *she* was doing now, but with one major difference: Emily had known that she possessed his heart as well as his body.

In that moment, Jessie knew that what Ben was offering her was not enough. *It was not enough!*

"No! No, don't!" she cried brokenly, tearing her lips from his and setting up a frantic struggle to escape.

"Damn it, Jessamyn, what is it?" he demanded in a resonant undertone. His gaze, smoldering with both desire and anger, searched her face while he continued to hold her captive beneath him.

"Let me go! Please, let me go!" She fought him like a veritable tigress now, for cold reality had finally triumphed over the heat of passion. "I will not do this! I will *not!*" she vowed, her eyes blazing their brilliant deep green fire while she pushed at him with all her might.

"What sort of game are you playing now, you little

witch?" Ben ground out, still easily overpowering her.

"It's no game! Now get off of me, damn you!" she hissed, punctuating her furious words with a well-aimed kick at his shin. "Let me go!"

For a moment he was seized by the urge to take her anyway, to force her to accept what he knew they both burned for. But it suddenly dawned on him that he didn't want her that way. He wanted her to accept him willingly, to respond with all the fire and passion she had displayed only moments earlier. No, by damn, when he took her, it had to be because she wanted it as much as he did. *He would settle for nothing less.*

So, even though it was one of the hardest things he had ever done, Ben forced himself to release her. He relaxed his iron grip upon her and rolled to his side. Only the intense, savage light in his eyes betrayed the supreme effort it cost him.

Jessie blinked up at him in astonishment. She opened her mouth to speak, but no words would come. Feeling heartsore and frustrated and more humiliated than she'd ever felt before, she scrambled from the bed and hastily smoothed her nightgown back down into place upon her trembling body. She snatched up her wrapper as she flew on unsteady legs to the door. Her hand had just closed about the brass knob when she heard Ben's deep voice, surprisingly calm, reaching out to her from where he still lay amidst the rumpled covers of the bed.

"You can't run away forever, Jessamyn. You're mine, and I mean to have you."

"*Never!*" she denied vehemently, hot tears springing to her eyes. She gave an abrupt shake of her head, which sent her long golden tresses cascading wildly about her face and shoulders. Her beautiful rose-tipped breasts were all too visible beneath the fabric dampened by the attentions of Ben's loving mouth.

His handsome features tightened as desire flared

within his virile body once more. Muttering an oath, he watched as Jessie wrenched open the door and disappeared into the hallway.

He heard another door closing seconds later, and then the faint yet unmistakable sound of weeping from the room next to his. His heart twisted at the thought of her lying in the emptiness of her own bed and crying. He vowed to himself that someday it would be upon his breast she spilled her tears. *Soon, wildcat. Soon.*

Eight

Jessie was greatly relieved to find only Martha waiting for her at the breakfast table the next morning. The older woman greeted her with a warm smile of welcome as she entered the dining room. After glancing hastily about and satisfying herself that Ben was not there, she breathed an inward sigh and took a seat beside his cousin.

"Good morning, my dear. Would you care for some coffee or perhaps some cocoa?" offered Martha.

"Good morning," said Jessie, managing a smile of her own. "Coffee would be fine, thank you."

She had been dismayed to observe the faint telltale smudges beneath her eyes that morning when she looked in the mirror. The events of the night had come flooding back to her with a vengeance, whereupon she had subjected herself to yet another round of furious, self-deprecating introspection.

It was still difficult for her to believe what she had done, what she had allowed Ben Chandler to do, and she told herself that she would never be able to forget—or forgive—what had happened between them. It was one thing to be tempted; it was quite another to allow the temptation to run rampant.

"I trust you slept well last night?" Martha inquired as

171

she poured coffee from a newly polished silver pot and handed the steaming cup to Jessie.

"Yes," she lied.

"Well, then, you must have been the only one. Aside from James and Hannah, that is. Those two little angels can sleep through anything! Truly though, I am surprised the storm did not keep you awake."

"Storm?" She took a cautious sip of the hot liquid and lowered the cup back to the saucer. "Was there a storm last night?" As soon as she had asked it, a faint guilty flush crept up to the face. She remembered how Ben had explained about the windmill and predicted a storm.

"Why, yes, indeed there was! The winds howled something awful, and there was a good deal of thunder and lightning. I heard one of the men telling Ben this morning that the river has risen nearly six inches since yesterday."

Consuela came bustling amiably into the room just then, offering Jessie a choice of hotcakes or ham and eggs for breakfast. Once she had expressed her preference for the latter and the cook had returned to the kitchen, Jessie looked to Martha with a thoughtful frown.

"Where are the children?" she asked.

"Outside with their father," the older woman answered, her eyes twinkling with fond amusement. "They're usually up at first light, just as Ben is. James takes particular delight in helping the hands with the horses. Hannah loves to feed the chickens and pigs. She has given a name to each and every animal on the Chapparosa, including the cattle!" Martha laughed softly at the thought, adding, "Ben complains that we're getting overrun with stock because Hannah protests so loudly whenever one of her 'friends' must be sold."

"We were never allowed pets, though there once was a cat who lived underneath our house," recalled Jessie, a brief smile of remembrance touching her lips. "How

172

large is the Chapparosa exactly?" she questioned at a sudden thought.

"Oh, I suppose it's what one would call typical for this part of the Territory. Ben actually has title to more than a thousand acres, but the cattle are scattered across the range for some distance in all directions. We'll be having the fall roundup soon. I think I ought to warn you that school may get off to a slow start as a result. Fall is an especially busy time of year, and there will no doubt be some who must wait a few weeks before coming."

"So I've heard," Jessie murmured ruefully. She frowned down at the cup in her hands for a moment before asking, "Do you think your cousin will allow James and Hannah to attend right away?"

"Of course he will," Martha assured her. "The twins are not really needed to help with the work; there are fully half a dozen hands living here at the ranch. But even if they *were* needed, Ben would manage without them somehow. I am happy to say he believes in education as much as I do." She cast Jessie a keen, perceptive look. "It may surprise you to learn that he attended college for two years before running off to join the cavalry. His parents held the highest expectations for him. They wanted him to practice law as did his father and grandfather before him. It was always believed he would complete his studies, return home, and go into partnership with his father."

Jessie found it difficult to imagine him living such a staid and orderly life. He seemed so much a part of the wild, ruggedly beautiful land he had chosen as his home.

"And why did he not?" she prompted Martha, anxious to know more about the man whose unsettling image rose in her mind at every turn.

"For the simple reason that he was young and adventurous and determined to assert his independence," his cousin remembered with an indulgent smile.

173

"Ben Chandler was never one to sit idly by and wait for life to happen to him. Even as a child, he always went after whatever it was he wanted—and nearly always got it, too."

"He has not changed much," remarked Jessie, her gaze sparkling with a touch of ironic humor.

"Oh, but he has," Martha insisted solemnly. "He is no longer the headstrong, mischievous boy I once knew. The years of fighting, the discipline he learned as a soldier, his struggle to keep the ranch going, Emily's death . . . all have changed him to some extent." She released a long sigh and rose purposefully to her feet. "But enough of my prosing on for now! I hope you don't mind eating alone, my dear, but I promised Consuela I would help her with the wash this morning," she explained with an apologetic smile.

"No, of course not!" replied Jessie, adding in earnest, "I'm sorry I was so late in getting—"

"Nonsense!" the older woman cut her off good-naturedly. "There is no need for you to rise early. You'll be doing that soon enough, when school begins next week."

Jessie, concealing her disappointment, watched the other woman sweep gracefully from the room, then shifted her turbulent emerald gaze to the window. The storm had left behind a perfectly splendid summer day, with a sky of deep blue and the fresh, distinctive scent of the newly washed earth in the air.

Her spirits lifted somewhat at the sight of the sun's benevolent rays streaming in through the glass, but she knew nothing could completely dispel the heaviness of heart wrought by the memory of those few hotly impassioned minutes she had spent in Ben Chandler's bed. . . .

*　　　*　　　*

174

Later that same morning, Jessie, Martha, and two of Consuela's older daughters, who lived in a house not far from the Chapparosa's headquarters, took a wagonload of cleaning supplies and drove to the schoolhouse. The women were accompanied by one of the ranch hands, a quiet man of perhaps thirty by the name of Curly. He had been appointed by Ben to serve as a protective escort, a duty he discharged without complaint and with all the solemn vigilance expected of him.

Jessie, delighted with Martha's suggestion that they do whatever they could before the school board began *their* efforts, climbed down from the wagon with a determined light shining in her eyes. She was anxious to get to work on the building and anxious to forget all about Ben for as long as possible.

"Martha," she asked while the other woman alighted and moved to the rear of the wagon, "why is the schoolhouse so far from town? It seems terribly inconvenient to have it sitting out here in the middle of nowhere."

"I know, but it was actually out of consideration for your future pupils that this site was chosen. It's close to the road, and it truly does enable the greatest number of children to attend school, since a good many of them will not be coming from town at all. Besides," she added wryly, "the land was generously donated for its present purpose by an old miner, and the board will usually vote for anything that doesn't cost them money!"

Jessie smiled at that and helped her companions unload the wagon. The four of them, their arms laden with soap and brooms and buckets and the like, marched through the overgrown meadow to the schoolhouse. It was every bit as filthy and disordered as Jessie had remembered, but she squared her shoulders and charged resolutely ahead.

Consuela's daughters, Juanita and Elena, proved to be

charming companions as well as hard workers, while Martha was always willing to give advice and instruction whenever the others were uncertain about how to tackle a particular problem. Curly, meanwhile, remained at his post beneath the trees nearby, his hat tilted back upon his head and his eyes continually sweeping the countryside for any sign of approaching riders.

The morning wore on. Noon came and went. It wasn't until the sun hung low in the western sky that Martha finally proclaimed it time to leave. They had spent nearly an entire day within the confines of the log schoolhouse, which had at times been uncomfortably hot and filled with a choking cloud of dust.

But it had been worth it, thought Jessie as she trudged wearily back to the wagon with the other women. The interior of the building was as clean as human hands could make it. The windows sported temporary panes of cardboard—installed with Curly's invaluable assistance—while the big black stove stood gleaming proudly in anticipation of winter's cold fury. All that was required now were replacements for the desk and chair, a new blackboard, some extra books, and of course, students.

"I wish my brothers and sisters could come to your school, Miss Clare," Juanita wistfully remarked on the hour's drive homeward.

"Well, why can't they?" Jessie questioned in puzzlement. "Will your mother not allow them to attend?" She observed the swift, worried glance the girl shot Martha.

"No. But it is impossible," Juanita replied, her eyes falling in obvious disquietude.

"But . . . why do you say that?" persisted Jessie.

"She says it because it is true, Miss Clare," Elena interjected with a faint smile of resignation.

Jessie's bewilderment increased, and she instinctively looked to Martha for an explanation. The petite brunette frowned and gave an abrupt flick of the reins.

"It is true, I'm afraid," she told Jessie, heaving a sigh of displeasure. "Only white children are allowed to attend the school."

"Surely you're not serious?" Jessie demanded in stunned disbelief. "Why, how could such—such blatant injustice be allowed? For heaven's sake, this land is called *New Mexico,* is it not? The Spanish were here long before the white men came!"

"I know it's unfair, my dear, but there's nothing you can do about it," Martha cautioned gently. "Ben has tried speaking to the other members of the board, but to no avail. The people here . . . well, they are different from those you are used to. In some ways, they're different because they've had to be."

"And I suppose this is one of those ways!" she commented with a bitter little smile, her green eyes blazing at the thought.

"No." Martha shook her head sadly. "No, I don't think there can be any excuse for denying a child an education simply because he doesn't happen to be white. As you said, this land is the ancestral home of the Spanish—and the Indians, too, for that matter. It doesn't seem right that we would force them to share their home with us and yet not be willing to accept them as our neighbors. It isn't right, Jessie, but things cannot change overnight. To be honest, while I am quite sure there are many others who disagree with the board's decision, I cannot blame those who are of the opposite opinion."

"And why not? Why not, when you have just said yourself it isn't right?"

"Because in the past four years I have been here, I think I have come to understand them, at least a little. There have been hostilities on both sides. Far too much blood has been shed . . . far too many loved ones lost to Indian raids and to the white man's greed."

"Yes, but that has nothing to do with—"

"With Consuela's children?" Martha provided, her mouth curving into another soft smile of understanding. "It shouldn't, but it does. The barriers were erected years ago, Jessie, and as a result, the settlers are on one side, the Indians and the Spanish on the other."

"Then those barriers will simply have to come down!" Jessie insisted, her determination growing stronger as her mind raced to formulate a plan.

"What do you mean, my dear?" Martha asked worriedly.

"As Cimarron's duly appointed teacher, I am in charge of the school," she declared in a quiet, calculating voice. "And as such, it falls to me to keep an orderly, well-behaved class. Well, I intend to do precisely that! I intend to see to it that every child—*every* child—desirous of an education is allowed to pass through the door of the schoolhouse and into the midst of that orderly, well-behaved class. I will tolerate no disruptions, no unpleasantness. I have come here to teach, Martha, and that is what I intend to do, regardless of a student's position in life!"

"But, Jessie, you must not go against the board's decision!" warned Martha, noticeably taken aback by her young friend's stated defiance. "Why, they might very well dismiss you if you dare to cross them in this matter!"

"I consider the likelihood of that to be extremely remote," she responded with unwavering confidence. The seed had been planted in her mind, and the light of battle shone in her eyes. "If they found it necessary to advertise for a schoolteacher outside the boundaries of the Territory and then to arrange for my passage all the way from St. Louis, I cannot help but think they were quite desperate to find someone with my qualifications."

"Not desperate," the older woman amended, a wry smile tugging at the corners of her mouth. "Only

178

determined. You see, they wanted a teacher who could offer the children something the frontier is still struggling to achieve."

"And what is that?"

"Oh, sophistication, I suppose. A way of life left behind but not forgotten. Very few of the people were born here, you know. Most remember childhoods spent much the same as yours."

"Which is all the more reason for them to allow everyone the freedom, the enlightenment attained through a cultivation of the mind!" She sighed heavily and allowed her fiery gaze to make a broad sweep of the surrounding countryside. "Nothing else can match the wild beauty of this land, Martha," she remarked in a low, deceptively calm tone. "Just as nothing else, I'm sure, can match the stubbornness and stamina of its people." She was plagued by the sudden unbidden thought of Ben, a thought that she perversely consigned to the devil. "But I have come here to open another world to the children," she continued. "And I will allow no one—*no one*—to keep me from my purpose!"

Martha's heart swelled with both affection and admiration for the young woman beside her. Jessie reminded her so very much of what she herself had once been like, of that spirit and tenacity and complete assurance only the young possess . . . but all too often lack the ability to control.

"If you're really that determined," she prudently advised her, "then you might try speaking to Ben about it. But even if he agrees to bring it up before the board again, that will not by any means ensure success. His relationship with the other members has been . . . well, a bit troubled, I'm afraid. My dear cousin has never been anything but *decided* in his opinions!"

"That I can well believe," mused Jessie, unable to refrain from smiling at the thought. She sobered again in the next instant. "But I believe I will take your suggestion and speak to him as soon as we get back to the ranch. At the very least, perhaps I can persuade Consuela to let her children accompany me to school."

"It's certainly worth a try," agreed Martha. She suddenly remembered what had happened when Ben and Jessie had attempted conversation in the parlor the previous night. Ben, in his usual exasperating way, had refused to discuss it after Jessie had gone to bed.

What is there between the two of them? wondered Martha, at the same time telling herself she had absolutely no right to pry. She heaved an inward sigh and tightened her grip on the reins. Whatever it was, there was no denying life at the Chapparosa had become a good deal more interesting since Jessie's arrival.

The sun was already beginning to set by the time the wagon rolled to a halt in front of the house again. Juanita and Elena hurried inside to speak with their mother, carrying with them Martha's request that water be heated for a bath right away.

Jessie, offering only a weak, ultimately useless argument when the older woman insisted she take first turn at the bath, went to her room in glad compliance and peeled off everything but her chemise. She wrinkled her nose in distaste at the grimy dust-cloaked garments she had worn that day, bundling them inside out before tossing them to the floor. She removed the pins from her hair and shook her head, then ran her fingers through the thick mass of curls and perched on the edge of the bed to wait. Consuela soon arrived with the bathtub, while Elena and Juanita followed close behind with the water.

Swiftly stripping off her chemise after they had gone, Jessie gratefully lowered her tired body into the soothing warmth of the metal hip bath. She leaned back and closed her eyes for a moment, languidly reflecting that nothing else could ever feel as good as the water did upon her naked skin.

Nothing?

Her eyes flew open at the thought, and a rosy blush crept over every inch of her bare, beguilingly shaped form.

"Two weeks," she whispered to herself. She would have to endure two more weeks under Ben Chandler's roof, two weeks in his disturbing presence . . . two weeks sleeping in the room next to his.

With an inward groan of dismay, she straightened and took up the cake of soap. She proceeded to scrub hard at her body, as if by doing so she could somehow obliterate the burning memory of Ben's touch. Her efforts produced clean and glowing skin, but nothing else. Rising from the soap-clouded water, she wrapped a towel about her, then knelt to wash her hair as well.

It was while she was bent over the tub that she heard Ben's footsteps in the hallway. He paused in front of her door for several long seconds, during which time Jessie held her breath and stared toward the door through the wet, dripping curtain of her hair. She listened, hearing nothing but certain his piercing blue gaze was fixed on her door. A tremor shook her, for she suddenly felt as though he could see right through the door, right through to where she sat kneeling with only a towel to hide her strangely tingling curves. Finally, he resumed his steps, and she heard his boots clumping softly on the floor as he disappeared into his own room.

She released her breath in a long pent-up sigh. Hastening to finish with her hair, she could not help but think about the man whose every movement on the other side of the wall seemed to reach her ears. She could envision him drawing off his shirt and splashing his face with water at the washstand in the corner, then snatching up a towel to dry the tanned, devastatingly handsome features that haunted her dreams.

It occurred to her that he might be suffering just as much remorse as she over what had happened between them. She felt a sharp twinge of pain in her heart when she realized that she had been on the verge of giving herself to him entirely. If not for her fateful glimpse of that wedding portrait, she might very well have ended up as his mistress, a shameless creature deserving of his secret possession but not his affection.

Would that really be so terrible? that inner voice of hers took delight in taunting.

The answer was an unequivocal yes. She could not and would not allow a repeat of what had happened. Every fiber of her being told her she must resist. Her romantic girlhood dream of being loved completely and without reservation had only deepened through the years. How could she even think of abandoning it now?

She would have all of Ben Chandler or none at all, she vowed to herself.

But she was not yet prepared to fully examine her own feelings about him. She was not yet ready to admit why the certainty of his love mattered so much. All she knew was that she had to be strong and guard against the sweet insanity his bold, masterful touch provoked. . . .

Her second supper at the Chapparosa was a trifle more subdued than the first. The twins, having willfully ignored Consuela's admonitions and overindulged themselves with leftover *biscochitos,* managed only a few bites before begging to be excused from the table. Neither Martha nor Ben had the heart to scold them, for it was obvious they were paying for their mistake in the most effective way known to rebellious children and their eminently wise parents.

The three adults repaired to the parlor again following the meal, but Martha did not tarry long. She rose with a conspiratorial smile at Jessie and a meaningful sideways glance in Ben's direction.

"I'm afraid the two of you will have to make do with one another's company tonight," she told them. "I must confess to being a little worn out from the day."

"Oh, Martha, I'm sorry," Jessie apologized, her eyes full of contrition. "I should not have allowed you to work so hard!"

"And why not?" the other woman retorted with mock severity. "I may not be as young and sprightly as I used to be, but I think I can still hold my own against you and the girls!"

"You did considerably more than hold your own!" Jessie admitted with a soft laugh.

"Well, then, I am entitled to my rest. Good night to you both," she said as she sailed from the room.

Ben waited until Martha had gone before turning away from his pensive stance at the window and wandering over to take a seat across from Jessie. She glanced up at him but hastily averted her gaze when he stretched his long legs out before him, crossed one booted foot over the other, and negligently folded his arms against his chest. He had changed into a clean white cotton shirt and dark blue trousers. The faint scent of soap, mingled with a trace of shaving lather, emanated from the hard warmth of his tall, splendidly masculine frame.

Since the night was unseasonably cool, there was a comforting blaze crackling softly in the big stone fireplace. The flames cast intriguing shadows in the room, for the only other source of light was the crystal-trimmed oil lamp on the table beside the sofa. Jessie could not help being reminded of quiet evenings spent at home with her family . . . with one significant difference. There had been no Ben Chandler to bedevil her in her own parlor.

"Martha told me you still need a few things for the school," he remarked quietly. "I'll see that you get them."

"Thank you," she murmured, still trying to prevent her eyes from straying toward him. She had battled alternate feelings of panic and resentment all through supper. Facing him again had been only slightly less difficult than she had thought it would be. He had certainly done nothing to help alleviate her discomfort.

She knew she had to look at him eventually, but it was easier to talk to him when his gaze wasn't boring relentlessly into hers. She smoothed a hand along the gathered folds of her lilac crepon skirts, her heart pounding against the scooped bodice that revealed a tantalizing but properly modest glimpse of the full, satiny roundness swelling above the lace-trimmed neckline of her chemise.

"There is something else we need to discuss, Mr. Chandler. Something else that concerns the school."

"Damn it, woman, don't you think it's time we dropped this ridiculous formality?" he grumbled with a dark scowl. "Under the circumstances, it seems—"

"Under the circumstances, *Mr. Chandler,* it is imperative that we keep things on a level of—of distant civility!" She raised her flashing emerald eyes to his face at last and felt an invisible current pass through her.

"And how the hell do you propose we do that?" challenged Ben, only the ghost of a smile playing about his lips.

"By forgetting what lies behind and forging ahead!"

"I'm willing to accept that," he agreed with surprising equanimity.

"You—you are?" she stammered, experiencing a sharp, contradictory mixture of relief and disappointment. She swallowed hard and raised her head proudly. "Very well then, let us get on with the subject at hand. I have learned of a grievous wrong that needs righting, and I—" She paused for a moment and searched for the right words. "I require your assistance, Mr. Chandler. I am asking for you to support me in a course of action that may very well cause us both a good deal of trouble."

"What are you talking about?" he demanded, his brows drawing together in a puzzled frown.

"I'm talking about Consuela's children. I want them to come to school. Not only them, but any other children who have been unjustly prevented from doing so. Martha told me the school board ruled that only white children may attend. She also told me you were opposed to the ruling. That is why I am asking for your support."

"All right. You've got it. But it won't do you any good."

"Why not?"

"Because I've been through all this with the other members of the board before," he explained, his eyes darkening at the memory. "Some of them are hardheaded jackasses who wouldn't know good sense if it kicked them in the seat of the pants. There are a few who might listen to reason, but they'll still vote with the majority every time."

"But you could give it another try, could you not?" she persisted. "There's nothing to be lost by simply speaking to them about it!"

"I'll speak to them. But it won't do any good," he reiterated. His steely gaze softened as it traveled over her beautiful stormy features.

"Well, it certainly won't if you approach it with the attitude of inevitable failure!" she shot back resentfully. "Didn't anyone ever tell you, Mr. Chandler, that—"

"By damn, Jessamyn, I swear I'll turn you over my knee if you call me Mr. Chandler one more time!" he threatened, the dangerously intense look in his eyes leaving little doubt that he would carry through on the threat.

"You wouldn't dare!" she breathed furiously, her face aflame and her own eyes flinging invisible daggers at his handsome head.

"I'd dare anything where you're concerned," he vowed in a low, vibrant tone.

His expression was deadly serious, his gaze filled with such warmth and possessiveness that Jessie's pulses leapt alarmingly. Words failed her for the moment, and she found herself unable to do anything more than stare at him through a haze of conflicting emotions. The fire hissed and popped softly beneath the carved wood mantel, while somewhere in the house a clock struck the hour of nine.

Finally, after what seemed to her like an eternity, Jessie stood. Ben did the same.

"We cannot continue in this manner, Mr. Cha—Ben," she amended, then silently berated herself for her cowardice. "This inexplicable ongoing battle between us has got to stop! I have my school to think of, and you have a ranch and two children, and—"

"We can't stop it, Jessamyn."

"And that's another thing! No one calls me Jessamyn! No one save my father, that is, and I . . . well, I . . ." She could not continue, not with that devilish amusement lurking in the brilliant, fathomless blue depths of his eyes.

"You don't look like a Jessie to me. But I'll call you whatever you like," he offered, slowly advancing on her as he talked. "Any damned name you like."

Jessie raised her eyes to his. He towered above her, making her feel at once small and vulnerable and incredibly feminine. She had never wanted to touch a man as she wanted to touch him. Heaven help her, but she had never before been so tempted to boldly reach out and smooth a hand along the rugged, clean-shaven smoothness of a man's cheek, to trail her fingers lower to where the partially unbuttoned front of his shirt revealed an intriguing glimpse of the bronzed, powerfully formed male flesh that she knew would feel so very warm and hard beneath her hand.

"I—I think it's time I went to bed," she declared in a weak, tremulous voice.

"I think not," he disagreed, his chiseled lips curving upward into a soft smile. His eyes gazed deeply into hers, and his hands came up to close with tender forcefulness about her arms.

"Let me go," she commanded breathlessly, frightened of the way he was making her feel. *Don't do this, Jessie!* her mind screamed. She made one last desperate attempt to heed the warning. "I've no intention of making the same mistake I made last night," she forced herself to say in a cool, calm manner. Her troubled gaze searched his face for any sign of understanding. "It was wrong of me. It was wrong of you. And you know as well as I do that unless we forget this—this madness, we will both regret it!"

"Call it madness if you will, Jessamyn." His gaze was smoldering with passion's fire, his deep-timbred voice laced with raw emotion as he drew her closer. "But it makes us both come alive." His head lowered relentlessly toward hers. "Damn it, it makes us come alive!" he repeated in a hoarse whisper, just before his lips descended upon hers in a fiery demanding kiss that quite literally took her breath away.

Jessie, her senses reeling, swayed against him in unspoken surrender. She was grateful for the support of his strong arms, which slipped about her trembling body and tightened with fierce, impassioned urgency. His warm mouth plundered the willing softness of hers, while her arms came up to entwine about the corded muscles of his neck. She clung to him, her soft curves pressing intimately against his virile hardness. All thought of resistance had fled her mind by now, leaving her sweetly pliant for his pleasure—and hers.

187

Ben, glorifying in her acceptance, clasped her to him as if he would never let her go, his body on fire with passion's yearning and his heart singing with a triumphant joy he was not yet ready to acknowledge. His hands glided downward along the graceful, slender curve of her back to close about her buttocks. His fingers spread possessively, appreciatively across the feminine roundness of her bottom, and Jessie moaned softly as she was made aware of the state of his masculine desire. She gasped and felt a delicious shiver dance down her spine.

Please, God, let it go on and on. . . .

She was unprepared when Ben suddenly put an end to the wildly pleasurable embrace. Gazing up at him in breathless astonishment, she found herself unable to speak. Her countenance was becomingly flushed and wide-eyed, and her whole body ached to continue with the madness she had condemned only moments ago. If not for the lingering support of one of his arms about her corseted waist, she would have crumpled back down upon the sofa.

"A man can only stand so much, wildcat!" he explained in a low, husky voice. His searing gaze, straying momentarily to where the alluring curve of her creamy, ripe young breasts swelled above the rounded neckline of her gown, burned down into hers. "You're right about one thing, you know. . . . We can't go on this way."

"Please, just . . . let me go!" she pleaded brokenly, her eyes clouded with misery and embarrassment. A sob welled up deep in her throat, and she pushed at him in a desperate attempt to be free.

"No, Jessamyn. We have to talk." Before she knew what he intended, he took a seat on the sofa and pulled her down onto his lap. She struggled, her blush deepening as she looked swiftly toward the doorway.

"Someone will see us!" she gasped out, pushing herself upward.

"Let them," he retorted unconcernedly. He forced her back down, but her defiant struggles continued. Groaning inwardly when her wriggling bottom fanned against the front of his trousers, he muttered an oath and tightened his arms about her in a grip of iron. "Unless you mean for me to take you here and now, Jessamyn Clare, you'd damned well better sit still and hear what I have to say!" he warned in a quiet, authoritative tone, which indicated all too clearly he would brook no further resistance.

"There is nothing to be said between us!" she pronounced while staunchly blinking back tears. She refused to meet his gaze, and she held herself stiff and unyielding in spite of the temptation to melt against him. No, she mused bitterly, there had been far too much *melting* taking place already!

"Yes there is," he decreed in a deceptively low and level tone. His blue eyes gleamed with an unfathomable light, and his handsome features grew quite solemn, "I don't know what the hell's going on between us. But I know something has to be done about it."

"And what do you propose, *Mr. Chandler?*" she challenged with tearful, biting sarcasm, her eyes meeting his at last.

She was surprised to observe a slow, strangely crooked smile touching his lips. But it was the words he spoke that served to shock her to the very core.

"Marriage, Miss Clare. You and I are going to be married."

Nine

It was not a question. It was a bold, utterly confident statement of fact.

"*What?*" Jessie breathed in profound disbelief. She peered closely at him but could find no trace of derision. "You . . . surely you cannot be serious!"

"Dead serious," he asserted with another faint smile of irony. He resisted the urge to kiss the lips that were still parted so adorably in stunned amazement.

"But we don't even know one another!" she protested, her head spinning. "For heaven's sake, we only met four days ago!"

"I know." The memory of the night they had spent together provoked another blaze of desire within him. His eyes darkened, and it was all he could do to refrain from tumbling her back upon the sofa and covering her soft, supple curves with his burning hardness.

"Time doesn't seem to matter much, does it?" he asked, referring to the fact that they were caught up in something neither of them had managed to fight with much success. "You're young, Jessamyn and you don't know much about the ways of men and women. But too much has already happened for us to go back to being strangers. What I'm trying to say is . . . damn it, you're not the kind of woman a man takes without marriage!"

"So that's it," she murmured dazedly, half to herself. "You want to make me your wife because duty demands it, because your sense of honor tells you it's the only way you can make things right."

"And because I want you in my bed," he added honestly.

Jessie crimsoned and looked away in confusion. Murmuring something unintelligible, she pushed against him, then was surprised when he allowed her to rise. She stood staring down at him, her eyes full of pain, while a sharp twinge of betrayal sliced through her. Although she felt heartsick at the realization that he sought only her body and not her love, she told herself she had no right to demand more. No right at all.

Ben drew himself up before her, his hands reaching for her but falling back to his sides when she abruptly stiffened. He turned away and moved to the fireplace. Bracing a hand against the mantel, he stared deeply into the flames, his thoughts drifting back to the moment, earlier that same day, when he had made the decision to make her his wife.

It had come to him while he was out on the range. He had drawn his mount to a halt beside a stream, his gaze absently scrutinizing the rain-drenched countryside while the animal drank. Tilting his hat back upon his head, he had shifted in the saddle and loosened his hold a bit on the reins, intending to take a well-deserved break from the day's work.

But, as had happened with damnable frequency the past few days, Jessie's beautiful face swam before his eyes. The memory of the previous night's events had returned to haunt him once more. And he had suddenly known what he had to do. There had been no doubts, no hesitancy on his part. He had simply known and accepted, just as he was asking her to do now.

"Did you love your first wife?" Jessie queried softly, already certain of the answer. Ben jerked his head up at the unexpected question.

"What the hell does that have to do with it?" he demanded in a curt, angry tone.

"A great deal!" she insisted. "A very great deal, Ben Chandler!" She swiftly closed the distance between them, her eyes flashing as she tilted her head back to confront him. "Who the devil do you think you are? You offer me the *glorious* honor of your name, and yet the manner in which you do so makes a mockery of everything I hold dear! Am I supposed to be pleased to receive such a cold, dispassionate proposal? Indeed, I defy you to find any woman who finds pleasure in hearing that her lifelong partnership with a man is based on nothing else but—but mere physical attraction and a highly misplaced sense of duty!"

"It's more than a lot of couples start with, Jessamyn. A hell of a lot more!"

"Is that all you and Emily started with?" she retorted. A loud gasp broke from her lips when his hands shot out to seize her arms.

"Damn it, you go too far!" he ground out, his eyes gleaming almost savagely down into hers.

"No more than you! You go too far when you tell me I will be your wife because it is what *you* want, because it is something *you* have deemed to be the perfect solution to a problem that is both sinful and degrading! I will not be your wife, Ben Chandler!" she cried vehemently, the hot tears spilling over her lashes now to course down the flushed smoothness of her cheeks. "When and if I do marry, it will be because I love and am loved in return!"

"And can you honestly say there's no love between us?" he suddenly challenged. He yanked her closer, his smoldering gaze raking over her with the same fierce possessiveness he had displayed a few minutes earlier.

"Can you, Jessamyn?"

She stared mutely up at him. The question had thrown her into utter chaos. No words would come, for the simple reason that she did not know how to answer.

"Well, neither can I," Ben admitted truthfully. "I only know I've never felt this way about anyone before. It wasn't something I had planned to feel. God knows, I've tried not to. But it's there just the same. For both of us."

"No!" whispered Jessie, shaking her head in an emphatic denial. "No!"

"You're mine, Jessamyn," he proclaimed once more. "You've been mine from the first moment I set eyes on you. And by damn, no other man will have you!"

Jessie gasped as he swept her forcefully up against him. She was given no time to protest, for his lips came crashing down upon hers without warning. He kissed her with a hard, demanding passion, almost as though to punish her for either her resistance or her desirability— or perhaps even both.

By the time he relinquished the conquered softness of her lips once more, she was beyond caring about what had prompted his startling, highly irregular proposal of marriage. She knew only that she wanted him to kiss her again and again. The thought of sharing his bed each and every night made her tremble with the passion he had awakened within her, and she could not summon the strength to deny him when he commanded masterfully.

"Say it Jessamyn. Say you'll marry me."

"I—I will marry you!" She was rewarded for her acquiescence with another kiss, which proved to be even more compellingly, rapturously persuasive than the first.

Moments later, Ben scooped her up in his arms and bore her purposefully back to the sofa. He wanted to drive her to the very brink of human endurance, wanted her to feel the raw, burning desire that had plagued him since the first time he had held her close. He wanted to make certain she would not betray her promise.

Jessie, her emerald gaze suffused with the soft glow of passion, was surprised when Ben suddenly lowered her to the sofa and momentarily abandoned her. Wide-eyed and breathless, she sat up, watching in bemusement as he crossed to the door and closed it, then pocketed the key. When he turned back to her, his handsome face wore an expression of unwavering determinaton, while the look in his eyes could best be described as tenderly wolfish.

Jessie's pulses raced, her whole body atremble. She swallowed a sudden lump in her throat as her roguish tormentor began advancing on her again.

"Wha—what are you going to do?" she stammered weakly.

"I think you know." At that, her eyes grew enormous within the flushed delicate oval of her face.

"Oh, Ben . . . *no!*" she breathed in alarm.

She sprang up from the sofa and tried to dart past him to the door. He easily caught her, his hands pulling her mercilessly back to him. Lifting her in his strong arms again, he took a seat on the sofa and held her captive upon his lap, just as he had done earlier. Jessie murmured a halfhearted protest, which was cut off quite effectively by the pressure of his loving mouth upon hers. Her arms crept back up with a will of their own to encircle his neck, her body arching into even closer contact with his.

The kiss rapidly deepened, and Ben's caresses quickly became more inflaming. He impatiently raked up her skirts and petticoat, his hand sliding upward along the silken curve of her left thigh to roam boldly over her soft, shapely derriere. She inhaled sharply when his warm fingers delved within the gaping edges of her lacy open-leg drawers to touch her naked skin. He stroked across her delectably rounded bottom, then sought the moist pink flesh nestled within the delicate golden curls between her thighs.

194

"Oh, Ben!" she gasped, her lips released at last so that his mouth could press a spray of hot, urgent kisses across the tops of her heaving breasts. Her fingers came up to entangle within the dark sun-streaked thickness of his hair, while her eyes swept closed against the deliciously wicked sensations he was creating within her.

Then, intervention arrived in a most unlikely form.

There was a sudden knock at the door, followed by a small childish voice calling out to the most reliable source of comfort in the house.

"Papa?" It was Hannah. "Papa, are you in there?"

Her eyes flying to the door, Jessie caught her breath. She felt herself coloring in mingled guilt and embarrassment, felt her heart twisting in dismay at what she had very nearly done.

"Papa, I know you're in there!" the little girl on the other side of the door said more insistently. She punctuated her words with another knock. "Please, Papa, I need to talk to you!"

Ben hesitated for only a moment, then reluctantly set Jessie away from him without a word. He shot a quick look back at her as she stood and hastily set her appearance to rights. The sight of her flaming cheeks and seductively tousled hair made him groan inwardly. Although he loved his daughter with all his heart, he was tempted to do her bodily harm when he flung open the door to reveal her sweet, innocently wide-eyed features.

"What is it, Hannah?" he asked quietly.

"I'm not feeling very well, Papa. Would you come sit beside my bed?" Her eyes traveled past him, finally alighting upon Jessie. "Oh, hello, Miss Clare," she declared with a brief, unusually wan smile.

"Hello, Hannah," Jessie returned the greeting with genuine warmth. Her gaze full of compassion, she came forward to lay a gentle, remarkably steady hand upon the child's forehead. Only a faint blush betrayed her

195

lingering disquiet when she said to Ben, "I believe she has a bit of fever."

He would not admit how deeply affected he was by this simple maternal gesture of concern. Frowning, he bent and lifted Hannah in his arms as if she were nothing more than a babe.

"Come on, sweetheart. Let's get you back to bed."

"And will you stay?" the little girl requested again, her arms tightening their hold on his neck.

"Yes. I'll stay," agreed Ben. It was hard enough for him to deny her anything when she was well and full of mischief; much less when she was ill.

"Good night, Miss Clare," Hannah murmured as she lay her head down on her father's shoulder.

"Good night, Hannah. I hope you are feeling much better in the morning," Jessie responded, reaching up to smooth a wayward blond curl from the child's pale brow. She gave Hannah another warmly lit smile, but the smile faded when her gaze met the glowing intensity of Ben's once more.

"We'll talk more tomorrow," he promised in a resonant undertone. Then, cradling his daughter lovingly in his arms, he carried her from the parlor and back through the house to her room.

Jessie stared after him as if transfixed. She could not begin to comprehend what had just taken place between them. And in truth, she did not want to, at least not now. She did not want to try and analyze her own feelings, or Ben's, or anything else. Her head still swam, her whole body ached, and she was seized with the unaccountable urge to fling herself back down upon the sofa and dissolve into a storm of weeping. But something she had not yet considered was suddenly brought to mind as a result of Hannah's timely intervention, and she could not help but turn her turbulent thoughts to it.

The children. Good heavens, she had forgotten about

the children! How would James and Hannah feel about having her as their new mother . . . their stepmother?

"Stepmother," she repeated aloud, thinking of Lillian. Just as she had told Martha, her relationship with her own stepmother was not a close one. The prospect of being resented, even a little, by Ben's children threw her into yet another quandary. It would not be Ben Chandler alone she was taking on when she married him, it would be his family as well.

In truth, she realized she knew nothing whatsoever about being a mother to seven-year-old twins. She knew nothing about being a mother at all, for that matter. The responsibility did not frighten her; only the possibility that she would not live up to their expectations. Nothing she had ever done or learned had prepared her for the position Ben was asking—no *demanding*—that she accept.

"Dear God, what am I to do?" she whispered.

The first thing she did was turn out the lamp and go to bed. When she finally lay beneath the covers of the canopied four-poster, she searched her heart and soul for the truth. And when it came, it did not set her free at all.

She was going to marry Ben Chandler. For better or worse, she had made her decision and would see it through. She could fight against the madness no longer.

But what about love? her conscience demanded. She had vowed to marry only for love. But, she rationalized to herself, the type of love she had always dreamt of finding might not exist. There had been no knights on white chargers riding by to sweep her away. No, she mused with a soft smile of irony, only a tall, devastatingly handsome rancher on an Appaloosa.

It makes us both come alive, Ben had said about the mysterious, splendidly passionate bond between them. He was right, admitted Jessie with a ragged sigh. She had never felt so alive. Heaven help her, but she wanted to go

197

on feeling what Ben made her feel. And if love had to come later, then so be it.

"But what if it doesn't?" she murmured. "What if it never comes at all?"

The image of Emily's pretty delicate features suddenly rose before her eyes again. Her throat constricted, her emerald gaze filling with anguish as she thought of Ben's first wife. Did he still grieve for Emily? Was his heart held captive by a memory? Would he ever be able to love another?

The questions ran together in her mind. She closed her eyes and pressed her fingers to her temples, as if by doing so she could somehow restore order to the turmoil within. Finally, she drifted off into a troubled sleep that left her feeling far from rested when the new day dawned.

Unlike the previous morning, she was dressed and waiting in the dining room when the others arrived for breakfast. She smiled at Martha, who was followed by James and an apparently recovered Hannah. There was, however, no sign of Ben. Jessie was surprised to learn that he had already gone for the day—or rather, for the next *three* days, according to Martha.

"He left word with Consuela that he had business in Santa Fe," explained the older woman, obviously more than a little perplexed by it herself. "I must say, it isn't like him to leave without saying good-bye to me or the children."

"He did say good-bye to me," revealed Hannah.

"Me, too," added James.

"He did?" Martha echoed with a slight frown of bafflement. "When?"

"This morning," James answered. He and his twin exchanged quick secretive smiles. "It was still dark. He told me I'd be the man of the house while he was gone and to look after things." He gave an eloquent shrug of his small shoulders and confided to Jessie, "Papa always says

198

that when he's going away."

"He told me he'd bring me something special this time," Hannah announced in an excited voice, her face beaming at the thought. She turned to Jessie and said earnestly, "I'm feeling much better, Miss Clare. I'm sorry I interrupted you and Papa last night. He told me he would have skinned me alive if I hadn't really been sick. You know, he slept in the chair beside my bed all night long!"

"That is undoubtedly why you are feeling better," Jessie remarked with a brief, preoccupied smile.

Why did he go away without a word? she agonized silently. It hurt her more deeply than she cared to admit to think that he had changed his mind, that he perhaps regretted the impulsive proposal of marriage he had made her. Maybe he didn't want her for his wife after all. Maybe that was why he had suddenly taken himself off and left her with this awful uncertainty and confusion. It was really quite ironic, she thought bitterly. She had prepared herself to face him with the news of her acceptance, and he had run away. . . .

"Oh, and he told me to tell you something, Miss Clare," Hannah suddenly remembered.

Jessie's eyes widened in surprise. Dismayed to feel the warm telltale color staining her cheeks, she was all too aware of Martha's steady scrutiny.

"And what was that?" she reluctantly asked the little girl seated across the table from her.

"He said I was to tell you to remember your promise, and that he would continue his private discussion with you as soon as he got back. He asked me to tell you because he knew *I* would remember," Hannah declared with a significant superior look at her twin.

"I would have remembered!" James protested defensively, the blue eyes that were so much like his father's narrowing in brotherly indignation. "You know damn well I have a better memory than you do!"

"James Chandler!" Martha sternly admonished. "You will not use such language in this house!"

"Yes ma'am," he complied with a begrudging grace. His face brightened in the next instant. "But is it all right if I use it outside?"

"No, young man, it most certainly is *not*," insisted Martha, concealing her amusement.

"What promise?" Hannah suddenly asked Jessie.

"I—I beg your pardon?" she faltered, taken aback by the unexpected inquiry.

"What did Papa mean when he said you were to keep your promise?"

"Hannah, it isn't polite to pry into other people's affairs," Martha reprimanded, though she had in truth been sorely tempted to ask the same question. She cast Jessie an apologetic smile and confessed, "It's my own fault, you know. Ben has complained that I'm too much of a doting aunt, and he's absolutely right. They need someone young, someone who isn't afraid to risk their fearsome wrath," she finished with a teasing frown of severity at the twins.

Someone like me? Jessie wondered, her gaze traveling over James and Hannah. She was already quite fond of them, and she sensed that they liked her in return. It was usually easy to tell with children, she mused, for they had not yet learned to hide their true feelings. But simply because they liked her didn't mean they would welcome her as their new mother and their father's new wife.

If their father still wants you, that inner voice pointedly reminded her. The message he had conveyed through Hannah led her to believe that he had not changed his mind after all. What else could have precipitated his abrupt departure?

"I just hope Papa gets back before Monday," sighed Hannah, her long blond pigtails framing her angelic features. "It will be my very first day of school ever!"

"Mine too!" James piped up. At a sudden thought, he asked Jessie, "Is it true that whenever we misbehave at school, you're going to make us strip down to our birthday suits and climb a tree and stay there until the sun goes down?"

"Why, of course not!" she breathlessly asserted, her eyes growing very wide at the question. "Where in heaven's name did you get such an idea?"

"From Billy Shelton," replied James. "He's nine. You can tell him apart from all the other Sheltons because his hair's redder than theirs and he's got the most freckles."

"I've never believed anything Billy Shelton said!" Hannah proclaimed with a childish disdain. "He told us the new schoolteacher was going to be old and ugly. And he said his father could whip our father, but I don't see how, since Mr. Shelton doesn't even come up as high as Papa's shoulder. Billy isn't very smart, Miss Clare, but Aunt Martha says we have to show tol . . . tol . . . oh, yes, *tolerance* for people like him!"

"Your Aunt Martha is quite right," she declared, valiantly striving to suppress a laugh. She looked to Martha, whose eyes twinkled back at her in shared, secret amusement.

"But I can assure you both," Jessie then avowed to the sadly misinformed twins, "that I have every intention of being a fair and reasonable teacher. I will mete out punishment only where it is due, and even then, I doubt if I will ever find it necessary to employ the drastic means Billy Shelton described to you."

"You'd better watch out for those big boys, Miss Clare," James warned solemnly. "Some of them are meaner than snakes."

"Some of the girls are, too," proclaimed Hannah. "Especially Mary Sue Mooney. She—"

"Now, children, there's no use in filling Miss Clare's

201

head with so much advice before school has even begun," Martha chided gently, then changed the subject. "As soon as you've had your breakfast, I want the two of you to help Consuela with the dishes. After that, you, James, may go outside and help Curly with the horses, and you, Hannah, may go outside and gather the eggs."

"But doing dishes is girl's work!" James objected, his expression comically mutinous.

"It is not!" Hannah shot back. "Who do you think washes dishes when the cowboys are out on the range?"

"That's different. There aren't any girls around out there."

Jessie smiled, shaking her head in wonderment at the twins as they continued to argue for several moments longer. Finally, Martha put a stop to things, and Consuela came in with breakfast. The remainder of the meal passed in relative harmony, at least outwardly. The emotional turmoil raging within Jessie interfered with her appetite, so that she could manage only a few bites before excusing herself from the table.

"Three days," she murmured, standing before the mirror in her room. She raised her eyes to her reflection, only to glimpse the disappointment shining in their fiery emerald depths. Although she was loath to admit it, the prospect of spending the next three days without Ben Chandler was a dismal one indeed.

By the time Sunday rolled around, Jessie was almost too excited to eat or sleep. Ben was due back that day, and school would be starting the next. Those two impending events combined to keep her feeling jumpy and on edge throughout what was a typically lazy Sunday for everyone else at the Chapparosa.

The past two days had been anything but lazy for either Jessie or Martha, who had decided to make curtains for

202

the schoolhouse. With Curly riding behind, they had taken the wagon into Cimarron on Friday to purchase the required materials, in addition to a few other things needed at the ranch. James and Hannah had declined Martha's offer to go along, both of them claiming there was far too much "exploring" to do before summer was over and they had to spend most of their time indoors.

Recalling the visit to town, Jessie's eyes filled with a troubled light. Things had not gone at all the way she had expected. . . .

"I would like to pay a visit to Lissa Boone before we leave," Jessie told Martha as the wagon drew up before the mercantile. "That is, if you don't mind."

"Mind? Not at all!" the other woman assured her.

The two of them climbed down and quickly smoothed the creases from their skirts. Curly, promising to return within the hour, had already turned his horse back toward Lambert's Saloon. He was neither a frequent nor heavy drinker, but he made no secret of the fact that he liked a shot of whiskey every now and then. Curly, Jessie had decided, was a real enigma. He was attractive in a lean, roughcast way, his sand-colored hair always neatly combed and his boots always polished. He spoke only when necessary, but he seemed to miss little.

"Why don't you go on over to the St. James now, my dear?" Martha suggested. "To tell the truth, I promised to look in on . . . well, on an old friend of mine the next time I was in town. We can meet back here in half an hour and choose whatever we need then."

"Very well," agreed Jessie. She set off along the boardwalk, turning back to Martha with a smile. "I'll not be late!"

It took her longer to reach the hotel than she thought it would. She was pleasantly surprised at the way so many people greeted her along the way. Unlike that first day, nearly every one of the women she passed offered her a friendly hello. Her spirits, which had admittedly been low since Ben had gone away, lifted at the thought that she was apparently no longer a source of irreverent speculation. Happily, it seemed that curiosity had given way to acceptance. She remembered Ben's warning that her association with him might very well damage her reputation; she certainly saw no evidence of that.

Finally arriving at the St. James, she paused in front of the large pink adobe building and gathered up her skirts with the intention of going inside. But she happened to turn her head and catch sight of Lissa through the window—Lissa and Curly.

They were standing beside the front desk, their gazes locked while they shared what appeared to be an urgent conversation. Lissa shook her head at something Curly said while he in turn frowned and took a step closer. He and the tall redhead were well matched in height, and it was obvious to Jessie from the way they looked at one another that they shared much more than a polite acquaintanceship.

Mentally upbraiding herself for her spying, she forced her eyes away from the window and wandered a short distance farther down the boardwalk. She did not want to interrupt the strangely intimate scene she had just witnessed, and yet she could not help being curious about her friend's relationship with the quiet, solemn ranch hand.

She was so engrossed in her thoughts that she did not realize she had moved to stand in front of the saloon. It was not crowded at that time of day, but there were always enough customers pushing through its swinging double doors to justify its being open in the late morning hours.

"Well, now, I didn't know schoolmarms were allowed

204

to drink," a familiar voice suddenly spoke behind her.

Jessie's eyes flew wide in alarm. She whirled about to face the man she had prayed never to see again.

"*You!*" she gasped in disbelief.

"The name's Hagan. Cole Hagan," he supplied with a slow, insolent smile. "And yours is Jessamyn Clare." His gaze flickered meaningfully up and down her body. "I asked about you."

"What are you doing here?" she demanded sharply, her eyes kindling with angry defiance in spite of the fear that had risen within her.

"That's my business. But I'll let you make it yours if you show me those pretty legs again," he offered with a soft, derisive chuckle. He reached up and swept the hat from his dark head in a mocking gesture of gallantry. "I forgot. . . . You're a lady, aren't you?"

Jessie drew herself up proudly and turned away. He grabbed her arm.

"I tried to forget other things, too, *Miss Clare*." Disregarding her efforts to pull free, he jerked her closer. His features took on a hard, sinister look. "Why don't you and I go on back out to that schoolhouse and have ourselves another *lesson?*"

"Let go of me!" she hissed furiously. His grip tightened until she winced with pain.

"What's the matter? Are you afraid you'll like it too much?" he sneered. "Maybe you've had a man's hand up your skirts before, schoolmarm! Just maybe—"

"Damn you, let me go!" she raged. Desperate to escape, she brought her hand up with all her might against his face. He bit out a vile oath and grabbed her other arm, twisting it behind her back until she cried out. His face loomed before her terror-filled eyes, so close she could smell the whiskey on his breath and see the menace reflected in his hotly glittering gaze.

"I like a woman with spirit!" he rasped out. "I knew

205

you had it in you, little schoolmarm! Yes, sir, *Miss Clare,* I'll bet you're a regular wildcat underneath those clothes of yours! I'll bet you scream good and loud when—"

"Let her go." It was a man's voice, full of deadly calm.

Cole jerked his head around at the sound of it. Jessie ceased her struggles and gazed incredulously across at Curly, who stood a few feet away in front of the hotel. His face was grim, his lean body tensed in defensive readiness.

"I said to let her go," he repeated quietly.

"You aiming to make me?" Cole challenged with a malevolent, unconcerned grin. His right hand was already inching down toward the fancy tooled leather holster he wore buckled low on his hips.

Jessie was scarcely aware of the fact that she had been released. She stood as if frozen to the spot, her heart pounding and her eyes fastened on Curly's dangerously set features.

"Move aside, Miss Jessie," directed Curly, his own gun within easy reach of his hand.

His words brought her to life once more. Hastening to obey, she stepped away from Cole Hagan and into the street. It was then that she noticed Lissa standing in the doorway of the St. James. The redhead's face was noticeably pale, and her expression was one of heart-stopping dread as her gaze shifted anxiously back and forth between Curly and the insolent stranger who had dared to lay hands on Jessie.

"Who the hell are you, anyway?" Cole demanded, his mouth twisting into another smile of malignant humor as he prepared to kill the older man.

"I'm your judge and jury, boy," Curly replied solemnly.

Cole Hagan laughed at that. He sobered in the next instant and shifted his booted feet a bit farther apart on the dusty boardwalk. The look in his eyes became one of cold-blooded intent.

Jessie held her breath, horrified to realize that the two men actually meant to draw on one another. She looked helplessly about, her gaze searching for anyone who might be able to put a stop to things before it was too late. Dear God, she could not simply stand by and watch while a man was killed!

"No!" she cried out. "No, please don't—"

"Hold it right there, you two!" a man suddenly ordered nearby.

Faint with relief, Jessie watched as the town's sheriff strode forward. He came up behind Cole, holding his own gun in an inarguable position of authority. Having already sized up the situation—similar to dozen of others he had seen—he placed the end of his six-shooter up against Cole's back.

"Let's have 'em, mister," he commanded, referring to the other man's guns.

"The name's Hagan. And I've broken no law," Cole ground out.

"I know who you are. Now do as I say, damn it!"

With eyes full of fury, Cole Hagan reluctantly did as he was told. The sheriff took his guns and looked to the other participant in the would-be gunfight.

"Better watch out for this one, Curly," he cautioned the man he'd known for years. "I got word he's a mean four-flushing son of a bitch hired by the company."

"That's a lie!" growled Cole, his mind racing to think of who might have been responsible for blowing his cover. Whoever the bastard was, he'd be made to pay!

"Is it?" the sheriff drawled contemptuously. He jabbed the barrel of his gun into Cole's back. "You're hightailing it out of Cimarron right now, Hagan. If I see you here again, by damn I'll let the men you're trying to run off their land have a go at you!"

With that, he marched the gunslinger away. Jessie

watched until they were out of sight, then hurried across to where Curly still stood tensed and watchful on the boardwalk. Lissa had already moved to his side, and she clasped his arm with trembling fingers.

"Oh, Curly, he—he would have killed you!" exclaimed Jessie.

"Maybe," allowed Curly, the ghost of a smile playing about his lips. "Maybe not."

Lissa said nothing. Several conflicting emotions crossed her face as she gazed up at him. He raised his hand to cover hers, but she murmured something unintelligible and drew away. His eyes glowing dully and his lips compressing into a tight, thin line, he gave Jessie a silent nod. She turned to watch as he strode past them, then disappeared inside the saloon.

"Lissa, what is it?" she asked her friend, noting the stricken look on the other woman's face. "What's wrong?"

"Nothing," Lissa denied hastily. Her troubled gaze fell before Jessie's wide, concerned one. "Nothing at all." There was a telltale catch in her voice. In the next moment, she embraced Jessie and asked, "Are you all right? He didn't hurt you, did he?"

"No. No, I'm fine," Jessie assured her. She shuddered involuntarily at the memory of the hot, predatory look in Cole Hagan's eyes, but she did not speak of it as she and Lissa walked together into the hotel.

Meeting Martha again a short time later, she forced herself to behave as if nothing had happened. She was glad for the fact that Curly did not mention the incident when they were on their way back to the ranch. Vowing to thank him for his intervention when she got the chance, she suddenly thought of Ben. She would not tell him what had happened, she decided. Just as before, she sensed that if he knew of Cole Hagan's assault, he would not rest until he had hunted the man down and exacted revenge. She had already learned enough about the ways of the frontier to know that such villainy would never be allowed to go unpunished.

So she would keep quiet about it. And she could only hope that Curly did the same. More than ever, the thought of Ben in danger made her heart twist painfully. . . .

Jessie's thoughts were drawn back to the present when a knock sounded at her door. Her pulses leaping at the possibility that it was Ben who summoned her forth, she made a last hasty inspection of her appearance and hurried to answer the knock. Her silken skirts rustled softly as she went, and her eyes were aglow at the thought of seeing him again when she opened the door.

But it was not Ben who stood grinning up at her. It was his children.

"Papa's back!" James and Hannah announced in perfect twinly unison.

"He—he is?" stammered Jessie, trying to conceal her disappointment. She frowned in puzzlement as her gaze made a quick sweep of the hallway. "But . . . where is he?"

"Outside," James answered.

"He's unsaddling his horse right now," added Hannah. "Aunt Martha has already gone out to see him. We thought you might want to see him, too!"

"Come on!" James grabbed her hand and gave it an insistent tug.

With a soft laugh of surrender, Jessie allowed herself to be led through the house and out into the bright sunshine. She looked for Ben once she stood with Martha and the children in the front yard, but she was denied the sight of him until several long seconds later, when he emerged from the nearby barn.

He strode toward her with the same easy masculine grace she had noticed the first time she saw him, in Gray Wolf's camp. Strangely enough, that night seemed long ago now. Its memories had been replaced by new ones . . . new ones that kept her tossing restlessly in her bed at night and yearning for a man whose feelings for her were as perplexingly undefined as hers for him.

She found herself trembling in anticipation while he closed the distance between them. A sudden warmth crept over her when her wide, luminous gaze finally met the penetrating steadiness of his. She caught her lower lip between her teeth and looked away in mingled confusion and embarrassment, certain that he could see how nervous she was.

"What did you bring me, Papa?" asked Hannah, fairly bursting with excitement. Her eyes fell upon the package he held in one hand. "Is that it? Oh, Papa, is that it?"

"It is," he confirmed with a soft, crooked smile. She took the bulky brown paper square from him and immediately whirled about to disappear back inside.

"I brought you something, too," Ben told James, who was trying not to look too crestfallen.

"You did?"

His son's face brightened right away, and he smiled again as the little boy accepted a small box he revealed in his other hand. James quickly opened the box and withdrew a bone-handled pocketknife.

"A knife!" he breathed in perfectly boyish wonderment and delight. Grinning from ear to ear, he looked up at his father again. "Thanks, Papa! Now I'll be able to whittle as good as Curly!" He scampered off to show his new treasure to the hands, while Martha shook her head in disapproval and battled an indulgent smile.

"Ben Chandler, you really shouldn't have given him a knife! He might very well cut his finger off with it!"

"He knows how to use it," Ben assured her casually,

then disclosed, "I brought you a couple of those Navajo blankets you've been wanting. They're still in my saddlebag."

"Oh, Ben, how very thoughtful of you!" His cousin was obviously quite pleased. "It's good to have you back, my dear boy," she proclaimed with true affection. "I trust your business went well?"

"Well enough." His eyes strayed to Jessie, who had yet to say a word.

"I'm glad of that," said Martha. She frowned as she scolded affectionately, "But I do hope you'll give us all a bit more notice the next time you see fit to deprive us of your company for so long!"

"I'll try," he promised with an undeniable air of preoccupation.

Martha, who had not failed to notice the direction of her cousin's gaze, cleared her throat gently and gathered up her skirts.

"Well, if you two will please excuse me, I think I'll see what Hannah is doing. I shudder to think what you may have brought *her!*" she teased Ben, making another pointed reference to James's knife.

Jessie and Ben were alone at last—or at least as alone as two people can be when surrounded by a ranchful of people who might interrupt them at any moment. Jessie stole a look up at him from beneath her eyelashes, reflecting that he was even more wickedly handsome than she had remembered. She could endure the silence between them no longer. If he had changed his mind, if he no longer wanted her, then so be it. Anything was better than standing before him like some foolish schoolgirl who is afraid to face the prospect of being alone with her first beau

"Was it because of me you went away?" she blurted out, then groaned inwardly at her own presumption. *For heaven's sake,* she chided herself, *he has a great many other*

211

things to think of besides you!

"Partly," Ben confessed, his mouth curving into a faint smile of irony. His gaze was filled with a disturbing, unfathomable light.

"It—it was?" Jessie faltered in surprise. She looked away again and swallowed a sudden lump in her throat. Misery welled up deep within her at the possibility that her worst suspicions might prove true after all. Though she hated herself for it, she could not refrain from asking, "And have you changed your mind about—about us?"

"Yes." He stepped closer and stared intently down into the thunderstruck, wide-eyed beauty of her countenance. "Yes, by damn, I have!"

Ten

Jessie felt as though her whole world suddenly came crashing down about her.

"I see," she murmured in a weak voice. "Well, then, I suppose that's the end of it." She gasped sharply when Ben's hands closed about her arms.

"No, Jessamyn," he disagreed, his eyes burning fiercely down into hers now. "It's the beginning."

"What are you saying?" As always, his touch sent a plethora of wild sensation blazing through her.

"When I said I'd changed my mind, I didn't mean I no longer wanted you for my wife."

"You didn't?" she echoed, hope rising in her breast once more.

"No," he answered with exasperating simplicity.

"Then what *did* you mean?" she demanded impatiently.

"Only that we're not going to wait. We're going to be married next week."

"Next week?"

"You're repeating everything I say, wildcat," he pointed out, his eyes brimming with wry amusement—and something else she dared not name.

"But we cannot be married next week!" she protested

breathlessly. "Why, that's much too soon, and I—"

"As far as I'm concerned, it's not soon enough." His deep voice was tinged with such underlying warmth that Jessie blushed anew. "But," he admitted reluctantly, his brow creasing into a frown, "I promised myself I wouldn't rush things too much."

"And you don't think a wedding in only seven days' time is rushing things?" she challenged in disbelief. She felt a sharp pang of disappointment when he released her arms.

"No." His jaw was set in grim determination. "No, I don't."

"But what about the school? Tomorrow is only the first day, and I have so much—"

"I'll allow you to continue teaching until the board finds a replacement."

"You'll *allow?*" echoed Jessie, her eyes growing very round before kindling with the fire of indignation. She balled her hands into fists and planted them on her hips, raising her head in the characteristic gesture of proud, spirited defiance that Ben never failed to find enchanting. "In the event you have forgotten, Ben Chandler, the very reason I came to Cimarron in the first place was to teach!" she declared feelingly. "You have no right to demand that I abandon my duties and—"

"You'll be my wife, Jessamyn. That gives me the right!" he asserted in a voice that was whipcord sharp. Unable to keep his hands off her, he seized hold of her arms again. "I want you here at the Chapparosa where you belong, not over at that blasted school!"

"That *blasted school* is where I belong!" she retorted hotly, her temper flaring to match his.

"Damn it, woman," he ground out, his strong fingers clenching about her soft silk-covered flesh, "I'll not have you defying me in this!"

"Then you'll not have me at all!" she declared, provoked to rashness by what she perceived to be his

214

infuriating, inexcusably overbearing manner toward her.

"Will I not?" he countered in a low, dangerously level tone. A faint smile touched his lips, while his smoldering blue eyes held the promise of passion unleashed.

Jessie felt a sudden powerful tremor course through her. She was surprised to find herself released, and she stared dazedly up at Ben as he lifted his hat to his head again.

"Tell Martha I'll be in after I've had a talk with the hands," he directed with maddening calm.

She was tempted to reply scathingly that he could damned well tell Martha himself, but then admitted to herself how childish such a response would be. She settled for tossing him a murderous look, which merely caused him to give a low, resonant chuckle as he turned and sauntered away.

Jessie drew in a ragged breath and folded her arms across her chest. Drat it! she seethed inwardly. She had just been thrown headlong into yet another quandary. If she did marry Ben Chandler, she faced the difficulty of trying to convince him to change his mind about her teaching. And if she did not marry him, she faced the agonizing possibility that she would never again feel what he made her feel . . . heart and soul, body and mind.

Heart and soul? Body and mind? she asked herself silently, frowning in puzzled astonishment as she wondered where in the world that had come from.

She was given no further time to contemplate it at the moment, however, for Hannah suddenly materialized in the doorway and called to her. Giving herself a mental shake, she pivoted about and forced a smile to her lips.

"Look, Miss Clare!" bid the little girl, her eyes dancing with pleasure as she indicated the new embroidered muslin dress she wore. "Look what Papa brought me! Isn't it beautiful?"

"It most certainly is," Jessie agreed in all honesty. She

215

could not help but marvel at a man who was thoughtful enough to purchase a pretty ruffled pink gown for his daughter, and yet who was so completely bullheaded and unreasonable when it came to other matters. Dear Lord, would she ever understand Ben Chandler?

The night held few surprises . . . and very little excitement. Indeed, Jessie was quite bewildered when, following supper and an all-too-short visit with Martha, herself, and the twins—their bedtime was postponed an extra hour in celebration of their first day of school— Ben announced that he had to pay a visit to a neighboring rancher. He favored Jessie with little more than a passing glance before he took himself off, leaving her emotions in as much turmoil as ever and her mind preoccupied with thoughts of him.

"Those meetings are always at the most inopportune times!" Martha opined, half to herself. She and Jessie sat in the parlor alone after finally tucking the children into bed. "It isn't fair. Ben no sooner gets home than he has to leave again." She sighed and took up the knitting in her lap.

"Has he gone to a school board meeting then?" asked Jessie.

"No," Martha answered with a slight shake of her head. "I wish he had. But I'm afraid it's a meeting for the Settlers' Organization." At the younger woman's inquisitive look, she smiled and explained, "I suppose I should have told you something about it before now, but I thought I'd give you time to get settled in first. Now that I think of it, though, you really should be aware of what is going on before school begins."

"Aware of what?" Jessie probed in growing bemusement.

"Have you by any chance ever heard of the Maxwell Land Grant?"

"Yes, as a matter of fact, I have. I read something

about it on my way here from St. Louis." She frowned thoughtfully for a moment, then related what she had learned. "A man by the name of Maxwell owned nearly two million acres of the Territory at one time." She remembered mentioning the subject to Ben when they were riding into Cimarron that first day, but he had been strangely unwilling to speak of it.

"That's true. Lucien Maxwell acquired the land upon his marriage to the beautiful young daughter of a man who had in his possession an old Spanish grant. It was this particular document that assigned ownership to Maxwell's father-in-law, and then in turn to Maxwell himself. But Maxwell sold the entire acreage to a company of foreign investors a few years ago, shortly before his death. And that's when the trouble began." Martha released another faint sigh and set her knitting aside. "You see, the legality of the grant has been under dispute for some time. It only made things worse when everyone learned the new owners are foreigners who do not even reside here. Tensions have been escalating in the past few months, and no one is sure where they will lead or when they will stop."

"What sort of tensions?"

"Between those who are in favor of the grant and those who are opposed to it. The settlers—the ranchers and farmers and miners—believe the grant is invalid. The company, which is quite powerful, I'm afraid, claims that those who have settled upon the land are nothing more than squatters. Or trespassers, in the company's opinion," she clarified with a frown.

"But if the grant is indeed legal, then—"

"That's the whole issue, my dear. Most of the men who brought their families here and built homes honestly believed the land they were claiming was in the public domain and therefore open to them as homesteaders. The question of the grant's legality has been before the courts for a number of years, and there have been so many reversals. . . . It's such a complicated matter. But the company is demanding that the settlers either buy the property they are occupying or move out."

"What about the Chapparosa?" asked Jessie, her throat constricting painfully at the thought that Ben was among those who might be forced out.

"The Chapparosa is in no danger," Martha hastened to assure her. "Ben purchased the land from Maxwell himself. But he isn't one to stand by and do nothing while his friends and neighbors are threatened." Her eyes sparked with an angry glow. "We've heard that the company is bringing in hired gunmen to drive the people off their land."

Jessie drew in her breath sharply as Cole Hagan's face swam before her eyes again. Hadn't the sheriff warned Curly that Hagan was suspected of being a "company" man? If what Martha had just said about hired gunmen was true, then she had little doubt Hagan was one of them. The thought struck renewed fear in her heart.

"What do Ben and the others plan to do?" she asked Martha, her emerald gaze clouding with worriment.

"I don't know yet. I'm not sure they do, either. But I *am* certain they will not surrender without a fight!"

"Fight? Dear God, you don't mean they're planning to—"

"They will do whatever is necessary, my dear," Martha declared somberly.

"And what if innocent people are killed as a result?" demanded Jessie.

"Innocent people have already been killed," the petite brunette revealed sadly. "A minister who spoke out against the company's methods was murdered on his way back from delivering a sermon at a nearby mining town. A man was tortured and lynched as a result. Another man was shot in Lambert's Saloon because he had accused

218

certain men of the lynching. And then yet another lost his life while under armed escort on his way to the county jail in Cimarron. So you see, Jessie," concluded Martha, "things have already gone too far."

"Yes," she murmured. "Yes, I—I suppose they have." She had never known anything of violence or hatred or terror before coming to New Mexico; she had never known anything of passion. At every turn, there was a new dilemma facing her, a new challenge to be met. *But wasn't that what she had wanted?*

She could not deny that it was. The desire for adventure and excitement had led her west. And she suddenly knew that she would never go home again.

"Well, now, let's talk of something else," the older woman suggested brightly. She proceeded to engage Jessie in a conversation about the school and the many improvements they had made. The new desk, chair, and blackboard had been delivered the previous day—it was Ben's doing, Martha had confided to her—and all was in readiness for the first day of school.

All save the teacher, mused Jessie.

Later, as she lay wide awake beneath the covers of her bed, she heard the familiar sound of Ben's footsteps in the hallway. He had not returned from the meeting before she and Martha retired for the night. Recalling the violence Martha had told her about, she had found herself tormented with visions of him lying dead or wounded somewhere.

She glanced toward the door, her breathing quite erratic and her whole body growing warm in the darkness. It bothered her more than she cared to admit, the way he had suddenly grown aloof toward her again. He had as yet to tell anyone of their impending marriage—*if* there was going to be a marriage, she corrected herself. It was insane to think of actually going through with it, especially in only one week's time.

"Impossible!" she proclaimed in an unsteady whisper. But she knew that with Ben Chandler, nothing was impossible. Nothing at all. . . .

Jessie rose early the next morning. Filled with excitement for the day ahead, she hurried to don the white lawn shirtwaist and navy cotton suit she had set out the night before. She drew on the purposely simple ensemble and adjusted it to perfection about her slender curves, then vigorously brushed her long golden tresses and arranged them in a loose chignon resting low on her neck. As a final touch, she pinned Andrew's gift, the small gold watch, above her left breast.

Facing her reflection in the mirror one last time, she smiled in satisfaction. She looked as much like a schoolteacher as she ever would! With that thought, she swept forth to meet the long-awaited challenge.

The other members of the household were already seated in the dining room when she arrived. Hannah wore the new dress her father had given her, while James was once again reluctantly attired in the suit Martha made him wear on special occasions. The first day of school, she had insisted firmly, was indeed a special occasion.

"Good morning, Miss Clare!" the twins sang out when she appeared in the doorway. They were in the process of attacking the scrambled eggs Consuela had just brought in.

"Good morning, Hannah. Good morning, James," she responded, smiling at each of them in turn as she moved to sit in her usual place beside Martha. She was scarcely aware of the older woman bidding her good morning, for her gaze was instinctively drawn to Ben. He offered her a faint mocking smile and a silent nod. A dull flush rising to her face, she murmured a response to Martha and sank

220

down into the ladder-back chair.

"Papa's going to take us to school today!" Hannah told her.

"He is?" She stared at Ben in surprise.

"Yes," James confirmed before his father had the chance, "and he said we can ride our own horses there and back!"

"But I thought we would be going in the wagon," said Jessie. The prospect of traveling on horseback was not a happy one for her; she remembered all too well how sore she had been the last time she had ridden.

"It's time you learned to ride, Jessamyn," Ben decreed as if reading her mind. His eyes were alight with devilish amusement when he added, "It won't take long for your backside to get used to the feel of a saddle beneath it."

"Well, I've certainly never gotten used to it," commented Martha with a soft, rueful laugh. "I still much prefer the comfort of my buggy." She turned to Jessie and admitted, "But it really is much faster to ride. You'll reach the school in half the time a wagon would take."

"Are Consuela's children coming with us?" Jessie questioned with a sharp, challenging look at Ben.

"No," he replied simply.

"Why not?" she then asked, her gaze kindling with righteous indignation. When he did not immediately answer, Martha cast him a worried glance and hastened to intervene.

"Because Consuela has decided it would be best if they do not," she told Jessie. "She is afraid there will be trouble. One certainly cannot blame her for wanting to spare her children the sort of unpleasantness which might occur."

"But when I spoke to her about it the other day," Jessie recalled, her brows knitting together in perplexity, "she seemed in favor of their going!"

"Well, I suppose she thought it over and changed her mind," Martha said soothingly. "Perhaps you can try talking to her about it again soon."

"Are you going to stay here forever, Miss Clare?" Hannah suddenly queried. Her eyes were wide and searching as they fastened upon an astounded, rosily blushing Jessie.

"I—I don't really know," she stammered uncertainly. "You see, I . . . well, I certainly intend to remain in Cimarron . . ." She broke off when her gaze flew in guilty confusion to Ben's handsome face. A wry smile tugged at the corners of his mouth. He did not appear in the least discomfited by his daughter's curiosity.

"Later, Hannah," he commanded quietly. His eyes traveled back to Jessie, but she quickly looked away. She wondered exactly what he meant by *later*.

"Come now, children, eat your breakfast!" Martha urged the twins, feigning impatience. "You don't want Miss Clare to be late, do you?"

Soon the foursome left the Chapparosa and headed off to school across the rolling sunlit plains. James and Hannah chattered excitedly together as they rode just ahead within eyesight of the two adults, while Ben and Jessie spoke little. It was a beautiful morning, with the scent of pine woodsmoke and wildflowers filling the air. As always, the nearby mountains drew Jessie's gaze, and she became so lost in her thoughts that Ben's deep voice startled her.

"You can use that old sidesaddle in the barn next time if you prefer," he offered. His blue eyes gleamed with mingled humor and wholly masculine appreciation as they moved over her shapely stockinged limbs, the lower half of which were exposed beneath the ruffled flounce of her petticoat.

"Sidesaddle?" She looked to him in accusing resentment. "Why didn't you tell me about it before now?"

222

"Because it's better if you're astride. It's easier on you and the horse both."

"I fail to see how anything about riding could be easy!" she retorted, frowning as she shifted uncomfortably on the hard leather again. Ben gave a low chuckle.

"Lots of things are hard till you get used to them," he drawled lazily.

"I seem to recall your telling me that life here was too hard for me!" she pointedly reminded him. "You told me I was not at all suited to it, remember?"

"I remember." All traces of amusement vanished, and his gaze darkened at the memory.

"Then what prompted this sudden reversal in your opinion?" she demanded.

"Damn it, Jessamyn, you already know the answer!"

"Do I?" she taunted recklessly, ignoring the fiery gleam in his eyes. "How is it, Ben Chandler, that I am *unsuited* to this country one week and entirely capable of living here the next?"

"Because I want you here, you little witch!" he ground out. "Because you're mine and I'll be damned if I'll ever let you go!"

Without warning, he brought his mount closer to hers and reached over to seize her about the waist. She gasped in surprise, then felt the familiar weakness descend upon her as he captured her lips in a hard, fiercely demanding kiss. When he released her again, she sat weakly back in the saddle and struggled to regain control of her highly erratic breathing.

They reached the schoolhouse a short time later. James and Hannah dismounted without assistance, while Ben swung down and moved to Jessie's side. She trembled when his strong hands closed about her waist and lifted her effortlessly to the ground. Instead of relinquishing his hold upon her, however, his fingers tightened with intoxicating possessiveness.

223

"If you have any trouble," he directed her solemnly, "ring the bell three times or send one of the boys over to O'Leary's place. It's only a couple of miles away."

"I'm quite certain there will be no trouble," she insisted, determinedly extricating herself from his grasp in spite of the temptation to prolong the contact. "Now, if you don't mind, Mr. Cha—" She broke off at the sudden warning look in his eyes, and though she bristled, she took heed. "*Ben*, I have work to do!"

"I'll send Curly to bring you home," he told her with a faint smile.

She was tempted to ask him why he would not be coming himself, but she merely nodded and gathered up her skirts. She had already turned to join Hannah and James in front of the log building, when his voice detained her.

"Remember what I said about the school, Jessamyn," he cautioned in a low tone. "You'll teach only until a replacement can be found."

"We shall see about that!" she countered with another flash of spirited defiance. She opened her mouth to say more, but clamped it shut and whirled away to march proudly across the newly cut meadow, clutching the reins of her gentle, obediently following mount in one hand.

Ben watched as she and the twins led their horses beneath the trees behind the schoolhouse, where a hitching post had recently been erected beside the stream. Then, battling the urge to stay, he swung back up onto his own horse and headed off to Cimarron. His eyes glowed with a purposeful light, his heart as well as his passions stirring at the thought that Sunday was only six days away.

By the time Jessie sounded the big iron bell, making sure to ring it more than three times, a small group of children had already gathered in the front yard. Having either walked, ridden, or been delivered by their parents—some of whom tarried for a few moments in order to have a word with the teacher—they now stood eyeing her dubiously. Their youthful faces displayed a wide array of emotions, from trepidation to simple childish curiosity to outright mulishness.

Taking a deep breath, Jessie climbed up the steps and threw wide the door. She was standing at the front of the room beside her desk when the first eager pupils shuffled inside the schoolroom. Facing them with a smile, she clasped her hands in front of her and announced, "Welcome, children. Please have a seat on one of the benches for now. I shall make seating assignments later."

Once the parents had disappeared and the initial commotion had died down, Jessie finally closed the door. She was anxious to commence with the duties for which she had been trained but had at times despaired of ever being able to put to good use. She returned to take up her stance at the front of the room, making note of the fact that there were ten pairs of eyes fastened upon her. James and Hannah sat side by side in the front row, and she cautioned herself against showing them any partiality.

"Very well, class. I should like for each of you to stand and tell me your name and age, and also the last grade of school you completed," she instructed with another smile.

"Miss Clare?" A plump dark-haired girl of about eight raised her hand.

Jessie recalled that the girl clad in an expensive dress of white dotted swiss was Horace Mooney's daughter; she could not help but remember it, since she had practically forced Horace and his wife out the door a few minutes ago.

"Yes?"

"*I'm* the only one here who has ever been to school before!" the little girl boasted with a superior, disdainful look at the children around her.

"That's a lie, Mary Sue Mooney, and you know it!" a boy to her left vigorously protested. "Me and my brother went to school here last year!"

"Well, my father says last year doesn't count because the teacher ran away!"

"Children, please!" admonished Jessie.

"One of the big boys shot at him," another girl, a year or two older than Mary Sue, told Jessie.

"Shot at him?" Her eyes grew wide with incredulity.

"Yes, ma'am, and nearly hit him, too!"

"My pa says there's always been men teachin' here," a boy whom Jessie immediately recognized as Billy Shelton spoke up. "He says a woman ain't got no business—"

"That's quite enough!" Jessie pronounced sharply. "Now all of you will cease this nonsense at once and do as I say." She nodded down at James and said, "James, we will start with you. Please rise and state your name and age."

He willingly complied. Hannah was next, followed by a girl who was undoubtedly another member of the Shelton clan. As it turned out, all of the children in attendance were under the age of ten, a fact that puzzled Jessamyn until she remembered what Ben had said about a number of students, particularly the older ones, not being able to come until later in the fall. She vowed to bring the matter before the school board without delay.

The second order of the day was to separate the girls from the boys. Although James and Hannah were reluctant to part with one another's company, they did as they were told, with James taking his place on one of the benches to the left and Hannah remaining with the girls on the right. Once that minor feat was accomplished, Jessie set about discovering exactly how many of the basic educational skills each child possessed.

She was pleased to learn that more than half of the

students knew how to read and write, if only a little, and that three of those had a very good grasp of arithmetic. James and Hannah, who had been tutored by Martha throughout the past year, were among the more advanced. None of the Sheltons had ever attended school on a regular basis, and even Horace Mooney's daughter, who had claimed the distinction of the only "real" school attendance, was unable to read on a first-grade level.

Their clothing, mused Jessie, was as varied as their skills. They could all be classified as neat and clean on this first day of school, but that was where the resemblance ended. Mary Sue Mooney was without a doubt the best-dressed, followed in order by James and Hannah, a girl in red calico by the name of Kristen Humboldt, a boy named John O'Leary in a blue cotton work shirt and denim trousers, and the infamous redheaded Sheltons. Martha had told her that their father was a poor but honest farmer; Jessie could not help but admire the man and his wife for seeing to it that all five of their children—three boys and two girls—were in school.

The morning went smoothly enough, until Mary Sue raised her hand and announced that she had to pay a visit to the privy. Jessie had been dismayed to learn that there was only a single outhouse—a small ramshackle frame structure—to be shared by both boys and girls; Martha had laughingly told her the local term for it was a "one-holer." Although she and Elena had scrubbed it from top to bottom, she still frowned to think of the children having to use such crude facilities.

"Very well, Mary Sue. You may go," she consented, then remembered to add the warning she had also learned from Martha, "But please be certain to check for spiders first."

"Yes, Miss Clare." The little girl hurried outside and down the narrow, well-worn path leading from the back of the school to the front door of the privy.

Seconds later, a bloodcurdling scream shattered the order inside the schoolhouse. Jessie's eyes flew wide in horrified astonishment.

"Dear God!" she gasped. *Mary Sue!*

Hesitating only an instant, she spun about and flung open the door. The children were hot on her heels as she went racing outside to where Mary Sue now stood in benumbed terror beside the privy.

"Mary Sue, what is it? What happened?" Jessie demanded breathlessly. She knelt and took hold of the little girl's arms. "What *is* it?"

"A—a snake! There's a snake under there!" cried Mary Sue, pointing to the privy. The words were no sooner out of her mouth than the other girls shrieked and took off for the safety of the school building again.

Jessie was tempted to take off as well, but she bravely stood her ground. She stared down toward the rocks piled up around the bottom of the outhouse, her heart pounding and her mind awhirl with indecision. Wondering if she should fetch the shotgun Ben had insisted be kept inside the school at all times, or if she should simply ignore the snake and hope it would go away, she was startled when Billy Shelton suddenly drew a pistol from his pocket.

"I'll get 'im for you, Miss Clare!" he proclaimed heroically. The other boys moved closer to the outhouse, shouting encouragement to Billy while their eyes shone with gleeful anticipation.

"Children! Billy, no!" Jessie breathed in alarm. "For heaven's sake, what are you—?"

But it was too late. John O'Leary and one of the other Shelton boys had already started pounding on the walls of the privy with sticks, standing as far away as possible and taking care to watch their feet. Their efforts achieved the desired result, for within seconds the snake slithered

228

from beneath the rocks.

A scream rose in Jessie's throat. Before she could make a sound, however, Billy Shelton took aim and blasted the unfortunate reptile's head from its body.

"That's damn good shootin', Billy," his brother Ned drawled approvingly.

"It's a rattler!" declared John O'Leary in triumph. He dropped to his knees on the ground to make a closer inspection. "Holy Joe, look at all those rattles! There must be dozens of them!"

"Come on, Miss Clare!" said James excitedly, grabbing her hand. "Let's go have a look!"

Too stunned to protest, she allowed herself to be led forward to where the rattlesnake's lifeless diamond-scaled form lay in the grass beside the privy. She shuddered involuntarily at the sight of it.

"Does this happen very often?" she was almost afraid to ask.

"Depends on the weather," replied John, giving a nonchalant shrug of his small shoulders.

"I'm the one that shot 'im," Billy Shelton reminded the other boys, "so I'm the one that gets to take the rattles home." Grinning cockily at his own accomplishment, he started to return the gun to his pocket.

"I will take that, Billy," Jessie insisted with a stern frown. She held her hand out for it. "I am exceedingly grateful to you for your assistance, but I cannot allow you to carry a firearm while you are at school!"

"But I never go anywhere without my gun!" he protested, his freckled face displaying acute open-mouthed disbelief.

"Well, you will simply have to alter your habits for the duration of the school year," she told him calmly. With great and visible reluctance, he placed the pistol in her hand. "Tell me, Billy, does your father know that you brought a gun to school?" she asked.

229

"Yes, ma'am. He's the one that gave it to me!"

"He gave one to all of us," revealed Tom Shelton, a year older than Billy. "Pa says since we got to light out 'cross open country on our way, we'd better make damn sure we get here with our scalps."

"I understand your father's concern," conceded Jessie, her brow creasing at the thought of the danger the children had to face. "But I really must insist that, during school hours, you allow me to take charge of your guns."

The prospect of her students being armed was highly unsettling. Musing wryly to herself that the last thing she needed was for them to start shooting up the place in pursuit of phantom rattlesnakes, she collected weapons from the other two Shelton boys. John O'Leary assured her he would not be receiving a gun of his own until his ninth birthday, while James complained that *his* father had taught him to shoot but still refused to let him have a gun.

Mary Sue's nerves quickly recovered from the blow they had been dealt, and it wasn't long before Jessie was able to resume her assessment of her first pupils' abilities. At noon, she recessed the class for an hour so that the children could eat and then play.

She was intrigued by the variety of foods contained within the dinner buckets, most of which were nothing more than syrup or lard pails with slitted lids that each student had carried to school and left waiting on a low shelf just inside the door. There were sausage and biscuit sandwiches, boiled eggs, fried butter pies, tins of cornbread and molasses, large chunks of smoked venison, jars of buttermilk, sweet potatoes, turnip greens and black-eyed peas, syrup cookies, assorted pieces of fruit grown on their family's trees, and other frontier delicacies Jessie did not recognize.

230

She stood in the doorway, her arms folded across her chest as she smiled at the children sitting on the grass in front of the school. Consuela had provided her with a cold chicken sandwich, sweet cakes, an apple, and a jar of freshly brewed tea, but she found she was still too excited to eat much. So far, except for the incident with the snake and the absence of half the pupils, the day had proven quite successful. She was beginning to believe that the academy had prepared her well after all, even if her instructors had never expected her to put her training to use in the wilds of New Mexico Territory.

Her heart swelled with both pride and pleasure as she turned her head and allowed her gaze to travel about the room. It would not seem like much by St. Louis standards, she reflected, but it was hers. And God willing, it would remain hers.

"You mean *Ben willing,* don't you?" she challenged herself softly, realizing that there might soon also be an earthly master of her destiny. She had almost been too busy to think of him the past few hours. Almost.

How was it possible for her to feel so torn? she agonized silently. She had never before encountered such trouble in making up her mind. Ben Chandler had told her they would be married in only one week's time, and yet no arrangements had been made and no one else but the two of them knew of it. She had always dreamt of a small, intimate church wedding, unlike the elaborately formal affair Lillian had insisted she must have. But she had most definitely *not* envisioned a wedding without any guests whatsoever!

When Sunday came, would she really go through with it? Would she really become Ben Chandler's wife? Painfully divergent emotions warred within her breast, and she cursed herself anew for her incertitude before resolutely turning her attention back to her pupils.

231

Once they had virtually gobbled down their dinners, the children devoted the rest of the hour to their play. The girls chose to remain in the front yard and enjoy a game of "drop-the-handkerchief," while the boys set off to take turns on the rope swing hanging from a tree down by the stream. Jessie was initially reluctant to let them go, but she gave her permission when Ned Shelton, the oldest, assured her it was something they had all done many times before and never yet "cracked any bones."

The hour of one o'clock brought with it a return to studies. Jessie enlisted the aid of Hannah and Billy to help pass out the McGuffey readers and simple alphabet books she had brought with her. Those who could read were assigned to familiarize themselves with the words on the first several pages of the readers, while those who could not were told to peruse the other books and try to memorize as many of the letters as they could.

After an entire afternoon of reading and spelling and storytelling and singing and privy-going, with another fifteen minutes of outside play in between, the first day of school came to an end. It was almost four o'clock by then, and Jessie felt nearly as tired as the students. Tired but more determined than ever, she thought with an inward sigh of satisfaction.

Curly was waiting when she led the children outside. After she had seen the last of them off, she and the twins mounted up and rode back to the Chapparosa. She was, for once, glad that her solemn, lean-muscled escort didn't speak much, for she had too many things to think about as she clung to the saddlehorn and tried to ignore the increasing soreness Ben had teased her about. James and Hannah, as usual, were so absorbed with one another that they took little notice of her preoccupation.

The trip homeward was achieved without incident. Martha, gathering the twins close when they swung down

232

from their horses and bounded into her arms, listened with great interest to everything they told her while she ushered them through the front doorway. Ben was nowhere in sight, a fact for which Jessie was grateful as she tried not to limp on her way into the house.

She felt considerably better after soaking in the bath Consuela provided for her without delay. Her tired, aching muscles were soothed by the hot water. By the time she drew herself upright and stepped from the tub, there was only a faint lingering tenderness to remind her of the time she had spent in the saddle that day.

Taking up the towel she had left atop the washstand, she first patted her face dry and then began doing the same to her wet, glistening curves. She turned her back toward the door and lifted her right foot to the edge of the metal hip bath. The thick, luxuriant golden tresses, caught up with a blue ribbon high upon her head, danced riotously about her face as she bent to her task.

Without warning, the door behind her swung open.

Jessie gasped, her face flaming as she snatched the towel up against her bare breasts and spun about. Her eyes widened in stunned disbelief when she saw that it was the handsome young master of the Chapparosa who had entered the room without bothering to knock.

"Ben!" she breathed. She frantically tried to cover herself with the towel while demanding, in a furious undertone, "What the devil do you think you're doing here? Get out of my room at once!" It did not occur to her that it was, in actuality, *his* room. All that mattered was that he had violated her privacy and thereby caught her in the most damnably vulnerable position she could think of.

Ben said nothing at first. His handsome face inscrutable, he stepped farther inside the room and closed the door. His blue eyes smoldered with hot, raging desire as they raked over her beautiful, indignant form. Although her womanly charms were concealed from his searing gaze now, he had been treated to the provocative sight of her naked backside a moment ago, as well as a tantalizing glimpse of the soft triangle of dark golden curls between her pale, slender thighs. The memory of what he had seen did nothing to help him in his battle to control the fiery, all-too-masculine passions threatening to drive him over the very edge of reason.

"Get out!" Jessie seethed again as she clutched the towel to her heaving breasts. "Good heavens, what if Martha or one of the children—"

"They're all outside." His deep, resonant voice sent chills up and down her naked spine. "But it wouldn't matter if they knew."

"Wouldn't matter?" she echoed, her eyes growing very round before kindling with outrage. "Why, it most certainly would! This may not be St. Louis, Ben Chandler, but I do not for one blessed moment believe it is the custom for guests here to entertain their hosts while wearing nothing but a towel!"

"You're a hell of a lot more than a guest, Jessamyn," he pointed out in a low voice. He advanced upon her now, his movements unhurried yet dangerously purposeful. "I came to tell you I've made all the arrangements for Sunday."

"You—you have?" she stammered in breathless surprise, temporarily forgetting the shocking circumstances of their present encounter. "But when? How?"

"Today," he replied, his eyes burning down into hers as he came to a halt mere inches away. "I rode into Cimarron this morning." The merest suggestion of a smile touched his lips when he added, "No one will dare to condemn us if we're married in the church, schoolmarm."

"But I haven't even decided if I'm going to—" she protested weakly, her senses reeling at his nearness.

"Yes you have," he masterfully cut her off. "You're going to marry me, Jessamyn Clare. You're going to be my wife." His eyes traveled caressingly over her face. Though he had yet to touch her, she felt branded by the warmth in his gaze.

"Please, I—I don't see how we can do this!" she tried one last time. Her own eyes filled with tears of helpless confusion. "Dear Lord, I don't know what's happening!"

"One of the reasons I went to Santa Fe," Ben confessed quietly, "was to give us both time to think. Damn it, Jessamyn, I tried to fight it. I used every argument you're using, and more. But it didn't do any good. And I know now that it never will."

His hands finally came up to draw her close. She offered only a brief, halfhearted resistance before his arms swept her up against him and his mouth descended upon hers. A low moan rose in her throat as he kissed her with a passion that was surprisingly gentle in its insistence. His arms tightened about her, molding her soft, trembling body to the hard warmth of his.

Jessie's arms crept up about the corded muscles of his neck, and she swayed against him in the sweet, unspoken surrender that never failed to fire his blood. She forgot about everything but Ben . . . about everything but this strong, forcefully captivating man who demanded so much more of her than she had ever demanded of herself. The rest of the world receded, leaving the two of them completely alone for a few precious moments that would burn forever in their minds.

Desire flamed hotter and brighter between them. She gasped against his mouth when his hands suddenly glided downward to the beguiling roundness of her buttocks. His strong fingers crept beneath the towel to curl

235

possessively about the bare satiny flesh that had taunted him when he had opened the door.

She moaned softly as his hands set up a gentle kneading of her bottom, pressing her into bold, intimate contact with his hardness before lifting her farther upward into his wildly compelling embrace. His mouth roamed feverishly, hungrily over her upturned face, returning once more to claim her parted lips in a kiss that literally stole the breath from her body.

Jessie clung to him as if she were drowning and he were the only means by which she could be saved. Thus, she was left feeling totally bereft when the rapturous bewitchment came to an abrupt end. Clasping the towel to her before it fell, she blinked up at Ben through a haze of lingering passion and sharp, near painful disappointment when he suddenly and quite firmly set her away from him.

"No more!" he ground out, his handsome features looking particularly thunderous. His eyes gleamed with a savage fury directed at himself, not her.

Damn, but he would have taken her there and then if not for the fact that his children were waiting for him in the barn. And that was something he had vowed not to do. He didn't want their first time together to be hurried and wrought with guilt. No, when he finally claimed the woman who had been his since that night in Gray Wolf's camp, he wanted all barriers between them to be toppled, all fears and doubts conquered. When he took his angel-faced temptress, he wanted all of her. . . .

"Get dressed, wildcat," he commanded in a low voice that still simmered with passion. He forced his arms back to his sides, and his mouth curved into a sardonic half smile. "I believe, Miss Clare, we have an announcement to make to the rest of the family."

Wide-eyed and breathless, Jessie watched as he moved to open the door. He paused, turning back to her for a

236

moment before leaving.

"Come Sunday, nothing will save you," he promised. His eyes, looking more than ever like molten steel, blazed across into the softly glowing virescence of hers. "Come Sunday, Jessamyn Clare."

With that, he was gone. But his words echoed throughout the turbulence of Jessie's mind long after.

Eleven

"But, Papa," Hannah protested, "you can't marry Miss Clare. She's our teacher!"

"Fathers don't marry teachers!" seconded James, frowning at the ridiculous idea.

"Children, please," Martha chided gently. She, too, had been more than a little taken aback by the news Ben had just given them, and she was anxious to hear the rest of what he had to say. "Allow your father to continue."

With a faint smile of gratitude at his cousin, Ben crossed the room to Jessie's side and claimed her trembling hand with the steady warmth of his. She stood beside the fireplace in the parlor, a knot of anxiety tightening in her stomach as she faced Martha and the twins. Their reaction came as no surprise to her; there was no way they could have anticipated Ben's announcement.

"The wedding will be on Sunday," he added, then smiled wryly again at his cousin's widening eyes. "In the church, Martha. Legal and proper."

"I'm sure of that, my dear boy, but . . . my goodness, Sunday is only a few days away!"

"Six days, to be exact. And there's no reason to wait." His hand tightened about Jessie's, and his eyes were glowing with an unfathomable light as he gazed down into her pale, somber features.

"Does that mean Miss Clare is going to be our mother?" asked Hannah in wonderment.

"Stepmother, you big silly," James corrected her with brotherly disdain. His expressive blue gaze shifted back and forth between Jessie and his father. "Teachers can't be stepmothers," he insisted with a stubborn shake of his head.

"Why not?" challenged Ben, his deep voice brimming with amusement.

"Because they can't."

"They can so!" Hannah argued. Although not fully understanding what she was arguing *about*, she was determined not to let her brother have the upper hand. "If Papa says they can, then they can!" she finished with a lofty, superior look and a defiant toss of her pigtails.

"Jessamyn will be your mother," Ben told them, his handsome brow creasing into a frown. "And she won't be teaching much longer."

"You're going to give up the school?" Martha asked Jessie in surprise.

Jessie cast a sharp look up at the man beside her. Taking note of the sudden, grim set of his jaw, her eyes flashed with spirit.

"I have no intention of abandoning my post," she answered Martha in willful disobedience of Ben's commandment. She felt the way his whole body tensed with anger, and she stifled a protest when his fingers clenched almost painfully about hers.

"A replacement will be found," he pronounced in a dangerously low and level tone. The look in his eyes promised later retaliation for her defiance, but she refused to be intimidated. Raising her head proudly, she was about to express further rebellious thoughts upon the subject when Martha spoke again.

"I must say, I had no idea the two of you had formed an attachment for one another!" the petite brunette remarked a trifle breathlessly, her head still spinning at the realization that her cousin was to marry a young woman he had known for such a short time. She was genuinely fond of Jessie, however, and could not find it in her heart to offer any condemnation. Rising to her feet, she moved to embrace the younger woman. "Congratulations, my dear! I hope you will be very happy here at the Chapparosa."

"Thank you, Martha," said Jessie, releasing a sigh of relief as she hugged her warmly. "You have been so kind, and I—I am glad you will be here." She *was* glad; for some inexplicable reason, she felt the need for an ally. Indeed, she mused with an inward smile of irony, someone needed to make certain she and Ben Chandler did not kill one another!

"Will we still call you Miss Clare?" Hannah questioned Jessie, her brows knitting together in a frown of childish perplexity.

"You may call me whatever you like," she responded with a warm smile, her emerald eyes aglow with true affection. She moved to take a seat beside the little girl on the sofa. James, never one to be left out, scrambled around to sit on Jessie's other side. She reached down to clasp one of each twin's hands in hers. "But I would prefer if it were not Miss Clare," she admitted.

"You mean we can call you just plain Jessie?" James asked in disbelief.

"Of course."

"Or even *Mother?*" Hannah queried dubiously.

"Even *Mother,*" Jessie confirmed. *Mother,* she repeated silently. Her heart stirred at the sound of it, and she suddenly realized how very much she wanted the love and acceptance of Ben's children.

"I think I'll call you Jessamyn, like Papa does," the

little girl proclaimed with a decisive nod.

"Not me," said James, shaking his head. "*I'm* going to call you just plain Jessie. For now, anyway."

"Then you—you won't mind my living here?" she asked the two of them, faltering a bit as her eyes anxiously searched their faces for any sign of disapproval or resis-tance.

"Well, you're going to marry Papa, aren't you?" Hannah pointed out, then added quite reasonably, "Married people always live together."

"Not always!" James hastened to disagree. Flinging a quelling look at his sister, he told Jessie, "John O'Leary's mother and father are married, and *they* don't live together. Mrs. O'Leary lives at home with John and his big brother, but Mr. O'Leary lives over at E-Town."

"E-Town?" echoed Jessie.

"He means Elizabethtown," Hannah provided. "But no one around here calls it that."

"Well, that's where John's father lives," James continued, "and John said it's because Mr. O'Leary came home drunk one night and hit Mrs. O'Leary, and then Mrs. O'Leary beat the living daylights out of Mr. O'Leary, and then—"

"I think you've said quite enough about the O'Learys, James," Martha finally intervened. She exchanged a smile of understanding with Jessie before bidding the twins, "Come now, it's time the two of you were abed."

"Oh, Aunt Martha," complained Hannah, "couldn't we stay up a little while longer?"

"No, my love, I'm afraid not. You've another day of school tomorrow, remember?" She came forward now, extending her hands to the children. "Say good night to Miss Clare and your father."

With unmistakable reluctance, they stood and did as they were told. Martha led them away, tossing a good night of her own over her shoulder as she left the room with her young charges.

Jessie, alone with Ben once more, felt his penetrating gaze upon her as she rose to her feet and drifted rather aimlessly over to the window. She stole a look back at him, only to see that his deep blue eyes were alight with both amusement and satisfaction.

"I—I suppose it went well," she murmured, suddenly feeling awkward. She turned back to peer outward at the rugged moonlit country that would now be her home. A strange restlessness crept over her, and she found herself yearning for something . . . something she did not recognize but that was there all the same, just beyond her reach.

"Well enough," Ben replied softly.

He came up behind her, his arms slowly enveloping her with their strong, sinewy warmth and pulling her close. With a faint sigh, she leaned her head back against his hard-muscled chest and brought her arms upward to rest upon the possessive circle of his.

"James and Hannah never knew their mother," he spoke in a low, wonderfully vibrant tone close to her ear. "They won't have any trouble accepting you." His mouth curved into a wry half smile when he added, "And any fool could see Martha likes you."

"What about you?" Jessie challenged in a voice scarcely above a whisper. Wishing she could see his face, she asked, "Do you like me, Ben Chandler?" Her voice held a note of such longing and uncertainty that Ben felt his heart twisting.

"Yes, Jessamyn," he answered quietly, holding back so much more. He gathered her even closer and pressed a tender kiss upon the top of her head. "I like you. I like you more than I've liked anyone in a long time."

It wasn't what she had been hoping for, but she told herself it was enough for now. In truth, she didn't know what she had been hoping for . . . perhaps some sign, some word or gesture to indicate that his feelings for her ran far deeper than he had led her to believe.

"I don't even have a wedding gown," she murmured at a sudden thought.

"I'll get you one."

"There are some things a woman prefers to do for herself, Ben Chandler!" She melted inside at the sound of his soft, resonant laughter.

"Then have at it, wildcat."

"Please stop calling me that," she objected weakly.

"Why?"

"Because it . . . Because I . . ." Her voice trailed away as he slowly turned her about to face him. His hands slid back up her arms to close about her trembling shoulders.

"It's what you are, Jessamyn," he declared in a rich, mellow voice. "A beautiful green-eyed wildcat who tempts me and taunts me and, by damn, who sets me on fire at every turn!"

"There is a good deal more to marriage than—than that!" she countered breathlessly, losing herself in the gleaming brilliant blue depths of his eyes.

"True," he allowed, his arms slipping about her again. She gasped when, with deliberate slowness, he fitted her pliant curves to perfection against his hard, undeniably virile frame. "But it's still a damned good place to start."

She was denied the opportunity to reply, for he lowered his head and captured her lips with his own. The kiss was long and ardent and sweetly, deliciously intoxicating. By the time Ben raised his head again, Jessie's beautiful face was flushed with passion.

"Go to bed, Jessamyn," she was surprised to hear him saying. "Go to bed and dream of me."

Her eyes flew open at that, and she bristled with indignation as she viewed the roguish humor in his gaze. She abruptly drew away from him.

"What makes you so certain I do not dream of another?" she retorted. A soft, breathless cry escaped her lips as he suddenly yanked her back against him.

"Because you're mine!" he ground out, his arm clamping like a band of iron about her slender waist. His eyes smoldered with jealous fury now. "If I thought for one minute there was someone else—"

He broke off and muttered a curse beneath his breath. Jessie, stunned by the utter savagery of his reaction, stared mutely up at him. She watched as a shadow of pain crossed his handsome features.

"I'm sorry, Jessamyn," he declared quietly, his temper cooling almost as quickly as it had flared. Though he ached to hold her all night, he forced himself to release her. He gave her a faint, humorless smile. "Take yourself off to bed, schoolmarm."

"But I—"

"Blast it, woman, can't you ever do what I tell you without arguing?"

"No, *Mr. Chandler*, it appears I cannot!" she shot back, her eyes flashing up at him. "I am not one of your children, nor one of your employees, nor one of your horses or dogs or cows. . . ."

"I've never thought of you as any of those," he told her, his voice brimming with renewed amusement as he resisted the urge to grab her again.

"And I will not be treated as such!" she finished with a proud toss of her head. She gathered up her skirts and marched to the door, whereupon she whirled to deliver one last spirited declaration of free will. "If we do indeed get married, Ben Chandler, you may rest assured that I will not allow you to forget I have a mind of my own!"

"There's sure as hell no danger of that," he drawled, then smiled to himself as she swept from the room amidst a feminine flurry of silk and lace and ruffles. He realized that he had taken to smiling more and more since she'd

244

come into his life. *If this kept on,* he mused wryly, turning back to the window, *she'd soon have him grinning like a fool.*

His amusement abruptly faded when the memory of the kiss they had just shared came back to torment him. With another muttered oath, he moved to the fireplace and lifted a hand to the mantel. His eyes reflected the light of the dwindling flames as he became lost in thoughts centered around the beautiful golden-haired woman who had finally brought him back to the world of the living.

A pleasant surprise awaited Jessie when she and the twins dismounted and led their horses up to the schoolhouse on Friday morning. In addition to the ten pupils who had attended the past four days, there were now three new boys waiting for her in front of the building. They were all older, perhaps as old as thirteen or fourteen, she judged, each of them greeting her with nothing more than a silent, solemn appraisal as she came toward them.

"Good morning, boys. I am Miss Clare, the teacher," she introduced herself with a polite smile.

James and Hannah, taking charge of the horses, continued on their way to the hitching post. Curly, who was standing in once again for Ben, had already swung back up into the saddle. Instead of reining about, however, he sat watching Jessie from a short distance away.

"Would you please tell me your names?" Jessie requested of the new students.

"Name's Foley Keech," said the tallest of the three. Older than she had first thought, he was big and brawny, with an unruly thatch of straw-colored hair and coarse, pockmarked features. His shirt and trousers were extremely dirty, and he wore heavy boots that smelled of the barnyard.

Jessie was discomfited by the look of belligerence in his narrow close-set eyes, but she gave no outward evidence of it as she turned to the slender boy standing at Foley's right. He was a full head shorter than Foley, and there was a likable openness to his gaze.

"I'm Peter O'Leary, Miss Clare," he told her, his mouth curving into a shy, tentative smile now. He looked like an older version of his brother John.

"Harmon Fielding," the last boy spoke up. Of more average height and build than the other two, he possessed a very dark and swarthy complexion, with eyes of brown and hair the blackest she had ever seen. "My ma says I got to come, but I don't want to!" he made clear right away.

"I am sorry to hear that, Harmon," Jessie replied calmly. "However, since you *have* come, I will do my best to see to it that neither you nor your mother are disappointed."

"We ain't got to stay, you know," Foley told her, already challenging her authority. His gaze traveled up and down her body with insulting boldness. "But I guess maybe we will, seein' as how we get to look at you all day, teacher lady!" he added, giving a derisive snort of laughter.

"How old are you, Foley?" Jessie demanded sharply, two bright spots of angry color riding high on her cheeks.

"Nigh on to sixteen," he boasted. He hooked his thumbs in the front belt loops of his dirty trousers and rocked complacently back on his heels. "How 'bout you?"

Jessie had known from the first moment she set eyes on him that he would prove troublesome, but she had not counted on the trouble starting so soon. Recalling James's warning that she "watch out for those big boys," she drew herself rigidly erect and asked, in a cold tone of voice, "Have you ever been to school before?"

"Nope."

"Then why are you here today?"

"Got nothin' else to do," he answered, negligently shrugging his shoulders.

"Well, then, I suggest you *find* something else to do!" she told him. "This school is for children who have a desire to learn or at least who are young enough to be taught. You could learn, too, Foley Keech, if you wanted to—but only if you wanted to. Your attitude is clearly one of impertinent unwillingness, and that is something I cannot and will not tolerate in my classroom!"

Foley backed down a bit at that. Unhooking his thumbs and standing up straight, he appeared more than a little surprised by Jessie's spirited defense. Courage was something he admired, even if it was in the schoolmarm.

"Now look here," he said, frowning, "you ain't—"

"*Aren't,*" Jessie pointedly corrected him. She turned her back on him and marched over to ring the bell. Suddenly, Foley was there beside her.

"Just who the hell do you think you are?" he growled. He pushed his face menacingly closer to hers. "Why, you ain't nothin' but an Apache's leavin's, that's what you are!"

"How dare you!" Jessie seethed in a furious undertone, her green eyes ablaze. If not for the fact that she wanted to avoid making an embarrassing scene in front of the children, she would have surrendered to the temptation to slap the teenager's sneering face as hard as she could. "You will leave the school grounds at once!" she commanded him.

"I ain't goin' nowhere till I—"

"You having any trouble, Miss Jessie?" It was Curly.

Jessie's gaze traveled past Foley to where the grim-faced cowboy had come to stand in the front yard. He clutched the reins of his mount in one hand, while he reached up with the other to tug the brim of his hat lower on his forehead. Foley Keech recognized the simple but nonetheless eloquent gesture as an indication that the older man meant business.

"There ain't no trouble," mumbled Foley. Like most everyone else around Cimarron, he knew better than to tangle with Ben Chandler's "right hand." He shot Jessie one last speaking glare, then flung angrily about and went stomping back down to the stream to retrieve his horse.

"Thank you, Curly," Jessie said, sighing with relief as Foley rode away moments later. "You always seem to be coming to my rescue."

"Just doing my job, Miss Jessie," he turned her thanks aside. He swung agilely back up into the saddle and touched a finger to the brim of his hat. Jessie could have sworn she saw a twinkle lurking in his unfathomable gaze. "Ben would have my hide if anything happened to you," he added unexpectedly. Before she could think of a reply, he had reined about and headed back to the road.

She smiled to herself, musing that she hadn't known him to be capable of speaking so many words at a single time. Then, releasing another sigh—and resolving to put the unpleasant incident with Foley behind her—she rang the bell to signal the start of school.

Although the day had not gotten off to a very promising start, it soon proved to be a very productive one. Jessie was pleased to discover that both Peter and Harmon knew how to read and write, and she presented them each with their own readers before setting to work with the younger children again. Later, immediately following the noon break, she treated the whole class to a reading of the first chapter of *Ivanhoe,* which fired their youthful imaginations and left them begging for more. After that there was more concentration on the three R's,

248

and then a lesson in American history and geography.

The pupils were still on their best behavior, due as much to the newness of school as to Jessie's disciplined control of the classroom. She had collected guns from all the boys at the door, had announced strict rules governing the use of the privy, and had already made a few changes in the seating arrangement because of the incompatibility of certain students, one example of which was Billy's shoving John onto the floor for no other reason than a stated dislike for the way the boy's elbows "stick out too far." All in all, however, she had encountered surprisingly little trouble thus far and was beginning to think, perhaps a bit naively, that the students had accepted her role of authority without challenge.

It was nearing three o'clock when the clouds began rolling in.

The children were all hard at work on the drawing exercise Jessie had just assigned them, while she was seated at her desk keeping a vigilant eye on the proceedings. Glancing toward the window, her attention was caught by the sudden darkness.

She frowned to herself, wondering if there would be rain before she dismissed school in an hour's time. It troubled her to think of the children having to make their way home in a downpour; adding to her disquiet was the thought of herself riding back to the Chapparosa while soaked to the skin. She had not yet mastered the technique of riding astride, but Ben had refused to make good on his offer of a sidesaddle. The prospect of arriving home both saddlesore *and* wet was a particularly dismal one.

Rising to her feet, she moved across to the window and pulled the blue calico curtains wider. She bent forward to peer up at the sky, only to discover that it was virtually boiling with thick, ominous gray clouds. Though unfamiliar with the sort of threatening weather New Mexico offered, she was convinced that the look of the darkening heavens warned of a coming storm. Alarm leapt in her breast, but she mentally chided herself for her fears and turned back to look at the children.

Her mind raced to make a decision. She knew that if she waited another hour, there was a very real likelihood that her pupils would be out on the prairie when the storm broke. At least by sending them home now, she reasoned with herself, she would probably spare them the full brunt of nature's fury. She gave silent thanks for the fact that, with the exception of Mary Sue Mooney, they had all traveled via horseback that day.

"Class, I am afraid there is a storm approaching," she announced calmly. "Just this once, I am going to dismiss school an hour early." Her words were met with a startling outburst of exuberance. "That is quite enough!" she admonished in a no-nonsense voice that immediately restored order. "Now, I want each of you to go directly home, as quickly as possible."

"Miss Clare?" Mary Sue Mooney raised her hand.

"Yes, Mary Sue?" Jessie responded with a patient smile, though inwardly her apprehension was growing with each passing second.

"My father is going to come for me in the buggy!"

"I know, but we haven't time to wait. James, Hannah, and I will take you back to town with us."

"You mean we're not going home?" asked James. He and his sister exchanged wide-eyed looks full of shared uneasiness and excitement.

"No," replied Jessie. She gave both of them a reassuring smile. "We will go to the St. James and wait there until the storm has passed. I'm quite sure Miss Boone will not mind."

Wasting no more time, she had the children line up and file quickly out of the building. The wind was well on its way to becoming a ferocious howl, mercilessly whipping hats from heads and flapping skirts about legs. The unmistakable scent of rain was heavy in the rapidly cooling air as everyone hurried down to the stream. Jessie helped some of the smaller children mount their horses, adding another caution for them not to tarry on their way home.

The five Sheltons were the first to leave, with the two girls riding double, Billy and Tom doing the same, and Ned, as the oldest, enjoying the privilege of riding alone. John and Peter soon left as well; Jessie was glad they lived only two miles away. Harmon promised to see Kristen home safely, since his route would take him almost directly past her family's ranch.

Once the other children were gone, Jessie lifted Mary Sue onto her horse and, after two failed attempts, hauled herself up into the saddle. The wind had ripped the pins from her hair, so that her long golden curls fanned wildly about her face and shoulders. She could not prevent her skirts and petticoats from flying up about her knees.

"Hang on tight, Mary Sue!" she shouted above the wind's roar.

Mary Sue, who was precariously balanced on the animal's sleek back behind her teacher, squealed in alarm and grabbed her about the waist as she gathered up the reins. It was difficult for Jessie to control the horse under such unusual circumstances—it was difficult for her even under *normal* circumstances—but she somehow managed to urge the gentle mare back to the road. James and Hannah followed close behind, their own skills at horsemanship standing them in good stead as they set off across the forebodingly dark and windswept countryside.

They had traveled no more than a mile or so whan the fierce norther suddenly calmed. A strange, almost eerie silence fell about them.

"It's about to get bad!" pronounced James, tossing a

worried look up at the sky. The clouds were still churning but had yet to release the torrent their highly charged density promised. "We'd better ride for cover!" he decreed in an authoritative manner that reminded Jessie of his father.

"Why? What is it?" Jessie demanded sharply. She had slowed the near frantic pace she had set for them and now turned her wide, apprehensive gaze to the turbulence overhead.

"It always gets quiet like this before it gets bad!" Hannah answered for her brother.

"Oh, Miss Clare, I—I want to go home!" sobbed Mary Sue, her eyes full of terror. She clutched frantically at Jessie and began to cry.

"I know, Mary Sue, and we will see that you get there as soon as possible," Jessie told her in a soothing tone. She did her best to conceal her own rising alarm as she looked anxiously about for any sign of shelter. There was none. "Perhaps we should return to the schoolhouse!" she suggested, not knowing what else to do. She was beginning to doubt the wisdom of her decision to dismiss school early. . . . *Please, God, let the children make it home safely!*

A sudden flash of lightning lit the strange darkness, followed almost immediately thereafter by a long, deafening roll of thunder.

"We've got to do something!" James pointed out. "We can't just sit out here and let it catch us!"

"We'll head back to the schoolhouse!" Jessie finally decided. Praying she was doing the right thing, she pulled on the reins and was satisfied when the horse obeyed her command to swing about. James and Hannah did the same, and the four of them rode with all haste in the opposite direction while lightning and thunder split the heavens above with ever-increasing fury. The brief period of calm had ended almost as quickly as it had come. The winds howled with relentless force down from the mountains once more, flinging dust in the riders' faces and leaving a trail of bent grass and stripped branches in its threatening wake.

Jessie felt a wave of relief wash over her when she spotted the familiar log building again. The first cold, stinging drops of rain began pelting the earth just as she and the twins pulled their mounts to a halt in the front yard.

"Hurry inside at once, children!" Jessie urged them, sliding from the saddle and reaching up for Mary Sue.

"We can't leave the poor horses out here, Miss Clare!" cried Hannah. "They might get hurt!"

"We have no choice, Hannah!" she insisted firmly. "The door is too narrow for them to pass through! But I—I'll take them around to the south side of the building. They will at least have some protection from the rain that way!"

Watching as Mary Sue and the twins dashed up the steps and into the school, she quickly snatched up all the reins and led the frightened animals away. She knew it was too dangerous to shelter them beneath the trees with all the lightning about. But it suddenly occurred to her that they might fare better if she allowed them to run free; they might stand a chance of finding their way home before any real harm befell them. Although she was far from an expert when it came to horses, she knew enough about them to believe their instincts would guide them to safety.

With the rain pounding her mercilessly, she slipped off the bridles of all three animals and sent them galloping off into the storm-tossed darkness. She gathered up her dampening skirts and made her way back around to the front of the school, bending her head against the wind and rain as she stumbled across the mud-slicked ground.

Once inside, she closed the door against the worsening tempest. She felt wet to the bone, with water coursing in rivulets down her face and her boots forming a muddy puddle on the floor. Shivering at the sudden chill that crept over her, she found it necessary to lean back against the wall for a moment in order to catch her breath.

"Are the horses going to be all right, Miss Clare?" Hannah asked with a child's typical misplacement of priorities.

"Yes, Hannah," Jessie replied, her breathing still ragged and uneven. "I—I believe they will be!"

"What are we going to do now?" James wondered aloud. His eyes made a quick, encompassing sweep of the room. "I guess we ought to build a fire. It's dark and it's getting colder by the minute."

"That—that is an excellent idea, James!" agreed Jessie. She shivered again before she pushed herself upright and crossed unsteadily to the big iron stove in the corner. A supply of wood and kindling rested on the floor beside it, in readiness for the first cold day of school. That day had come sooner than anyone had thought it would.

She dropped to her knees before the stove, her sodden skirts falling heavily about her. She opened the small vented door and tossed a handful of kindling inside, then hurriedly positioned several pieces of wood on top. Withdrawing a match from the ample supply in a decorative tin holder hanging low on the wall, she struck a flame and held it to the kindling. Within seconds, the fire was well on its way to a healthy blaze.

Heaving a weary sigh, Jessie climbed to her feet again and closed the door. The children came to gather close to the stove, holding their small hands out to its slowly spreading warmth. The rain drummed loudly on the roof above, while the wind hurled leaves and branches against the log walls with such force that it sounded as though someone were outside flinging handfuls of rocks at the building.

"I hope it's over with soon," Hannah remarked, casting another apprehensive glance up at the ceiling.

"I want to go home!" Mary Sue wailed again, obviously on the verge of hysteria as she began to cry almost uncontrollably. Jessie, her heart filling with compassion for the frightened little girl, placed a comforting arm about her shoulders. James, however, refused to tolerate such nonsense.

"Oh, don't be such a crybaby, Mary Sue!" he chided sharply. "It's only an old thunderstorm! Hannah and I have been in lots of thunderstorms, haven't we, Hannah?"

"Yes," his sister confirmed, "and once we got caught out on the range in one! Papa made James and me get down on the ground, and then he covered us with his duster—he wore it back when he was fighting Indians," she explained proudly, "and we had to stay there until the storm went away!"

"Do they have storms back in St. Louis?" James asked Jessie with a thoughtful frown."

"Yes, they certainly do," she answered, her features relaxing into a smile. "When I was very young, I used to hide beneath the covers and dream myself far away from the thunder and lightning."

"You *dreamt* yourself away?" both twins questioned in unified disbelief. Jessie gave a soft laugh and nodded down at them.

"But only in my imagination, of course," she clarified. "I would envision myself in a place of warmth and peace and security, someplace where there were no storms to frighten me. It didn't always work," she admitted, "but on most occasions I managed to fall asleep."

"Were—were your storms as—as bad as ours?" Mary Sue stammered through her tears.

"Almost," she replied, hugging the little girl close again. She glanced toward the window and tensed involuntarily at the sudden flash of lightning that set the glass aglow. Giving silent thanks for the fact that she and the three children had reached the schoolhouse in time, she could not help wondering again about the fate of the other students. She knew she would never forgive herself if anything happened to them.

More frightened than she cared to admit, Jessie shifted her gaze back to the stove. Mary Sue and the twins had fallen silent for the moment. There was nothing to be heard but the wrathful pounding of the storm. The awful din filled every corner of the room.

Ben, her heart suddenly cried out to him. She realized that, from the first moment their eyes had met across the firelit clearing in Gray Wolf's camp, he had been an unending source of strength and comfort for her. *Ben,* she repeated his name silently. Just as she had long ago imagined herself away from her childish terrors, she now closed her eyes and called forth a vision of his ruggedly handsome features. She imagined the feel of his strong arms about her and the sound of his deep, wonderfully resonant voice exhorting her to stand firm against her fears.

Outside, the storm continued to release its destructive fury upon the earth. Whenever it seemed the fierce cloudburst showed signs of lessening into a steady downpour, the wind would lash the rain into a rage again and thunder would split the boiling sky once more. Inside the schoolhouse, Jessie drew a bench close to the stove's warmth and then sank gratefully down upon it while her young charges did the same.

"I'm glad you're going to be our mother," Hannah suddenly murmured, releasing a sigh as Jessie slipped an arm about her shoulders.

"You are?" Her heart stirred at the unexpected

declaration of approval, and she gazed down at the little girl with eyes full of hope and happiness.

"Yes," affirmed Hannah, then frowned briefly. "But only if Aunt Martha doesn't have to go away."

"She won't be going away at all!" Jessie hastened to assure her. "Why, I honestly don't know how I would manage without her! You see, I . . . well, I've never been married and had children before, and I'm afraid I'm going to need a great deal of help."

"None of the others believed me when I told them you were going to marry my father," James confided, the corners of his mouth turning down in renewed annoyance at the memory.

"I still don't believe you, James Chandler!" Mary Sue piped up, leaning forward to make a particularly uncongenial face at him. She had apparently begun to feel like her old self again. "It can't be true, because teachers aren't allowed to marry fathers!" she proclaimed with a haughty toss of her dark curls.

"They are so!" cried Hannah. She turned back to Jessie for assistance. "Please tell her it's true, *Jessamyn!*" She shot Mary Sue a pointedly challenging look. "Tell her you really are going to marry Papa on Sunday!"

Jessie's silken brow creased into a frown of perplexity. She had not given much thought to how her students would react to the news of her impending marriage; she had naturally assumed they would not be concerned with her soon-to-be-altered status. Belatedly realizing that she should have made the announcement herself first thing that morning, she sighed and looked back to the plump little girl beside her.

"It is true, Mary Sue," she said gently.

"My father won't let you!" exclaimed Mary Sue, shaking her head emphatically. "He won't let you get married, Miss Clare!"

"Your father can't tell her what to do!" James countered. "Only *my* father can do that!"

"Children, please," urged Jessie, her emerald eyes sparkling with wry amusement at James's words. "Let's not discuss the matter any more at present. Instead, why don't we talk about—"

She broke off with a loud gasp when the storm suddenly worsened. The pounding on the roof grew almost deafening as rain turned to hail. Great chunks of ice began battering the countryside with a vengeance, threatening to smash everything in their path.

Jessie and the children leapt to their feet in alarm. Looking instinctively toward the windows, they watched in horrified disbelief as shingles from the roof were sent flying downward to be buried underneath a white sea of hail that rose higher and higher with each passing moment.

A panic-stricken Mary Sue screamed and clutched frantically at Jessie. James and Hannah held tight to one another, their faces paling with unspoken terror.

"Get under my desk!" Jessie shouted above the roar. Fearing that the roof would not hold, she dragged Mary Sue over to the desk and shoved her beneath it. She waited until the twins scrambled under it as well before she fell to her hands and knees and joined them. She tried to position her body protectively over the children, who were huddled together with their eyes tightly closed and their small hands pressed over their ears in a futile effort to shut out the dreadful noise.

Then, without warning, a large branch came crashing through one of the windows. Glass shattered everywhere, while the wind howled ferociously inside to fling water and grass and leaves across the room.

Both Hannah and Mary Sue shrieked in fright. Jessie clutched at the children, setting up a silent, desperate prayer for deliverance from the danger that threatened them. A tremor of sheer paralyzing fear shot through her as she closed her eyes against the sound of the storm's intensifying violence.

How long they remained under the desk she could not say. But, sometime later, she slowly became aware of a diminishment in the fury outside. Her eyelids fluttered open, and she blinked in stunned disbelief when she realized that the wind had died down and the torrent of hail had been replaced by a quiet, steady rain. She lay there and listened for a while, until finally satisfied that the worst had indeed passed.

"I—I think it's safe for us to get up now, children," she pronounced shakily.

She winced at the sharp pain in her cramped muscles as she climbed from beneath the desk and pulled herself upright in the damp, receding darkness of the room. Her eyes filled with dismay when she surveyed the damage before her, but she resolutely pushed it to the back of her mind and bent to help the twins to their feet. Mary Sue, still curled up into a tight ball on the floor, obstinately refused to emerge from the desk's security.

"Come on, Mary Sue, you're perfectly safe now," Jessie reassured her in a soft, soothing tone. She extended her hand to the child and waited patiently. Mary Sue finally raised her head, eyeing Jessie mistrustfully.

"It might start again!" she breathed, her eyes very round as they flew overhead.

"It might indeed," replied Jessie calmly, "but I do not believe it will. Now please, Mary Sue, come back to the stove and get warm." She was relieved when the little girl took her hand.

"Are we going home now?" asked Mary Sue, allowing Jessie to pull her to her feet.

"We can't just yet, I'm afraid. But someone will come

259

for us soon." She ushered the children back to the bench and was relieved to find the fire still burning in the stove.

"It's not so dark now," commented James, casting a quick glance about. "That means the storm's going away."

"Do you think the horses are all right?" Hannah asked Jessie in sudden worriment.

"They are more than likely back at the ranch by now, safe and warm in the barn," she answered, her lips curving into a soft, rueful smile. She would give anything to be safe and warm at the ranch at that very moment . . . with Ben's arms about her and his kisses making her forget the nightmarish ordeal she and the children had just endured. Until now, she thought with an inward sigh, she had not known how truly frightened she had been.

"If they do make it home, Papa will know something's wrong," said James.

"You don't suppose he was out on the range when the storm hit, do you?" Hannah asked Jessie, her worriment increasing now as she thought of her father. "You don't suppose he's hurt or anything, do you?"

"No, I am quite sure he is not." She sat down beside Hannah again and pulled her close. "Your father has lived here a long time. He is very familiar with the country, and I've no doubt he knows what to do in any circumstance." The possibility that Hannah's fears might prove true made her own heart leap in awful dread. *Dear God, please let him be safe.*

They sat, mostly in silence, for perhaps a quarter of an hour after that, listening while the rain dwindled into nothing more than a drizzle, then ceased altogether. Finally, once Jessie was satisfied that the children were calm, she moved across the room to make a closer inspection of the damage caused by the branch, which still rested halfway through the broken window.

Suddenly, the door was flung open. Jessie gasped, her

gaze darting across to where a tall, splendidly familiar frame stood outlined against the gray light outside.

"*Ben!*" she breathed, her whole body flooded with relief—and profound joy. Before she had paused to consider what she was doing, she gathered up her wet, muddy skirts and went flying straight into his outstretched arms.

Twelve

"I told you it was the truth!" James said with smug triumph to Mary Sue as he nodded toward the couple entwined in the open doorway.

"Papa!" exclaimed Hannah. Hesitating no longer—and disregarding the fact that her father was at the moment holding her schoolteacher as though he would never let her go—she raced across the room to hurl herself against him. Her arms clasped him about the waist as she feelingly declared, "Oh, Papa, I knew you'd come!"

Ben, whose eyes had already provided him with the evidence of his children's safety, smiled softly and lowered an arm to include Hannah in the embrace. Never one to be left out, James scampered forward to join the trio. Mary Sue stood watching them all with her brows pulled together in a deep frown.

Jessie, suddenly recalling the fact that there were three pairs of little eyes to witness her impulsive outpouring of affection, blushed fierily and attempted to draw away. Ben refused to release her. His arm remained securely about her slender waist as he gazed down into her beautiful upturned countenance.

"You look like a drowned kitten, schoolmarm," he

drawled, his eyes alight with a devilish amusement and no small measure of relief as they flickered briefly downward. His features grew solemn again when he told her, in a low voice brimming with raw emotion, "Damn it, Jessamyn, I thought something had happened to you and the twins! I was on my way here when I caught sight of your horses."

"Did you get them, Papa?" was naturally foremost on Hannah's mind.

"Only Jessamyn's mare. The others were too spooked by the storm." His mouth curved into a faint smile. "They'll be back at the Chapparosa by now."

"Were you out in the storm?" asked James in boyish excitement. "It rained and hailed and thundered something awful here! It even blew a tree through the window!"

"I missed the worst of it," disclosed Ben. He looked back to Jessie, and his eyes burned down into hers when he added quietly, "As soon as I saw the clouds, I headed this way."

"The—the children and I were able to make it back here in time," Jessie faltered beneath the smoldering intensity of his gaze. The canvas military slicker he wore had kept his clothing dry, but his hair curled damply across his forehead. She battled the temptation to lift a hand and smooth the dark glistening locks from his brow.

"What about the others?" He watched as her gaze clouded with renewed, heartfelt trepidation.

"Oh, Ben, I sent them home shortly before the storm hit!" she declared with a catch in her voice. "I—I don't know if they were able to reach safety in time or not!"

"I'll find out," he promised, reluctantly letting her go at last. "Curly's outside. He can ride over to the O'Leary place and spread the word from there. We can head back through town and—"

"Father!" Mary Sue suddenly cried at the top of her lungs.

Ben, Jessie, and the twins looked back to see that Horace Mooney stood on the front step. His anxiously searching gaze lit upon his daughter, and he quickly pushed past them to catch Mary Sue up against him.

"Thank God you're all right!" he proclaimed, his voice hoarse with relief.

"I didn't think you'd come!" Mary Sue choked out between a fresh onslaught of tears. "I was so—so scared, but Miss Clare said it—it would be all right!" She hugged him tight as he stood and lifted her in his arms.

Horace turned to face Ben and Jessie, then appeared somewhat embarrassed by the fact that his own eyes were wet. Clearing his throat noisily, he stepped forward and said, "I left town when I saw the storm coming. I had to stop at the Keeches and wait it out for a while, else I'd have been here sooner." He paused for a moment, glanced about the room, then frowned in puzzlement. "Where are the other students, Miss Clare?"

"I sent them home, Mr. Mooney."

"You sent them home?" he repeated, his eyes widening in disbelief.

Jessie flushed guiltily. Feeling sick inside, she nodded and stole a look up at Ben before meeting Horace Mooney's accusatory gaze again.

"I thought it would be better if they went home before—" she attempted to explain.

"Damn it all to hell, Miss Clare, don't you have any better sense than to send a bunch of young'uns out into a thunderstorm?" raged Horace. "Why, there's no telling—" It was his turn to be cut off, as Ben moved to stand protectively in front of Jessie.

"Leave her alone, Mooney!" he ground out, his blue eyes gleaming with a dangerously savage light. "She did what she thought best. Instead of wasting time arguing

264

about what's already past, why don't you get back to town and see what you can find out!"

"*I'm* chairman of the school board, Chandler, and that means I'm the one's got to answer to the parents! Not only did she send those children off into a storm, but I just found out from Lem Keech that she refused to let his boy come to school today!" He rounded on Jessie again and charged furiously, "Who the hell gave you the right to turn anyone away? You're paid to teach, damn it, and—"

"Take your daughter home, Mooney," Ben interrupted in a low voice full of deadly calm. His steely gaze narrowed inperceptibly, while a tiny muscle twitched in the bronzed ruggedness of his cheek. "This isn't the time or the place for discussing school policy."

"Maybe not, Chandler, but you can be damned sure I'm going to bring it before the board come Monday!" growled Horace, his face reddening. His wrathful gaze sliced back to Jessie in the next instant. "There's something else, too, *Miss Clare!* I just found out today that the two of you are planning to get married day after tomorrow! Well, let me tell you, young lady, we got a contract with you to teach for the full year! Just because Chandler here takes it in his mind to—"

"*Enough,* Mooney!" warned Ben. The smoldering look in his blue eyes gave evidence of the fact that he was on the verge of doing the other man bodily harm.

Horace Mooney was not a particularly wise man and he didn't always know when to quit, but he sensed that he had pushed Ben Chandler as far as he could push for one day. With one last spleenful glare that included both Jessie and Ben, he went stomping out of the schoolhouse with Mary Sue.

"It wasn't Jessie's fault about the storm, Papa!" James emphatically declared as soon as the Mooneys were gone.

"She was only trying to help!" seconded Hannah.

265

"She took care of us! It was wrong of Mr. Mooney to say those things!"

"I know." His handsome features still grim, he took Jessie's arm. "Come on. Let's go home."

"But the—the window," she stammered weakly, tears glistening in her eyes as she indicated the glass and debris strewn across the floor.

"It can wait."

She nodded mutely and allowed him to lead her outside. He exchanged a few words with Curly, who immediately set off for the O'Leary's place, then turned to the twins.

"You two ride Jessamyn's horse," he told them. He effortlessly tossed each of them, in turn, up to the saddle.

"Wouldn't it be better if I rode with one of the children?" Jessie asked him as he moved to her side. "I mean, perhaps you and I should not ride together. . . ."

"Afraid it'll drive you crazy, wildcat?" he challenged in a low, resonant voice just for her ears. She saw that his eyes were brimming with the roguish amusement she had come to know so well.

"Not in the least!" she retorted defiantly. A faint smile touched Ben's lips, for he was glad to see the healthy return of spirit.

His strong hands closing about her waist, he lifted her up to his horse's back. Jessie shifted her body forward in the saddle as he swung up behind her. A sudden involuntary tremor ran through her when he slipped one arm about her waist and gathered up the reins with his other hand. He pulled her against him, and she released a soft sigh as her back came into contact with the hard warmth of his chest.

Upon reaching the Chapparosa, they discovered that the ranch had been spared the full brunt of the storm's fury. The river was swollen with the rain and the wind had done some damage to one of the barns, but the severe weather witnessed by Jessie and the children had followed a more southerly route.

Curly did not return to the ranch until well after nightfall. Jessie was preparing to slip beneath the covers of her bed when she heard two familiar masculine voices drifting down the hallway from the front entrance foyer. She flung a gingham wrapper about her shoulders and hurried from the room, desperate for any news of her students.

"What did you learn, Curly?" she anxiously questioned as she came forward, pulling the belt of her wrapper tight. "Were the children able to reach home safely?" She spared only a passing glance at Ben, whose gaze darkened at the sight of her dishabille.

"Yes, ma'am, they did," the ranch hand affirmed in his usual quiet, solemn manner. "The Fielding boy's horse was killed, but he made it back to the Humboldts."

"Dear God," whispered Jessie, her face paling at the thought of what Harmon must have gone through. "Is he all right? Did any of the children suffer injury?" she then demanded in a tremulous voice.

"A few bruises and a lot of scare," Curly revealed with only the ghost of a smile. "Nothing worse."

"Thank heavens," she murmured. Tears of relief sparkled in her eyes as she told him earnestly, "Thank you, Curly. It seems I owe you yet another debt of gratitude."

"No, ma'am, you don't owe me anything." For one fleeting moment, a real smile spread across his lean, weathered features. "Come Sunday, you'll be the boss lady."

He and Ben moved back to the door. They shook hands, exchanged a few more brief words, and then Curly bid Jessie good night. Closing the door after the man who was much more than an employee, Ben turned back to his future bride.

She stared across at him, her heart beating quite erratically and her legs suddenly feeling very weak. She had no idea of the fierce desire raging within him as she stood there with her long golden locks tumbling down about her shoulders and her soft, beguiling curves clad in nothing but a thin nightgown and wrapper.

"I—I am so glad the children are safe," she faltered, flushing beneath the brilliant blue intensity of his gaze. Although she was seized with the sudden and quite shameless urge to fling herself upon his chest and implore him to hold her tight, she did not. He had scarcely touched her the past several days; she could only suppose it was because he thought it would make things easier for the both of them. But, heaven help her, she didn't want things to be easier! She wanted to feel his powerful arms about her, wanted to press her soft body against the compellingly masculine hardness of his and surrender her lips to the warm, enchanting mastery of his kiss. . . .

"You did right to send them home when you did," Ben responded in a strangely tight voice. "They'd have been caught in the worst of it if you had waited."

"Do you truly think so?" she asked, her eyes lighting with such wistfulness that Ben's heart twisted.

"I do," he confirmed hoarsely, his iron will bending with each passing second. Finally, he threw caution to the winds and closed the distance between them in three long strides.

Jessie offered no resistance whatsoever as he swept her up against him and brought his lips crashing down upon hers. She raised her arms to his neck and kissed him back with all the pent-up yearning deep inside her.

"Ben? Ben, was that Curly who—" Martha called out, only to break off in surprise when she rounded the corner and nearly stumbled upon the couple who stood in the midst of the most passionate embrace she had ever witnessed.

Jessie blushed crimson to the very roots of her hair and pulled away from Ben in acute embarrassment. He, on the other hand, did not appear at all embarrassed, but his handsome face looked dangerously thunderous as a result of his cousin's ill-timed intrusion.

"Oh, my dears, I *am* sorry!" offered Martha, feeling more than a trifle discomfited herself. "It's just that I thought I heard Curly's voice, and I wanted to know if he had been able to find out—"

"The children are all safe," Ben assured her without rancor. A soft, crooked smile of irony tugged at the corners of his mouth. "And I've got some work to do."

Jessie frowned in puzzlement, but she was not given the opportunity to question him about what sort of work could possibly demand his attention so late in the evening. His face was maddeningly inscrutable as he turned to her.

"Good night, Jessamyn," he declared.

"Good night," she murmured in a small, still breathless voice, her eyes falling before his. Her whole body ached with something she did not yet recognize, and she suddenly felt like crying. Although she had always despised weepy females, she now found herself moved to tears with increasing frequency. *And it was all because of Ben Chandler,* she mused with a touch of wholly feminine resentment.

"See you in the morning, Martha," Ben told his cousin. A roguish light suddenly danced in his eyes. "Don't forget. . . . We've got company coming tomorrow." He was satisfied to observe the faint telltale color rising to her face.

"At times, dearest cousin, you remind me very much of the incorrigible tease you were as a boy!" she countered with mock severity. He merely gave a low chuckle, then left the two women alone as he entered the study next to the parlor and closed the door.

"Well, Jessie, I suppose we had best get ourselves to bed," the petite brunette remarked, beaming a warm smile at her. "We have a great deal to do tomorrow, don't we?"

"Yes," sighed Jessie. Her troubled gaze wandered back to where Ben had just disappeared.

"I suggest we complete the fitting of your gown before we move on to anything else. And then there is the matter of the refreshments, of course. I believe Consuela has a number of questions about those. Good heavens, only one more day in which to get everything in order! How will we ever manage?" Martha wondered aloud.

Jessie certainly did not have the answer. The closer her wedding day loomed, the more confused and apprehensive and wickedly excited she became. She would be glad when Sunday was over with, so her life could return to normal.

Normal? her mind's inner voice challenged. She then realized that, with Ben Chandler as her husband, her life would never, ever be the same again.

The following day brought a flurry of activity to the Chapparosa. Although there were the usual chores to be done outside, preparations for the wedding ruled the household. The kitchen had not seen the like of such frenzied baking in a long time, just as Martha's treadle sewing machine had seldom pumped and whirred and stitched the way it was doing on this particular day in September.

By late afternoon, the bride-to-be felt an urgent need to escape. As soon as Martha had measured the hemline of the white silk gown one last time, Jessie changed into a pale rose shirtwaist and dove-gray cotton skirt and turned her steps purposefully toward the front door. She had no sooner emerged into the welcoming sunshine, however, than a horse and buggy pulled up in front of the house. The driver was a man she had never seen before, but the sight of his passenger made Jessie's face light with pleasure.

"Lissa!" She gathered up her skirts and hastened down the steps to greet her friend. "Lissa, what are you doing here?" she demanded happily, embracing the tall redhead.

"Hello, Jessie!" Lissa proclaimed with a soft laugh. She kept an arm about the younger woman's shoulders when she drew back to face her. "Mr. Easton was kind enough to drive me out." At Jessie's wide-eyed expression of lingering bewilderment, she smiled again and confessed, "Ben arranged for me to come today. He said you'd probably be wanting to talk to another female above the age of seven and below the age of fifty!"

"For once, he happens to be right!" quipped Jessie. In truth, she was touched by his gesture. Vowing silently to thank him for it later, she told Lissa with a sigh, "Martha and Consuela have been wonderful, but they're so terribly busy, and I . . . oh, Lissa, I *do* need someone to talk to!"

The man Lissa had called Mr. Easton came forward to join them now. He was an attractive, distinguished-looking gentleman of sixty, with thick gray hair and features that bespoke undeniable good breeding. His eyes were kind and full of warmth when the tall redhead presented him to Jessie.

"I am honored to make your acquaintance at last, Miss Clare," he declared in a mellow voice tinged with a faint southern accent. Impeccably attired in a frock coat and white high-collared shirt, he looked as if he would have been much more at home on some palatial antebellum estate than on a cattle ranch in this rugged land.

"How do you do, Mr. Easton," she responded politely. "Won't you please come inside?" Her lips curved into a

271

wry, apologetic smile as she led the way up the steps, "I'm afraid things are a trifle chaotic here today!"

"That's to be expected, isn't it?" said Lissa. "After all, this is the first wedding Cimarron's had in more than a year. Why, I wouldn't be at all surprised if the church was packed to the rafters tomorrow!" Her words struck renewed trepidation in Jessie's heart.

"I—I hadn't thought of that," she murmured. *She hadn't been able to think at all.*

Martha actually set aside her work for a while in order to visit with the guests in the parlor. Jessie could not help noticing the way the older woman seemed to pay particular attention to the man who had driven Lissa out to the Chapparosa, and it suddenly occurred to her that William Easton might very well be the "old friend" Ben's cousin had called on in town the previous week.

She was enjoying her conversation with Lissa immensely, and was glad when Martha suggested that the two of them take a stroll around the grounds. Glancing back over her shoulder as she and Lissa left the parlor, Jessie saw that Mr. Easton was already moving to take the seat she had just vacated on the sofa beside the petite brunette. She smiled to herself, her curiosity about their relationship growing.

"You know, Jessie, I think the folks in Cimarron could use a happy occasion right now," Lissa remarked once they were outside. "There's been a lot of trouble in town this past week."

"What sort of trouble?"

"Another man was shot in the saloon two nights ago. And there are some who say that Cole Hagan has come back and is making threats against some of the settlers." Her eyes filled with concern when she observed the sudden shadow crossing Jessie's face. "I wouldn't have told you about Hagan, but I thought you should know in case you have the misfortune to see him in town again."

272

"What about the sheriff?" asked Jessie, shuddering at the memory of the gunslinger's dark, predatory eyes. "Isn't there something he can do?"

"I'm afraid not," replied Lissa with a sigh. "So far, it seems he's broken no real laws. And even if he had, the company has some very powerful men on its payroll. This wouldn't be the first time they'd stepped in to take care of their own." She eyed Jessie closely for a moment. "You still haven't told Ben about Hagan, have you?"

"No, and I don't want him to know! I asked Curly not to mention it, but he—he offered no commitment one way or the other." Her brow cleared for a moment, and a knowing smile touched her lips. "Curly is certainly an unusual man, isn't he?"

"Yes, he is," Lissa agreed, unable to resist smiling in return. "It's always difficult to know what he's thinking." The smile faded, and her brows drew together in a troubled frown when she added quietly, "Most of the time I don't even try."

"He appears to like your company above all others."

"We've been friends for a long time."

"Only friends?" Jessie probed affectionately, then was contrite when she viewed the sudden pain in the other woman's eyes. "Oh, Lissa, I'm sorry! I shouldn't have teased you about it!"

"No, it's all right, Jessie." She gave a shaky little laugh as they paused beside the corral. Raising a hand to the top rail, she confided in an uncertain manner, "I don't know how to explain it, exactly—what's between us, I mean. He barely spoke to me for the longest time, and then . . ." Her voice trailed away for a moment; when she spoke again, her words were quite unexpected. "Curly has asked me to marry him."

"To marry him?" Jessie echoed, her eyes growing very round in astonishment. "Good heavens, I had no idea you and he were that serious about one another!"

273

"I'm not sure *he* is," Lissa murmured disconsolately.

"But, if he has asked you to be his wife, how can you have any doubt as to the sincerity of his affections?"

"Because he doesn't know—he doesn't know everything about me yet." She drew a ragged breath and turned her misery-filled gaze upon the three colts prancing about in the corral. "Do you remember that night at the meeting, when Abigail Higgins accused me of—"

"—of having been an Indian's woman," Jessie finished for her. "Yes, Lissa, I remember. It was unforgivable of her!"

"Unforgivable, but true," the redhead admitted with a bitter, humorless smile. "At least part of it. But not the way people think." She sighed heavily and looked at Jessie as the memories came flooding back to haunt her anew. "He was called Nakota. I first met him nearly four years ago when I came out here with a group of missionaries from Texas. He was an Apache, but not like the others. He had been educated at a mission school, then had gone back east for a time. When he returned, he was determined to do some good for his people. But he was, after all, only an Indian in the eyes of the white man, and he was resented by his own tribe for adopting the enemy's ways. In the end, he held no place in either world."

"What happened?" Jessie asked quietly.

"He was murdered one night. No one was ever brought to trial. It was said that the man who killed him was his own cousin. But it didn't matter. He—he was gone, and nothing anyone could do would bring him back." Tears gathered in her eyes, and the pain of utter heartbreak was reflected in their glistening opal depths. "I loved him, Jessie. I wasn't just his woman. . . . I was his wife. We were married in a secret Indian ceremony two months before he was killed. Our union was forbidden by the white man's laws, but I didn't care. I loved him so very much and I—I suppose I was foolish to think we could be together."

"Oh, Lissa," whispered Jessie, tears starting to her own eyes as her heart filled with compassion. She slipped an arm about the other woman's shoulders.

"No one ever knew about our marriage," continued Lissa in a distant voice. "Oh, there were plenty of rumors flying about when I came to live in Cimarron. I tried to ignore them, hoping the talk would die down after a while. It never mattered that much to me until now. Until—until I came to care for another man. I never thought I would, you see, but then I met Curly."

"And you fear he will not understand about Nakota." She watched as the redhead nodded in silent anguish. "You should tell him the truth, Lissa. If he loves you as I know he must, then he *will* understand!"

"No. No, Jessie, you don't know how things are here! The Indians are hated and feared. They have no home of their own any more. They have been driven from place to place while the government tries to decide what to do with them. The people in Cimarron want them out for good, and in some ways I cannot blame them. But the fact remains that no one would ever tolerate the notion of a white woman married to an Indian. And Curly—he would probably despise me if he knew! He wouldn't want the widow of Nakota!"

"How can you know that?" argued Jessie. "How will you ever know unless you tell him the truth?" She raised both hands to grasp her friend's arms, pleading insistently, "Don't do this, Lissa! Don't throw away your chance for happiness because of other people's hate and prejudices! You deserve to love and be loved again!"

"Oh, Jessie, you don't understand! You are certain of Ben's love for you! There is nothing standing between the two of you, nothing in his past or yours to be ashamed of or feared!" She calmed after that and gave Jessie a faint smile. "I wonder if you know just how lucky you really are. To have a man like Ben Chandler so in love with you he can't get you to the altar fast enough . . ."

You are certain of Ben's love, the other woman's words echoed throughout Jessie's brain. If only it were true. Dear God, if only he did love her the way Lissa was convinced he did!

For some, the truth hits like a bolt of lightning; for others, realization dawns slowly and only after a great deal of introspection. For Jessie, it was a combination of both.

She was in love with Ben Chandler. She could no longer deny what she had refused to acknowledge these past few days. *She loved Ben Chandler!*

It had started in the very beginning, she now realized dazedly. From the first moment she set eyes on him, love had been kindled deep within her, growing stronger all the time. Ben had not only stolen part of her innocence that night in Gray Wolf's camp, he had stolen her heart as well. That was why she had been unable to resist him, why she now yearned so desperately for his love. She wasn't so wicked and shameless after all; she was in love with the man whose very touch set her afire!

She loved Ben, she thought, repeating it to herself in wonderment. She loved him more than she would ever have believed possible. So much that she could not bear the thought of never being loved by him in return. Her whole being was filled with both exaltation and agony at the same time. Love, she had finally come to understand, was truly a double-edged sword.

"Oh, Jessie, please forgive me!" The tall redhead flushed guiltily when she glimpsed the sudden strangely conflicting emotions that crossed the younger woman's face. "I—I shouldn't be troubling you with my problems on the day before your wedding! You have enough on

276

your mind as it is." She forced a smile to her lips and drew Jessie's arm companionably through hers. "Why don't we walk to the river? I heard Martha telling Mr. Easton the twins are down there. The two of them might be feeling a bit left out right now."

Her senses still reeling from the truth, Jessie nodded mutely and went along with Lissa.

That night, as she lay in the loneliness of her own bed for the last time and listened to the familiar sounds of Ben moving about in the next room, she tried to imagine what his reaction would be if she suddenly burst through his door and declared her love for him. Would he be pleased . . . or not? It was difficult, she then mused with a deeply troubled sigh, to be in love with a man who was still a stranger to her in so many ways.

Heartsick at the thought of his rejection, she closed her eyes and became lost in a reverie that was half pleasure, half pain. She remembered all that she and Ben had shared, trying to convince herself that his feelings for her were more than those of a man for a woman—in the physical sense alone. Recalling what he had once said about neither of them being able to truthfully deny the presence of love, she clutched at that hope and opened her eyes again.

"I will make you love me, Ben Chandler!" she vowed in a low, tremulous voice. Her emerald gaze full of longing, she stared toward the wall that separated her from the man she would wed the next day.

"God willing, you shall love me!" This last was nothing more than a broken whisper, a whisper that rose in the darkness of the room and drifted out the open window to be borne heavenward on the cool, gentle breeze.

"You look absolutely beautiful, my dear!" Martha proclaimed, stepping back to admire the bride one last

277

time. "Ben will be the envy of every man in town this day!"

"She's right, Jessie," confirmed Lissa with a warmly lit smile. "Cimarron has never seen the likes of you!"

Jessie, her nerves strung tight, could manage only a weak smile in return. She had already subjected her appearance to a critical inspection before leaving the hotel with the other women and walking the short distance to the church.

They now stood waiting in the narrow cloakroom just to the left of the doorway. Abigail Higgins was playing a selection of what she deemed to be appropriately solemn hymns on the pump organ at the front of the sanctuary. True to Lissa's prediction, the church was filled to overflowing with guests from near and far.

"The gown is lovely, Martha," Jessie told her, making a determined effort to gather her rapidly fleeting courage. "You have performed a remarkable transformation!" She glanced down at the other woman's handiwork and smiled again.

What had once been a ruffled white silk ballgown trimmed in pink satin rosettes along the rounded neckline and black velvet ribbon around the bottom was now a plain but elegant wedding dress that fit Jessie's slender curves to perfection. Her long hair was drawn up and away from her face in a loose "waterfall" style, which allowed the thick golden curls to cascade downward in the back. She did not wear a traditional veil, but rather a small square of lace pinned atop her head. The simplicity of her ensemble lent an almost ethereal quality to her beauty.

"It's time, Miss Clare," announced William Easton as he unhurriedly rounded the corner to fetch her. Delighted to have been asked by Martha to give the bride away, he looked quite dashing in his well-tailored gray serge suit. He smiled at Jessie and tucked her hand in his arm. "It will be over with before you know it," he assured her kindly.

As Jessie's lone attendant, Lissa headed down the aisle first. Then, with Abigail striking up the requisite wedding march, Jessie allowed William to lead her forward. She caught her breath when she saw Ben waiting for her at the other end of the church. He looked so tall and handsome, his lithely muscled frame encased in a black coat and trousers, white linen shirt, black string tie, and polished cowboy boots. Curly stood beside him, his own appearance greatly altered by the exchange of work clothes for the one real suit in his possession.

It *was* over with almost before Jessie knew it. After repeating her vows with secret heartfelt conviction and listening as if in a daze while the minister proclaimed her to be Ben Chandler's wife, she felt her new husband draw her arm possessively through his. He led her back down the aisle and across the street to the meeting hall, the guests following them to the reception Martha and Consuela had arranged with Lissa's help.

The next hour passed in a never-ending whirl of hearty congratulations, mountains of good advice, and a number of toasts to the future happiness of the bride and groom. Even Horace Mooney put aside his differences with both Chandlers long enough to participate in the festivities along with the other members of the school board, who also temporarily forgot about the meeting they had planned for the following afternoon. It seemed that Lissa had been right about something else as well: Cimarron *had* needed a happy occasion to celebrate.

By the time Ben spirited Jessie away, she was beginning to feel as though the day would never end. She bent her head against the shower of rice that pelted them when they hurried outside. Ben handed her up into the waiting buggy, then took his place beside her and gave a swift, practiced flick of the reins.

Jessie looked back over her shoulder as the buggy rolled away. Her eyes widened when she caught a brief glimpse of Cole Hagan's face in the crowd. Unaware of the fact that she tensed in alarm, she started guiltily when Ben demanded, "What is it, Jessamyn?"

"Nothing!" she denied in a breathless rush, her eyes falling before his when she turned her head back around. "Nothing at all. I—I was just thinking."

"About us?" he asked quietly.

"Yes," she lied. She was dismayed to feel the telltale color staining her cheeks.

"You haven't even asked me where we're going." She looked up to see that a strange smile was playing about his lips, while his blue eyes were glowing with a warm, unfathomable light.

"I assumed we were going back to the Chapparosa," she responded with a slight frown of bewilderment.

"You assumed wrong, Mrs. Chandler."

Mrs. Chandler. The sound of her new name on his lips brought a rush of pleasure. Her heart pounded erratically within her breast at the thought of being alone with him. It was her wedding night—or soon would be, she amended, glancing toward the red-gold ball of fire sinking low on the horizon. She chided herself for the wicked turn her thoughts kept taking, then mused wryly that they would no longer be considered wicked now that she was married to the man who had prompted them.

"Very well then, where are we going?" she finally asked.

"To a place where I can have you all to myself," he replied enigmatically, his gaze darkening with thoroughly masculine anticipation at the thought. "You may never make it back to school."

"But I have to!" she protested, blushing rosily. "I promised to be there as usual in the morning. And you told me yourself that this is the busiest time of year at the ranch, so we—"

"I know, damn it!" he muttered darkly. He said nothing for several long moments, then his handsome brow cleared again. Turning back to Jessie, he vowed in a low, deep-timbred voice laced with barely controlled passion, "Soon, wildcat, I'll take you away on a real honeymoon. Just the two of us."

"Wha—what about James and Hannah?" she stammered weakly.

"Blast it, woman, I'll be damned if I'll bring my children along on our honeymoon!"

"*Our* children," she corrected without thinking. She was surprised to hear him give a quiet chuckle.

"You don't waste any time, do you, schoolmarm?" he challenged, his eyes alight with devilish amusement now.

"I haven't the faintest idea what you mean!" she countered with a proud lift of her head. Though she outwardly bristled at his laughter, she was melting on the inside.

"Yes you do. But I'm not complaining—not yet, anyway. You're welcome to rule my household, Mrs. Chandler, so long as you don't try to rule me."

"I have no intention of *ruling* anyone!" Her eyes flashed their brilliant deep green fire up at him. "You, of all people, Ben Chandler, have no right to accuse—"

"I have the right to do whatever I please now," he pointedly reminded her. The look on his face caused Jessie to fall silent and swallow a sudden lump in her throat. His gaze smoldered with passion when he reiterated, in a voice that was scarcely more than a husky whisper, "Whatever I please."

She watched as he shifted his gaze forward again and gave another abrupt snap of the reins. The horse obediently quickened its pace, while the buggy bounced and rocked over the dusty road. The setting sun cast a soft pale orange glow over the countryside. "Angel fire," Consuela had told her the Indians called it.

Jessie held tight to the back and side of the cushioned leather seat, her pulses racing every bit as much as the buggy's wheels.

Thirteen

"This is where we are—are going to spend the night?" Jessie faltered in disbelief. Her wide, luminous gaze traveled over the small log cabin nestled in a grove of cottonwood trees beside the river.

"It is," Ben confirmed. He came around to her side of the buggy and lifted her in his arms. Instead of putting her down, however, he pivoted on his booted heel and began carrying her toward the cabin.

"But all my things are back at the ranch!" she protested feebly. "And what about—?"

"Everything's been taken care of," he cut her off in his usual masterful way.

Jessie could only hold tight to him as he kicked open the door and strode across the threshold with his literally blushing bride. He set her on her feet, then stood gazing intently down at her for a moment, with his hands at her waist, before remembering the old adage of business before pleasure.

"I'll see to the horse," he said, releasing her with great reluctance. "You'll find whatever you need in the trunk over there." He gave a curt nod toward the far corner of the one-room cabin. "Light the lamp. I won't be long."

She waited until he had disappeared back outside, then

hastened across to the lamp on the table. With slightly trembling hands, she struck a match and held it to the wick, then replaced the globe and turned the knob to bring the flame to its full strength. That done, she turned to survey the room in which she would spend the first night of her married life.

It was no larger than she had first thought, but it was clean and warm and filled with the faint, pleasant aroma of pine and wildflowers. And old iron bedstead covered with a patchwork quilt took up nearly half of the room, leaving only enough space for a rough-hewn table, a couple of ladder-back chairs with laced rawhide seats, and a rather battered oak washstand that had clearly seen better days.

Musing that the cabin had a certain decidedly rustic charm that she could not help but find appealing, Jessie smiled to herself. She knew that any place would have been appealing to her as long as she shared it with Ben. Still, she wondered why he had chosen this particular location for their wedding night.

Wedding night. Those two words, at once thrilling and ominous, returned to the forefront of her thoughts. She crossed to the small leather trunk and bent to open it, her eyes widening when they beheld its contents.

A nightgown of the sheerest white lawn she had ever seen lay folded neatly on top. Underneath it she found a wrapper of pale green silk, a clean set of undergarments, a pair of stockings, and her dark navy suit. This last was apparently meant to serve as her attire for the next day. She frowned in puzzlement at the lack of her everyday corset, but her greatest curiosity lay in the direction of the nightgown.

Had Ben chosen it for her? she wondered, then grew warm at the possibility. She drew it out and straightened to her full height again, holding the nightgown up and watching as the gossamer folds spilled downward across the front of her body.

"I had to guess about the size," Ben remarked from the doorway, his deep voice startling her. She whirled to face him, her face flaming in embarrassment as she hastily thrust the nightgown behind her.

"So then you were the one who bought it!" she pronounced breathlessly, then demanded at a sudden suspicious thought, "How long has this—this *garment* been in your possession, Ben Chandler?"

"Since last week," he answered blithely. "I got it for you in Santa Fe." He stepped farther inside the cabin now and closed the door.

"Last week? But how could you know for certain I would go through with this?"

"I never doubted it." This was not entirely true; he'd been filled with a number of doubts when he had taken off for Santa Fe so abruptly. But he had doubted neither his feelings nor the intended course of his actions by the time he had returned.

Jessie fell silent. Feeling incredibly awkward all of a sudden, she could only stand and watch while Ben moved to the table with deceptive nonchalance and set a basket atop its cracked, unvarnished surface.

"Consuela packed a supper for us," he told her.

"I—I'm not hungry, thank you."

"Neither am I." His mouth curved into a brief crooked smile before he turned away and went down on one knee in front of the stone fireplace. Jessie's eyes were inexorably drawn to his broad back and the lean hardness of his thigh as he set about building a fire. Night was falling, and with it came the chill that always swept down from the mountains in the early fall.

"How did you come to know so much about women's clothing?" Jessie charged impulsively, then could have bitten her tongue. She had actually managed to forget that he had been married before.

"I haven't exactly lived the life of a monk these past seven years, Jessamyn," he confessed dryly. But he sure as hell hadn't had a great many dealings with women, either. He hadn't wanted to—until now.

"No, of course not," she murmured, then colored as the meaning of his words sunk in. She felt a sudden sharp pang of jealousy at the thought of those other women. *Had he bought them shamefully immodest nightgowns, too?* she mused to herself in bitter sarcasm, her green eyes blazing. Spinning about again, she flung the nightgown back down into the trunk with a vengeance. She knew it was a terribly childish thing to do, but she could not help it.

"You won't be needing it anyway," promised Ben.

Jessie's fiery gaze flew to where he was now drawing his tall frame upright before the strengthening dance of the flames. The look in his own eyes held such compelling warmth and desire and tenderness that she caught her breath on a soft gasp. With slow, almost deliberate movements, he drew off his jacket and tossed it heedlessly across one of the chairs. His fingers moved up to tug the string tie from about his neck, then began unbuttoning his white linen shirt. The shirt soon joined the jacket and tie, leaving the bronzed, powerful hardness of his upper torso completely bare.

As if mesmerized, Jessie stood quiet and motionless while he took a seat on the chair and removed his boots and socks. She had never watched a man undress before; she had never really had the desire to do so up till now. She could not tear her eyes away from Ben, until he stood and brought his hands purposefully upward to the waistband of his trousers.

Blushing hotly, she whirled about to face the other way. He abandoned his efforts for the moment and came up behind her, his hands closing gently about her shoulders.

286

"It's all right, wildcat," he told her in a low voice that brimmed with an intoxicating mixture of humor and passion. "We're man and wife now, remember?"

"Of course I remember!" she retorted with unexpected vehemence. "I also remember why you married me, Ben Chandler!" She had foolishly believed her love alone would be enough—but, God help her, it was not!

"What are you talking about?" He forced her about to face him again, his strong fingers tightening their grip on her soft flesh.

"What the devil do you think I'm talking about?" she countered, dismayed to feel hot tears starting to her eyes. Ben's gaze softened, and an affectionately wry smile touched his lips.

"You don't have to be afraid of me, Jessamyn."

"I'm not afraid of you!"

"Aren't you?" he challenged softly. He drew her stiff, unyielding body closer. "We both know why we're here."

"I don't!" she shot back, the pain in her heart fueling the turbulence of her emotions. "I don't know how I could have allowed myself to be—to be seduced into compliancy with this madness. You don't want me. You want my body, but you do not want *me!*"

"Do you really believe that, you little fool?" he demanded tersely, jerking her up hard against him now.

"What else am I to believe?" She tried to pull free, but he held fast. "I am not one of your *other women*, Ben Chandler, to be used and discarded when you—"

"You're my wife, damn it!" he ground out. A dangerously intense light burned in his gaze, but Jessie was too sick at heart to take warning from it.

"Just as Emily was your wife?" she taunted recklessly.

"Emily has nothing to do with this!"

"Doesn't she?" She drew a ragged breath before accusing, in a voice full of anguish, "You loved her,

287

didn't you? You loved her so much that you can never love another! That's why you married me, isn't it? Because I was willing to settle for marriage on your terms! And now—now you can have someone in your bed while you go on loving a woman who has been dead for—"

"Damn you, Jessamyn, that's enough!" he thundered, his eyes glittering hotly.

For a moment, she feared that he would strike her. But he did not. Instead, he abruptly released her as though the contact burned him, then turned away with a muttered oath. She watched him through her tears as he took up an angry, rigid stance before the fireplace and fixed his savage blue gaze upon the flames.

"I loved Emily," he admitted grimly, his tone one of foreboding calm. "I'll not deny it. I would have gone on loving her if she hadn't died. But I don't grieve for her the way you think. It's been seven long years, damn it! I've punished myself enough!"

"Punished yourself?" Jessie choked out in bewilderment. She was shocked at his next words.

"I killed her, Jessamyn," he declared in a voice edged with raw emotion. "I knew she was too frail, too delicate to be able to survive the hardships we had to face back then. She wasn't meant for the kind of life facing her in this wild country. But I brought her anyway. I was too damned selfish to acknowledge the danger. She didn't even make it through the first year." He paused and lifted a hand to the split-log mantel, his fingers clenching about its rough edge until his knuckles turned white. "I wasn't even with her when it happened. And afterward . . . I should have sent the twins back east. But I couldn't bring myself to do it."

"Oh, Ben," whispered Jessie, the tears coursing freely down her cheeks now. Her heart twisted painfully at the thought of his suffering. *He blames himself for*

Emily's death.

She now understood why, in the beginning, he had tried to make her leave Cimarron. It was because of Emily . . . because he had mistakenly believed her to be like Emily. But why had it mattered so much to him? she then asked herself. *Why?*

"Emily's parents tried to take James and Hannah from me," he continued quietly, his handsome features tensing anew. "They claimed I had killed their daughter and would do the same to her children. But I wouldn't give them up. They were all I had left." He allowed his arm to fall back to his side. "In the end, they stayed where they belonged. Consuela had come to live at the Chapparosa shortly before they were born. She took care of them while I was gone."

"Gone?"

"I had agreed to serve as a scout for the army whenever I was needed. Gray Wolf's band was much larger then. They had joined with some of the Utes in an uprising just north of here." His eyes darkened with renewed pain at the memory. "That's where I was when Emily died—leading the troops from Fort Union against the Indians."

"Is that why you and Gray Wolf are enemies now?" asked Jessie, slowly approaching him now. "Because—because of Emily?"

"That's part of it," he acknowledged with a curt nod. "But other things had destroyed our friendship even before that. Emily's death only strengthened the hate which had sprung up between us."

"And yet he let us go free," she recalled.

"I was almost certain he would." His mouth curved into a faint, sardonic smile. "As I said before, he may be a moody, scheming savage, but he still possesses a certain sense of honor. And there would be no honor in killing a man who was not only unarmed, but also an old friend.

So he played out his little game and made sure we'd never forget."

He finally drew his eyes away from the fire and looked at her as she came to stand close beside him. Their gazes met and locked. Silence rose between them for several long moments, a silence full of yearning and confusion and the awful pain of uncertainty.

"I married you for one reason only, Jessamyn," Ben finally declared, his deep, resonant voice filling the room.

"I know," responded Jessie, a sob catching in her throat. "Because I am suitable as a wife, and as a mother, and—and because you want me in your bed." She had known he didn't love her. She had known it all along. Why then did it feel as though her heart was breaking in two?

"No," he denied, giving a slight shake of his head.

"No?" she echoed in disbelief. Her glistening eyes became very round and she trembled when his hands closed about her arms. "You mean you don't—"

"What I mean, Mrs. Chandler, is that I married you because I love you," he confessed at last. "I've loved you from the very first, though I tried like hell not to. I didn't want to care for anyone again the way I'd cared for Emily. I didn't want to face losing you." He smiled softly down into the incredulous wide-eyed beauty of her countenance. "But I never had a chance. And the truth is, I don't love you the way I loved Emily."

"You—you don't?" Jessie faltered weakly, her head spinning wildly as a result of what she had just heard. *Ben Chandler loved her,* she repeated in the chaotic depths of her mind. He had married her because he loved her. Dear God, was it true?

"What Emily and I had together started when we were children and deepened as we grew older," he explained solemnly. "It was just something that had always been understood between us. I loved her, but it was a cautious love. She wasn't at all like you, Jessamyn. And I never burned for her the way I do for you!"

He swept her up against him now with such fierce possessiveness that Jessie felt her own blood turning to liquid fire in her veins. She gazed breathlessly up into the face of the man she loved, her whole body alive with joy and passion. *He loved her!*

"I love you with all my heart, wildcat," he reiterated in a low, vibrant tone of voice that sent a delicious shiver dancing down her spine. "I love you as a woman, not as some precious, fragile object to be cherished and stroked and then put carefully away on the shelf, but as a beautiful creature of flesh and blood who is more than a match for me. I've never felt this way about anyone before, and by damn, I'm going to make you feel it, too!" he vowed. "I'm going to make you love me!"

"Oh, Ben, I *do* love you!" she proclaimed, throwing her arms about his neck. Her eyes shone with the truth. "Don't you see? That's why I couldn't bear the thought of meaning so much less to you than Emily. I feared you would never come to care for me as you did for her. It was because I loved you that I was able to go through with the wedding; I don't think I'd have had the courage to do so otherwise. And then, when you brought me here, I—I discovered that I could not bear to give you only part of myself. I needed the assurance of your love!"

"Why the devil didn't you tell me?" he demanded, his own heart soaring and the glow of triumphant elation in his brilliant blue eyes.

"Why didn't *you?*" Jessie countered with loving reproach. "Why did you let me go on believing you were marrying me only because you had formed a—a physical attachment for me?"

"I've certainly done that," he drawled roguishly. "But I had promised myself to give you time. I didn't think you

291

were ready yet to hear—"

"Not ready yet?" she repeated, bristling with indignation. "For heaven's sake, why should any woman have to be *ready* to hear that the man she is to wed is in love with her? If you had only told me of your true feelings the night you proposed, it would have saved us both a great deal of trouble!"

"I didn't know then," he admitted with another perfectly devastating smile. His arms tightened about her. "At least, I wasn't prepared to face the truth then. I knew I wanted you more than I'd ever wanted anyone. And I was determined to have you for my own!"

"No matter what the consequences of your desire!" she retorted, endeavoring to look stern. "You took an awfully big chance, didn't you? It would have served you right, Ben Chandler, if you had found yourself married to a woman who would have nothing to do with you outside of the privacy of the bedroom!"

"If that had been the case, I'd have made every moment in that bedroom count," he parried. He delighted in her blush and reveled in the knowledge of her love. "Blast it woman, you have put me through absolute hell from the very first! I've never met anyone like you before—and God help me if I ever do again!"

"Sometimes, Mr. Chandler, you talk too damned much!" she murmured, raising up on tiptoe to press a soft, beguiling kiss upon his mouth. She was rewarded for her boldness in the very next instant, when he kissed her back with such warm, demanding mastery that she grew faint.

The next thing she knew, he was scooping her up in his powerful arms and carrying her to the bed. He did not lower her to the quilt as she had expected, but rather set her on her feet beside the bed and spun her about to begin unlooping the row of tiny pearl buttons on the back of her fitted bodice. With a swift dexterity that made Jessie wonder exactly how much practice he'd had with getting women out of their clothes, he unfastened the white silk gown and pushed it off her shoulders. It fell in a heap about her ankles.

She gazed downward but had no time to lament the terrible creasing of her wedding gown, for Ben's fingers next moved to untie the strings of her new satin lace-trimmed corset.

"From this day forward, Mrs. Chandler, you won't be wearing these damned things!" he decreed.

"But I must!" she protested breathlessly, her knees growing weak at the thought of what was to come. "It wouldn't be proper—"

"No, but it will be practical. And that matters more out here. Besides," he concluded when he impatiently yanked the corset free, "I like your natural shape better." As if to prove his point, he stripped off her two embroidered petticoats, turned her about again, and pulled her close with his strong, work-hardened hands at her slender waist. She was clad only in her chemise and drawers now, and she grew warm beneath the ardent look in her husband's eyes. "Loosen your hair, Jessamyn," he commanded softly.

Following only a moment's hesitation, she obeyed. She raised her hands to her hair and removed the square of lace, then, one by one, the hairpins. Ben's eyes followed her every movement. Finally, she shook her head, sending the thick curls of burnished gold cascading seductively downward about her face and shoulders. She trembled when Ben lifted a hand to tenderly brush a strand of hair from the silken smoothness of her brow.

"Every night, wildcat," he told her in a hoarse whisper, "every blasted night I lay alone in the darkness and stared at the wall between us, my whole body on fire and my mind tormented with visions of you looking as you do now. I love you, Jessamyn. Dear God, how I love you!"

He could wait no longer. Sweeping her masterfully up in his arms once more, he lowered her to the bed. He covered her body with his own while his mouth claimed the willing sweetness of hers. Jessie moaned softly and entwined her arms about his neck, her lips parting beneath the demanding pressure of his. The kiss rapidly deepened, firing their mutual passions to such an extent that they both yearned for release.

But Ben was determined to prolong the delectable agony. He had waited for what seemed like an eternity to make Jessie his; he had no intention of allowing their first union to be achieved with a haste they might both come to regret. No, he had vowed to make her want him as much as he wanted her, to unleash the fiery passions he knew raged within her, and it was to this purpose that he now forced himself to end the wildly intoxicating kiss.

Jessie's eyes flew open, and she gazed up at Ben in mingled disappointment and bewilderment as he drew away from her. She inhaled sharply when his fingers moved to the three small buttons on the waistband of her ruffled linen drawers. He unfastened them with remarkable ease, then suddenly rolled her facedown upon the quilt. Pulling her chemise free from where it had been tucked in beneath her drawers, he left it bunched up about her waist.

"Ben?" she asked tremulously. "What are you—?"

She broke off with another gasp when he began easing her drawers slowly downward. Kneeling beside her on the bed, he lowered his head so that his warm lips could brand the pale satiny flesh he was exposing. Jessie's face flamed at the bold intimacy of his actions, but she could not bring herself to utter a protest. She clutched at the pillow beneath her head, her eyes closing again and her breathing increasingly erratic as Ben's lips wandered across the small of her back, then lower to where her shapely hips were moving restlessly beneath his searing gaze.

"Oh, Ben!" she gasped, her eyelids fluttering open again at the first touch of his lips upon her bare bottom. Her fingers tensed about the pillow, and she caught her lower lip between her teeth to stifle a soft cry of mingled shock and pleasure.

He pulled the undergarment all the way down to her knees now, his hands smoothing appreciatively over her naked derriere before his lips returned to press a series of warm, wickedly provocative kisses across the rounded hillocks of flesh. She shivered, her skin tingling deliciously while he trailed a searing path downward over the back of her slender, quivering thighs.

Then, with her senses reeling, he tugged the drawers all the way off and purposefully turned her over to her back again. She lay gazing up at him with eyes full of passion's glow, her alluring form attired only in the sleeveless thin white chemise that was now twisted up about her waist. Suddenly realizing that her lower body was completely bare, she blushed from head to toe and brought her hands downward in an instinctive gesture of modesty.

Ben, however, would not be denied the long-awaited sight of her body in all its womanly glory. He gently but firmly took Jessie's arms and raised them above her head.

"Ben . . . please!" she implored feebly.

But he would not be swayed. Grasping the edge of the chemise, he tugged it upward and off. He felt his desire flaring almost beyond control as his smoldering gaze raked over her trembling naked curves.

"Damn, but you're even more beautiful than I'd imagined!" he murmured huskily.

Releasing her arms, he quickly stripped off the remainder of his own clothing. Jessie lay with her arms still above her head, her shyness conquered by her love for Ben and a desire that blazed nearly as hot as his. She did not turn her head away from his nakedness, but rather gazed boldly at him in loving fascination. His bronzed, hard-muscled body was more splendidly formed than she had remembered. She felt herself grow warm when her eyes were drawn to where his undeniably virile manhood sprang forth from a cluster of tight dark brown curls between his lean but powerful thighs.

The feel of her eyes upon him made Ben groan inwardly. He covered her body with his own once more, his hardness pressing her down into the feather mattress while his hands began an urgent, feverish exploration of her supple curves. His mouth claimed hers in a kiss that demanded a response—a response that she was only too willing to give. She clung to him, her fingers curling about his broad shoulders and her body straining instinctively upward against his. His tongue slid easily between her parted lips, and she delighted him with the innocently seductive manner in which she welcomed the ravishment of her sweet mouth.

Soon his lips roamed hungrily over the silken planes of her flushed, beautiful face, then followed an imaginary course downward from the graceful curve of her neck to the pulse beating at the hollow of her throat. She gave a low moan when he finally bent his head to her breasts, his hand cupping the fullness of her left breast from underneath while his mouth closed about the rosy peak.

She gasped sharply when his warm, velvety tongue snaked out to encircle the nipple, then flicked across it with light, tantalizing strokes that made her gasp again and again. Her fingers came down to thread within the sun-streaked thickness of his hair as he continued with the exquisite torment for a few moments longer, before moving to do the same to her other breast.

Just when she was certain she could bear no more, his

296

lips took to wandering again. They trailed a fiery path downward across the trembling smoothness of her belly, where his tongue came out again to dip erotically within her navel, then traced a hot moist line even lower still. . . .

"Oh!" breathed Jessie, a near painful ecstasy rising within her. She felt her passions being hurled forcibly higher and higher as Ben's strong, sensuously persuasive fingers finally touched her at the very core of her womanhood. His hand moved upon her with such gentle yet masterful strokes that she cried out.

Closing her eyes tightly against the shocking pleasure of his caress, she could not prevent her back from arching, could not keep her legs from spreading wider to allow him even greater access to her womanly secrets. He slid his tall frame upward upon her body again, so that his mouth, on a level with her breasts, could return to its rapturous conquest of the rose-tipped globes while his fingers, at the secret place between her thighs, elicited wildly enchanting sensations that intensified with each passing second and threatened to drive her utterly mad with longing.

It was her beloved tormentor, however, who could stand no more. He had held his own passions in check for as long as humanly possible, and he now sought to make his possession of the woman he loved complete. His heart as well as his body demanded their union. . . . Fate had decreed it the first time he had held her in his arms.

Sliding his hand beneath her buttocks, he positioned himself between her legs. The tip of his manhood readily found its mark, and he waited no longer before easing his hardness into his bride's honeyed warmth. Then, unable to deny the most powerful wave of desire he had ever known, he thrust forward until her flesh had fully accepted the consummately natural intrusion of his.

Jessie cried out softly at the sharp pain, but it was almost immediately replaced by the most intense pleasure she had ever known. She moaned as Ben skillfully tutored her hips in the age-old rhythm of love, and she soon began meeting his thrusts with all the answering passion he had aroused within her. Her fingers clutched almost convulsively upon his bronzed, granite-hard shoulders. She felt as though he touched her very womb, as though the two of them had truly become one while their passions were born heavenward.

Finally, they were rewarded with the joyful, satisfying completion only the truest of lovers can ever know. A soft, breathless cry burst from Jessie's lips, followed closely by Ben's sharp intake of breath above her. His tensed muscles relaxed, and he rolled to his side on the bed, drawing her pliant body close against him.

They lay together in the soft afterglow of their tempestuous loving, neither of them speaking for several long moments. The fire crackled and hissed softly, the lamp's steady flame filling the room with a comforting golden glow, while outside the wind had died down to a gentle stirring of the moonlit countryside.

"I love you, Jessamyn," Ben finally murmured. As always, the sound of his low, deep-timbred voice close to her ear sent a delicious tremor through her.

"And I love you," she happily reciprocated. Sighing in contentment, she lay with her head cradled upon his naked chest and her soft curves fitted to perfection against his lithe hardness. "Oh, Ben, I never dreamt it would be like—like *this*." She suddenly raised up on one elbow and peered closely down at his handsome face, a slight frown of worriment creasing her brow. "You weren't disappointed, were you?"

"Far from it," he assured her with a tenderly crooked smile. He drew her head back down and smoothed a hand across the bare satiny smoothness of her hip. "Hell, sweetheart, I don't think I could have endured it if it had been any better," he drawled in a tone brimming with loving amusement. "It was definitely worth the wait."

"It's just that I know so little of these things," she remarked with another sigh, then looked up at him and demanded with wifely severity, "*You*, on the other hand, possess a vast knowledge, do you not?"

"Enough to know I've never felt this way before," he replied evasively, his mouth curving into a disarming grin that made her legs grow weak again.

"Just make certain you confine any *practical application* to your wife from this day forward!"

"You've no worries on that score, my love," he promised, settling her back down against him once more. Jessie relaxed and allowed her eyes to wander about the room.

"Ben, why did you bring me here?" she asked, her curiosity returning. "Why didn't we go back to the ranch?"

"Two reasons. I wanted us to be completely alone. And this is where I lived when I first started the Chapparosa. I suppose my bringing you here was symbolic of our new life together."

Silence fell between them again after that. Each of them became lost in thoughts of the future they would share, a future full of love and hope and the bright, never-ending promise of tomorrow.

"I will do everything in my power to make you happy, Ben Chandler," Jessie finally vowed.

"As will I you, Jessamyn." His blue eyes glowed with all the love in his own heart. Passion soon followed, and he drew her atop him.

"But we just—" she pointed out in confusion.

"We've all night, wildcat," he effectively cut off her

protests. "And I mean to love you well!"

Jessie blushed at the shocking unfamiliarity of her position, but she could muster no further resistance. Her arms crept up about his neck.

"Then by all means, dearest husband, do your duty," she whispered provocatively.

He was only too willing to oblige. . . .

Fourteen

Ben reluctantly delivered his new wife to the school the following morning, then headed back to his own work at the ranch. Watching as the horse and buggy grew smaller in the distance, Jessie released a sigh and turned about to ring the bell.

The children were already gathered about in the front yard, and they came racing up to the steps at the familiar summons. Everyone was present, Jessie noted as they formed themselves into a line, except for the oldest Shelton boy. Making a mental note to ask Billy about his brother's absence, she watched the students shuffle inside in a reasonable facsimile of the neat and orderly manner she had made them practice a number of times.

Hannah and James, however, remained behind. They exchanged quick conspiratorial looks before James stepped forward.

"Jessie?"

"Yes, James, what is it?" she asked with a warm smile that included the two children who were now her own. Her heart swelled with love for them—and for their father as well.

"Aunt Martha told us you and Papa spent the night at the old cabin last night."

Much taken aback by his reference to the previous night, Jessie crimsoned and hastily averted her gaze. Vivid memories of those intimate, wonderfully passionate hours she and Ben had shared came flooding back into her mind, and she felt her pulses leaping anew. Her body ached in a dozen places she had not previously known to exist, and her skin still tingled from the kisses and caresses she had delighted in receiving. *Good heavens*, she thought with an inward groan, *she had to put such thoughts aside or else she'd never be able to get through the day!*

"Yes, James," she confirmed, finally managing to meet the little boy's eyes again. "It—it is customary for two people who are newly married to go away together."

"Aunt Martha said you'll be sleeping in the same room with Papa now," Hannah remarked solemnly.

"Yes, Hannah. I will." She could hear the voices of the other children inside the schoolhouse, and she took a deep, steadying breath before requesting, with another smile, "Please, may we not discuss this later? It's already after eight o'clock, and—"

"What we want to know is whether or not you're going to have a baby," James confided at last.

"*A baby?*" she echoed in stunned disbelief.

"When people are married and sleep in the same room, they get a baby," Hannah patiently explained.

"After the wedding yesterday, at the party, we heard Mrs. Higgins saying that the reason you married Papa so fast must be because you were afraid you were going to have a baby," revealed James. He and his sister looked at one another again before he added, "I told Aunt Martha about it, but she said not to pay any attention to Mrs. Higgins."

"Is it true?" Hannah asked, her eyes growing very wide in childish wonderment.

"I hope it is!" James proclaimed with an emphatic nod. "Hannah and I have never had a baby brother."

"Baby sister," his twin pointedly amended. James rolled his eyes heavenward in an eloquent gesture of brotherly exasperation.

"No, confound it! We don't need any more girls. . . ."

"Children, please!" Jessie finally recovered voice enough to intervene. "I am *not* going to have a baby—at least not yet—and I give you my word that you will be the first to know when I am! Now come," she said, slipping an arm about each of them, "we must get inside before the others think they have been abandoned."

Her blood boiled at the thought of Abigail Higgins spreading such a vicious rumor, but she firmly told herself there was nothing to be done about it. Evil would persist in the minds of some, she mused angrily, no matter how much she tried to deny its bitter harvest. Still, she could not help but hope the spiteful Mrs. Higgins had the tables turned on her one day.

The morning passed quickly, with the students displaying a bit more restlessness and defiance than usual. Several of them engaged in the time-honored custom of twisting their legs in intricate patterns upon the floor, staring dreamily out the windows, or simply tormenting one another. Billy Shelton tied Hannah's long braids to the back of the bench, causing her head to snap back when she tried to rise. He was assessed the humiliating punishment of being made to sit with the girls for a half hour's time. His brother Tom flicked ink at Harmon and Peter and received fifteen minutes in the corner for his troubles. John passed a love note to Kristen; Jessie confiscated it and then suppressed a laugh when her eyes scanned its contents: "A ball of mud on a stick of wood, a kiss from you would do me good, the road is wide and you can't step it, I love you and you can't hep it."

Fortunately, things began settling down after the noon break. Jessie had just finished leading the children in a recitation of one of Wordsworth's poems and had taken a seat at her desk when Foley Keech came sauntering boldly into the classroom. Reflecting that it seemed fate was determined to blight her happiness on this first full day of her married life, she stood again and demanded sternly, "What are you doing here?"

"My pa said I was to come," Foley told her with an insolent grin. He was every bit as dirty as he had been before, and his eyes were still full of contempt as they flickered over her. "He says I got a right to be here. He says you can't keep me out, so long as I don't cause no trouble."

"Your father is correct," Jessie agreed calmly, though she felt a lingering unease that would not be dispelled. "I will allow you to remain, but only if you give me your word you will be on your best behavior—and only if you have the desire to learn."

"He can't learn, Miss Clare!" Billy Shelton piped up. "He's too damn dumb!"

"It's Mrs. Chandler now!" James dutifully pointed out.

"You're the one that's dumb, Billy Shelton, you little jackass!" growled Foley.

"That's quite enough!" Jessie admonished sharply. "Foley, if you really do intend to stay, then you will keep quiet and take a seat on the bench beside Peter in the back row. Billy, we will have no more of your outbursts, do you understand?"

"Yes, ma'am, Miss—I mean Mrs. Chandler."

"Good. Now, class, suppose we—"

"Mrs. Chandler?" interrupted Mary Sue, her hand shooting up in the air.

"Yes, Mary Sue?" Jessie asked with sorely tested patience. "What is it?"

"Foley's got a sackful of chewing tobacco, and he spit some at me!"

"Foley, is that true?" demanded Jessie with a severe

304

frown. She walked forward to where he sat grinning unconcernedly behind Mary Sue. "Do you have a sackful of tobacco?"

"Nope."

"Then what *do* you have?"

"Nothin'."

"Indeed?" she challenged, glimpsing the top edge of the small brown paper sack stuffed in the front pocket of his trousers. She had known he would be trouble. And if she did not manage to win this first battle, the situation would only worsen. "Foley Keech, you will take that sack and—" She broke off for a moment and allowed her eyes to travel quickly about the room. The big iron stove caught her attention. Someone—probably the older boys—had started a fire to chase away the morning's chill. Her emerald gaze sparkled with satisfaction, and she turned back to Foley to finish decisively, "You will place it in the stove!"

"You sure you want me to do that?" sneered the brawny mischief-maker.

"Quite sure!"

"All right," he surprised her by capitulating without further argument. "You're the boss, ain't you?" A smile of malicious amusement played about his lips, and his eyes wre full of a strangely triumphant light as he rose to his feet. He sauntered across to the stove in the front corner, turning back to Jessie to ask one last time. "You want me to put the whole sack in?"

"I most certainly do!"

"All right." He opened the door of the stove, pulled the sack from his pocket, tossed it into the fire, slammed the door shut again . . . and suddenly ran like hell to the back of the room.

"Foley!" exclaimed Jessie in alarm. "What in heaven's name do you think you are—"

Without warning, the sound of a gunshot rang out.

Then another, and another, and another. The room erupted into screams, muttered curses, and the frantic scramble of children diving under overturned benches. Jessie spun about, her eyes wide and full of alarm as she tried to discern where the gunfire was coming from. Her gaze was almost immediately drawn back to the stove, and it dawned on her that no one was shooting at all. The furious sounds of battle were coming from the stove.

Foley!

"Foley Keech!" she shouted, rounding on him where he stood laughing beside the door he had flung open in preparation for a hasty retreat. "What was in that sack?" she demanded. Her eyes blazing with wrathful fire, she stormed forward to confront him as the mock warfare continued to rage behind her. "What did you put in that stove?"

"Hell, teacher, it wasn't nothin' but a sackful of chawin' tobacco!" he chortled.

"That's a lie!" She stood directly before him now, too angry to be frightened of the boy who stood nearly a head taller than herself. "Now, what was in that sack?"

"Bullets!" he finally revealed with another sneer.

"Bullets?" she echoed, belatedly lamenting the fact that she had not even bothered to inspect the sack's contents.

"You're so smart, why the hell didn't you figure it out for yourself?" Foley taunted scornfully, then swung about and went lumbering outside.

Jessie, by this time infuriated beyond reason, followed the impulse to give chase. She gathered up her skirts and raced furiously down the steps after him. The other children came spilling out of the schoolhouse close on her heels, anxious to escape the terrifying din inside *and* to see what happened when their teacher caught up with the big bully who had intimidated them for years.

"Foley Keech, you will stop right there!" ordered Jessie.

"You go to hell!" he growled over his shoulder as he kept on walking.

"I said *stop!*"

She caught up with him midway to the road. A loud gasp broke from her lips when he came to such an abrupt halt that she collided forcefully with the brawny hardness of his back. He gave a low, malevolent chuckle and flung about to grab her arms. Bringing his face close to hers, he yanked her up hard against him.

"You want me to stay, schoolmarm? You want me to stay and be the teacher's *pet?*" he snickered lewdly.

Jessie struggled in his offensive grasp, her stomach churning at his foul-smelling breath and the stench emanating from his filthy clothes.

"Take your hands off me!" she cried in outrage, trying desperately to pull free. Her hair tumbled down from its pins, and she winced with pain as Foley's hands tightened with bruising force about her arms. "Take your hands off me at once, or I—"

"You'll what?" he broke in with another derisive laugh.

The other students had gathered in a semicircle behind Jessie, where they stood watching the confrontation in shocked, openmouthed amazement. If any of them were tempted to come to their teacher's aid, they were too frightened of Foley to do so.

Except James. Vengeful fury welled up deep within his breast at the sight of his new mother being manhandled by Foley Keech. He hesitated no longer before charging forward and shoving his small, slender body protectively between Jessie and her assailant.

"You leave her alone!" yelled James. "Let her go!" He punctuated his demands with vigorous kicks at Foley's unprotected shins. Pushing with all his might against the boy who was twice his size as well as twice his age, he did not consider the danger to himself. He could think only of helping Jessie. "Let her go!"

307

"Why you little—" bit out Foley. Releasing Jessie, he seized James's arm with one large hand and brought the other smashing with merciless force against the side of the little boy's face.

Jessie, staggering backward, could only watch in mute horror as James crumpled to the ground. He lay conscious but stunned from the blow. A low moan came from his throat, and there was a widening trickle of blood at the side of his mouth.

"James!" screamed Hannah. She flew to his side and dropped to her knees on the grassy earth. Jessie would have gone to him as well, but Foley was not yet done with her.

"Who's gonna help you now, *teacher?*" he spat menacingly, advancing on her again with deadly purpose in his eyes.

Fired by the example of James's courage, Peter and Harmon finally sprang into action. They moved to block Foley's path, standing together with their hands clenched into fists and their youthful faces grimly determined.

"Get inside, Miss Clare!" directed Peter, forgetting the unimportant detail of her new marital status.

"Peter, Harmon . . . no!" she choked out. Fearing for their safety, she implored, "Please, stand aside!" Dear God, what was she going to do?

"You pissant coyotes think you got enough guts to take me on?" Foley sneered at the two boys who, though almost the same age as himself, were still a good deal smaller.

Wracked with indecision, Jessie whirled about and raced back inside the schoolhouse. She battled tears of helpless dismay as she searched frantically for something with which to stop Foley. Her eyes lit upon the shotgun Ben had made her promise to keep handy near her desk.

She did not pause to consider the fact that she had

never handled a gun before, much less fired one. Her one thought to help the children, she took up the shotgun and hurried back outside. Its weight felt strange and uncomfortably heavy in her hands, but she nonetheless raised the stock to her shoulder. She took up a defiant stance and aimed the barrel directly at Foley, who was at that moment preparing to hit Peter for the second time.

"Get out of here, Foley Keech!" Jessie commanded with as much bravado as she could muster. "Get out of here at once, or I—I'll shoot!"

"Ha!" he snorted in derision. "You ain't gonna shoot! Look at you. . . . . "You're just a scared little bitch! You're so damn scared your hands are shakin'!"

"That may well be," she responded with deceptive calm. "But I do not believe you want to run the risk of testing me, Foley. My hands *are* shaking, and as a result of that this thing might go off at any moment!"

Foley scowled at that. He visibly wavered, tempted to stay and show everyone no schoolmarm could get the better of him, yet unable to deny the truth of Jessie's warning. Experienced or not, he reluctantly conceded to himself, there was nothing more dangerous than a female with a gun.

He shot Jessie a murderous glare, cursed Peter and Harmon, then finally took himself off. Jessie breathed a loud sigh of relief and lowered the gun.

"He won't come back," predicted Harmon, his gaze full of admiration as he looked at her. "Once word gets around that you bluffed him down, he won't show his face here again."

"Yeah, and besides that, he's got to worry about that husband of yours," added Peter, remembering Ben now. He picked himself up off the ground and rubbed at his painfully throbbing jaw.

Jessie handed the gun to Harmon and flew to where James still lay. Hannah was weeping softly as she cradled her brother's head in her lap.

"Oh, James, are you all right?" asked Jessie tremulously, kneeling beside him. She lifted a hand to the cut on his mouth. Tears threatened to blind her. "Do you—do you hurt anywhere else?"

"My arm hurts, Jessie," he answered weakly. His eyes were suffused with a dull glow as he battled the pain, and his little face was alarmingly pale—except for the red, swollen imprint of Foley's hand. "He twisted my arm."

As gently as possible, Jessie inspected his injured arm. She tried to urge him to bend it at the elbow, but he cried out sharply.

"I'm afraid it may be broken," she pronounced, fighting back a sob. She smiled soothingly down at the little boy through her tears and told him, "We need to get you to the doctor, James. Do you think you can ride?"

"I could ride before I could walk," he murmured, his eyes twinkling up at her in spite of the pain. He reminded her so very much of his father at that moment that she could not help but laugh softly.

"Very well then, my brave little champion." She stood again and summoned Harmon, then told James, "Even though you are an excellent horseman, I must insist that you ride with me. And I would prefer it if you allowed Harmon to carry you down to the stream."

"Carry me?" James repeated, his eyes moving to the older boy in horrified disbelief. "I can walk!" To prove his point, he held onto his arm and climbed to his feet. He was a bit unsteady, but there was no doubt he was determined to make it under his own power. *True Chandler obstinancy*, Jessie mused to herself, her heart swelling with love and pride.

She dismissed school for the remainder of the day, sending the children home with the promise that studies would resume the next morning. Both Peter and Harmon offered to ride back to town with her but she declined, insisting that they look after the younger students instead.

Soon, she and the twins were on their way to Cimarron. With the recent ordeal fresh in her mind, she had tied the shotgun to the back of Hannah's saddle. She did her best not to touch James's injured arm as she handled the reins with surprising confidence. Hannah, who had remained unusually quiet since Foley's attack, rode beside them. She was still pale, and her eyes were full of lingering apprehension.

"Do you think Papa will kill Foley?" she asked Jessie solemnly.

"Why . . . no, of course not!" answered Jessie, her eyes wide with surprise at the question. "Wherever did you get such an idea?"

"Papa always said he'd kill anyone who hurts us."

"Well, he will not kill Foley! While there can be no excuse for Foley's behavior, he is still only a boy. Your father will undoubtedly be angry, but I can assure you he will not kill him."

"You were going to shoot him," the little girl reminded her.

"I'll bet you could have done it!" James interjected, the pain in his arm only a dull ache now. His eyes gleamed with boyish pleasure at the memory of Jessie's defiant stand against the bully. "I'll bet you could have blasted that old Foley Keech clear to kingdom come!"

"I had no intention whatsoever of shooting him!" Jessie hastened to deny. "I was merely trying to—to frighten him into leaving!"

"Well, I hope Papa *does* get angry!" Hannah declared with an emphatic nod.

"He will," her brother asserted, then heaved a sigh of regret. "I wish I could have been the one to make Foley go away."

"Oh, James," said Jessie, resisting the urge to hug him

tight, "you did everything within your power! You are without a doubt the bravest person I have ever known, and I want you to know how very grateful I am for the way you came to my defense," she proclaimed in all sincerity.

"The bravest?" he echoed, his face beaming with delight when she reaffirmed it. "I'm not really braver than Papa, you know. He fought Indians."

"And Yankees," added Hannah.

"Not Yankees—Rebels!" her twin corrected.

"What difference does it make?"

"A whole lot!"

Jessie smiled to herself and nudged the horse's flanks gently with her heels. She gave silent thanks once more for whatever it was that had prompted her to leave St. Louis and go west . . . west to Ben Chandler and the two children she had grown to love.

By the time they reached the doctor's house on the edge of town, James was beginning to complain of a headache as well. Jessie reached up and lifted him from the horse, then carried him up the neat picket-fenced front walk. Hannah rushed forward to ring the bell. A short blond-haired woman opened the door.

"Yes?" The moment her eyes fell upon James she gasped and swung the door wider. "Why, James Chandler, what happened to you?"

"May we see the doctor, please?" Jessie requested urgently. "I think James may have a broken arm!"

"Oh, dear heavens! Please, come this way!" The doctor's wife led them quickly through the house to a room at the back where her husband performed his examinations. "Place him on the bed there!" she bid Jessie, her eyes full of concern for the little boy she had known since birth. "I'll fetch the doctor at once!"

Jessie lowered James to the bed in the far corner of the small sunlit room. She frowned at the spasm of pain

312

that crossed his face. Hannah, who looked suspiciously close to tears, moved forward and slipped her small trembling hand into the comforting warmth of Jessie's.

"Is he going to be all right, Jessamyn?"

"Yes, Hannah," she assured the little girl with a smile that belied her own trepidation. "He's going to be just fine."

The doctor came into the room a moment later. He was a large, kindly man with a graying brown beard and a full set of hair to match. With a polite but firm request for Hannah and Jessie to leave the room, he closed the door and set about examining James with his wife's able assistance. He emerged shortly, his countenance looking quite solemn.

"Fortunately, Mrs. Chandler, your suspicions concerning his arm did not prove to be true," he told Jessie. "It is badly sprained, not broken. But he has suffered a slight concussion. I am afraid he will have to remain in my care overnight."

"Overnight?" she repeated, her heart pounding in alarm.

"Yes. It is only a precaution. If all goes well, he should be able to return home tomorrow."

"I see." She swallowed a sudden lump in her throat and placed an arm about Hannah's shoulders. "Well, then, is it possible for me to stay with him?"

"It is possible, but entirely unnecessary. As a matter of fact, I would advise against it. James needs to be kept as quiet as possible. My wife and I are well-known to him, so I don't believe he will be in the least bit apprehensive about remaining here with us."

"Very well," Jessie reluctantly agreed.

"But we can't leave him here!" Hannah protested with surprising vehemence. "James and I have never been apart, not even once in our whole lives!"

"It will only be for tonight," the doctor reassured her gently. "You can come back to fetch him after dinner tomorrow. I give you my word, Hannah, that he will be well treated."

Although it was apparent Hannah still dreaded the prospect of being separated from her twin, she nodded in capitulation and went along with Jessie to say good-bye to James. He was resting peacefully at the moment, his eyes closed and his breathing steady. Jessie's heart twisted at the thought of leaving him.

In the end, however, they had no choice in the matter. Jessie gave the doctor a brief report of how James had received his injuries, then returned outside with a visibly despondent Hannah. She drew the little girl close again and remarked, "I suppose we should ride back to the Chapparosa and tell your father what has happened." She released a troubled sigh when she pondered what his reaction would be when he learned of Foley's attack. There was no way she could keep the news from him, she reflected unhappily.

"I'm not going," insisted Hannah.

"Oh, Hannah, we must go!" She looked down at her with eyes full of compassion. "I know you don't want to leave James, but your father needs to know about him and—"

"Papa will come to town when he finds out we're not at the school," Hannah pointed out in a perfectly reasonable manner. "We can wait for him here. That way, we'll be close by in case James needs us."

Jessie could not deny the sense of her suggestion. There was nothing Ben could do for his son at present, and she knew he would not want them to ride all the way back to the ranch alone.

"We can tell the doctor we'll be over at the St. James," added Hannah. She gazed expectantly up at Jessie, her eyes wide and full of entreaty.

"All right," Jessie finally agreed. Pausing only to inform the doctor of their plans, she and her new

314

daughter led their horses down the street to the hotel.

Lissa was in the process of handing one of the regular customers his key when they entered. She sent the old miner off with an affectionate smile, then hastened forward to greet her friends.

"What brings the two of you to town today?" she asked once she had exchanged quick hugs with them both. She frowned at a sudden thought. "Isn't there any school today?"

"There was," Jessie replied as she and Hannah moved to take a seat on the sofa. "But I had to dismiss class early." She raised a hand to tuck a wayward curl back into place; although she had hastily pinned her hair up again while at the doctor's house, it threatened to come loose again.

"What happened?" The tall redhead sank down upon a chair opposite them.

"Foley Keech grabbed Jessamyn, Miss Boone!" provided Hannah. "And he put bullets in the stove!" She drew in a ragged breath. "And he hurt James!"

"James?" gasped Lissa, looking at Jessie.

"He tried to protect me," she explained, her voice quavering as tears sprang to her eyes once more. "Foley knocked him to the ground. He—he's over at the doctor's house right now. His arm was injured, and he has a concussion, but he should be able to come home tomorrow."

"Oh, poor James!" Lissa murmured, her own eyes full of anguish at the thought of the little boy's suffering. In the next instant, however, her gaze kindled with vengeful fury. "What are you going to do about Foley?"

"I don't know," admitted Jessie. "I haven't given him much thought since it happened, other than to wonder what Ben is going to do when he finds out!"

"The sheriff ought to be told about this right away!" Lissa opined decisively. "That Keech boy has been a

315

menace for years, and it's about time someone put a stop to it!" She paused for a moment, recalling something she had heard earlier that same morning. "Isn't there a school board meeting scheduled for this afternoon?"

"Good heavens, I forgot all about that!" exclaimed Jessie. Telling herself that the last thing she needed right now was to be hauled before the board and raked over the coals for any number of real or imagined misdeeds, she frowned and stood to her feet again. She wandered aimlessly over to the window, then suddenly spun about when it occurred to her that it might be best to let the school board deal with the problem of Foley Keech. Her eyes glowed with a purposeful light, and Lissa smiled at the sight of it.

"Horace Mooney will have to eat his words when he finds out what Foley's done," she remarked dryly.

"Eat his words?" Hannah echoed in bewilderment. Jessie sat back down and slipped an arm about the little girl's shoulders.

"Hannah, I would appreciate it if you would remain here with Miss Boone. I think I'm going to take her advice and pay a visit to the sheriff." She shifted her gaze back to Lissa. "You're right, you know. The proper authorities must be informed. Foley's treachery cannot be allowed to go unpunished; he has to be stopped before he hurts someone else."

Only a short time after she had returned from the jail, Jessie looked up to see Ben striding through the hotel's doorway. Her eyes filled with both relief and alarm as she hurried forward to meet him. His features were dangerously grim, and his gaze darkened as it moved over her.

"What happened?" he demanded, his strong arms closing about her when she stepped gratefully into his warm embrace. "There was no one at the school. Damn it, Jessamyn, I nearly went out of my mind when I

316

discovered you gone!" He held her so tightly against him that she could scarcely breathe, but her heart soared at the knowledge that he cared so much. "Where are the twins?" he then asked, drawing her away so that his eyes could search her face.

"Hannah is resting upstairs. James is—is over at the doctor's house," she reluctantly answered. She had dreaded this moment; now that it had come, she felt her courage rapidly fleeing.

"At the doctor's house?" His fingers clenched about her arms. "What happened to him?"

"There was an incident at school. James was injured while trying to protect me. He's going to be fine, Ben! The doctor said he had a mild concussion and he suffered a bad sprain to his arm, but—"

"What the devil do you mean, trying to protect you?" he demanded tersely. "Who was it, Jessamyn? Who did this to James?"

"One of the older boys," she murmured, her eyes falling before his. She gasped when he yanked her back against him.

"Who was it, damn it?" he ground out, his gaze smoldering now.

"Foley Keech," she finally revealed. "He—he had caused some trouble and I foolishly went after him! James stepped between us, and Foley struck him! Oh, Ben, please don't do anything rash!" she pleaded. "I've already reported the incident to the sheriff, and—"

"Stay here!" he commanded in a voice simmering with rage.

"Why? Where are you going?" asked Jessie, fear gripping her as his long, angry strides led him back to the door.

"To see my son," he stated in a deceptively low, level tone. "And to find Foley Keech!"

"Ben, no!" she gasped in horror. But it was too late. He

had already gone.

She sank wearily back down upon the sofa. Offering up a silent, fervent prayer for help, she buried her face in her hands and let the tears come at last.

Foley Keech, it turned out, had disappeared. His family had seen nothing of him since he had left for school earlier that day, and no one had any idea where he might have gone.

Ben, forced to abandon his quest for vengeance—at least for the moment—rode away from the Keech's place and back to town. Lem Keech watched him go, then cursed his boy for being so stupid as to get tangled up with the likes of Ben Chandler. He'd heard it said Chandler was a man who never forgot; he could only hope the talk was wrong. He didn't aim to pay for Foley's mistakes, and he told himself it would be just as well if the damned boy never came home.

Jessie revealed the whole story to Ben upon his return to the St. James. His blue eyes gleamed savagely when she told him of Foley's attack upon her. But when he went upstairs to speak to Hannah, his manner toward his daughter was loving and tender. The little girl cried while he held her, and he assured her, as only a father can, that everything would be all right.

By the time Ben and Jessie left to attend the school board meeting, Hannah was perched happily on a chair at Lissa's side behind the front desk. Lissa had professed a genuine delight in her company and had declared herself only too willing to look after Hannah for the duration of the meeting.

Horace Mooney, growing impatient, had just called the meeting to order when Ben and Jessie arrived.

"You're late as usual, Chandler!"

"Calm down, Mooney," Will Grant urged with his

usual reasonableness. He and the five other members, all of them male, stood gallantly to their feet as Jessie moved forward to take a seat in the front row. Ben, however, stepped directly up onto the platform, prompting Horace's face to redden with anger.

"What in tarnation do you think you're doing, Ben Chandler? I'm in charge here, and I'll be—"

"My wife was attacked by Foley Keech at school today," Ben announced grimly, disregarding the other man's furious presence at his side. "If not for her quick thinking, as well as the intervention of some of the other boys, the news might be far worse. As it is, my son is at Doc Prater's and Foley Keech has lit out in an effort to escape justice." The room erupted in masculine curses and emphatic demands that something be done, with everyone talking at once and Horace's fancy gavel pounding uselessly.

"Does the sheriff know about this, Ben?" asked Will Grant, raising his voice in order to be heard above the others.

"He does," Ben affirmed with a curt nod.

"I say we form a posse and find the little bastard!" suggested the man seated behind Jessie.

"Hell, Fielding, that won't do no good!" another man exclaimed in disgust. "He could be clean out of the Territory by now!"

"You got a better idea, Humboldt?"

"Yes, by damn, I *do!* It's too late to do anything about the Keech boy, so I say we just leave it to the law and get on with the blasted meeting!"

"You wouldn't be sayin' that if it'd been your woman that got manhandled and your boy lyin' hurt over there at the doctor's."

"Gentlemen, please!" Jessie stood to her feet and whirled to face them. Clasping her hands tightly together in front of her, she cast a troubled look in Ben's direction

319

before saying, "If there's any good to come out of this unfortunate incident, then we must set aside all thoughts of vengeance!"

"Beggin' your pardon, Miss—Mrs. Chandler," said the man whom she recognized as Harmon's father, "but you're an outsider *and* a female. You just plain don't understand these things!"

"I understand enough to know there's nothing to be gained unless we learn from our mistakes!" she countered, her eyes sparkling with indignation at his condescending attitude.

"What mistakes?" challenged Horace Mooney. He refused to be quelled by the fierce gleam in Ben's eyes. "If anyone's made any mistakes here, Mrs. Chandler, it's been you! You're paid to keep your students under control!"

"I cannot be expected to keep them under control if they are like Foley Keech, and I refuse to do so at the point of a gun!" she maintained with a flash of spirit. "You must allow me to practice discretion when it comes to who will pass through the schoolhouse door!"

"Hell, woman, if we—" Horace burst out, only to break off and take an instinctive step backward when Ben rounded on him.

"Talk to her like that again, Mooney," he warned in a voice of deadly calm, "and you'll answer to me."

"If we let you choose your own students, ma'am," another man told Jessie while shooting a worried glance at her tall, powerfully built husband, "then the next thing we know you'll be bringing in greasers and redskins and we'll have a war on our hands!"

"Why, that's absurd!" pronounced Jessie. "If I were free to teach any child who desired an education, then there would most assuredly be no war because of it! And if their parents would but give me the chance then, yes indeed, I would admit *Spanish* and *Indian* children to my school!"

"You do that, Mrs. Chandler, and we'll have to send you right back to St. Louis!" Fielding threatened.

"No we won't," Will Grant dissented quietly, his eyes twinkling as they traveled across to meet Ben's. "I don't think her husband would let her go."

"Let's stop with this claptrap and get on with business!" insisted Kristen's father.

"Humboldt's right!" said the man beside him. "I got to get home and feed my stock!"

Everyone finally agreed on something at that point. Ben gave way to Horace's exalted position of authority and told Jessie he wanted her to step outside for a few minutes while he discussed certain matters with the board. She bristled at his dismissal, but she nevertheless obeyed.

In truth, relieved to escape the tense atmosphere inside the meeting hall, she stepped out onto the boardwalk and wandered over to the hitching post. She raised a hand to one of the horses tied there, idly stroking her fingers down across the long diamond-shaped patch of white on its nose. A faint smile touched her lips when her thoughts drifted back to the way Ben had jumped to her defense a moment ago, then had proven himself to be a typical male in other ways when he had sent her off so he and the others could get on with "man's talk."

Musing wryly that she should be pleased he had allowed her the opportunity to speak at all, she released a sigh and turned back toward the building. A sharp gasp broke from her lips when she came face to face with the man whose dark, hawkish gaze never failed to strike fear in her heart.

"Howdy, schoolmarm," drawled Cole Hagan.

Fifteen

"Get out of my way, Mr. Hagan!" Jessie ordered sharply. Her eyes darted past him to the doorway of the meeting hall. She drew courage from the knowledge that Ben was within earshot if she needed him, then groaned inwardly in dismay at the thought of what might happen if she did call for his intervention. Cole Hagan, she now knew, was a cold-blooded killer.

"I've got something to say to you, *Mrs. Chandler!*" he stated with a quiet, malicious chuckle. All traces of humor vanished in the next instant, however, and his features grew forebodingly sinister. "Your husband's right square in the middle of a fight that isn't his. Either he backs off, or you're going to find yourself a widow before too long!"

"Are you threatening to kill my husband, Mr. Hagan?" she demanded. Although her heart leapt in alarm, she concealed her fright behind a show of proud defiance. "Because if you are, I will not hesitate to inform the authorities. . . ."

"You say a word of this to the sheriff, and that boy of Chandler's won't make it through the night!"

Dear God, James! The color drained from her face, and she clutched at the hitching post for support.

"Surely you—you wouldn't harm an innocent child?" she faltered in horrified disbelief.

"Not if you do as I say," he promised, his eyes narrowing in satisfaction.

"Very well," she murmured, her mind racing. She swallowed hard and forced her gaze to meet Hagan's again. "What is it you want me to do?"

"Just tell Chandler to cut his ties with the Settlers' Organization."

"But . . . why? Why should it matter so much to you that he is involved?"

"Because he's the one leading them, damn it!" the gunslinger muttered through tightly clenched teeth. "Because without him, those bastards'll be nothing more than a bunch of useless, hot-winded steers!" His hands suddenly shot out to grip her arms, and he brought his face so close to hers that she could see the feral glint in his dark eyes. "I'd kill him right now, teacher lady!" he rasped, his voice a strident whisper that burned in her ears. "I'd kill him right now and be done with it if I didn't have orders to bide my time! You'd make a pretty widow, by damn, and I'd see to it you didn't stay lonely! You'd be hot to have a man between your legs again, and I'd be—"

"Stop it!" she cried out hoarsely. "I'll do as you say! Now let me go!"

She twisted in his grasp, then fell heavily against the post when she was abruptly released. No sooner was she free than the sound of Ben's deep voice startled her. Her eyes flew to where he stood framed in the doorway, his gaze fixed upon Cole Hagan with murderous rage.

Suddenly, he lunged forward and brought his fist smashing up against the gunslinger's jaw. Jessie drew in her breath upon a gasp, her eyes growing very wide as she watched Hagan stagger backward to lay sprawled in the dusty street. Ben was on him again in an instant, his handsome features a mask of relentless fury and his

323

whole body tensed for battle. He never gave his wife's persecutor a chance to rise, landing another hard, punishing blow against Hagan's face before the other man had climbed off his knees.

"Ben!" Jessie gathered up her skirts and hurried out into the street. "Ben, please!"

But he would not stop—not yet. He twisted his hand about the front of Hagan's shirt and yanked the man up again.

"Touch my wife again, and I'll kill you!" he ground out.

Hagan tried to fight back, but it was too late. Ben raised his fist one last time and knocked him unconscious. Jessie stared down at the gunslinger who lay bleeding in the dust, and a tremor of heart-stopping dread shot through her.

"What did he say to you, Jessamyn?" demanded Ben, moving forward to tower above her. His face was still a tight mask of fury, his eyes still smoldering at the memory of the other man's hands upon her.

"Nothing!" *God help her, but she couldn't tell him the truth. . . . She couldn't!* "It seems he had mistaken me for someone else!" she lied in a breathless rush. She flushed guiltily beneath his penetrating gaze. Desperate to convince him, she added, "He told me his name is Cole Hagan and that we—we had met before, in Santa Fe!"

"Hagan," echoed Ben, half to himself. Though he had never met the man, he was all too familiar with the name. He looked back to Jessie, but the arrival of the sheriff upon the scene prevented him from questioning her any further at the moment.

Jessie grew faint with relief when the sheriff announced Cole Hagan would be spending the next three nights in jail for "disturbing the peace." She immediately thought of James and gave silent thanks for the fact that he would be safe.

324

If only Ben were safe, she then told herself. She shuddered to think what Cole Hagan might do to avenge himself for the beating he had just received at Ben's hands. Recalling his warning about the Settlers' Organization, she vowed to do everything in her power to persuade Ben to break his ties with the group. Her conscience told her it was wrong to give in to the man's threats, but her heart told her she must. In that moment, she knew she would give her very life to save the man she loved.

Hagan's words continued to burn in her mind as she rode back to the ranch with Ben and Hannah. They drew up in front of the house shortly before nightfall. Martha was, as could be expected, quite distraught at the news of James's injuries. She would have driven her buggy to town right away if Ben had not convinced her that they had to follow the doctor's advice and wait until tomorrow.

Supper at the Chapparosa that night was a somber affair. Afterward, Martha took herself off to bed early and left Hannah sitting on Ben's lap in the parlor. Jessie stood at the window, her emerald gaze full of lingering trepidation as she stared outward and tried, unsuccessfully, to forget about the two separate ordeals of the day.

"Papa, I miss James something awful!" sighed Hannah.

"I know. But he'll be home tomorrow." His features tightened anew at the memory of his son's slender little body lying in the bed at Doc Prater's house. James had awakened only briefly when he had gone in, but he knew he would never forget the way the boy had told him he'd done his best to keep Foley Keech from hurting Jessie.

"Will you sleep in the chair beside my bed tonight?" Hannah pleaded with her father. Her eyes were shining with tears of abject misery. "Please, Papa? I—I don't think I can sleep unless you're there with me!"

Jessie turned away from the window and met her husband's gaze. Her heart pounded crazily when she glimpsed the unmistakable glow of desire in his deep blue eyes.

"It's all right," she assured him, managing a weak smile. "Hannah needs you." She hated the prospect of spending the night without him, but she consoled herself with the thought that they would have a whole lifetime of nights together.

"Maybe it would be better if you slept in Aunt Martha's room," Ben suggested to the little girl. Obviously reluctant to agree, his brow creased into a slight frown when Hannah shook her head.

"No. I don't want Aunt Martha. I want you!"

He knew he was beaten. He couldn't bear to deny her, not when she looked so damnably small and forlorn. Looking back at Jessie, he stood up from the chair and cradled his daughter in his arms.

"Well, Mrs. Chandler, it appears you've been granted a reprieve for tonight—*but only for tonight*," he remarked, his eyes darkening with the promise of passion. Her cheeks grew warm, and she felt a sudden shiver run the length of her spine.

"Good night, my love," she murmured. She would have moved forward to kiss him, but she sensed that would only make things harder for them both. "Good night, Hannah. I hope you sleep well."

"Good night, Jessamyn," the little girl responded, then yawned sleepily. She lay her head down upon her father's shoulder and closed her eyes. "Let's go, Papa."

He sent his beautiful bride one last long, hungry look, then took Hannah off to bed. Jessie heaved a ragged sigh once they had gone. She battled the sudden urge to cry as she left the parlor and sought the loneliness of her own bed, a loneliness she had foolishly believed she would never know again.

It took her a long time to fall asleep. Sometime after midnight, she was awakened by the sound of her door being eased slowly open. Her eyes flew open, and she sat up in bed.

"Ben?" she whispered, her lips instinctively forming his name. She was both surprised and delighted when his deep, wonderfully resonant voice came up to meet her in the starlit darkness.

"Damn it, woman, were you expecting someone else?" he demanded in mock outrage, closing the door behind him.

"Oh, Ben, what are you doing here? What about Hannah?"

"Hannah is sound asleep and has been for hours."

"But . . . why aren't you sleeping?" She moved to the other side of the bed as he lifted the covers and took a seat on the edge of the canopied four-poster. Her pulses raced when she saw that he was wearing nothing but a pair of trousers.

"How the devil could I sleep?" he countered, reaching for her. Although she was already melting inside, she made one last valiant attempt to make them both see reason. She brought her hands up to push weakly against his bare chest before he could pull her against him.

"Hannah will expect you to be there when she awakens in the morning!"

"I will be." In no mood to be denied, he seized her wrists and lifted her arms to entwine about his neck. "It's a long time till morning, wildcat. She'll never know I was gone." He gave a low chuckle of irony and wrapped his strong arms about her nightgown-clad softness, drawing her close. "I guess I ought to be ashamed of myself, sneaking into my wife's room for a few stolen hours of passion while my daughter lies sleeping."

"It—it does feel incredibly wicked, doesn't it?" whispered Jessie, her eyes nonetheless sparkling with delight. She gasped when he pulled her across his lean, granite-hard thighs.

"No, my love," he disagreed, smiling softly down at her. "It feels right."

He lowered his head and took her lips with his own. She gave a low moan of complete surrender and pressed her body into even more intimate contact with his, her arms tightening about his neck and her thinly covered breasts tingling as they came up against the hard warmth of his chest. His hand swept down to tug her nightgown higher, his fingers delving beneath the voluminous folds of sheer white lawn to slide upward along the satiny smoothness of her thigh, then over the bare, alluring curve of her hip.

"Oh, Ben!" she breathed, his mouth relinquishing hers to brand the graceful column of her neck. His large hands roamed appreciatively across her naked derriere.

"You have the most damnably taunting backside, Mrs. Chandler," he murmured. His lips traveled lower to where the deep rounded neckline of the gown revealed a shocking expanse of womanly flesh. "And beautiful breasts," he added in a husky undertone. "Sweet, beautiful breasts." He pressed a series of warm, tenderly provocative kisses across the uppermost curve of her breasts as they rose and fell rapidly beneath the thin cotton.

Jessie stifled another moan when he suddenly tugged the neckline lower, thereby completely freeing one silken rose-tipped globe. His mouth feasted upon it, his warm velvety tongue teasing at the nipple while his lips tenderly suckled. Her head fell back, her long golden tresses shimmering down to her hips while her eyes swept closed in response to the exquisite, near painful ecstasy building to a fever pitch deep within her.

Growing impatient to have all of her, he suddenly left off with the delectable torment and toppled her back

328

upon the bed. He stood and swiftly divested himself of his trousers, then pulled her almost roughly to her knees on the bed and stripped the nightgown from her body with thrilling masterfulness. She shivered as the cool air swept across her naked curves, but she was almost immediately warmed as Ben pressed her back down to the feather mattress and covered her soft body with the powerful, splendidly virile hardness of his.

"I love you, Ben Chandler!" she whispered fervently, her arms curling about the corded muscles of his neck as her body strained upward against his. "I—I love you so very much!"

"I love you too, Jessamyn," he declared in a quiet, solemn tone. He peered closely down at her in the darkness, his eyes able to make out the look of impassioned sincerity on her beautiful face. "More than I ever thought possible. So damned much that I would kill any man who tried to take you from me!"

Her mind was plagued by the sudden unbidden image of Cole Hagan's malevolent features. But she hastily pushed all thought of him aside, determined that nothing should spoil the precious moments she and Ben were able to share.

"I am yours forever," she assured him, her luminous emerald gaze reflecting all the love in her heart. "As you have claimed more than once, my dearest husband, I have been yours since the night we were *married* in the Apaches' camp!"

"You've no idea how much I wanted to take you then," he confided hoarsely, his eyes darkening at the memory. "I did everything in my power to fight against it. Little did I know I had already lost the battle."

"Do you think Gray Wolf knows?" she asked, her silken brow creasing into a slight pensive frown. "Do you think he knows how well his plan succeeded?"

"He knows," Ben affirmed. His mouth curved into a

329

faint sardonic smile. "But for once, we share the same victory."

Jessie moaned softly when his lips finally descended upon hers. She clung to him as desire flared between them. His hands set up a bold, ardently persuasive exploration of her naked curves, while his mouth ravished the willing sweetness of hers. She grew emboldened after a few moments and began smoothing her hands down across the magnificent hard-muscled expanse of his back, then lower to the lean roundness of his hips. He gave a low groan when her fingers crept around to the front of his taut thighs with beguiling innocence, and she heard his sharp intake of breath when her hand suddenly closed about his manhood. Her eyes glowed with feminine triumph at the realization that her touch was capable of returning the favor of passion's sweet torment.

"Damn it, woman, do you want to drive me mad?" he growled with pleasure, his mouth traveling across to tease at the delicate flesh of her earlobe.

"Yes!" she retorted breathlessly.

It was her turn to beg for mercy soon thereafter, when he made it clear he intended to kiss every square inch of her pliant, captivating body. Only after he had rendered her nearly mindless with longing did he relent. Her eyelids fluttered open when she found herself being turned facedown again, but the unspoken question in her mind was answered in the most deliciously satisfying manner in the next moment.

His hands gripping her slender waist, he pulled her firmly up to her knees and back against him where he knelt behind her. She felt her thighs spreading wider when his strong fingers insinuated themselves between the soft pink folds of womanly flesh to stroke gently at the tiny bud of passion. Her breath was coming in short gasps by the time his hands curled about her shapely bottom and held her ready for the final blending of their bodies.

Jessie cried out softly when the hard instrument of his masculine desire sheathed up to the hilt within her feminine passage. She strained back against him, her face flushed with the most intense pleasure she had ever known as she met his loving thrusts. Her hips matched the skillful, rapturously demanding rhythm of his, and she moaned in delight when his hands came up to close upon her breasts. Together, she and her beloved were borne ever upward to reach the very pinnacle of fulfillment, the two of them tensing almost in unison as they achieved the ultimate satisfaction that was a perfect combination of heaven and earth.

Hannah never suspected a thing. When she awoke the following morning, her eyes immediately sought her father. She was greeted with the welcome sight of him in the chair, unaware that he had only returned there to fall asleep less than two hours earlier.

Three new students, all girls, were waiting in front of the schoolhouse when Jessie rode up with Ben and Hannah later that same morning. Discovering that they were the daughters of the talkative young matron who would have been her hostess if not for Ben's fateful intervention, Jessie battled the temptation to ask them why they had not come before. She suspected that it was because their mother had been greatly offended by the abrupt change in the schoolteacher's living arrangements. Whatever the reason, she was happy to welcome the three fair-haired sisters to school.

Ben rode away with the promise of returning that afternoon. Hannah could scarcely contain her excitement at the prospect of fetching James home, and she proceeded to ask Jessie the time of day at least a half-dozen times throughout the morning alone.

The children spoke little of the previous day's incident, a fact for which Jessie was relieved. She wanted nothing more than to put the ordeal behind her and get on with the business at hand. Although she met with almost complete success in regard to Foley Keech, she was unable to keep her thoughts from straying frequently back to Cole Hagan's threats.

Two days, she recalled, her pulses racing with dread at the thought. *Hagan would be free in two days time.* She vowed to speak to Ben about the Settlers' Organization when they were alone at the ranch later; she would not allow herself to even consider the possibility that he would deny her request. He had to agree. . . . He had to!

Four o'clock finally came. Jessie dismissed school for the day, an indulgent smile touching her lips when Hannah bounded impatiently up from the bench and went flying outside to where Ben waited. He had brought the wagon so that James could lie down if need be.

He tied the reins of the two other horses to the back of the wagon, then lifted Jessie and Hannah up to the wooden seat. Clouds had gathered in the sky to blur the sunlight, but there was fortunately no sign of rain.

"As soon as we get James back to the Chapparosa, I'll be heading out again," Ben told Jessie before they had traveled far along the rough, deeply furrowed road. Hannah sat between them, appearing unusually preoccupied as she stared down at the book in her hand.

"Heading out?" echoed Jessie, frowning in puzzlement. "Where are you going?"

"Elizabethtown. I'll be back tonight, but it may be midnight or after." He smiled at the sudden look of consternation crossing her features. "Don't worry, I'll be careful not to wake you." His pulses leapt when he glimpsed the rosy color warming her cheeks.

"Oh, I wouldn't mind," she murmured softly, her eyes

332

falling in embarrassment when she recalled Hannah's presence. Ben merely chuckled.

"Aren't you even curious, Mrs. Chandler, about what's taking me away from you?" he challenged, his blue eyes full of loving amusement.

"I naturally assumed, Mr. Chandler, that you would enlighten me!" she retorted saucily. Her own humor abruptly faded at his answer.

"I've got to attend a meeting. Martha said she'd told you something of the problem the settlers' are facing." His gaze kindled with sudden anger, and his handsome features tensed. "Things are getting worse. I'm going to do all I can to see that no one gets hurt."

"But why must you get involved?" she demanded, feeling sick inside as Hagan's face swam before her eyes again. "I—I have heard the company will not hesitate to employ violent means to get what they want. Oh, Ben, please don't go!"

"I have to, Jessamyn," he told her quietly. There was a set, grimly determined look about him that sent a tremor of alarm coursing through her.

"Why? The ownership of your land is not under question! Why then must you—"

"Because these people are my neighbors. They deserve a chance to make a life for themselves here. That's all they're asking, just to be left in peace to raise their stock and grow their crops. Damn it, I can't stand by and do nothing while they're driven off their land!"

"But what if it *isn't* their land?" she pointed out. "What if the final ruling is in favor of the company?"

"We'll deal with that if and when it comes. But I wouldn't be in this if I didn't believe in the settlers' cause, Jessamyn," he declared, a dull glow in his eyes now. "And we've come too far to turn back now."

"Even if it means your own life is in danger?"

"A man can't allow fear to rule him, especially not in

333

this country."

"If you refuse to consider yourself, then perhaps you will stop to consider your family!" she remarked feelingly, desperation making her temper flare. "What would we do if something happened to you? For heaven's sake, Ben Chandler, your children need you. . . . *I* need you!"

"I've no intention of letting anything happen to me," he asserted with unwavering confidence. "But neither do I intend to back down just because some unscrupulous bastards decide to make a show of force." He, too, thought of Cole Hagan, as well as the other hired guns the company had brought in to the Territory. "We'll fight fire with fire if we have to, Jessamyn. And we'll not stop until this thing is settled once and for all," he vowed in a low tone edged with steel.

Although Jessie was sorely tempted to say more, she was forced to concede that she had lost this first round. She fell silent and turned her flashing troubled gaze upon the passing landscape.

"Papa?" Hannah looked up at him at last. "Maybe the Indians could help."

"The Indians?"

"Yes," she confirmed, nodding her head so that her long blond pigtails swept forward across her shoulders. "I'll bet they would like the company to lose, too."

"What makes you think that?" he asked, schooling his features to remain perfectly serious in spite of the urge to smile down at her.

"Because I heard Aunt Martha say the company wants to take away the land they're supposed to get. She told Consuela that Mr. Easton and some other men were trying to make the government give the Indians the land to live on, but that the company was going to take it away. So," the little girl concluded, "maybe the Indians would

334

like to help you."

"They might," allowed Ben, a faint smile touching his lips now, "but I'm afraid their help wouldn't be enough."

"All the same," she persisted, "you should ask them." She turned to Jessie then and questioned, with a child's usual flight of thought, "Do you think Aunt Martha is going to marry Mr. Easton?"

"Why, I—I don't know!" Jessie stammered in surprise. She met Ben's gaze, and her anger with him was conquered by the warmth in his eyes.

"He hasn't asked her yet, but Aunt Martha told Consuela she thinks he's going to," Hannah went on to reveal. She heaved a sigh and leaned against Jessie, who placed an arm about her shoulders. "I don't want her to leave, but I don't want her to be sad. People are sad when they can't be with people they love." She was thinking of her brother again, but Ben and Jessie were thinking of one another.

"That's very true," said Jessie, her heart twisting painfully at the thought of anything happening to the stubborn, devilishly handsome man she loved. She hugged the little girl close as the wagon's wheels rolled and bounced on their way across the beautiful cloud-shadowed prairie.

James, as the three other Chandlers soon discovered, seemed quite his old self again. The only visible evidence of Foley's aggression against him was a faint purplish bruise on the side of his face and the sight of his arm in a sling. He was in high spirits by the time they arrived at Doc Prater's house to fetch him, although Mrs. Prater declared him to have been a model patient.

Hannah made no secret of her delight in seeing him. Although he displayed typical boyish embarrassment at his sister's outburst of affection, he returned the bear hug she gave him and did not even turn his unbruised cheek away from her kiss. The doctor assured Ben and Jessie that James was completely recovered from the concussion he had suffered. His arm would have to remain in a sling for a day or two longer, but there was fortunately no permanent damage.

Hannah insisted upon riding in the wagonbed with her brother as they headed toward home. Ben drew his wife close beside him on the seat and held the reins with one practiced hand.

"You'll sleep in my room tonight, schoolmarm," he decreed in a deep-timbred undertone meant only for her ears.

"I'm not at all certain I should," she responded with a dramatic little sigh.

"And why the devil not?"

"Because I recall all too clearly what happened the last time I set foot in your room!"

"We're married now, damn it," he reminded her with a disarming grin. "You don't have to worry about what anyone else thinks."

"It isn't that." She had just thought of a new tactic with which to try and prevail upon him to stay home from the meeting. It was not a particularly clever one and certainly not one she wished to resort to, but she knew of no other. And heaven help her, she had to do *something!*

"Then what is it?" demanded Ben, his dark brows knitting together in a frown.

"Don't expect me to welcome you with open arms when you return from the meeting," she threatened with deceptive composure. "If you insist upon going— knowing full well that I am strongly opposed to your involvement—then you might as well be prepared to spend the night alone!"

"You don't mean that, Jessamyn." His voice dropped to a low, dangerously even level.

"Oh, but I do!" she asserted, forcing herself to remain adamant. She was tempted to tell him about Cole Hagan's threats but admitted to herself that he would be even more determined to go if he knew. Thus, although she was heartsick at the idea of denying them both the physical closeness they yearned for, she warned him, "I mean it, Ben. Either you have your meeting—or you have me." To emphasize the point, she slid to the opposite end of the seat.

He said nothing for several long moments. Facing straight ahead, with his attention seemingly focused on the road before them, he gave no hint of the battle waging within him. Hurt and fury mingled in his breast. It required every ounce of self-will for him to refrain from pulling the wagon to a halt and having it out with his damnably headstrong bride right there and then. If not for the presence of his children, he would have done just that.

When he finally turned his head to look at Jessie again, she blanched inwardly at the fierce, smoldering gleam in his eyes. An involuntary shiver of alarm coursed down her spine, and she realized that she had made a terrible mistake.

"I love you, Jessamyn," he told her in a quiet, simmering tone that was scarcely more than a whisper. "I love you more than life itself. But so help me, if you ever make such a threat again, I'll not hesitate to beat your pretty backside until you can't sit for a week. I won't let you run roughshod over me, wildcat, no matter how much I love you."

Jessie swallowed hard and felt a wave of pure misery washing over her. It was all she could do to keep from cyring out that she was sorry and hadn't meant a word of it. But she was both too proud and too much in love to let herself give in. She had to be strong if she ever hoped to sway him. Dear God, she had to save him from his own accursed sense of duty and honor!

Stealing a quick sideways look at him, she was dismayed to observe the grim set of his jaw. She battled the sudden urge to cry as an awful silence rose between them, a silence that remained unbroken for the duration of the trip home.

Sixteen

"Don't worry, my dear, I'm quite sure he will be home soon," Martha assured Jessie, though her words lacked the necessary conviction. She cast a glance toward the clock on the mantel, noting with an inward frown that it was only a little after nine. As she knew only too well, the meetings could drag on for hours. It was not at all unusual for Ben to get home after midnight.

"If only that were true," murmured Jessie. She heaved a disconsolate sigh and wandered back to the fireplace.

The twins had been abed for over an hour. Normally, Martha would have retired by now as well. But she had sensed the younger woman's need for company. It had not escaped her notice how the newlyweds had parted earlier that evening with scarcely a word to one another.

"Oh, good heavens!" Martha now exclaimed at a sudden thought. "I completely forgot to tell you. . . . A letter came for you! Curly brought it back with him from town earlier today." She smiled, and her eyes glowed with a knowing light as she rose to her feet. "I don't think he had planned on riding into Cimarron. William was here this morning, however, and happened to make mention of the fact that Lissa Boone had taken a spill down a flight of stairs at the hotel yesterday afternoon."

"Lissa?" Jessie hastily turned away from her pre-occupied scrutiny of the flames. Her emerald gaze was wide and clouded with sharp concern. "Dear God, is she—"

"It's nothing serious," the petite brunette hurried to set her mind at ease. "Only a twisted ankle. She and James would make quite a pair right now." She smiled ruefully before adding, "Curly did not remain in town very long. I don't think his visit there was a particularly satisfying one."

Martha swept gracefully from the room, only to reappear a few moments later with the letter addressed simply: *Miss Jessamyn Clare, Cimarron, New Mexico Territory.*

Jessie took the proffered missive and quickly opened it. Her face lit with pleasure when she saw that it was from her brother Andrew. She had only written to her family once, to tell them of her marriage, but Jessie knew that it would probably not reach St. Louis for several days, perhaps even weeks.

She scanned the letter first, then read it word for word. Finally, she sank down into the chair beside the fireplace and battled a sudden wave of homesickness. Her eyes glistened with unshed tears, and her hand trembled a bit when she lowered Andrew's hastily penned communication to her lap.

"Is it bad news, Jessie?" Martha probed gently.

"No," she answered, her mouth curving into a rather wan smile. "My brother writes that all is well. It's just that—that I hadn't realized how very much I missed them." Indeed, she had been so busy with the school of late, and so blissfully happy with Ben—until now. His angry remoteness had pained her to her very soul.

"Perhaps you will be able to visit them some time in the near future," the older woman offered soothingly.

"Perhaps," murmured Jessie. Perhaps sooner than

340

she hoped, she thought, her heart feeling almost unbearably heavy. Like many another bride, she was devastated by the first real quarrel with her new husband and feared nothing would ever be right again.

By the time she said good night to Martha and trudged wearily down the hallway to her room, her sorrow was beginning to give way to resentment. She still feared for Ben's safety, but she would not allow herself to face the possibility of anything but his safe return. Plagued by a combination of anxiety and bitter hurt, she unfastened her lavender muslin gown and virtually yanked it up over her head.

She told herself, in growing indignation, that Ben had no right to treat her like a child. His attitude toward her had been inexcusably overbearing and unfair. Her green eyes flashed as she recalled the fact that he had actually threatened to subject her to the humiliation of physical chastisement.

"You wouldn't dare, Ben Chandler!" she murmured defiantly. She stripped off her undergarments, pulled on her nightgown, and turned out the lamp. Gaining some small measure of satisfaction by slipping beneath the covers of her own bed—*not* Ben's—she punched at the unresisting softness of the pillow and lay down.

She tossed and turned restlessly for what seemed like hours. Her mind refused to grant her a respite from her troubles. Tormented alternately by visions of Ben in terrible danger and the irrational but nonetheless persistent fear that her marriage had suffered irreparable damage, she gazed toward the window and listened to the various distinctive sounds of the night.

Finally, sleep conquered the merciless state of wakefulness. Her belated slumber soon became such a deep and dreamless state of unconsciousness that it was several long moments before she awakened to the reality of being lifted from her bed and carried down the darkened hallway by two strong, familiar arms.

"Ben?" she whispered drowsily. Her eyelids fluttered open to reveal the sight of his handsome face as he bore her into the lamplit warmth of his room. Alarm shot through her when she then became aware of the grimly determined look upon his features and the fierce, almost savage gleam in his eyes. "Ben, wha—what are you doing?" she demanded in a small, breathless voice.

"Taking you where you belong, damn it!" he ground out. He kicked the door shut with his booted heel and strode over to the bed with his shocked, unprotesting burden. A loud gasp broke from her lips when he tossed her unceremoniously down upon the quilt-covered mattress.

Her anger with him came back to hit her full force. She scrambled up to her knees on the bed, her long hair cascading down about her face and shoulders in glorious disarray and her eyes blazing their magnificent deep green fire. Though her heart exulted in her beloved's safe return, her mind and the recent memories of hurt and resentment contained within its turbulent depths reigned supreme.

"I will not remain here with you!" she vowed hotly. "If you think you can bend me to your will so easily, then you are very much mistaken!"

"You're my wife, Jessamyn," he reminded her in a dangerously even tone, his gaze burning down into the storminess of hers. With slow, deliberate movements, he began unbuttoning his blue cotton shirt. "A man must be master of his own household. And I'll be damned if I'll let you defy me in this or anything else!"

"Why, you—you are not my *master!*" she sputtered in furious denial. "We are no longer in the Dark Ages, and I am a grown woman, not a child!"

"Then act like one!" he shot back. He yanked off the shirt and flung it aside. A sudden warmth crept over

342

Jessie, and she had to swallow hard before continuing.

"You are without a doubt the most dictatorial, pigheaded, infuriating man I have ever known! I warned you what would happen if you went to that meeting, but you would not listen! I refuse to play the role of a docile, mousy wife who waits meekly and obediently at home while her 'lord and master' is off doing whatever he pleases! As I told you before, Ben Chandler, I have a mind of my own and I intend to use it!"

She sprang from the bed and flew to the door in a desperate, ultimately futile attempt to escape. Ben was in no mood to let her go. His hand seizing her about the arm, he spun her about and sent her tumbling facedown over his broad shoulder. She kicked and twisted as he carried her back to the bed, then cried out sharply when his large hand came up to administer a hard, punishing smack upon the squirming roundness of her conveniently placed bottom.

In the end, she was powerless to prevent him from flinging her back down on the mattress. She landed with a hard bounce, and her eyes kindled with even more anger as a result of such rough treatment.

"I won't let your blasted stubbornness deny us both what we want, you little witch!" Ben told her, his voice whipcord sharp and his gaze smoldering with a highly volatile combination of fury and desire as it raked over his willful young bride. Tempted to either spank her or kiss her until she begged for mercy, he groaned inwardly and sought to regain control over his perilously rising temper.

"I don't want this!" countered Jessie, too enraged to admit the truth. Pushing herself back up to her knees, she lifted her chin in a gesture of dauntless spirit and met Ben's fiery, penetrating gaze without flinching. She had no idea how incredibly desirable she looked, with her full breasts heaving angrily beneath the thin cotton of her nightgown and her beautiful face flushed with the force of her emotions. "If you truly loved me, you would not have gone to that meeting and you—you would not be doing this to me now!"

"I love you, wildcat," he declared in a low, vibrant tone, his passions inflamed almost beyond endurance. "You've no cause to doubt that. But I still have to do what's right. It was right for me to take a stand against tyranny—and it's right for me to have my wife in my bed." His hands closed firmly about her waist.

"No!" She was dismayed to feel the familiar weakness descending upon her, and she made a valiant attempt to fight against it. Struggling in Ben's possessive grasp, she pushed at his bronzed sinewy arms and tried to slide from the bed again. "We cannot settle our differences this way!" she insisted weakly.

"We can and will."

She gasped when he suddenly yanked her up hard against him. His arms were like bands of steel as they imprisoned her on the edge of the bed, and she murmured an unintelligible protest before his mouth came crashing relentlessly down upon hers.

A low moan of passion rose in Jessie's throat. She could not prevent her own arms from wrapping tightly about his neck, and she pressed feverishly against him as though her soft body could not be fitted close enough to the hard warmth of his. Desire, greatly heightened by their anger, flared wild and hot between them. Their lips met in a fiery, ravenous kiss that left them both gasping for breath.

One of Ben's hands moved urgently to the fastening of his trousers, while the other swept down to clasp his bride about her thinly covered buttocks. Before she quite knew what was happening, he had turned around and taken a seat on the edge of the bed, pulling her down upon his lap so that she faced him. Her silken limbs were parted to rest on either side of the powerfully muscled length of his, and she blushed rosily at the bold intimacy of her position.

But she was not in the least bit inclined to deny him whatever he wished to do with her. She clung to his shoulders while his lips, finally relinquishing the well-conquered softness of hers, seared a fiery path downward to the rapid rise and fall of her full young bosom. She inhaled sharply when his hands suddenly came up to close upon her breasts, and her eyes flew open when, in the next instant, he impatiently ripped the sheer white fabric in his efforts to bare the satiny rose-tipped globes. His mouth roamed hungrily, ardently across her naked breasts, while his hands curled about her hips to urge her farther upward for his moist caress.

"Ben . . . *please!*" she begged, her passions demanding a release from the delectable torture he was inflicting with such loving mastery.

She caught her breath on another gasp when he moved his legs farther apart, thereby forcing her thighs to spread even wider. He yanked up the hem of her nightgown so that her bare bottom rested on the taut denim-clad leanness of his thighs.

"*Oh, Ben!*" she whispered raggedly as his strong fingers took full advantage of her shocking position and closed upon the silky triangle of golden hair, setting up a splendidly, rapturously compelling exploration of the delicate pink flesh concealed within.

Jessie moaned softly, her naked hips squirming restlessly upon his thighs and her beautiful breasts tingling beneath the warm, exquisitely skillful adoration of his lips and tongue. Her breath was nothing but a series of gasps now, and she was certain she would faint with the sheer pleasure of the sensations her husband was creating within her.

Just when she was certain she could bear no more, Ben

lifted her hips and brought her down upon his throbbing masculinity. Her hoarse cry was silenced by the returning pressure of his lips upon hers. His hands remained clasped about her smooth, firmly rounded derriere as she rode atop him. Her hands clutched almost convulsively about his shoulders, and she met his demanding thrusts with an impassioned fervor that both delighted and surprised him.

Passion took flight, spiraling ever upward to fulfillment, then subsiding into the sweet aftermath that knew no equal. Ben wrapped his arms about the languid, trembling body of his wife and lowered her back to the bed. He stretched out beside her, his own head still spinning from their wildly impassioned union as he drew her lovingly against him.

When she was finally able to speak again, Jessie released a sigh of utter contentment and remarked, in a tremulous little voice, "It seems, Mr. Chandler, that I am completely powerless to resist you."

"And I you, wildcat," he responded with a soft chuckle, his hand smoothing downward to where her nightgown was tangled up about her hips. "Damn it, woman, I hope you've learned your lesson once and for all."

"Oh, I doubt very seriously that I have." She sighed again and snuggled closer to his hard warmth. "I fear you will be forced to remind me on a regular basis." The prospect delighted them both.

"Things will sure as hell never be dull," he murmured, his gaze brimming with wry amusement.

"Would you want them to be?"

"Maybe in another fifty years I will."

"And then what?" she challenged, raising up on one elbow to cast him a saucy smile.

"Then, Mrs. Chandler, I'll be doing my damnedest to keep up with you." His deep blue eyes twinkled roguishly

346

across at her, then darkened with renewed passion when they strayed lower to where the torn neckline of her gown revealed a tantalizing glimpse of her breasts. Jessie, noting the direction of his gaze, flushed warmly again and settled back down against him.

"You're a wicked man, my dearest husband!" she charged affectionately.

"Maybe. But I must have done something good sometime, since Providence saw fit to give you to me." He gathered her up against him, his lips pressing a tender kiss upon the top of her head while his eyes swept closed. "I love you, Jessamyn. Dear God, how I love you!" His deep voice was full of raw emotion, and Jessie felt tears springing to her eyes.

"I love you too, Ben. And I—I'm sorry for the way I behaved. It's just that I can't bear the thought of anything happening to you!"

"Nothing is going to happen to me," he assured her.

"How can you know that?" she argued feelingly. "You are not invincible, Ben Chandler!"

"What's got you so worried all of a sudden?" he demanded, his handsome brow creasing into a frown. "Why did it matter so much to you that I stay home tonight?"

"I've heard so much talk of violence, and I was afraid you would be in danger," she answered truthfully.

"I'm in no more danger than any of the other men—probably less."

"What do you mean?"

"The company doesn't want to see me dead," he answered with a faint smile of irony. "There's already been one martyr to the settlers' cause; they don't want another." His features tightened, and his voice was edged with a sudden fury when he said enigmatically, "I didn't want to tell you, but I know you'll find out about it in the morning."

347

"Find out about what?" She raised up again and peered closely down at him as the lamp's soft golden glow cast long shadows on the wall.

"Humboldt's barn was burned while he was at the meeting tonight," he disclosed, his tone one of deadly calm. "His wife and children were awakened by the sound of gunshots. The barn was already engulfed in flames by the time they got outside. They saw four men riding away, but it was too dark for them to be able to identify the bastards."

"Oh, Ben, no!" Jessie breathed in horror, shuddering to think of Kristen and her family in such peril.

"We've no proof that it was the company," added Ben. "But Humboldt had paid a visit to the office of their attorneys in Santa Fe last week and demanded they do something about the eviction notice he had been served with."

"Eviction notice?" she echoed. "Good heavens, you mean they're trying to make him leave?"

"They are. And he's not the only one." He gazed solemnly across at her, his hand smoothing a wayward curl from her face. "Maybe now you can understand why I can't do as you ask. Damn it, Jessamyn, you can't expect me to stand by and watch while Humboldt and all the others are driven from their homes by a few greedy, powerful men who want to make the Territory their own personal kingdom. I wouldn't be who and what I am if I allowed that to happen without lifting a hand to prevent it. This land is my home—it's your home now as well—and I'm going to do everything I can to make sure it doesn't fall under the control of those 'foreign investors' who haven't a clue what it means to those of us who live here!"

Jessie swallowed a sudden lump in her throat and lowered her head back to his chest. She listened to the strong, steady pounding of his heart and knew herself defeated. Though she still feared what Cole Hagan might do, she realized there was no way she would ever be able to convince Ben to abandon the cause he so fervently believed in. Her heart swelled with love and pride for the man she had married, and she prayed that what he had said about the company wanting him alive was true.

Kristen was absent from school the following day. None of the Sheltons were in attendance, either, a fact that puzzled Jessie greatly. Except for Ned, she reflected, they had not missed a single day since the beginning. She wondered if they had perhaps been subjected to the same sort of treachery as the Humboldts, then told herself it was useless to speculate. Determining to pay a visit to their farm on her way home that afternoon, she climbed the steps of the schoolhouse and opened the door.

Billy Shelton provided the answer to the mystery when he came riding up just as she was preparing to ring the bell. She grew worried when she observed the unusually somber look on his impish freckled features.

"What is it, Billy?" she asked urgently. "What has happened?"

"Ned's got the measles, Mrs. Chandler," he replied without dismounting.

"The measles?" she echoed, her pulses leaping in alarm.

"Ma said I was to come tell you we won't be back in school for a while," he announced with genuine regret. "Doc Prater says Ned's just the first; the rest of us'll probably get sick, too. I reckon he'll be by to talk to you when he gets done talkin' to Ma."

"Thank you for coming, Billy," Jessie responded calmly, though her mind was awhirl with terrible thoughts of an epidemic. She knew all too well that an outbreak of measles could prove deadly. "And please give

349

my regards to Ned. Tell him I—I hope he is feeling better soon."

"I will, Mrs. Chandler." He appeared to want to say more, but instead reined about and urged his horse back down to the road. Although he lifted his hand in a wave when Harmon and the two O'Leary brothers called after him, he did not look back.

Jessie's throat constricted as she watched him go. *Measles,* her mind repeated the dreaded word. Dear God, she thought, what if some of the other students fell ill? . . . What if James and Hannah . . .

"Mrs. Chandler?" She looked down to see that Mary Sue was on the verge of tears.

"What's wrong, Mary Sue?" she asked in a pre-occupied manner.

"John said I was fat!"

"Well, you're not. You're just . . . pleasingly plump," Jessie assured her. "And the next time John or anyone else makes such an unkind remark, you would do well to behave as though you were not in the least bit affected by it."

"My father says the O'Learys are nothing but Irish hooligans!" the little girl proclaimed in a lofty manner, her recovery amazingly rapid. "He says that Mr. O'Leary is a drunk who—"

"That's quite enough, Mary Sue!" Jessie reprimanded sharply. "If you do not wish to be insulted yourself, then you must not go about saying hurtful things about others."

"Even if they're true?" retorted Mary Sue. "My father says—"

"And you must not keep repeating everything your father says!"

"Yes, ma'am," Mary Sue agreed with obvious reluctance.

Jessie lifted her hands to the rope and proceeded to

350

ring the bell at last. The children filed inside. She led them in the pledge of allegiance, then instructed them to take their seats and open their primers. Doc Prater appeared in the doorway soon thereafter, and she hastened forward to speak to him.

"I understand Billy Shelton has already told you of his brother's illness," the doctor said quietly. Jessie nodded.

"How serious a case is it?" she asked, her eyes full of concern.

"From all indications thus far, it does not appear too bad. But he could easily take a turn for the worst before it's over with." He paused for a moment, his brows knitting into a thoughtful frown while he ran a hand over the graying thickness of his beard. Tossing a glance toward the children, he told Jessie, "I'm afraid you'll have to close the school for a while, Mrs. Chandler."

"Close the school?" she repeated in dismay.

"At least until this thing has run its course. You never know. . . . Ned could be the only one, but we can't take that chance. I've instructed Mr. Shelton to keep her children at home. It's best if the remainder of your students avoid contact with one another as well."

"But, how long do you think—?"

"A week. Maybe two. And you should send them home now, without delay." He sighed heavily, his frown deepening and his gaze troubled. "There's very little any of us can do. We can only pray the illness does not sweep the area's entire population. It's always the children who suffer most. And the Indians."

"The Indians?" She watched as he nodded grimly.

"They have far less immunity to our diseases than we do," he explained. "To make matters worse, most of them won't allow themselves to be tended by the white man's medicine." Turning to leave again, he lifted his hat to his head and smiled faintly. "Good day, Mrs. Chandler. Send the children home. God willing, I won't be seeing any of them again for a while."

"Good day, Doctor," murmured Jessie. On legs that suddenly felt very heavy, she moved back to the front of the room and stood beside her desk. Her gaze traveled over the bright, innocent young faces of her students, and a knot tightened in the very pit of her stomach. Her heart twisted painfully at the thought of any of them being struck down by the disease. *Please, God, please don't let anything happen to them.*

"Children," she said, her voice betraying none of the alarm she was trying so hard to quell, "the doctor has advised me to close the school for a time. Ned Shelton has come down with a case of the measles, and we must take every precaution to make sure the disease does not spread among you. It is necessary for you to avoid contact with one another. Therefore, I must suspend our studies indefinitely. I will send word when the doctor thinks it safe for us to resume. Please go directly home now and relate to your parents all I have said."

"Is Ned going to die?" John blurted out.

"We—we must pray that he recovers," answered Jessie, choosing her words carefully. "He will be very ill and in need of our prayers." She could not in all honesty deny the possibility of his death, and yet she did not want to frighten her students. "You may take your books with you," she told them, forcing a smile to her lips, "and please don't forget your lunch pails. Good-bye, children. I have every confidence we shall see one another again soon."

She fought back tears as she watched them leave. James and Hannah waited for her on the front steps while she cast one last wistful look inside and closed the door.

"What are we going to do now, Jessie?" asked James.

"Papa won't like it if we ride all the way back to the ranch by ourselves," Hannah pointed out.

"I know," Jessie admitted with a troubled sigh. "But

we have little choice in the matter."

"We could catch up with Doc Prater!" suggested James, his eyes lighting at the idea. "He wouldn't mind if we rode along with him to town!"

"All right," Jessie agreed, smiling down at him. "I should like to pay a visit to Miss Boone, anyway, and I did hear your Aunt Martha say she was planning to take the wagon into Cimarron for supplies this morning."

"We can buy Papa a birthday gift while we're there!" Hannah proclaimed at a sudden thought.

"When is his birthday?" asked Jessie, musing once again that she still had so very much to learn about the man she had married.

"Next Tuesday," supplied James. "Aunt Martha said she remembers when he was born. I'll bet he used to look just like me!"

"Not when he was born he didn't!" Hannah retorted with typical sisterly exasperation.

They each took one of Jessie's hands and led her down to the stream to fetch the horses. She was actually beginning to feel comfortable in the saddle and no longer suffered from the embarrassing soreness that had plagued her for a number of days. Of course, she then reflected with an inward blush at the wicked turn of her thoughts, she no longer awakened with the soreness caused by other "activity," either.

Martha and Curly had already arrived in town by the time they got there. Curly was nowhere in sight, but they spied Martha preparing to step inside Hunt's General Store.

"Aunt Martha!" the twins called out as they slid from their horses and looped the reins about the hitching post. Jessie dismounted as well, endeavoring to keep her skirts down about her stockinged legs when she swung to the ground.

"Why, what on earth are you two doing here?"

Martha asked in surprise when James and Hannah bounded up onto the boardwalk in front of her.

"Ned Shelton's got the measles and we're not going to have any more school!" James told her in an excited rush.

"Measles?" she echoed breathlessly. The word struck fear in her heart, just as it had Jessie's. Her gaze shifted to the younger woman. "Oh, Jessie, is it true?"

"I'm afraid so. The doctor stopped by this morning on his way home from the Shelton's place. He advised me to close the school."

"Thank God the twins have already had the measles!" remarked Martha. At Jessie's expression of surprise, she explained, "They were much too young to remember. It was only a few months after I had come to live at the Chapparosa." She shook her head at the awful memory. "The poor little things were so terribly ill. Ben was like a man possessed. He refused to leave their side, neglecting his own health until the worst had finally passed. They recovered very quickly, but I'll never forget how close we came to losing them." She sighed, then smiled down at the children again and said, "Since you're here, perhaps you'd care to help me choose the supplies we need."

"We have to get a gift for Papa!" reiterated Hannah.

"We certainly do," Martha agreed. She looked back to Jessie, and her eyes sparkled mischievously when she told her, "Curly has taken himself off to the St. James."

"In that case, I suppose I had better postpone my visit to Lissa," Jessie responded with an answering twinkle. Hoping her friend would finally gather the courage to tell Curly the truth, she accompanied Martha and the children into the store.

At that same moment, Lissa and her lean, would-be suitor were facing one another across the front desk in the lobby. Curly stood gazing down somberly at the tall redhead, who sat with her bandaged ankle propped up on a footstool and the account books spread before her on the surface of the massive walnut desk.

"I'm sorry, Curly, but it's no use!"

"You're stubborn, Lissa. Too damned stubborn for your own good."

"Maybe for mine, but not for yours!" she retorted with a defiant toss of her head. Her titian locks threatened to spill out of their pins, and her small but well-rounded bosom heaved beneath the bodice of her white shirtwaist. "There are so many things you don't know about me, and I—"

"I don't need to know."

"Yes you do!"

"Why?" he countered, his eyes darkening. "I don't care what you've done or where you've been. All I care about is the way you are now."

Lissa's heart stirred at his words, and her eyes glistened with sudden tears. Dropping her gaze back down to the books, she forced herself to say coolly, "Thank you for your kind offer, Mr. Taylor. I regret, however, that I cannot accept."

She was unprepared for what happened next. With uncharacteristic violence, Curly bit out a curse and came storming around the desk. Lissa gasped as he grabbed her by the arms and yanked her up from the chair, his steely arm clamping about her waist so that he literally swept her off her feet.

"Curly!" she breathed, her eyes flying about in alarm. "Someone might—"

"You listen to me, woman!" he commanded in a low, furious tone. "I love you! I've never loved anyone before, and I'm damned sure not going to stop now just because you've got some fool notion you're not good enough for me!"

"It isn't that!" she protested weakly. "It's just—"

"Shut up and let me finish!" he ground out, his gaze

355

searing mercilessly down into hers. "Either you get it through your head once and for all that you're mine, or I'm going to have to prove it to you!"

"Wha—what do you mean?" Another gasp broke from her lips when his arm tightened about her.

"I mean, Lissa Boone, that I'm going to grow tired of waiting!" he threatened. "One day, I'm going to throw you across my saddle and carry you off! By damn, I'll make you forget all about whatever it is that's making us both miserable!"

With that, he brought his lips crashing down upon hers. Lissa felt her head spinning wildly, and she trembled as he proceeded to kiss her with more demanding thoroughness than she had ever been kissed before. She was blissfully unaware of the fact that the Lamberts had just strolled into the lobby from the dining room; at first startled by the sight of their trusted employee locked in a passionate embrace with Ben Chandler's normally undemonstrative ranch hand, they smiled at one another and turned about to retrace their steps into the other room.

By the time Curly set her firmly back down in the chair, Lissa was almost totally incapable of rational thought. She struggled to regain control of her highly erratic breathing. Her face was becomingly flushed, her eyes aglow with passion's delight as she stared up at the man who had made her feel things she had never expected to feel again.

"One week," he decreed quietly. "I'll give you one week to make up your mind. Then I'm coming for you!"

She watched as if in a daze while he replaced the hat atop his head, tugged the brim low in the front, and strode back outside. Lissa raised a hand unsteadily to her lips, which still tingled from the kiss she had felt with every fiber of her being.

I'm going to have to prove it to you, Curly had vowed.

She realized that he had done just that. Heaven help her, she thought with a ragged sigh, but how could she resist him any longer?

The following day was a busy one at the Chapparosa. The time for the fall roundup was fast approaching, and the men were already riding out with more frequency in an effort to estimate the size of the herd.

Jessie insisted upon continuing with the twins' studies at home, in spite of their argument that none of the other students had the misfortune to possess a schoolteacher for a mother. She could not help but laugh when, upon appealing to their father for assistance, he told them they had better obey because she was the scariest thing he'd ever seen when she was riled. James and Hannah apparently believed him, for they settled down with their lessons and did not once complain for the duration of the afternoon.

Later, Ben informed his wife that the two of them were going for a ride—alone. She offered no resistance, hurrying to change into the new divided riding skirt Martha had so thoughtfully made for her. Of dark blue cotton, it fitted smoothly over her hips, then flared outward to just below her ankles. Donning a white cotton shirtwaist, a navy serge jacket, and a pair of boots, she tied her long golden tresses back with a ribbon and hastened outside.

Ben eyed her new riding costume with thoroughly masculine approval. He moved to help her mount, his hand lingering upon the roundness of her bottom after he had tossed her up into the saddle.

"Good thing we're not riding into town," he drawled, his eyes brimming with roguish amusement as she colored delightfully. "I don't think I'd like the kind of attention you'd attract in this getup."

"Behave yourself, Mr. Chanlder, or I shall remain at home!" she threatened with mock severity.

"Liar," he retorted with a crooked smile. He swung up onto his own horse and announced, "We'll head toward the mountains. There's something I want to show you."

"What is it?" she asked, her curiosity aroused.

"Patience, wildcat," he commanded affectionately.

The rugged prairie landscape was ablaze with the colors of an early autumn. In the nearby mountains, the ridges were splashed with the brilliant gold of the aspen and the heads of the canyons turned a rusty red by scrub oak. Snow, blinding white, topped the majestic peaks all the way down past the treeline. The days were cool and bright and made for riding, the nights chilly enough so that a huge, comforting blaze roared in the fireplace and sent showers of sparks spiraling up the chimney.

Jessie breathed deeply of the cool, fresh air and reveled in the feeling of absolute freedom as she rode beside Ben. He did not set a difficult pace, so that they were able to talk while the horses beneath them snorted and pranced with high spirits. Crossing the rolling plains, they traveled onward to the foothills of the Sangre de Cristo.

"Are we still on your land?" Jessie asked Ben, her emerald gaze moving appreciatively over the wildly enchanting countryside about them.

"*Our* land, Mrs. Chandler," he corrected, then told her, "We won't cross the Chapparosa's boundary for another mile yet."

"Why don't you tell me now where you're taking me," she suggested with a purposefully engaging smile. He gave a low chuckle.

"Sheath your feminine wiles, you little witch—at least until we get there."

"Do you mean to tell me, Ben Chandler, that you are taking me someplace with the intention of—"

"Guilty as charged," he confessed without any trace of

358

repentance. His deep blue eyes glowed with passion at the thought of what he had planned. He and his beloved would lie naked beside the stream in the secluded glen that had long been a favorite retreat. . . . He would kiss her sweet lips until she clung to him and pleaded to be taken. . . . He would drive them both nearly mindless with pleasure as he stroked and caressed her whole beautiful body.

Jessie grew warm all over at the look on his handsome face. Her pulses racing, she caught her lower lip between her teeth and shifted restlessly in the saddle.

Suddenly, Ben tensed beside her. Her eyes widened, and she quickly turned her head to follow the direction of his intense gaze.

"What is it?" she demanded with a frown of bewilderment.

"Indians."

"Indians?" She drew in a sharp breath, her grip loosening on the reins. Ben reached over and pulled her mount to halt in unison with his.

"Whatever you do, don't panic," he cautioned her. His eyes narrowed as he looked toward the approaching riders in the distance. "Apaches," he pronounced quietly. "Six of them."

"Dear God, do you think it's Gray Wolf?" asked Jessie tremulously, her heart pounding in alarm.

"I do," he confirmed with a curt nod. He met her frightened gaze. "You can bet they saw us long before now. They mean us no harm, Jessamyn."

"How—how can you be certain?"

"Because they're in no hurry to get here," Ben replied with a faint smile. "And they damned sure don't ride up to a man in the open if they're planning to kill him."

Although far from convinced, she nodded mutely and turned to watch as the Apaches drew closer. A shiver ran down her spine when she caught sight of Gray Wolf's familiar features. He and the other braves with him were clad in loose cotton shirts, buckskin breeches, and moccasins that were laced up about their knees. They wore their long raven hair parted in the middle and plaited into two braids wound with strips of deerskin. Each of them was armed with a bow and arrows slung horizontally over his chest and shoulders, as well as a Winchester saddle carbine in one hand.

Please God, Jessie implored in silent desperation, *please help me to have courage!* Her mind flew back to remember the terror she had felt when Gray Wolf had attacked the stagecoach and carried her off. Valiantly fighting down the panic that rose within her now, she drew strength from Ben's calm presence beside her.

"Let me do the talking," he commanded her in a low voice.

Gray Wolf and the other Apaches drew their mounts to a halt a few yards away. They said nothing, their dark gazes moving over Ben and Jessie for several long, agonizing seconds. Finally, Gray Wolf looked to his former friend and allowed the merest ghost of a smile to touch his chiseled lips.

"You still have your woman, Chandler," he stated, his eyes gleaming with something akin to humor.

"She is my wife," Ben told him solemnly. "What are you doing on my land, Gray Wolf?"

"Hunting." A couple of the braves smiled at that, but Gray Wolf did not.

"Hunting for what?" asked Ben with deceptive nonchalance. In spite of the fact that he believed there was no danger, his gaze remained watchful and his body tensed in defensive readiness.

"Our women and children are hungry. They must have fresh meat. So, we hunt," Gray Wolf answered simply.

"If your women and children have need of them, I will

give you cattle," Ben offered the other man, knowing full well that he would refuse.

"My people do not take the white man's charity!" the fierce Apache leader growled, his dark eyes glittering hotly. "You know this, Chandler, and yet you ask!"

"I meant no insult, Gray Wolf." His gaze locked in silent combat with that of his onetime ally. When he spoke again, it was to issue a warning. "There has been an outbreak of measles among the children at my wife's school. Your people would do well to stay away from Cimarron for a while."

"Why do you warn us, Chandler?" demanded Gray Wolf with a rancorous scowl. "Would you not be pleased to learn my people have died? Would your heart not be glad at such a victory over us?"

"No," he answered truthfully. "No, Gray Wolf, the news would give me no pleasure. My heart is no longer filled with hate for you."

The tall, powerfully built Apache searched the face of his long-ago brother for the truth. What he saw in Ben's eyes led him to believe the other man's words. He was taken aback by the realization and found himself seized by a rare uncertainty about his next move.

Casting Ben one last hard look, he raised his hand in an unspoken gesture of command and reined about, his men obediently following suit. They rode back in the same direction they had come, the thundering hooves of their horses leaving only a thin cloud of dust to be borne away on the cool wind sweeping down from the mountain.

"Oh, Ben, thank goodness they've gone!" breathed Jessie, feeling faint with relief as she watched them growing smaller in the distance.

"I'm sorry you were frightened, wildcat. But at least you kept your mouth shut this time," he remarked dryly.

"Do you think his people really are going hungry?" she asked in concern, too preoccupied with what she had heard to offer him a suitable retort.

"He would never have mentioned it otherwise," Ben told her with a frown.

"But . . . isn't there some way we can help?" It no longer mattered that Gray Wolf and his band had once held her captive. Compassion stirred within her breast at the thought of them starving. "We've got to do something!"

"I'll do what I can."

"And what is that?" she persisted.

"Curly and I will drive a few head of cattle up into the mountains tomorrow." A wry smile tugged at the corners of his mouth, and his blue eyes filled with appreciative humor. "Gray Wolf won't hesitate to steal them. He may be stubborn, but he's not so stubborn he'll let the 'strays' wander back home."

"I hope not," she murmured. Releasing a sigh, she asked, "Would you mind if we returned to the ranch now? I—I think I would prefer just going home."

"All right," he consented without argument. He knew she had been pretty badly shaken by the encounter, and his heart twisted at the look of entreaty in her beautiful green eyes. "But don't think you're going to get off that easily, wildcat. I still mean to love you well this day, even if it *is* in the comfort of our own bed!"

"Is that a threat, my dearest husband?" she taunted, her eyes sparkling with delight now.

"It's a promise." He leaned over and pressed a tender, sweetly provocative kiss upon her lips. "Let's go home, Mrs. Chandler."

Seventeen

Jessie sighed in utter contentment and pressed closer to Ben's hard warmth in the bed. It occurred to her that she would have to get some sleep eventually; Martha and the children would be sure to take note of her increasing drowsiness of a morning sooner or later. But she was certainly in no mood to complain about that or anything else at present, for her handsome, thoroughly masculine husband had made good on his promise to love her well.

She rolled to her back and pulled herself into a sitting position while Ben continued to sleep beside her. Taking care not to wake him, she slipped from the bed and padded barefoot across to where her nightgown lay discarded on the floor. She hurriedly drew it on over her head, then retrieved her wrapper from the mirrored wardrobe and flung it about her shoulders.

Seized with a powerful thirst and belatedly lamenting the fact that she had forgotten to fill the pitcher with water, she tiptoed over to the door and eased it open. The house was very quiet as she moved down the darkened hallway to the kitchen; the only sounds to be heard were the steady ticking of the clock, which had recently chimed the midnight hour, and the soft, monotonous pumping of the windmill outside.

Jessie smiled at the sight of the *sopaipillas* Consuela had left arranged neatly on a tray atop the kitchen table. The children, she knew, would smother them with honey at breakfast in the morning and consume unbelievably large quantities for such small creatures. Indeed, she mused with an indulgent sigh, the only person capable of matching their enjoyment of the squares of puffy deep-fried bread was their father.

Crossing to the sink, she grasped the pump handle and positioned a pitcher beneath the spout. Her eyes traveled up to the window in front of her as the water began to flow. She frowned to herself when she glimpsed a sudden spark of light near one of the barns.

"What in the—?" she whispered in puzzlement, then broke off with a sharp gasp as the spark of light blazed to life on the barn's roof.

Fire! her mind screamed. *Good heavens, the barn was on fire!*

She dropped the pitcher into the sink with a loud clatter and whirled about, flying back down the hallway before she became aware of the sound of hoofbeats growing fainter in the distance. Ben was still sleeping peacefully, but she clutched at his arm with urgent trembling hands.

"Ben! Ben, wake up!"

He came bolt upright in the bed, his whole body tensed in defensive readiness. His piercing gaze fell upon Jessie, who stood leaning anxiously over him in the darkness.

"Damn it, Jessamyn, what is it?" he demanded with a frown.

"Fire!" she gasped out. "The barn is on fire!"

With remarkable swiftness, he sprang from the bed, drew on his trousers, and grabbed his gun. Jessie was close on his heels as he raced toward the back door.

"Stay inside!" he thundered.

He headed straightaway for the barn, where the flames

364

had by now spread nearly all the way across the roof. His deep voice raised the cry of alarm. Within seconds, the ranch hands spilled from the bunkhouse. They cursed as their sleep-drugged gazes were met with the sight of the deadly blaze, but they wasted no time before obeying their employer's terse, authoritative commands to fill buckets with water and form a line of offense to fight the fire.

"Jessie?" Martha's eyes were wide and full of worriment as she stood framed in the kitchen doorway. "Jessie, what is it?" she asked breathlessly, her fingers shaking a bit while she tied the belt of her wrapper. "I heard a noise, and then Ben—"

"Oh, Martha, one of the barns is on fire!"

"On fire?" she echoed, her pulses leaping in dread. She hurried across to the door Ben had just flung open on his way outside. Lifting a hand to her throat, she looked back to Jessie in dawning horror. "God help them, they've made a terrible mistake!"

"They?" Jessie immediately moved to stand before the other woman. "What are you talking about?" she demanded sharply, her hand lifting to Martha's arm.

"Don't you see, my dear? They burned Humboldt's barn two nights ago!"

"You—you mean the *company* is responsible for this?" Jessie faltered in stunned disbelief.

"Yes!" Martha confirmed with an emphatic nod. "But this time they have chosen the wrong man to provoke! Ben will not rest until he has avenged this attack and . . . oh, Jessie, I am afraid of what he might do!" she finished, shuddering at the thought of her cousin's fury.

Jessie, a sudden impulse leading her to disregard Ben's orders, gathered up the folds of her nightgown and wrapper and flew outside. She shivered as her bare feet came into contact with the hard cold ground, but she did not waver on her way across the yard to where the barn was now well on its way to being completely engulfed by the roaring flames.

"Dear God!" she whispered hoarsely, her eyes narrowing against both the fire's heat and its blinding radiance. She finally caught sight of her husband, who was leading the last of the terrified, wildly straining horses from the building.

Suddenly, there was a loud splintering crash, and a shower of sparks fell across Ben just as he reached the doorway with the animals. Jessie's horror-filled gaze was drawn swiftly upward, and a tremor of sheer paralyzing fear shot through her when she saw that the section of wood forming the top of the frame was threatening to give way at any second.

"*Ben!*" she screamed in shrill warning, her legs refusing to obey the frantic commands of her mind.

If he heard her, he gave no indication of it. He remained in the doorway, his tall frame outlined by the fire's virulent glow as he struggled to lead the horses to safety. Jessie's heart pounded in rising panic, and she looked back up in helpless desperation while the flames swept ever downward about the door frame.

Finally, she sprang into motion. Coughing at the choking cloud of smoke that came up to hit her, she stumbled forward until reaching Ben's side. His eyes glittered with a savage, near murderous light when he jerked his head around and saw her.

"Get back, damn it!" he yelled, bringing his hand up to give her a forceful shove that sent her staggering backward. Fearing for her safety a good deal more than he feared for his own, he sliced her a furious speaking look before turning his attention back to the horses who reared and snorted with dangerously intensifying fright.

Jessie hastily regained her balance and flew back to her husband's side. Hot tears stung against her eyelids, and she gasped for breath as she cried out, "It's going to give way!" She clutched frantically at his arm and pointed overhead. "Please, Ben, you've got to—"

She broke off as the wood splintered farther apart, hurtling another torrent of sparks downward. Ben, his one thought to save Jessie from the impending danger, suddenly clamped an arm about her waist and released his hold on the horses' bridles. He lifted his wife in his strong arms and bore her swiftly away from the front of the barn. In the very next instant, the brace of wood came crashing downward in a merciless tumble of flames. The horses, their shrill screams piercing the night air, were driven back into the burning barn.

Curly rounded the corner. Without hesitation, his long strides led him directly across the path of the fire. The flames shot up around him as he disappeared inside the raging inferno in a courageous attempt to save the animals.

"Stay here!" Ben told Jessie, setting her on her feet a short distance away before spinning purposefully about to go help Curly.

"Ben, no!" she pleaded, but to no avail. She could do nothing but watch in anguished terror as he, too, battled the flames on his way back inside the barn. After what seemed to her like an eternity, she saw the horses finally bursting outside to scatter into the night. Ben emerged from the flames soon thereafter, miraculously alive but with his face and clothing blackened from the smoke . . . and his arms supporting the weight of Curly's unconscious body.

Jessie's eyes filled with joy at the sight of her beloved, then with startled dismay when they fell upon Curly. She hastened forward to meet Ben as he lowered his friend to the ground.

"Oh, Ben, what happened?" She dropped to her knees beside the injured man, her wide, anxious eyes meeting the savage intensity of Ben's. "Is he—?"

"He's alive," he told her grimly, his voice full of deadly calm. "But he took a hard blow on the head before we could get out."

"Curly!" breathed Martha as she came scurrying outside now. Kneeling on the ranch hand's other side, she made a hasty inspection of his injuries while Ben returned to help the other men fight the inevitably hopeless war against the fire. Jessie's eyes followed him, then shifted back to Martha's face when the older woman pronounced, with a sigh of relief, "I don't think his injuries are too serious."

"Thank God!" murmured Jessie, her voice breaking.

The twins, no longer held in check by Martha's presence, raced across the yard in their nightclothes. They drew up short at the sight of Curly's prone body.

"What happened to Curly?" asked Hannah, frowning worriedly down at the man with whom she and her brother had always shared a special relationship.

"Is he dead?" James queried while his little face paled at the thought.

"No, he's not dead," Jessie assured them. "He—he was injured while saving the horses from the fire."

"The two of you should not be out here!" scolded Martha, rising to her feet. "But since you are, you can help me fetch some water and bandages."

Jessie remained on the ground with Curly's head cradled in her lap, her emerald gaze suffused with a dull glow as she watched the walls of the blazing structure crumble beneath the fire's destructive wrath. She looked at Ben, who now stood with his men and stared in helpless fury at what was left of the barn.

Martha and the twins returned shortly, and they set about tending to the cuts and burns suffered by a number of the weary firefighters. Curly moaned when he finally came to again. His eyes were clouded with pain as he opened them. Disregarding Jessie's insistence that he lie still, he pulled himself into a sitting position, then grimaced and put a hand to the back of his head. Ben, moving to his side again, went down on one knee and rested an arm across the other one.

"Hurts like hell, doesn't it?" he remarked with a faint smile, his nonchalant attitude belying the profound relief he felt at the other man's return to consciousness.

"I've had worse," murmured Curly, his own eyes sparking with a hint of wry amusement in spite of his pain. Stubbornly shaking his head at Ben's attempted help, he climbed to his feet and turned his somber gaze upon the barn. "Looks like we got ourselves a bonfire." Waiting until Ben had pulled Jessie upright beside him, he asked quietly, "The horses?"

"They got out," affirmed Ben. His arm slipped about his wife's slender waist and pulled her close as he told Curly, "I found this around back." He held up the broken feathered shaft of an arrow.

"Indians?" gasped Jessie, her eyes growing very round at the sudden image of Gray Wolf's face.

"No." Ben's gaze locked with Curly's in silent understanding. "The Indians didn't do this. Someone else just tried to make it look like they did. The fire was started with Apache arrows all right, but the tracks I found were made by the horses of white men."

"Martha said it was the company!" Jessie recalled. "Oh, Ben, do you really think—"

"I do," he replied grimly, his eyes gleaming with a dangerously foreboding light. "And I'll be damned if I'll let them get away with it!"

"You've got no proof," Curly pointed out.

"Neither did Humboldt!"

"But why would they do this to you?" Jessie wondered aloud. "You're not like the others! There is no dispute over the ownership of your land!" It then dawned on her that she already knew the answer. Cole Hagan had given

369

it to her.

"This is their way of warning me off." His blue eyes smoldered with both vengeful fury and steely determination. "They can burn every damned barn in the Territory; it still won't make any difference."

"What are you going to do?" Jessie now asked, her pulses leaping in renewed alarm.

"I think I'll pay a visit to the company's headquarters in town tomorrow morning," he told her in a low, deceptively even tone.

"I'll ride along," insisted Curly.

"No." Ben shook his handsome smoke-blackened head. "I want you to stay here and keep an eye on things. Besides, they'll be less likely to pull anything if I go alone."

"Well, I'm coming with you!" Jessie obstinately declared. "They will certainly not consider *me* a threat!"

"Damn it, woman, I don't want you involved in this!"

"I'm already involved!" she countered, her eyes flashing up at him. "I have no intention of allowing you to go alone, Ben Chandler, so you might as well accept that fact here and now and—"

"You'll do as I say!" he ground out, his own gaze darkening.

"She's right, Ben," Curly offered his unexpected support. He looked to Jessie, and an ironic smile tugged at the corners of his mouth. "She's probably the best insurance you've got."

"And how do you figure that?" demanded Ben, his fingers tensing around his wife's softness.

"No one wants to get tangled up with a schoolmarm from back east. The company wouldn't want that kind of publicity."

Although Jessie did not fully comprehend what Curly was talking about, she was grateful for his intervention and saw no reason to press the issue—especially since

Ben reluctantly agreed to let her accompany him to Cimarron the next day.

He and Curly spoke a few moments longer about the recent incident, then decided it was safe to call it a night. By the time everyone returned to the comfort of their beds, it was well after two o'clock in the morning and the barn was nothing more than a glowing pile of embers outlined against the starlit darkness of the sky.

"Is that where the company has its local headquarters?" Jessie asked in surprise. Her eyes widened as they traveled over the magnificent adobe mansion across the street. She had been curious about it since the first time she had ridden into Cimarron with Ben, but she had never remembered to ask him about it again. "But it's the old Maxwell estate!" she exclaimed, having heard at least that much about it from others in town.

"It is. The company took it over when Maxwell sold out," replied Ben. His hand closed about her arm as he led her down the boardwalk toward the St. James.

"I thought I was supposed to be going with you!" she protested with a frown.

"I changed my mind." His mouth curved into a faint, mocking smile. "I don't think the poor bastards would know what to do if you took it into your head to fly off the handle."

"I would not 'fly off the handle'!" she denied, her beautiful green eyes kindling with anger. "In the event you do not remember what Curly said—"

"I remember." All traces of humor vanished now, and his handsome features tightened as he said, "I let you ride along, Jessamyn, because it pleased me to do so. But, damn it, I'll not hide behind a woman's skirts when I go in there and face those cowardly sons of bitches who are responsible for last night's attack!"

371

"You still have no proof to bear out your suspicions!" she pointedly reminded him, her heart twisting in fear of what he might do. She drew to a halt and turned to place a restraining hand upon his arm. Her bright gaze was full of entreaty when she tilted her head back to look up into his face. "Please, Ben, don't provoke them any more than is necessary!"

"Provoke them?" His eyes darkened, and he almost roughly urged her along with him again. "They've got hired guns terrorizing the countryside, Jessamyn! They're not going to stop at burning barns and delivering a few blasted eviction notices! The men sitting over there in Maxwell's house and in those fancy offices in Santa Fe don't even have the guts to carry out their own treachery; they pay others to do it for them!"

"But where is it all going to end?" demanded Jessie, sick at heart when she realized he could be plunging himself into even greater danger than before.

"I don't know," he admitted grimly. "On the side of justice, I hope. On the side of the decent, honest, hard-working men who believed they were doing the right thing when they came to this land and made it their home!" He finally stopped when they were directly in front of the hotel. "Wait for me inside. I won't be long."

"If it's all the same to you, I would prefer to spend the time at Dr. Prater's, inquiring about my students," she announced, drawing herself rigidly erect. She wanted to plead with him not to go but knew it would do no good.

"All right." Ben released her arm, and his blue eyes glinted down at her like cold steel. "I'll meet you back here at the hotel in half an hour's time." Watching as she nodded mutely and refused to meet his eyes again, he muttered an inward curse. He spun about on his booted heel, striding across the wide, dusty street toward the walled mansion Lucien Maxwell had built many years ago.

Jessie resisted the temptation to run after him. Once he had disappeared through the open gateway, she released a long, pent-up sigh and turned her steps toward the doctor's house. It required only a few minutes for her to learn that two more of the Shelton children had broken out with the distinctive red rash signifying the onslaught of measles, and that poor little Kristen, whose family had already known so much trouble, was also showing signs of the disease. There was still, unfortunately, nothing to be done but wait.

"What about Ned, Dr. Prater?" she asked, her gaze full of concern. "Has his condition worsened?"

"I'm afraid so," the kindly bearded man answered with a frown. "To tell the truth, Mrs. Chandler, he may not recover."

"Oh no!" she breathed in dismay. Sudden tears sprang to her eyes, and she felt a knot tightening in the pit of her stomach. "Will—will you please keep me informed?"

"Of course. But it may be several days before—" He broke off and heaved a sigh. "I've seen more than my share of pain and death, but I will never get accustomed to the suffering of children." The responsibility of his profession weighed heavily upon his shoulders at that moment, and he found himself longing for the burden to be lifted.

Jessie left soon thereafter. Her thoughts flew back to memories of Ned Shelton and the other students she had come to know so well in the past few weeks. She realized how very much they meant to her, and she prayed more fervently than ever for all of them to make it safely through the crisis.

When she got back to the hotel, Ben was nowhere in sight. Her gaze was instinctively drawn to the adobe mansion, but she would not allow herself to consider the possibility that anything was wrong. She stepped inside the hotel and went in search of Lissa . . . anxious to try and keep her mind from straying to thoughts of the stubborn, opinionated, thoroughly exasperating man she loved with all her heart.

A short time later, Ben was on his way out of the company's headquarters. Filled with luxurious furnishings that had been freighted over the Santa Fe Trail by Maxwell, the house boasted of two grand pianos, gaming rooms and a billiard room fitted with green baize-covered tables, and other rooms decorated with deep-piled carpet, heavy velvet draperies, and gilt-framed oil paintings.

This opulent estate, which covered an entire block in town, was considered by the settlers to be a perfect example of the company's greed and unquenchable thirst for power. Ben's visit to the men enthroned within its walls had only served to fuel his dangerously flaring temper. He had expected them to deny any involvement in the burning of his barn—or Humboldt's, for that matter—but he had nonetheless been determined that they should know neither he nor anyone else would tolerate the sort of methods they were employing. If it took an all-out war within Colfax County to settle the matter, then so be it.

He was on his way past Lambert's Saloon when he caught a glimpse of Cole Hagan leaning negligently against the bar inside. Without hesitation, he turned and pushed through the swinging double doors.

"Well, now, if it isn't the pretty little schoolmarm's husband," Cole sneered as he took note of the other man's approach. His hand itched to reach for the gun holstered low on his hip, but he fought the impulse and settled instead for casting Ben a look full of contempt.

"I heard you got out of jail this morning, Hagan," said Ben. A faint sardonic smile touched his lips. "Too bad your friends across the street couldn't spring you any sooner."

"I don't know what the hell you're talking about," the

gunslinger denied with studied nonchalance. He kept one booted foot on the brass rail that ran along the base of the bar and raised the glass of whiskey to his mouth. He was filled with a murderous rage at the memory of the beating he had suffered at Chandler's hands, but he had orders to keep his cool.

"Don't you?" Ben, his own gaze unfathomable, stepped closer. He was a good six inches taller than the other man, his experience with danger at least that many times greater. "Remember what I said, Hagan. . . . Stay away from my wife," he warned in a low voice edged with barely controlled violence. "If you ever try to use her to get to me again, I'll kill you." He had not believed Jessamyn's hastily concocted story; once he'd learned the identity of the man who had dared to lay hands on her, he had immediately known the reason for her lie.

"I still don't know what the hell you're talking about." Cole downed the shot of amber liquid, then lowered the glass slowly back down to the polished wooden surface of the bar. There was nothing to indicate his burning desire to kill Ben other than the hot, feral gleam in his dark eyes.

"Play it however you like," Ben countered with another faint smile that was totally devoid of humor. "But we both know why you're here. You can tell whoever's calling your shots that it won't work. I'm not backing down. And neither is anyone else in this town." His eyes narrowed imperceptibly, the grim set of his jaw leaving little doubt that he meant what he said. He turned his back on the other man and moved, almost leisurely, toward the doors again. "Take my advice and go back to Santa Fe, Hagan," he added in a dangerously low and level tone without bothering to look back.

"You threatening me, Chandler?" Cole gave a soft, derisive chuckle. "Hell, man, you've got me quaking in my boots!" he taunted, swinging about to brace himself

375

back against the bar with his elbows. His features grew particularly ugly as he glared at the tall broad-shouldered man who kept walking.

Emerging outside, Ben turned his steps toward the hotel next door and thought of the gunslinger he had just left behind. It had required every ounce of self-will he possessed to keep from smashing his fist into that black-hearted son of a bitch's face again. He knew he would never forget the fear in Jessie's eyes the day he had sent her assailant sprawling in the street. *Someday, he might have to kill Hagan after all.* . . .

"Ben!" Jessie breathed in relief when she looked up and saw him striding toward her. She sprang up from her seat on the red velvet sofa, hurrying across the lobby to impulsively throw herself upon her husband's chest. His strong arms came up about her, and his fierce gaze softened.

"You act as though I'd been gone for days," he murmured, his deep voice brimming with loving amusement.

"I was beginning to think you would be!" she retorted, drawing away a bit and tilting her head back to look up at him. Her sparkling emerald gaze was full of wifely reproach. "You said half an hour; it's been nearly twice that!"

"Where's Lissa?" he asked casually, his quick glance encompassing the room.

"Upstairs," she replied, then demanded, "What happened? Did you speak to the—"

"I spoke to them." His eyes glittered like molten steel again.

"Well, what did they say? What did *you* say?" she prompted insistently.

"It doesn't matter."

"Of course it matters! I happen to be your wife, Ben Chandler, and as such am fully entitled to know—"

"—whatever I decide to tell you," he finished for her. A soft smile of irony played about his lips, and he pulled her back against him for a moment. "Nothing happened, Jessamyn," he lied, having already decided not to reveal the heated discussion between himself and the company's representatives. "They pretended to know nothing about the barn burning."

"What are you going to do now?"

"For the moment . . . not a damned thing." Setting her reluctantly but firmly away from him, he cast a look toward the stairs. "I need to have a word with Lissa before we head back to the ranch."

"Why?" Jessie asked with a slight frown of bemusement.

"So I can let her know about the celebration we're planning for Sunday after next."

"*What* celebration?"

"The one we're going to have for her and Curly out at the Chapparosa."

"And why are we going to do that?" she questioned with an air of sorely tried patience, her eyes flashing up at him in growing exasperation.

"Because they're getting married," Ben finally revealed. "Curly told me last night."

"But Lissa has said nothing about it to me!" she exclaimed in surprise. As a matter of fact, she recalled, Lissa had determinedly avoided the subject of Curly while they had talked a short time earlier. "I find it difficult to believe she would have kept such important news from me!"

"According to Curly, she hasn't exactly made up her mind yet," he confessed with another brief smile. "He asked me to tell her about the celebration anyway. I guess he thinks it will count for something."

"This is absurd!" protested Jessie, her mind spinning as a result of what she had just heard. "How in heaven's name can we plan a celebration when they aren't even—"

"Curly said to go ahead, and that's just what I plan to do," Ben declared with maddening calm.

He left her staring after him in openmouthed disbelief while he sauntered over to the corner and up the stairs to find the hotel's flame-haired manager. When he returned shortly thereafter, it was with the news that Lissa had been struck speechless.

"I hope you and Curly know what you're doing!" Jessie told him with a stern frown. He took her arm and led her outside.

"Never doubt it, wildcat," he murmured, his magnificent blue gaze full of an unfathomable light.

An uneasy peace fell over the countryside for the next several days. There were no further outbreaks of violence, no additional eviction notices delivered, and no more threats traded by the two opposing factions. Many, however, feared that it was the calm before the storm— and that the worst was yet to come.

Ben and his neighbors worked together to rebuild the Humboldts' barn. The new one at the Chapparosa, meanwhile, was already half finished three days after the original had been burned. These buildings were necessary not only to provide shelter for the horses, but also to store the hay that would be needed with ever increasing frequency during the coming winter. Each man who owned stock prayed that it would be a mild one.

Jessie's spirits were lifted immeasurably when, at the end of the week, Dr. Prater stopped by the ranch with the news of Ned Shelton's recovery. She embraced him in an impulsive burst of joyful relief, and the good doctor reciprocated with a broad grin and the additional assurance that the crisis had passed for the other children as well. Giving her permission to open the school again on Monday, he climbed back up into his buggy and headed homeward with a generous supply of Consuelo's famed cornhusk-wrapped tamales in a basket on the seat beside him.

By the time Monday rolled around, Jessie was fairly bursting with impatience to resume class. None of the Sheltons were quite well enough yet to attend, but all of the other students—even Kristen, who had fortunately suffered only a mild form of the disease—were in attendance that first day back.

The children were soon up to their old tricks again. Harmon and Peter crawled under the schoolhouse to smoke during the noon break, then took it into their heads to rock the privy when Mary Sue was inside it. John remarked afterward that you could have heard her screaming all the way to E-Town.

Someone, their identity remaining a mystery for the time being, had decided it would be a splendid idea to place a live creature in the teacher's desk drawer. Jessie did not discover the prank until mid-afternoon; opening the drawer to make an entry in the journal she kept to record her student's progress, she was startled when a small opossum jumped out and began running about the room. A terrible commotion ensued, some of it caused by the teacher herself, and it was a number of minutes later before things settled down again inside the paper-and-book-strewn schoolhouse.

Jessie, musing to herself that their high spirits were in all likelihood due to the lack of school the past week, announced to her pupils that her leniency would end the very next day. Starting then, she added firmly, she would mete out appropriate punishment for each and every infraction of the rules.

They must have taken her warning to heart, for there was not a single occurrence of any real mischief on Tuesday. Considerable progress was made in regard to their studies as well. Jessie was filled with a sense of great satisfaction at the end of the day, but her students' good behavior was not the only reason for the glow in her beautiful green eyes.

It was Ben's birthday. She had something very special planned for him, something she was certain would please him—and herself. There had been so much to trouble them both of late, and he had been occupied until long after dark at the ranch. Although they had managed to steal a few hours together before drifting off to sleep at night, she longed for a time, however brief, when they could forget about everything else and think only of one another.

Just you wait until tonight, my dearest husband, she vowed silently, a soft flush rising to her face and a delicious shiver of anticipation dancing down her spine.

Arriving back at the Chapparosa with the twins after school, Curly and Jessie exchanged quick conspiratorial glances. Ben, they both knew, was going to be surprised.

"I wonder what Consuelo is planning to make Papa for supper," Hannah mused aloud. She slid from the saddle and smiled at Curly, who gathered up the reins of all four horses and led them toward the newly finished barn.

"Probably flapjacks," opined James, taking Jessie by the hand as they climbed up the front steps of the house. "He always says he likes flapjacks better than anything."

"She wouldn't make flapjacks for *supper!*" his sister insisted with a quelling frown.

"I'm afraid your father and I won't be having supper with you tonight," Jessie finally revealed to them, a secretive little smile playing about her lips.

"Why not?" asked Hannah.

"Because we're going to have our supper someplace else, just for this one night. And it's meant to be a surprise, so please try not to let him suspect anything when you see him," she cautioned, her smile deepening.

The three of them stepped through the doorway into the comforting warmth of the house. Martha hastened forward to greet them, her eyes meeting Jessie's in shared excitement for what lay ahead.

"Children, go on out to the kitchen," the petite brunette bid the twins with a fondly maternal look. "There are fresh cookies waiting for you, but mind you do not eat so many you spoil your supper." As soon as James and Hannah had willingly taken themselves off, she turned back to Jessie and proclaimed, "Consuelo and I have everything ready, my dear!"

"Thank you, Martha! Curly promised to deliver him to the front steps in exactly one hour, so I had best hurry up and bathe!" She affectionately brushed Martha's cheek with her lips, then gathered up her skirts and flew down the hallway to the room she now shared with Ben.

She drew off her jacket and skirt, removed her pin-striped blouse, and hurried across to the wardrobe. Her eyes lit with renewed satisfaction when they fell upon the riding costume Martha had pressed and hung there for her earlier that day. Taking it out, she draped it carefully across the bed and began unfastening her petticoat. Consuelo brought in hot water a moment later, pouring it into the bathtub she had already filled with cold water and left sitting in readiness in the middle of the floor.

Once she was alone again, Jessie quickly stripped off her chemise and drawers and lowered her body into the tub. She scrubbed at her naked skin until it was pink and glowing, then stepped out and knelt to wash her hair. Afterward, she dried the long, shimmering golden tresses as best she could with the towel and secured them in a single braid that hung down her back all the way to her slender waist.

Having already donned fresh undergarments, she buttoned on a tucked-front white shirtwaist, stepped into the divided riding skirt and pulled it up over her hips, and

381

slipped her arms into the fitted long sleeves of her jacket. She knelt on the floor beside the bed, withdrawing the carpetbag she had stowed there the night before. Her eyes sparkled in almost guilty delight once more at the thought of what she had planned.

Finally, she left the room and turned her steps toward the kitchen, where Martha and Consuelo waited for her. They had packed a light supper and a bottle of champagne—though Jessie had never even tasted strong spirits before—into a thin woven hamper that could be secured on the back of a saddle.

"Well, it's almost time!" Martha pronounced as the younger woman came into the room. "I do wish you and Ben could go away for more than a night. Perhaps after the roundup . . ."

"I fully intend to still be teaching then," Jessie insisted with a smile of determination. She thanked both women quite earnestly once more for their assistance as she took up the hamper and carried it, along with the carpetbag in her other hand, toward the front doorway.

"Good-bye, my dear!" Martha called after her. "Don't worry about the twins; they'll be fine!"

Adios, señora!" added Consuelo. She sighed, remembering with pleasure the time when she had been a young bride like Jessie. Well, not quite like Jessie, she told herself with an inward smile. She had never been brave enough to do what *this* young bride was doing—but she wished she had.

Jessie hurried down the front steps, arriving only seconds before Curly and Ben did. The two men were leading their saddled horses behind them, and Ben frowned in puzzlement when he saw his wife waiting before the house in her riding costume.

"Where are you going?" he asked.

"With you," she replied simply.

"Curly and I were just heading out to check on the

herd," he explained, his sun-kissed brow creasing into another frown. "I'm sorry, Jessamyn, but—"

"There's absolutely no reason to be sorry," she cut him off with an engaging smile. "You and Curly aren't going anywhere, Ben Chandler. You're coming with *me!*"

"What do you mean?"

"I'm kidnapping you, my dearest husband!" she confessed, her green eyes alight with beguiling mischief. "In case you have forgotten, it happens to be your birthday, and I have planned a very special evening for the two of us—*alone!*"

"Have you indeed?" he challenged as a slow, devastatingly warm smile spread across his handsome features. He turned to the man beside him and remarked, "This is only the second time you've lied to me, Curly."

"What was the first?" the ranch hand demanded solemnly, though his eyes glimmered with a touch of wry amusement.

"A little more than a year ago," Ben recalled easily, "when you told me you'd just as soon ride off a cliff than get yourself tied down to a woman."

Jessie was surprised to observe a dull flush rising to Curly's face. Musing that she had rarely seen him display emotion of any kind, her thoughts returned to the visit she had paid to Lissa on Saturday. The tall redhead had confirmed the fact that she had finally told Curly the truth, and that she had been assured of his unwavering devotion—in spite of her "checkered past." There was going to be a celebration on Sunday after all.

"You've no right to tease him!" she scolded Ben with mock severity. "I seem to recall a certain amount of resistance on your part to admit that you had fallen hopelessly in love with me!"

"Maybe," he allowed with an unrepentant grin. "But I sure as hell didn't waste any time once I'd made up my mind."

He moved to toss her into the saddle, while Curly took charge of the carpetbag and hamper. The horse she had chosen was a beautiful roan filly.

"Are you sure you don't want me to saddle your old mare?" Ben asked her, his gaze full of roguish humor.

"Quite sure!" she retorted saucily. Gathering up the reins, she shifted her weight to a more comfortable position in the saddle and reached down to pat the spirited young animal's neck. She was proud of her newly acquired equestrian skills and anxious to put them to the test.

"Where are you taking me, Mrs. Chandler?" her husband demanded while he agilely mounted his own horse.

"Patience, my love!" she took great pleasure in telling him. He gave a low chuckle, then sobered when he turned back to Curly.

"If anything happens . . ."

"I know where to find you," the ranch hand assured him with a curt nod.

"Damn it, woman, does everybody on the whole blasted ranch know about this?" the handsome young master of the Chapparosa grumbled, casting his wife a scowl that was far from convincing. Even his own children, excitedly presenting him with their gift a short time earlier in the barn, had managed to keep the secret from him.

Jessie merely smiled complacently and reined about. Ben, his heart feeling lighter than it had in days, offered no further complaints before following her lead.

Eighteen

"I should have guessed," remarked Ben as they approached the old cabin where they had spent their wedding night.

"You don't mind that we came here, do you?" Jessie queried a bit apprehensively.

"Quite the contrary."

He drew his mount to a halt while she did the same. The sun hung low upon the horizon, and the wind had stilled to nothing more than a gentle pine-and-sage-scented breeze. Overhead in the brilliant blue sky that was like no other, a flock of geese flew southward to escape winter's rawness, while somewhere in the distance a coyote set up a long, plaintive howl that echoed mournfully across the rugged land. For Ben and Jessie, however, there was nothing bleak or melancholy about the coming night.

"I'll go inside and start a fire while you wash up at the stream," she told him as he lifted her down.

"Aren't you going to join me?" he asked with a soft, meaningful smile.

"I've already had my bath. And besides, that water is in all probability ice cold!" Sparing him no mercy, she opened the carpetbag. "I came prepared, as you can see," she declared, handing him the bar of soap and the towel she had just withdrawn.

"Yes. I can see." Tugging the hat from his head, he shifted his amused gaze to the hamper she was now retrieving from the back of his saddle. "Supper?" he asked.

"Courtesy of Martha and Consuela," she confirmed. She opened it as well and took out the bottle of champagne. "Your cousin insisted upon including this with instructions to place it in cold water for at least half an hour."

"You didn't forget anything, did you, wildcat?" he lovingly challenged, his lips curving into another appreciatively wry smile.

"Nothing at all!" She whirled about and headed into the cabin, leaving him to shake his head in admiration of her delightful little scheme of seduction. It pleased him even more than she had hoped.

When he returned to the cabin a short time later, his hair still damp from his efforts and his body feeling chilled to the bone in spite of the fact that he had drawn on his clothes again, it was only to find Jessie on her knees before the fireplace. She was still struggling to light a fire. An even dozen discarded matches lay on the hearth where she had thrown them in disgust.

"Here. Let me do that," offered Ben, his eyes brimming with indulgent humor. He went down on one knee to take over, while she rose to her feet and frowned reproachfully at the uncooperative stack of wood.

"I found it necessary to evict an owl from the chimney!" she disclosed, then sighed. "But the cabin appears to be in remarkably good condition otherwise." Her gaze traveled to the table, and she smiled in satisfaction at the meal she had set out. "At least we have a nice supper. And the champagne, of course."

"You've gone to a lot of trouble, Jessamyn," he

386

remarked softly, his deep voice sending a warm color to the smoothness of her cheeks. She suddenly felt a trifle embarrassed by her boldness, and her eyes fell before the fathomless blue intensity of his.

"Well, it *is* your birthday, and I—I honestly couldn't think of anything you either wanted or needed, and—"

"You're what I want and need." He drew himself up to his full, ultimately superior height now and faced her. The fire had sparked to life at last, setting up a soft hiss and crackle that filled the cabin with the pleasant aroma of woodsmoke.

Without a word, Jessie went into her husband's outstretched arms. Her eyes swept closed, and she trembled as he held her close. After several long, wonderfully pleasurable moments, she forced herself to draw away.

"First things first," she decreed with a captivating smile. "Supper awaits, my lord and master."

"Hell, woman, I can *eat* anytime," he drawled, his arm slipping purposefully back about her waist. She was tempted to give in but did not.

"Nevertheless," she said, firmly disengaging herself, "I must insist that we proceed in the proper order of things. If you will please retrieve the champagne, we—"

"I'll make you pay for this, you little witch," he vowed, his gaze holding the promise of a sweet revenge. Casting his recalcitrant bride one last tenderly wolfish look, he turned and headed back outside to fetch the bottle he had left submerged in the frigid waters of the stream.

Jessie sighed unevenly. She wandered back to the table, only to draw to an abrupt halt when a sudden idea occurred to her. Her eyes widened, her cheeks flamed, and her whole body tingled from head to toe.

Good heavens, dare she do such a shameless thing? she wondered breathlessly.

387

She already knew the answer. After all, she reasoned with herself, she had planned this little celebration for Ben. Loving him as she did, she was naturally anxious to please him. And besides, she concluded as her heart pounded erratically within her breast, she knew she need feel no shame with her own husband. His love had freed her from the usual constraints society placed on the bedroom. She did not merely endure his masculine affections the way she had always been taught a wife should; she reveled in them!

Feeling splendidly wicked, she raised her hands to the buttons of her shirtwaist. . . .

Ben made his way back through the trees to the cabin. Musing that he would have done well to plunge *himself* in the cold water again, he clutched the chilled bottle of champagne in one hand and raised the other to the cabin door. He swung it open, only to be met with the startling, undeniably enchanting sight of his wife standing before the fire, wearing nothing but a blanket and a smile.

"I—I decided that since it was your birthday, you should get your wish," explained Jessie, blushing all over in spite of her resolve to be bold. "Supper can wait." Hesitating only a moment, she allowed the blanket to slide downward. It fell about her ankles, leaving her soft, alluring curves completely bare.

Ben's gaze, smoldering with the force of his raging passions, raked hungrily over her exposed loveliness. He had seen her naked before, but never quite like this. She stood before him in all her womanly glory, proud and unashamed, the look on her beautiful face stirring his heart and firing his blood. Love and desire mingled hotly together within him, coursing through his body like wildfire as he read the sweet surrender in his wife's eyes.

Jessie was the first to move. An innocently seductive little smile played about her lips when she began advancing upon him. Her thick, luxuriant curls of burnished gold, freed from the braid, shimmered gently back and forth across the naked curve of her back as she walked. She shivered suddenly as the cool night air swept inside the cabin to touch her bare skin.

"Close the door, Ben," she directed softly.

He obliged, then tossed the bottle of champagne to land on the bed. But when he finally reached for her, she brought her hands up to press against his chest in loving restraint.

"No, my dearest husband," she said, her emerald eyes aglow. "Now yet." Still amazed at her own daring, she lifted her hands higher and began unbuttoning his shirt. His lips curved into a soft, crooked smile, and his gaze darkened with pleasure.

"Do you mean to undress me, wildcat?" he asked in a low, vibrant tone brimming with humor as well as passion.

"I do," she confirmed, her fingers trembling a bit. "You've performed the service often enough for me, and I—I think it's time I returned the favor." Melting inside at the look in his eyes, she told herself she'd have to concentrate on what she was doing or she would never be able to go through with it.

Ben fell silent. His penetrating blue gaze traveled possessively over her face and downward across her beguiling nakedness while she worked to strip off his shirt. Although delighted by her boldness and willing to let her have her way, he knew he could not bear much more of the delectable torment. He groaned inwardly when, upon reaching up to smooth the unbuttoned shirt from his shoulders, she unwittingly caused her bare breasts to sweep across his chest.

"Damn it, Jessamyn," he growled, "how much more of this do you expect me to take?"

"You've made me beg for mercy often enough, Ben Chandler," she murmured, then cast him a soft, taunting smile. "Tonight, it's your turn," she added in a voice that was scarcely more than a whisper.

She urged him back to take a seat on the bed, then attempted, unsuccessfully, to tug off his boots. Growing impatient to have his angel-faced temptress in his arms, he pushed her aside and removed his boots and socks. He stood again, his hands moving to the front of his trousers. Jessie, however, was determined to complete the task herself.

Her eyes full of bewitching challenge, she drew his fingers insistently away and replaced them with her own. He indulged her, for the simple reason that he could not resist seeing how far she would let things go.

The next thing he knew, she had unfastened his trousers and was easing them downward with tantalizing slowness. He muttered a curse beneath his breath, his handsome features tightening as she bared his manhood. His desire for her was unmistakable, and she trembled in anticipation while continuing to pull the trousers all the way down to his ankles.

Her head was on a level with his throbbing hardness as she knelt before him and tugged the last of his clothing free. Suddenly, just as she was about to rise again, she found herself giving in to the mischievous impulse to press a light kiss upon the instrument of her husband's pleasure—not to mention her own.

Ben tensed and suffered a sharp intake of breath at the touch of her warm lips upon him. He endured two more such loving tributes, then bent and almost roughly hauled his startled bride up before him again.

"No more!" he ground out.

She gasped as he tumbled her unceremoniously back upon the bed and covered her body with his own. Jessie gave a low moan of surrender as his mouth claimed hers in a fierce, hotly demanding kiss that threatened to make her forget all about her desire to take the lead.

She surprised him when she suddenly ended the kiss and pushed against him. He was about to yank her close again, when the soft, enticing smile on her face told him she was not yet ready to cease her exquisite torture of him. Before he knew what she intended, she squirmed from beneath him and came up to her knees on the bed. He rolled to his back for the purpose of pulling her down onto the mattress beside him, then clenched his teeth against a forceful wave of desire as she lowered her body atop his.

Fitting her curvaceous softness against the length of his virile hard-muscled form, she pressed a series of light, provocative kisses across the rugged perfection of his face. But when he would have recaptured her lips with his own, she began searing a path downward along his neck to the broad nakedness of his chest. Her mouth traveled lovingly across the warm, bronzed expanse of his skin, dipping ever lower until it was once again on a level with his masculine hardness. This time, however, she had done no more than trace her fingers along the fully aroused length of hard flesh before Ben seized her arms in a firm grip and brought her swiftly upward again. Certain he intended to claim her lips again, she was surprised when his strong hands came down to curl about her naked hips and urge her even higher.

She drew in her breath upon a sharp gasp when his mouth closed about the rose-tipped fullness of her breast. Her fingers threaded tightly within his thick hair, and her eyes swept closed as she trembled with the force of her own passions. Ben's warm velvety tongue encircled the delicate peak, flicking erotically across it while his fingers spread across the pale satiny roundness of her derriere and held her captive for his pleasure. His hands kneaded her adorable bottom while his mouth continued to tease at her breasts.

Jessie moaned and squirmed in near painful ecstasy

atop him, her silken limbs straddling his lower body. She gasped sharply when her feminine softness suddenly came into contact with his throbbing male counterpart. His hands brought her into even closer contact, his lips branding all across her beautiful breasts.

"Oh, Ben!" she pleaded brokenly.

"Tell me, Jessamyn!" he commanded in loving triumph. "Tell me what you want!"

"I—I want you to take me! Please, Ben, I can bear no more!" Her voice was nothing but a ragged whisper now, and he knew that he had indeed brought her to the very brink of passion's madness.

She was scarcely aware of the moment when he lifted her hips, but she cried out when he brought her down upon his hardness. Her honeyed warmth willingly accepted the full pulsing length of his masculinity. Instinctively arching her back, she rode atop him, bracing herself upright with her hands upon his chest. Her long hair streamed down across her breasts as she met his thrusts with an equal fire and felt the heavenly sweetness of fulfillment approaching. When it came, she collapsed weakly down upon her magnificent beguiler, whose own body felt completely sated with what the two of them had just shared.

"Now, Mrs. Chandler," he demanded a short time later as they lay entwined amidst the wildly rumpled covers of the bed, "what was it you said earlier about someone begging for mercy?"

"You would have done just that, Mr. Chandler, if not for the fact that you put a stop to my efforts beforehand!" she retorted. She released another soft sigh of contentment, her eyes straying toward the table. "I should like to have supper now, if you don't mind."

"I don't mind," he was in a mood to agree. "We've got plenty of time. I still have several hours of my birthday left." He smiled roguishly down at her before teasing, "I

392

can hardly wait to see what else you've got planned."

Jessie blushed delightfully but did not offer a response. She slipped from the bed and moved to retrieve the blanket she had left on the floor before the fire. Ben drew on his trousers, frowning when his gaze fell upon a suspicious lump in the bed. He uncovered the bottle of champagne he had earlier tossed aside. Surprisingly enough, it was still cool.

"As a member of the board," he told Jessie while sauntering across to the table, "I feel it's my duty to remind you, schoolmarm, about the clause in your contract forbidding the consumption of strong spirits." A smile of ironic amusement tugged at the corners of his mouth.

"I believe there is another clause wherein I am also forbidden to display 'wanton behavior of any kind,'" she pointed out. She wrapped the blanket about her again and sank down into a chair at the table. "It appears you have led me astray on both counts!" she charged in mock reproach, then smiled. "To tell the truth, I only brought the champagne because Martha insisted upon it. And the other . . . well, I suppose I shall have to throw myself on the mercy of the board." She heaved a dramatic little sigh.

"The hell you will," he drawled with a soft chuckle. He lifted the bottle to the surface of the table. "I think, however, that you can throw yourself on the mercy of one particular member and—"

Without warning, a shot rang out. The bottle in Ben's hand was shattered by the bullet, which tore through the window to become embedded within the log wall.

Reacting on instinct, Ben hurled Jessie down onto the floor and covered her body protectively with his own. His gaze flew to his gun, which he had left beside the door.

"Stay down!" he told his wife, pushing her into the front corner just below the window. The glass was not broken, but there was a neat bullethole near the center of it.

Jessie's eyes, wide and full of alarm, followed Ben as he made his way swiftly across the room. Keeping himself low in the event that another bullet followed the first, he took hold of his rifle and drew himself upright in the narrow space between the window and the door.

"Dear God, Ben, what's happening?" Jessie whispered hoarsely. "Who would do such a—?"

"I don't know! But whoever it is, he's either a damned good shot—or a miserably poor one!"

His hands clenched in defensive readiness about his gun, he stood motionless beside the door while his mind raced to think of a way to ensure Jessie's safety. Realizing that the two of them had little choice for the time being but to stay inside the firelit cabin and wait for the unknown marksman's next move, he cursed their vulnerable position and looked to where his wife sat huddled in the corner. The terror in her eyes filled him with a murderous rage toward the person who had put it there.

"We can wait him out if we have to," he told her quietly. "The bastard's alone. He won't stay past first light."

"How—how do you know there aren't any others?" she asked, pulling the blanket closer about her and shuddering involuntarily as her eyes traveled back to the shattered bottle on the table.

"The cabin would be shot full of holes by now if there were," he replied grimly.

Jessie fell silent. Her blood pounded in her ears, and she looked back to her husband while her throat constricted in growing dread. *Please, God, please help us!* she prayed fervently.

Seconds seemed like hours as they waited. Finally, their ears detected the lone rider's sudden retreat. Ben did not wait any longer. He flung open the door, emerging outside with his rifle already raised to his shoulder. His eyes were able to make out the dark form of a man spurring his shrilly protesting mount into a gallop. Firing a shot at the rider, he was satisfied to hear a sharp curse of pain rise in the darkness.

He fired again, but the man did not stop. He rode off into the night, his horse's hooves thundering into the distance while Ben resisted the urge to give chase.

Jessie flew impulsively to the doorway, her body gripped with heart-stopping alarm at the thought that something had happened to her husband. She stood staring dazedly across at him in the darkness while he muttered a blistering oath and reluctantly lowered his rifle.

"Oh, Ben, are you all right?" she asked in a tremulous voice. He gave her a curt nod, his mouth compressing into a tight thin line of fury.

"He was moving too fast for me to get off a clean shot. But he's hit, which might at least make it easier for me to discover his identity." He stepped forward and gathered her close. She swayed weakly against him, her eyes sweeping closed as she offered up a silent heartfelt prayer of thanksgiving. Ben's arms tightened about her, and he said his own prayer for assistance in bringing the wounded man to justice.

"We'll have to stay here till morning," he told Jessie, his gaze full of a savage light when he thought about how close the coward's bullet had come to hitting her. "It's too dangerous to travel now. Come on," he said, leading her back inside the cabin. "You might as well try and get some sleep. I'll stand guard."

"Do you think he might come back?" she demanded anxiously, her face paling anew.

"No," he assured her with a faint smile. "But I'm not going to take any chances." He lifted her in his strong arms and placed her beneath the covers. His hand tenderly smoothed a strand of golden hair from her face, and his fierce gaze softened when he commanded, "Close your eyes, my love. I'll be able to hear if anyone else approaches."

"Wouldn't it be better if I stayed up with you?" she suggested, fearing for his safety as well.

"That's the last thing I need," he replied. She glimpsed the sudden wry amusement lurking in his deep blue gaze. "If not for the distraction you so ably provided, I wouldn't have been caught off-guard. Now go to sleep, wildcat."

She watched as he drew a chair up beside the door. He bent his tall frame down upon it, positioning his rifle within easy reach at his side. Jessie drew in a shuddering breath and obediently closed her eyes. The flames danced in the fireplace nearby, but their warmth failed to chase the chill from her body. Recalling the enchantment she and Ben had shared only a short time earlier, she shuddered again at the memory of how it had been so abruptly shattered. She felt sick inside at the possibility that the man who had fired the shot had witnessed their intimacy beforehand.

"Ben?" she asked, opening her eyes again.

"Yes?"

"You think it was one of the company's men, don't you?"

"I do," he replied, then added with a deep frown, "Once again, however, I have no proof."

"You don't think he meant to kill us, do you?"

"If he did, he sure as hell didn't try very hard." He cast her another faint smile. "They meant to warn me off, Jessamyn—nothing more. First the barn, now this."

"But how did they know where to find us?" she questioned in growing confusion.

"We were followed." He thought of Cole Hagan, but

396

then discarded the notion that the gunslinger had been the one. No, he told himself, Hagan wouldn't have settled for a single shot through the window.

"Oh, Ben, how long is this going to go on?" cried Jessie, her heart twisting at the thought of further violence. "There must be a way to settle things before someone gets hurt!"

"There might be," he responded enigmatically. Declining to elaborate, he told her once more, "Go to sleep, my love."

Certain she would never be able to do so, she nonetheless closed her eyes and turned her head on the pillow. . . .

Ben awakened her at dawn. Her eyes traveled to the window, where she was surprised to observe the first rays of sunlight warming the glass. She slipped from the bed and hurried to dress, while Ben stepped outside to saddle their horses.

When they reached the school, it was to find three men waiting along with the children. Jessie immediately recognized two of the men as Mr. Fielding and Mr. Humboldt, but the third looked only vaguely familiar to her.

"We thought you ought to know we had some trouble last night," Fielding told Ben as he helped Jessie dismount in front of the building.

"What kind of trouble?"

"Someone fired a shot through my window."

"And mine!" added Humboldt. "They damned near hit one of the children!"

Jessie inhaled sharply, her eyes flying to Ben. His own gaze had taken on the look of cold steel.

"They *did* hit Reed here!" Kristen's father disclosed angrily, giving a curt nod toward the man beside him.

"They just winged me," insisted Reed. He flushed beneath Jessie's look of concern before telling Ben, "But they like to've scared my poor woman clean out of her wits. I don't think there's any call for that, do you, Chandler?"

"No. I don't," he agreed grimly. "Did any of you get a look at them?"

"It was too dark," answered Harmon's father with a regretful shake of his head. "From the sound of it, though, there was only one of them."

"Same at my place," said Humboldt. "I haven't heard if anyone else got a 'visit' or not."

"I did," Ben finally revealed. His gaze moved to Jessie, who stood beside him "Or rather, *we* did," he amended.

"What are we going to do about it?" Humboldt demanded. "Hell, we can't let them keep plugging away at our houses and burning our barns.

"I say we get our hands on those bastards sitting on their backsides in Maxwell's house and ride them out of town on a rail!" suggested Humboldt.

"That'll only make things worse," Reed cautioned gravely. He looked back to the man who was leading them in the fight against tyranny. "What do you think we ought to do, Chandler?"

"For now . . . nothing."

"Nothing?" Humboldt echoed in disbelief.

"Chandler's right," Fielding reluctantly conceded. "They're just trying to put the scare in us. They'd probably like nothing better than for us to do something stupid; it would give them that much more to use against us in the courts."

"The courts!" Humboldt remarked with a gesture of disgust. "This thing won't be settled in the damned courts! It will be settled right here in Colfax County, with more fighting and more killing and—"

"I got work to do," Reed broke in to announce calmly. He smiled at Jessie. "And Mrs. Chandler's got youn'uns to teach." He pulled on his hat and nodded silently at

Ben, then mounted his horse again.

Fielding and Humboldt exchanged a few more words with Ben before swinging up into their saddles as well. The three men rode off together, leaving Ben and Jessie to be greeted at last by the twins. He headed back to the ranch soon thereafter, while she summoned the children inside with the bell. There was a good deal of excitement over the previous night's treachery, and it took a while before the class finally settled in to the day's routine.

That same evening, Jessie argued to no avail with her husband about his planned attendance at an emergency meeting of the Settlers' Organization. She still could not help thinking of Cole Hagan, and she watched with a heavy heart as Ben rode off after supper. He awakened her with a kiss when he returned home to find her asleep in a chair in the parlor. Carrying her to bed, he tucked her lovingly beneath the covers and joined her moments later, pulling her against him while the two of them drifted off to a well-deserved respite from their worries.

Jessie was surprised when, after school the following day, she saw that both Curly and Ben were waiting to provide escort for her and the twins. She approached the two men with a mild frown of bemusement, James and Hannah skipping happily alongside as she made her way across the yard.

"Curly's taking the twins home," Ben informed her, smiling briefly. "You and I are riding into town."

"Into town? But why?" she asked, her eyes moving to where the solemn ranch hand was already tossing each child in turn up onto their horses.

"I've got to talk to a man who was due to arrive on the stage today. I don't want to arouse any suspicion, so I need you to pay a visit to Lissa."

"Who is this man? And what do you mean about not wanting to arouse—"

"I'll explain everything later." His hands clasped her

about the waist, and he lifted her easily up into the saddle. Mounting beside her, he told Curly, "Don't look for us back till after dark."

Curly gave a nod and set off with the twins. Plagued by a sudden inexplicable uneasiness, Jessie rode beside her husband and waited for him to explain. When he did, her disquietude only increased.

"The man's name is Summerville, and he's a special investigator sent here by the federal government. No one else is aware of his true identity. It could be dangerous for him as well as for us if it became public knowledge. That's why I'm taking you along, Jessamyn. Summerville's supposed to be waiting at the hotel."

"But . . . surely no one would dare—"

"They would and will," he asserted, his blue eyes full of a particularly grim light. "They're capable of doing anything to get what they want."

His words burned in her ears. She felt a sharp tremor of fear course through her, fear for the man she loved and for all the other men involved in the perilous struggle.

"But how do you know about this man?" she asked at a sudden thought. "And why is he coming here to meet with *you?*" She watched as Ben's lips curved into a soft smile of irony.

"Let's just say my father has a lot of friends in Washington."

"Of course," she murmured, recalling what Martha had once told her. "He is an attorney, isn't he? I suppose he could provide invaluable assistance in this matter."

"Unfortunately, that's not the case. He uses his influence as best he can, but the company has plenty of their own high-ranking associates in Washington. And in Santa Fe," he added, his eyes suffused with a dull glow now. He tightened his grip on the reins and met Jessie's bright, troubled gaze.

Arriving in Cimarron, they immediately headed for the

St. James. Lissa, as they soon discovered, had left her post momentarily in order to purchase some supplies at the general store. Ben checked the hotel's register, then led Jessie upstairs with him to the room at the far end of the hallway. He knocked brusquely on the door, which was opened by a dark-haired man whose appearance was purposely nondescript.

"Summerville?" Ben asked quietly.

"Who are you?" the man first demanded.

"Ben Chandler." He was satisfied to see the investigator's features relax into a faint smile.

"I'm Summerville. I thought you'd never get here," he said. He swung the door wider, then smiled again as Ben introduced him to Jessie. She returned the man's polite greeting before shifting her emerald gaze back to her husband.

"You'd better go see if you can find Lissa," he told her.

"Perhaps I should simply wait downstairs," she suggested, suddenly reluctant to leave him.

"No. Now do as I say and go on," he insisted. Too worried about him to take offense at his summary dismissal of her, she gathered up her skirts and left him alone with the man whose presence had been ordered cloaked in secrecy for his own protection.

Jessie emerged outside, her eyes narrowing a bit against the sun's brightness. She sighed, then turned her steps toward the general store. Engrossed with thoughts of Ben and his involvement in something she knew to be dangerous, she did not at first notice William Easton approaching from the opposite direction. By the time she looked up to see him a short distance away on the boardwalk, his path was being barred by a raven-haired man whose dark eyes gleamed with deadly intent.

Though his back was turned toward her, Jessie immediately recognized him. *Cole Hagan.* Her pulses leapt in alarm as she drew up short. She was not yet close

enough to hear what he was saying to William, but sh
could tell from the way he stood so insolently in front
the older man that he meant him no good. Althoug
tempted to intervene, she forced herself to remain wher
she was.

"I beg your pardon, sir, but you happen to be in m
way," William Easton said politely enough, though h
tone was very cold. He knew who Hagan was, but he wa
not afraid of him.

"It sure looks like it," Cole drawled with a so
malevolent laugh. He lifted a hand to negligently tilt h
hat farther back upon his dark head. "Your name'
Easton, isn't it?"

"Yes. And yours is Hagan. Now, if you don't mind,
William concluded with a frown, attempting to pass. Col
moved squarely in front of him again.

"But I do mind, you old bastard. I heard tell you're on
of those 'Indian lovers' trying to take land away from th
white and give to the red-skinned sons of bitches who—'

"I don't care for your language, Hagan, nor for th
tone of your voice," William interrupted in rising ange

"Then why don't you do something about it?" th
gunslinger taunted with a sneer. "Why don't you dra
on me, 'Grandpa'? Why don't you show me what the
teach all you stinkin' Johnny Rebs back home?"

"If you think to provoke me into drawing my weapon
Mr. Hagan, then you are headed for disappointment,'
the older man responded with a faint sardonic smile
"Your reputation with a gun precedes you, and I an
neither as old nor as foolish as you seem to believe.'
He did not wear a holster as did the other man, bu
instead carried a pearl-handled derringer within th
inside pocket of his coat. Hagan was aware of this; he had
made it a point to research the job thoroughly.

"You got a cigar, Easton?" he asked unexpectedly.

"A cigar?" William repeated, his brows drawing

402

ogether in puzzlement. His eyes narrowed imperceptibly, but he gave a curt nod of affirmation.

"Then why don't you give me one? Hell, old man, if you're not going to draw on me, we might as well call a truce," offered Cole. The smile on his lips belied the murderous plan he was about to play out.

Though William Easton was quite naturally suspicious of the gunslinger's sudden change of attitude, he was too generous in spirit to deny the man such a simple, harmless request. He raised his right hand to his coat pocket to retrieve one of the cigars he always kept there.

Something prompted Jessie to move forward at that point. But it was too late.

Cole Hagan seized advantage of the older man's actions. Shouting a curse as though in anger, he drew his gun and shot William. His dark predatory gaze shone with triumphant satisfaction as his unwitting opponent crumpled to the boardwalk.

Jessie screamed when the shot rang out. Unmindful of her own safety, she raced along the boardwalk and fell to her knees beside William. Other people came running as well, so that a crowd had already gathered by the time she called out for someone to fetch a doctor, then raised her head to glare vengefully up at Hagan.

"Why did you do it?" she demanded, tears of outrage glistening in her fiery green eyes. "He never meant you any harm! He didn't even have a gun!" Some of the men grabbed Cole at the sound of her accusations, but he appeared strangely unconcerned.

"If you'll look in his coat pocket, you'll find a gun," he insisted smoothly. "He was going for it when I drew mine. It was nothing more than self-defense." He cast Jessie a slow derisive smile when one of the men hastened to either confirm or deny Hagan's claim.

"Easton's got a gun all right," the man announced, rising to his feet again.

403

"That don't prove nothin'!" one of the onlooker protested.

Lissa pushed her way through now, and she pale when she caught sight of William's unconscious form Meeting Jessie's stormy horror-filled gaze, she kne down as well and lifted William's hand to press he fingers against his wrist. His pulse was weak, but he wa at least still alive. She, too, set up an anxious plea fo someone to get the doctor, then placed her han comfortingly over Jessie's.

"I seen the whole thing!" a young man suddenl proclaimed above the crowd's roar. Everyone quieted t hear his story, which he proceeded to relate in an excite rush. "I was across the street, and I seen Mr. Easto talkin' to this feller here"—he jerked a thumb to indicat Cole—"and then I seen Mr. Easton reachin' into hi coat! He was outdrawn, clear as day!"

"Let me through, damn it!" the sheriff thundered arriving upon the scene at last. His narrowed, examinin gaze traveled from William's prone body to Cole Hagan "Did you shoot him, you bastard?" he demande wrathfully. William Easton was well liked by everyone i town, and he himself counted the man as a persona friend.

"I did," Cole admitted, then allowed the meres suggestion of a smile to touch his lips. "In self-defense."

"That's right, Sheriff," the man beside him seconded though with obvious reluctance. Musing that he an most of the townfolk would like nothing better than t see Cole Hagan and all his kind dancing at the end of rope, he added, "Hagan's got himself a witness."

"Some of you men get Easton over to Doc Prater's!" the sheriff now commanded harshly. His gaze was full o fury and contempt when he looked back to Cole. "Let' go, Hagan! You and your damned 'witness' are coming

404

ver to the jail so I can make a full report. And self-
efense or not," he cautioned in a low, simmering tone,
you'd better get out of town and stay out!"

"Thanks for the warning, Sheriff," Cole drawled
azily. His eyes met Jessie's one last time. "But I don't
im to move on till I've got what I want."

His words struck fear in Jessie's heart, but she was
etermined that he should not know it. She shot him
nother venomous glance, then stiffened when he merely
ave a low chuckle and sauntered away.

She and Lissa followed along as four men carefully
fted William and carried him down the street. Dr.
rater met them halfway, instructing them to bring the
ounded man inside the house at once. The two young
omen waited in the hallway outside the examining room
hile the doctor and his wife began their efforts to save
he gray-haired Southern gentleman who was known for
is unfailing kindness and generosity.

"I saw Hagan talking to Mr. Easton, but I—I never
uspected he meant to kill him!" Jessie confided brokenly
o Lissa, her eyes full of mingled anguish and guilt.

"How could you possibly have known?" The tall
edhead slipped an arm about her shoulders. "I don't
elieve Hagan's story of self-defense, witness or no
itness. William Easton is not a man who's easily
rovoked, Jessie."

"I know. I just don't understand why Cole Hagan did
t! Mr. Easton isn't a member of the Settler's Organiza-
ion, and—"

"No, but he's involved in the struggle to get the
icarilla Apaches their own reservation. And it's company
and that's in question," Lissa pointed out.

The doctor's wife emerged a short time later to tell
hem that although William had been shot in the chest,
he bullet had missed his heart. She added that it was

405

entirely too soon to be able to discern the true extent of his injuries, and that she would send word to them at the hotel as soon as she knew something.

They returned to the St. James to wait. Jessie hurried upstairs to tell Ben what had occurred. He was still closeted with the federal investigator, but he stepped outside into the hallway when she insisted upon speaking with him.

"What is it, Jessamyn?" he demanded with a frown, his features tensing at her visible distress.

"It's William Easton," she told him. "He's been shot! The doctor is tending to him now, and Mrs. Prater has promised to keep us informed about his condition."

"Who did it?" asked Ben. His tone was deceptively low and level.

"Cole Hagan." She blanched at the savage gleam in his eyes, and she hastened to explain. "Hagan claims it was self-defense, but I don't believe it! I saw the two of them talking together moments before it happened." She shuddered involuntarily at the memory. "A witness stepped forward to bear out Hagan's story. The sheriff said he would file a report, but I—I fail to see what purpose that will serve."

"Wait for me downstairs," he instructed, his handsome face dangerously grim. "Summerville and I are almost finished."

"What are you planning to do?" she was almost afraid to ask. She knew he had been friends with William Easton for years; so had Martha. *Martha*. Her heart twisted at the thought of what the older woman's reaction would be to the news.

"Whatever needs to be done" was all he would say.

When he came downstairs, he headed immediately over to the jail. Jessie was surprised when he returned only minutes later. Alarmed at the look on his face, she

406

stened forward to ask him what had happened.

"Hagan's already gone," he revealed with barely
ntrolled fury.

"Gone?" she echoed in disbelief. "But how can that
?"

"The sheriff had no choice. With the witness to back
m up, Hagan couldn't be charged."

"Dear God," she murmured, dazedly realizing that the
nslinger could strike again. She could not bear the
ought that Ben might be his next victim.

"I'm going over to the doctor's now. So help me God, if
illiam dies . . ." He broke off and muttered a curse, his
es burning with helpless rage. Jessie's hand closed
ntly about the tensed hardness of his arm.

"He isn't going to die, Ben," she asserted, though she
ew it could well be a lie. She was glad when he pulled
r close.

It was nearly midnight by the time they finally
turned to the Chapparosa. But at least they returned
ith the assurance of William Easton's recovery. Dr.
rater had told them that William Easton was in
markable health for a man his age; his recovery would
slow but nevertheless complete.

The dangers Ben and Jessie were facing almost daily
w made their time together that much more precious.
he longed for the time when they could settle into a
ore normal routine, when they could concentrate on
ving their lives to the fullest without the shadow of
nstant peril hanging over them.

That night, after they had found Martha waiting up for
em and told her what had happened, Ben took his wife
bed and made love to her with incredible tenderness.
he clung to him as though she would never let him go,
r body responding without restraint to the loving
astery of his.

407

Afterward, when they lay together in the big brass be with their passions fully sated and their naked bodie gloriously entwined, they spoke of their hopes an dreams for the future. It was a future clouded for th moment, yet they refused to believe it held anything bu happiness for them.

Nineteen

Sunday arrived at last, bringing with it friends and neighbors from miles around. They came on horseback, in buckboards and wagons and buggies, gathering beneath a clear blue sky on the grounds of the Chaparosa to celebrate the coming marriage of Lissa and Curly. The wedding itself would not take place until after roundup, but the betrothal provided a good excuse for everyone to forget their troubles for a day and enjoy the fellowship of others.

Tables had been set up in the front yard, offering a vast array of food and drink for the nearly two hundred guests. A fiddler was on hand to provide his particularly energetic brand of music for the dancing that would commence after dinner. Families brought their own blankets and quilts to spread upon the ground, and many of the women insisted upon adding their own "special recipe" concoctions to the already overflowing bounty of refreshments.

Children scampered energetically all about, while babies cried and were fed or cuddled. Men talked politics and weather and crops and cattle, while the womenfolk gossiped and traded advice on everything from cooking to child-rearing to handling men. People temporarily set aside their grudges and differences, the strong pioneer spirit they all shared bonding them together in harmony for at least this one day.

The bride-to-be looked especially lovely, with her slender figure encased in a fitted pale blue silk gown that had been a gift from Martha. There was a glow about her, a certain sparkle in her eyes that made her look much younger than her two and thirty years. Jessie knew it was because Lissa's heart had finally been set free to love again.

Her own attire was undeniably becoming, consisting of a violet gown trimmed with a deep flounce and narrow lengthwise tucks, a Brussels straw bonnet, and black kid shoes featuring bows of narrow black silk ribbon. Ben had teasingly admonished that it wasn't fair to the other women for her to be so beautiful, but she had retorted that his opinion was biased and therefore not to be trusted.

Spotting Lissa near the front steps, she gathered up her skirts and made her way across the yard. The sun blazed with a particularly bright radiance overhead, but a light breeze ensured the day would not grow too warm.

"Where is Curly?" asked Jessie, approaching Lissa with a smile. As mistress of the Chapparosa, she had willingly performed the duties of welcoming guests when they arrived and making frequent rounds through the crowd. Ben was an equally attentive host, so that she had now been denied the pleasure of his company for nearly half an hour.

"I'm not exactly sure," the tall redhead admitted, her eyes lighting with both pleasure and relief at the sight of her friend. She was at present enjoying a brief respite from the overwhelming flood of congratulations and warm wishes for future happiness. "He wandered away several minutes ago, and I've not seen him since!"

"Ben has disappeared as well," Jessie revealed with a

410

dramatic little sigh, then smiled again. "But I suppose they'll return eventually. Meanwhile, you and I can console one another!"

"Oh, Jessie, I—I can scarcely believe this is happening!" Lissa exclaimed, her opal gaze very wide as it traveled over the lively throng of celebrants. "I never expected such a response from these people. So many of them have avoided me all these years, and now things have changed overnight! Did you know that Abigail Higgins actually made a point of telling me how happy she was for me?" Lissa shook her head in wonderment. "I don't understand it at all."

"It's quite simple, really," Jessie replied, her green eyes twinkling. "You have gained instant respectability as a result of your betrothal! Indeed, Miss Boone, you are about to join the ranks of married women, and that apparently entitles you to the belated respect of the good people of Cimarron."

"Well, it doesn't make sense to me. *I* haven't changed. But I suppose I should be grateful for whatever it is that's brought about this unforeseen miracle!" she commented with a soft laugh.

"You and Curly deserve your happiness, Lissa," Jessie told her earnestly. "And I'm so very glad you'll be living nearby."

"I am, too, though I honestly wish I didn't have to leave my position at the hotel. The Lamberts have been so good to me. But I am looking forward to having a home of my own." She smiled at Jessie, then impulsively hugged her. "You and Ben are the dearest, most generous people in all the world! I still can't believe you've given us the land!"

"Ben says Curly has more than earned it," insisted Jessie. "And he told me your house should be completed by the end of the month. I suspect Martha's sewing machine will be given little rest. In fact, I wouldn't be

411

at all surprised if you had curtains long before you had windows!"

"I told her I didn't want her going to so much trouble, but she said it would give her something to do while William Easton recuperates. I think there's more between those two than meets the eye," opined Lissa. She grew solemn, her gaze clouding with sudden worriment. "There's been a lot of talk in town about what happened to him, Jessie. A fight broke out in the saloon Friday night, and I heard it was because some foolish young cowboy made the mistake of saying Mr. Easton got what he deserved. Mr. Lambert keeps threatening to close the saloon, but it's very profitable and we probably couldn't keep the hotel open without it."

"I know," sighed Jessie. "Perhaps something will occur to improve the situation soon. Even the children are being affected by these tensions that are running so high. They're very sensitive to what's going on, even more so than their parents seem to realize."

"What about the school, Jessie? Are you going to continue to teach?"

"I hope so." Her lips curved into a smile and her eyes sparkled with wholly feminine mischief. "Ben Chandler doesn't know it yet, but he's going to be persuaded—"

"Did I hear my name mentioned?" Ben demanded amiably as he came up beside his wife and favored her with a warm look that sent the color flying to her cheeks. To Jessie's eyes, he appeared more devastatingly handsome than ever, his blue chambray shirt and denim trousers fitting his hard, lithely muscled body to perfection. He was wearing no hat, so that the sunlight set his thick chestnut hair afire with glints of gold.

"You did," Jessie affirmed without a trace of remorse. "It is a wife's prerogative to speak about her husband when he is safely out of earshot!"

"And it's a husband's prerogative to tell his wife to

shut up and come dance with him." He took her by the hand and smiled at Lissa. "Curly said to tell you to save him the first dance. He's doing his damnedest to get away from Mooney and some of those other—"

"But no one's dancing yet!" Jessie broke in to protest.

"Precisely, Mrs. Chandler. It's traditional for the host and hostess to start things off." He firmly tucked her hand through his arm, his magnificent blue eyes gleaming affectionately down at her. "It may surprise you to learn that I dance very well, my love."

"You do everything well!" she insisted loyally.

"Some things better than others," he retorted in a low voice meant only for her ears. He chuckled in delight at her blush, then led her forward to where a space had been cleared for the dancing. At a signal from him, the fiddler struck up a reel, its lively strains filling the air and lightening the hearts of all those who heard it.

Jessie soon discovered that her husband's playful boast was not unfounded. He was an excellent dancer. His fingers tightened possessively about hers, and his strong arm encircled her slender uncorseted waist while they whirled together in the graceful movements of the dance. Other couples joined in, while those who merely sat and watched gained almost equal enjoyment from the sight before them.

Curly and Lissa, meanwhile, were finally reunited. He wasted no time before catching her up against him and spinning her out into the midst of the other dancers. Lissa was pleasantly surprised at her future husband's abilities, for she had never imagined he would be so adept. He seemed to have been born to ride, not dance, and she eyed him with loving suspicion while demanding to know where he had acquired such skills—and from whom.

"From my mother," he replied seriously, though his eyes were brimming with wry amusement.

"Really?" Lissa challenged with one archly raised eyebrow. "And did 'Ma' happen to teach you anything else I don't know about?"

"Nope. But I learned a few things here and there."

"I'll just bet you did!"

"I don't think you'll have any complaints." His lips curved into a thoroughly disarming smile when he observed the faint color rising to her face.

"You're a wicked man, Curly Taylor," she scolded though without any conviction whatsoever. Her eyes softened, her hand trembling a bit within the work-hardened strength of his as she vowed, "I'll make you a good wife. You'll never have cause to regret marrying me."

"Never thought I would," he drawled, another rare smile making her legs feel weak. He pulled her closer and murmured against her ear, "I'll be glad when roundup's over with."

"So will I." She smiled tremulously up at him when he gazed down into her face again, her heart swelling with more love and joy than she would have believed possible. The pain and horrors of the past had been vanquished by this unlikely hero, who was no knight in shining armor but the most sensitive, caring, loving man she had ever known. Let other women have their handsome, dashing beaux, thought Lissa happily. She would have Curly.

Ben finally took mercy on his wife, who claimed to have eaten nothing since breakfast, and led her back to the tables in front of the house. The twins came bounding up soon thereafter, their little faces beaming with pleasure and excitement.

"Papa, can we go down to the river now?" asked Hannah.

"John and Peter told us they know how to catch a fish with nothing but their bare hands, but I don't believe them!" declared James. "They said they'd prove it if I'd

414

come down to the river!"

"All the others are already there!" Hannah added by way of persuasion. "We told them we couldn't go because Aunt Martha said she didn't want us getting soaked to the skin, but we *promise* not to get wet!"

Ben and Jessie exchanged looks full of parental understanding and fondly indulgent humor. James and Hannah waited anxious for the verdict, which caused their blue eyes to light with triumph when it came.

"All right," their father urged, then cautioned sternly, "But tell everyone to stay together."

"We will!" they sang out in unison as they took themselves off again.

"I'm not at all sure you should have let them go," Jessie told Ben, her silken brow creasing into a frown.

"They'll be fine. Hell, if one of them does fall in, there'll be no lack of volunteers to fish them out," he proclaimed dryly.

"Oh, Mrs. Chandler!" Abigail Higgins suddenly called out behind them. Jessie rolled her eyes heavenward, prompting Ben to smile in devilish amusement before she turned to face the troublesome woman who bustled forth to claim her attention.

"Yes, Mrs. Higgins?" she asked politely.

"Several of the ladies wish to have your opinion about a matter concerning the school." Without waiting for a response, she took Jessie's arm and demanded rather imperiously, "Come along, please. I'm sure your husband won't mind sparing you for a few minutes!"

"Not at all," he assured her solemnly, though humor still lurked in his gaze. Jessie cast him a look that promised revenge, but she had little choice but to go with Abigail.

Curly and Lissa joined Ben at the table just as Jessie was disappearing into the crowd. A square dance had begun, with Will Grant calling the steps and a number of people who had not previously danced now feelir themselves moved by the spirit to do so.

"It's nice to see everyone having a good time," Liss remarked as Curly handed her a glass of punch.

"There's been little enough cause for celebration, Ben said quietly. His handsome features relaxed into grin when he told Curly, "You've done us all a great favc by deciding to get yourself hitched."

"My pleasure," the ranch hand drawled.

Several others gathered around the tables now, the appetites evidently stimulated by all the fresh air an activity. Jessie returned to her husband's side in remarkably short amount of time, her eyes full c reproach but a smile playing about her lips.

"Mark my words, Ben Chandler," she threatened, " will—"

The loud report of a gunshot suddenly rang out abov the music. The startled fiddler abruptly ceased hi efforts, while everyone turned in stunned astonishmen toward the unmistakable sound of hoofbeats drawin closer. Without warning, more than two dozen maske riders came thundering down upon the crowd.

Screams filled the air as men, women, and childre scattered everywhere in a frantic attempt to get out of th way. The horsemen rode forward with relentless fury the lower part of their faces covered by brightly covere kerchiefs, their hands clasping six-shooters that the fired into the air with ever increasing fervor.

None of the celebrants were armed; they had no expected trouble while in the force of so many number in broad daylight. Their guns were at the moment sittin uselessly in scabbards, below wagon seats, or in one o the barns designated for that purpose. Thus, they coul do nothing more than watch in mingled horror an outrage as the intruders trampled the quilts and blankets sent the tables crashing to the ground, and added blood urdling yells to the already terrifying din of the gunfire.

Ben, who had instinctively pushed Jessie to the ground and shielded her body with his own, was the first to take action. Telling his wife to stay put, he and Curly darted up the steps and into the house. They each quickly grabbed a shotgun from the rack beside the door, then stormed back outside to take aim at the riders.

But it was too late. The horsemen had already taken flight, leaving behind a trail of fear and destruction as they rode away across the sunlit prairie. It had all happened so quickly, and it had ended as abruptly as it had begun.

Battling the urge to go after the men who had dared to terrorize his guests, Ben looked to Jessie. She was already climbing to her feet, her eyes flying to him in renewed alarm at a sudden thought.

"The children! Dear God, Ben, *the children!*" she cried hoarsely.

He ground out a curse and headed for the river. Jessie was close on his heels, as were a number of other worried parents. They discovered their children still gathered along the water's edge, frightened but unharmed.

"Those men told us they'd shoot us if we made any noise!" Hannah burst out when Ben caught her up gratefully against him. Jessie knelt to draw James close, closing her eyes and repeating a silent prayer of thanksgiving.

"They came riding up through the river!" the little boy explained in a breathless rush. He had been so scared he could hardly move, but he wasn't about to let on about it. "We couldn't see much of their faces, but they had the meanest eyes I ever saw!"

"What was all the shooting about, Papa?" asked Hannah, trying her best not to cry. "Did they hurt anybody?"

"I don't think so," he answered grimly. He lifted her in

his arms and carried her back toward the house, th[e]
gave both of the twins over into Jessie's care while
hastened to discover if anyone had been injured in t[he]
attack. There were a few cuts and bruises but nothi[ng]
worse, only badly strained nerves and a burning desi[re]
for revenge.

Several of the families left right away, while othe[r]
remained behind to help survey the damage and clean [up]
the mess. Ben found himself being confronted by [a]
veritable mob of angry settlers, who demanded that th[ey]
band together and do something to put a stop to t[he]
company's scare tactics once and for all.

"This time they've gone too far!" Humboldt insiste[d.]
His words were met with a roar of approval from t[he]
others.

"You're right," Ben surprised them by agreeing. H[is]
eyes smoldered with a savage light. "This time they'[ve]
gone too far." Twice now, they had dared to send me[n]
onto the Chapparosa. And now, he mused with bare[ly]
controlled rage, they had thrown off the cover [of]
darkness and imperiled innocent women and childre[n]
while carrying out their treachery. *No more!* he vowe[d.]
By damn, no more!

"What are you going to do about it, Chandler?"
another man demanded. Like most of the others, h[e]
looked instinctively to Ben for the solution.

"I'm going to ride to Santa Fe and pay a call on th[e]
governor."

"What the hell good will that do?" Fielding countere[d]
with a scowl of disapproval.

"More than you think." He was thinking of Summe[r]
ville, who would have plenty to offer in his report t[o]
Washington. The federal investigator, he knew, woul[d]
be more than willing to help him convince the governo[r]
to call in the troops from Fort Union. The presence [of]
the military would buy them some desperately neede[d]

me . . . Time to press the matter before the courts. Time to gather their own forces to put an end to the company's reign of terror.

"I say we form a posse and go after those yellow-bellied bastards!" another man in the crowd piped up.

"We could kill every damned one of them," Ben responded in a quiet, clear tone, "and it still wouldn't make any difference. The company would only send more, and then more, and then more after that. The only way to win this is to keep our wits about us and outmaneuver them."

"Yeah, well, you go ahead and do what you can to *outmaneuver* them!" the man retorted with disdain. "Me, I'm going to shoot first from now on and ask questions later!"

There were a few others who embraced this hopeless strategy, but the majority sided with Ben. By the time the last of his guests took themselves home, it had been decided that he would leave for Santa Fe the next morning.

"Santa Fe?" Jessie repeated, her pulses leaping in alarm when he told her of his plans. Alone with him in their bedroom, she was in the process of changing into another gown. The violet had, unfortunately, been ruined during the frenzied charge of the horsemen. "Surely you're not planning to go alone?" she asked in disbelief.

"I have to," Ben insisted. "Curly's got to stay here and keep an eye on things. And besides, I can travel faster if I'm alone."

"But what if someone tries to prevent you from reaching Santa Fe?" she pointed out. She was surprised at the faint smile that touched his lips.

"I learned how to take care of myself a long time ago, Jessamyn."

"As I have found it necessary to remind you before, Ben Chandler, you are *not* invincible!"

419

"Maybe not. But I still have to go." He drew her close his arms enveloping her with their warm, comforting strength. "I want you to close the school again."

"Close the school?" she echoed in disbelief. She tilted her head back to look up at him. "But why?"

"Because I don't want you in danger."

"For heaven's sake, I have already been in plenty danger and have come through it unscathed!" she declared quite feelingly, her emerald gaze flashing up into the piercing blue intensity of his. "Surely you don expect me to sit at home, cowering in fear at what might happen! That would be a fine example for my students! do not intend to surrender to defeat so easily, and—"

"Easy, wildcat," he murmured with a low, resonant chuckle. "If I believed for one minute you'd have an trouble at the school, I'd not hesitate to bolt the damned door. But," he admitted, pulling her head back down to rest upon his chest, "I don't think the company woul ever resort to using innocent children to get what the want."

"When—when will you be back?" Jessie faltered sudden tears starting to her eyes.

"A couple of days. Maybe three. I've arranged for Summerville to meet me there; Curly took him th message when he drove Lissa back to town thi afternoon."

"There's nothing I can do to keep you from going, there?" she asked, drawing in a slightly ragged breath

"No. But you have my permission to try," he willingly consented, taking a seat on the edge of the bed an pulling her down upon his lap. His eyes brimmed with a intoxicating mixture of passion and amusement. "Supper's not for an hour yet."

"You are impossible!" she lamented, though her own gaze was soft and full of an answering glow. In spite of the trepidation she still felt over his coming journey, she

uld not help responding to his determination to make
ght of the matter. She would welcome a time, however
ief, in which to forget the horrors of that afternoon.
First you tell me my endeavors will avail me nothing,
en you tell me I may go right ahead and employ them
onetheless!"

"I did," he readily admitted. "And you're wasting
me."

His lips came down upon hers, while his hand crept
urposefully upward to the inner edges of her ruffled
en-leg drawers. She moaned softly, her hips squirming
delight upon his hard thighs. . . .

Ben set out for Santa Fe at first light the following
orning. Jessie watched him go with a heaviness of spirit
at would not be dispelled. She knew that her heart
ould not be at peace again until he had returned.
either her teaching nor the comforting presence of
artha and the twins could provide her with the solace
he needed.

The next three days were mercifully uneventful.
lthough the memories of that terrible Sunday afternoon
ad not yet faded, the children were at least able to
esume a normal routine at school. Jessie knew they
eeded those hours when their minds were occupied by
omething other than the escalating talk of revenge
round Cimarron—talk that was being perpetrated by a
umber of settlers and townsmen who advocated
iolence as a means of defeating the company.

Tensions were at an all-time high by the time Ben
eturned on Thursday. His visit to the governor had
roven successful; troops would be arriving from Fort
Inion in two days time.

"Oh, Ben, does this mean there will finally be an end to
he trouble?" Jessie asked hopefully, her whole being

flooded with joyful relief as she rested within the war
circle of his arms.

"Most of it," he replied, a faint smile touching his lip
"The matter of the grant has yet to be settled, but t
presence of the military should help put an end to t
company's tyranny."

"What about Cole Hagan and the other mercenaries?
She shuddered involuntarily at the thought of the ma
who had tried to kill William Easton. The memory of h
cold-blooded actions, as well as the way he had gazed
covetously upon her afterward, had returned to hau
her many times. "Surely now that the troops are comi
to Cimarron—"

"I don't know, Jessamyn," he said grimly. His blu
eyes were suffused with a fierce light. "If Hagan know
what's good for him, he'll get the hell out of the Territor
without delay."

Unaware that those words were a foreshadowing
what was to come, Jessie released a long pent-up sigh ar
pressed her soft curves closer to his undeniab
masculine hardness. She gave silent thanks for his sa
return and for the news he had brought with him. H
mind was still spinning at the realization that the dang
had finally passed.

Telling herself that she and her beloved could begin t
fulfill their dreams of a happy future at last, she close
her eyes and felt Ben's lips claiming hers in a kiss s
gentle in its insistence that she trembled with the swe
flood tide of passion it evoked within her.

The following afternoon, Jessie stood before the clas
shortly before dismissing them for the day. Her eye
traveled with pleasure over the eager young faces of he
students. The five Sheltons had finally returned t
school on Monday, and she smiled inwardly at the sigh

their red heads glistening in the sunlight that streamed
ough the windows.

"Now remember, children," she exhorted them all,
e're to have our first recitation program and spelling
e here at the schoolhouse next Friday night. That gives
one full week in which to prepare."

"Mrs. Chandler, do our folks *have* to come?" Harmon
elding complained.

"Yes, Harmon, they do. I'm sure they will very much
joy observing how much progress you've made in these
w short weeks."

"Mrs. Chandler?" Mary Sue's hand, almost perenially
the air for some reason or another, shot up again.

"Yes, Mary Sue?"

"My father says—"

"Dangblast it, Mary Sue Mooney, nobody gives a hoot
r holler what your pa's got to say!" Billy exclaimed,
owling in disgust.

"Billy Shelton!" Jessie admonished with a stern look.

"Well, hell—I mean *heck,* Mrs. Chandler," he offered
his own defense, "she don't never shut up about him!"

"Doesn't ever," corrected Jessie, trying very hard not
smile. "Regardless of what you think of her comments,
u must not interrupt—and certainly not with such
atant incivility."

"Huh?" he burst out in confusion.

"She means you're not supposed to be so rude,"
nnah obligingly explained.

"Well, then, if there's nothing else . . ." began Jessie,
ly to break off when she heard the sound of ap-
oaching hoofbeats outside. She did not grow alarmed
til they drew closer, at which time she was able to
scern that a large number of riders were bearing down
on the schoolhouse at a full gallop. Wondering
pefully if perhaps it was Ben and some of the settlers,
e turned her wide, anxious gaze back to the children.

"Please remain in your seats!" she directed. Her hea[rt] racing, she gathered up her skirts and started for t[he] door.

She got no farther than the first row of benches.

The door suddenly burst open, and Cole Hagan stepp[ed] into the room with his six-shooter drawn.

"*Hagan!*" Jessie breathed in horror.

Several of the girls screamed at the sight of the arm[ed] intruder. Billy Shelton, however, sprang up from his se[at] and raced instinctively toward the table in the fro[nt] corner where Jessie placed the weapons she collect[ed] each morning. He was already reaching for his gun wh[en] Cole fired a warning shot dangerously close to his han[d].

"Hold it right there, you little bastard!"

At the sound of the shot, most of the other childr[en] scrambled toward Jessie, who gathered them protective[ly] about her and faced Cole with her head held at a proud[,] defiant angle.

"What is it you want, Mr. Hagan?" she demanded, h[er] emerald gaze full of wrathful fire.

"*You,* teacher lady," he answered with a broa[d,] malevolent smile, then warned, "Do as I say, a[nd] nobody'll get hurt."

Jessie paled, her blood pounding in her ears as sh[e] realized that he meant what he said. She looked at th[e] children. *No, please God, no!* In that moment, she kne[w] she would do anything to keep them from harm.

"Very well," she told the gunslinger calmly, thoug[h] panic threatened to send her courage fleeing.

He advanced on her now, his steps slow and marked b[y] a sinister confidence. Jessie caught a glimpse of the oth[er] men waiting on horseback outside, and she felt her le[gs] grow perilously weak.

"We're going for a ride," Cole informed her with [a] sneer. His dark predatory gaze raked over her as she stoo[d] bravely before him.

424

"She's not going anywhere with you!" declared Peter, moving toward the man in a foolhardy attempt to save Jessie. She cried out in protest as Cole brought his hand back against the boy's face with bruising force. Peter fell heavily to the floor.

"No more!" Jessie insisted furiously, glaring up at Hagan. "I will go with you!"

She gazed briefly at the children again, her eyes filling with tears when she saw the stricken look on the twins' faces. Forcing a smile to her lips, she hugged both James and Hannah close.

"Don't worry," she reassured them tremulously. "I'll be fine. Tell your father—"

"Let's go!" Cole growled impatiently. Seizing her arm, he jerked her against him. He kept the gun pointed menacingly toward the children, who could only watch in helpless fear and rage and confusion as he forced Jessie outside.

Her bright, terror-filled gaze fell upon the horsemen, and she hastily noted that there were ten of them in all. Cole grabbed her about the waist and lifted her up onto his horse, then mounted behind her. Although every instinct screamed at her to fight him, she would not allow herself to do so.

The children, she repeated silently. She had to think of the children.

"Where are you taking me?" she demanded with admirable composure. She stiffened when Cole gave a soft, derisive laugh close to her ear.

"It doesn't matter," he replied evasively. His arm tightened about her waist until she could scarcely breath. "You'll be with me from now on, schoolmarm!"

"My husband will find me, Mr. Hagan," she vowed. "He will find me—and he will kill you." She knew that he spoke the truth, for Ben would never rest until he had accomplished both objectives. She would not allow her-

425

self to consider the possibility of his failure. Her hea
cried out to him, and she fought back the sob tha
suddenly welled up deep in her throat.

"You've got that wrong, *Mrs. Chandler,*" he drawle
his voice full of scorn. "If he follows us, he's a dea
man."

Jessie's heart twisted painfully. Still unable to believ
what was happening, she clutched at the saddlehorn fo
support and closed her eyes. Cole Hagan spurred hi
horse forward, leading the others as he rode away fron
the schoolhouse with his silent captive, heading towar
the beckoning mountains in the near distance.

Twenty

Jessie shivered and moved closer to the fire's warmth.
he flames cast long shadows that danced eerily up the
ck-spired walls behind her. Stars glowed with an
nbelievable brilliance overhead in the deepness of the
ght sky, while the chilling wind that swept down
rough the surrounding red sandstone palisades carried
ith it the scent of spruce and wild grapevines.

Wondering anew why Hagan had chosen to make camp
the very midst of the Cimarron Canyon, Jessie looked
ward the rushing waters of the river and felt a knot
ghtening in the pit of her stomach. The past few hours
ad been wrought with an almost unbearable anticipa-
on as she waited for the inevitable moment when the
nslinger finally decided to exercise what he had said
as his right as her new "husband." His evil laughter still
urned in her ears. Fighting against a fresh onslaught of
tter tears, she turned her thoughts back to the man she
ved more than life itself.

She knew that he would have learned of her abduction
ours ago. Was he already on his way to save her? Would
e even know where to search? What if Hagan had
ready exacted his own cruel revenge upon him? What if
e . . .

No! she screamed inwardly. She could not all
herself to think of the possibility that he was lyi
injured or even dead somewhere. *Ben!* his name echo
in the turbulent depths of her mind. *Dear God, please*
him be safe. . . . Please help him find me!

Her glistening emerald gaze shifted toward the gri
coarse-featured men who had risen to their feet on t
opposite side of the fire. They had shared a supper
beans and bacon a short time earlier and now sudden
began arguing amongst themselves about their ne
course of action. Cole Hagan was obviously their leade
but the plans he had just outlined were being met wi
staunch resistance from several of the others.

"We're makin' a clean break with the company, air
we?" challenged a member of the opposition. "Hell, ma
it ain't safe for us to stay in these parts no more!"

"Buck's right!" another hired gun seconded. "I'm f
hightailing it on down into Texas! They won't be lookir
for us there!"

"I'm the one giving the orders here!" Cole ground ou
his dark eyes blazing. "We're heading for Santa Fe, ju
like I said! The company owes us money—plenty of it-
and I'll be damned if I'm going to light out before I g
what's coming to me!"

"We could've been playin' this job out for a long tim
yet if not for that sonofabitch Chandler!" a young ma
with a pockmarked face and lank greasy hair reiterate
vengefully. "If it hadn't been for him gettin' the troop
called in, we—"

"It don't make much difference now," the olde
among them pointed out solemnly. He stood at Cole
right, and his cold gaze moved slowly over the faces of th
others. "Hagan's got Chandler's woman; that square
things. I'm going to Santa Fe to get my money. The rest o
you bastards can do what you like."

Jessie listened with a sinking feeling of dread as the

428

scussion grew more heated at that point. Although she
und herself wishing someone else would replace Cole
agan in the position of authority, she knew the
elihood of it was remote. And it wouldn't necessarily
ake things any better, she conceded. The other men
ppeared to be every bit as ruthless as the one who had
aimed her as his own.

Her heart leapt in alarm when Hagan broke away from
e group and strode toward her. She clutched the
anket more tightly about her and instinctively retreated
few steps, almost stumbling over one of the low scrub
nes that dotted the land along the river.

"Did you think I'd forgotten you, teacher lady?" he
eered as he came around the fire. Glimpsing the lustful
tent that burned in his dark gaze, Jessie fought down
e impulse to turn and run.

"I was hoping perhaps you and your *friends* would kill
1e another off!" she retorted with biting sarcasm,
etermined that he should not know how very much
raid she was. She held herself rigidly erect, her gaze
nflinching as it moved over his sinister, firelit counte-
ance.

"You're a sharp-tongued little bitch, aren't you?" he
marked, his own eyes narrowing as he gave a quiet,
ppreciative chuckle. "But as I told you before, I like a
oman with spirit." He loomed menacingly over her
ow. "By damn, I'm going to enjoy taming you and
nowing you what it means to be Cole Hagan's woman.
ll be the teacher from here on out!"

"Why are you doing this?" she demanded, desperately
alling for time while her mind raced to think of a way to
scape. "The company did not order you to abduct me!
ou can gain nothing by my presence here, so why don't
pu allow me to go—"

"I had a score to settle with your husband," he
eminded her. "And I decided the first time I saw you

raise your skirts that you might be worth the r
involved. I've been watching you, schoolmarm. I've be
biding my time." He paused and edged even closer.
figured I ought to get something extra for my trouble
he told her with a hard look. "This way, those fan
suited bastards in Santa Fe get what they want, and so
I. That husband of yours won't put up a fight agai
them so long as I've got you with me. The only thing i
don't aim to let you go."

"You cannot hold me captive forever!" she cr
hotly. "I will find a way to escape you eventually, a
then I will see you brought to justice for your crime
Recalling the way he had gunned down William East
and struck Peter O'Leary, her eyes kindled with ev
more righteous fury. "You are nothing but a cowar
blackguard who preys on women and old men a
innocent children! Tell me, Mr. Hagan, have you ev
faced an opponent in a fair fight?" she taunted, st
frantically trying to think of a way she could prevent h
from carrying through his vile intentions.

"What difference does it make? The only thing th
matters is who wins." A slow, baneful smile spread acro
his features as he moved closer. "And I won, scho
marm," he decreed, his voice edged with desire as
finally reached for her.

Panic gripped her at the mere thought of his touc
She correctly sensed that his ravishment of her wou
be devoid of tenderness, devoid of mercy. *Ben!* she cri
out in the very depths of her soul. What they had shar
in love, Cole Hagan would seize in brutal lust. God fo
give her, but she would die before she allowed it
happen!

"No!"

She whirled about to take flight. Cole easily caug
her, his fingers closing about her arm with brutal forc
She screamed in protest when he yanked her back again

m, and she immediately set up a violent struggle to be
ee. Her hand doubling into a fist, she hit him with
arprising vehemence squarely on the jaw. He cursed,
omentarily relaxing his grip.

Jessie stumbled away, then rounded on him again
hen he grabbed her skirt and jerked her backward. She
ruck him wildly about the head and shoulders, while he
rought his arms up in an attempt to ward off her blows.

The men watching on the other side of the fire laughed
1 raucous enjoyment at the sight of their leader's
ifficulty in subduing the beautiful golden-haired spit-
re.

"You want some help, Hagan?" one of them called out.

"Hell, Cole, I think she's too much for you to handle!"
nother said gleefully.

"Looks like Chandler's got his brand stamped too
eep!"

"I'll ride her for you, Hagan!"

"Use your spurs, man!"

Jessie was impervious to their derisive taunts, for she
ould think only of denying her would-be conqueror his
oal. She cried out when he suddenly gave a vicious tug
n her skirt, tearing half of the gathered folds free of the
vaistband. He finally caught one of her arms again and
wisted it cruelly behind her back. She tried to strike at
iim with her other hand, but he brought about an end to
ier struggles by jerking her arm farther upward and
angling a hand within the mass of golden curls that
treamed riotously down about her face and shoulders.

"Damn you!" he rasped out, his face a mask of
vengeful fury. "I might have gone easy on you, but not
1ow! Now, you stupid bitch, I'm going to make you pay
or making a fool of me in front of my men!"

"Let me go!" she seethed. Another sharp cry of pain
oroke from her lips when he twisted her arm again.

"They'd like nothing better than to watch me take you!

431

How about it, *schoolmarm?* How about I give you a less[ ]
you'll never forget?" he threatened.

Without waiting for a response, he released his h[ ]
upon her hair and brought his hand around to the fr[ ]
of her white lawn blouse. She screamed when he tore [ ]
delicate fabric all the way down to her waist. Struggl[ ]
futilely in his grasp, she gazed down in horror as [ ]
fingers traced a cruelly tantalizing path along t[ ]
rounded neckline of her chemise.

"You can make me stop right here," he offer[ ]
huskily, his eyes glittering with a hot, feral light. "G[ ]
in, and I'll take you over into the bushes so they ca[ ]
see!"

"I won't let you do this!" Jessie countered with[ ]
proud defiance that made him feel a begrudg[ ]
admiration for her. "I'll never surrender to you, C[ ]
Hagan! If you had any decency at all, you'd—"

"Have it your own way, then!" he bit out. He w[ ]
goaded on by the boisterous encouragement of his men [ ]
strip her. His fingers delved beneath the neckline of h[ ]
chemise, then took hold to yank it downward. T[ ]
thought of baring her breasts made his eyes gleam wi[ ]
anticipation.

In spite of the throbbing pain in her arm, Jessie st[ ]
refused to admit defeat. She raised her free hand a[ ]
slapped Cole as hard as she could.

"Why you—" he muttered between tightly clench[ ]
teeth, breaking off and growing visibly enraged as [ ]
rubbed at the stinging bright red mark on his fac[ ]
"You've settled your own fate!"

She gasped sharply when he suddenly flung her dow[ ]
on the cold, hard ground and drew his gun from t[ ]
holster buckled low on his hips. Her eyes grew ve[ ]
round, and she felt a shiver of very real fear run th[ ]
length of her spine. *Dear God, did he mean to kill her[ ]*

"Take off your clothes!" he ordered.

432

"No!" she cried breathlessly, shaking her head in a frantic denial. With slow deliberateness, Cole pulled back the hammer.

"Do it, damn you, or I'll put a bullet right between those pretty green eyes of yours!" It was difficult to tell if he meant it, for his lips were curled into a smile of malicious amusement, as though he were merely toying with her again.

"Now hold on a minute, Hagan," the older man standing with the others felt compelled to intervene at this point. "I'm not against you having your fun, but I can't stand by and let you kill her."

"If you don't want her no more," jeered another, "I'll sure as hell take her!"

Jessie had pulled herself up into a sitting position, her gaze locked with Cole's as she clutched the ripped bodice of her blouse against her thinly covered breasts. Though virtually paralyzed with fear, she was still capable of resistance. It was instinctive; everything she held dear, everything she believed and felt, made it impossible for her to surrender to what this man was demanding of her. At that moment, she realized the utter hopelessness of her situation. And yet she could not give in. *Ben* . . .

Cole glimpsed the steadfast determination in her eyes. He hesitated, wavering between admiration for her courage and white-hot fury for her defiance. Growling another curse, he seized her arm and jerked her back to her feet.

"No woman's ever got the better of me, and I don't aim to let you be the first!" he hissed furiously.

Before she knew what he had intended, he holstered his gun again and withdrew the knife concealed within his boot. Jessie abruptly ceased her struggles and caught her breath, the color draining from her face as she watched him brandish the knife before her. Its cold steel glinted dully in the firelight.

433

Cole pressed the tip of the blade against the holl[ow] between her breasts. She made a desperate attempt [to] pull away, but his hand shot out to grasp the neckline [of] her chemise. In one swift motion, he brought the bla[de] ripping upward. The edges of the parted fabric fell ope[n] exposing the satiny, rounded flesh beneath.

The onlookers grew quiet now. Their eyes filled wi[th] unbridled lust as they gazed upon Jessie's naked breas[ts.] Recovering from the initial shock of Cole's actions, s[he] snatched at the torn garment to cover herself. But it w[as] too late. Her wide, horrified gaze swept over the grim[,] purposeful faces of the men who had begun movi[ng] slowly toward the spot where their leader held her.

"Get on with it, Hagan," one of them prodded in a lo[w,] tight voice.

"Show us the rest!"

"Strip her, damn it! Strip her and let us have a look [at] what else she's hidin' under them clothes!"

To Jessie, they seemed like a pack of wolves closing [in] on their prey. She strained against Cole's brutal grip, h[er] eyes filling with tears of bitter defeat as the mercenar[ies] bore down on her. *Please, God, no! No!* she scream[ed] inwardly. She thought of Ben, her heart crying out [for] him once more as panic threatened to overwhelm he[r.]

A strange sound rose in the night. Suddenly, one of t[he] men gave a strangled cry of pain and fell to his knees [on] the ground. The others spun about to see that an Apac[he] arrow was imbedded in the flesh of his shoulder.

"Indians!" breathed several of the men in terrifi[ed] unison. That one word struck fear in the hearts of eve[ry] one of them, but they were given no time to ponder i[ts] significance.

Another arrow sliced through the cold air to bury itse[lf] in the center of the older man's back. Already dead, [he] crumpled into a lifeless heap beside the fire.

"The fire! Get the fire, damn it!" Hagan ordered. [He]

anked Jessie up in front of him and drew his gun again,
is gaze shifting frantically all about through the
arkness in a futile attempt to spot the Indians.

The other men drew their guns now as well. Some of
hem hastened to kick dirt over the flames, aware just as
ole was that they were all easy targets with the fire's
low lighting them.

Two more arrows found their marks, sending their
ictims sprawling in the dirt. At that point, Cole and the
emaining men began shooting randomly into the starlit
arkness, the blazing din of their gunfire thrown back
ith near-deafening fury by the canyon's walls.

"Where are they, damn it?" shouted the young man
ith the pockmarked face. He spun this way and that in
errified indecision, wasting his bullets as he finger
erked on the trigger again and again. "Indians ain't
upposed to attack at night! Hagan said we'd be safe at
ight!"

"Take cover behind the rocks!" someone else yelled.

Still shooting, they made a frenzied dash for the
oulders beside the river. Except for Cole Hagan. His arm
lamping about Jessie's waist, he used her body as a
hield while he headed toward the horse he had left tied
o a tree on the edge of the clearing.

"Do as I say or neither one of us will get out of this
live!" he snarled close to her ear.

His arm was cutting off her breath, so that she could
ffer no resistance as he literally dragged her across the
learing. Strangely enough, no arrows came their way.
essie dazedly wondered if it was Gray Wolf and his band
ho were attacking. Her heart filled with renewed hope,
or she could not help but prefer captivity among the
paches Ben knew so well to being Cole Hagan's
risoner.

Reaching the horse, Cole unlooped the reins from
bout the tree. The animal, frightened by the gunfire,

snorted nervously and tossed its head, but its owner ga
a vicious jerk on the reins and told Jessie to mount u
When she did not obey, he jabbed the end of his gun in
the soft flesh of her side.

"Do you want to know what Indians do to whi
women?" he ground out. "Chandler might have sav
your skin before, but not this time! Now mount up or I
damn well leave you to those—"

"Hold it right there, Hagan!"

Jessie's heart leapt at the sound of the familiar dee
timbred voice. *Ben! He had come for her!* Her ey
desperately searched for him in the surrounding dar
ness.

"Chandler?" His name broke from Cole's lips in
strident whisper of disbelief.

"Let her go, Hagan!" Ben commanded, his tone one
barely controlled fury. His blue eyes were full of a sava
gleam as they moved over Jessie and her captor. "Relea
her and you'll go free!"

"That's a lie, Chandler! We both know I'm a dead ma
if I let her go!" yelled Cole. His dark predatory ga
followed the direction of the other man's voice as h
fingers tensed in anticipation about the gun he still he
against Jessie's side.

Ben finally emerged from the concealing darkness
the trees just ahead. Jessie was flooded with profound jo
and relief at the sight of his beloved features, but h
happiness at seeing him was swiftly replaced by fear fo
his life. She knew the gunslinger would not hesitate t
kill him.

"Ben, no!" she cried out hoarsely, then drew in
sharp, ragged breath as Cole jabbed the gun cruelly int
her soft flesh again. He clutched the reins in the sam
hand that was gripping her arm, his fingers bruising he
and leaving the imprint of the narrow leather straps upo
her skin.

"She's coming with me, Chandler!" he declared, his voice rasping out above the sound of the continuing gunfire in the near distance. "Make one move to stop me, you son of a bitch, and I'll put a bullet in her!"

"She'll only slow you down," said Ben. His own voice was full of deadly calm. "You won't have a chance with her along."

He could not fire at Hagan; even if he got off a clean shot, there was still the danger of the other man pulling the trigger. Burning with vengeful rage, he could do nothing more for the moment than stall for time while his mind raced to think of a way to save Jessie. *Jessie . . . God help the bastard who had dared to take the woman he loved!*

"The Apaches will be hot on your trail, Hagan," Ben told him, his smoldering gaze fastened on the gunslinger's face. "You'll never get out of this canyon alive."

"Don't try to follow us!" was Cole's only response.

He suddenly released Jessie's arm and gave another jerk of the reins. The horse moved forward, blocking them from Ben's view. Cole wasted no time. He grabbed Jessie and tossed her up into the saddle, then swung up behind her. Keeping the gun positioned threateningly at her side, he cast Ben a smile of malevolent triumph.

"See you in hell, Chandler!" he proclaimed with a sneer. He spurred the horse into action, its hooves flying across the cold ground toward the head of the canyon.

Jessie cast a look back over her shoulder at Ben, her eyes full of mingled fear and love and heartache. She could not believe that fate could be so cruel as to part her from him now. . . .

Suddenly, a figure came hurtling out of the darkness toward the two riders. Jessie, clutching the saddlehorn with all her might, felt her captor being torn from the saddle behind her. She instinctively grabbed at the reins to slow the horse's frantic gallop as Cole was sent crashing to the ground by the unknown assailant.

437

Within seconds, she had brought the animal to a halt a
reined about, then saw that it was a tall, powerfully bu
Indian who had come to her aid.

"*Gray Wolf!*" she whispered, her eyes round wi
incredulity.

Still lying on the ground where he had fallen, Co
Hagan was not yet beaten. He brought his booted fo
sweeping against the Apache's legs just as Gray Wolf w
preparing to plunge a knife in his throat. Gray Wo
tumbled downward, but quickly recovered his balan
and stood again.

Cole had by now lunged forward to retrieve the gun
had dropped. He rolled onto his back and took aim at t
Indian.

"Come on, you red-skinned bastard!" he taunted, l
eyes glittering with hatred as he cocked the hamme
"Come on, damn you!"

There was no trace of fear in the Apache's steady ga
In fact, his lips curved into a faint, mocking smile.

"No, Hagan, don't!" screamed Jessie, watching
horror as the gunslinger prepared to kill the man who h
once been her enemy.

A shot rang out. But it was not Gray Wolf who gasp
in horrified disbelief as the life drained from his body;
was Cole Hagan.

Jessie's eyes flew to where Ben stood with his Colt st
aimed at Hagan. The bullet he had fired was now lodg
deep within the other man's heart. The gunslinger
features were contorted gruesomely in death as he lay
Gray Wolf's feet.

"Ben!" Jessie started toward him at last, only to be m
more than halfway. He swept her up against him, h
strong arms holding her close as her legs threatened
give way beneath her.

"Jessamyn!" he murmured, his deep voice brimmin
with raw emotion. "Dear God, I nearly went out of m

438

nd when I heard you'd been taken!"

"Oh, Ben, I—I love you so much! I could not bear the
ought of never seeing you again!" she choked out, the
ars coursing down her beautiful face now.

"I love you, Jessamyn!" he whispered hoarsely. "By
mn, Hagan wouldn't have gotten far!"

"How did—did you know where to find me?"

"Gray Wolf told me. His men spotted you with Hagan
d the others when they rode into the canyon. He got to
e ranch just after the twins arrived home and told me
at had happened."

"But why did he risk his own life to—"

"Because he's a man with a peculiar sense of honor. It
ems he felt he owed me something for the cattle I
anged for his men to *steal*. And we shared a common
emy—the company. These men were known to the
aches, Jessamyn. Thank God for that," he added, his
ms tightening about her as though he would never let
r go.

The swift and furious battle ended with Cole Hagan's
ath. The few gunmen who were still alive surrendered
en they realized that it was Ben Chandler who
manded they throw down their weapons. Relieved it
s not the Apaches who would be deciding their fate,
ey offered no further resistance as they mounted up for
e ride back to Cimarron.

Ben and Jessie moved to speak to Gray Wolf while the
ners prepared to leave. The tall Apache leader stood
side the river, his dark, fathomless gaze observing the
proach of the man who had just saved his life and the
man he had once intended to make his own.

"Thank you, Gray Wolf," Jessie told him earnestly.
hank you for helping us."

"She speaks for the both of us," said Ben, his own
atures solemn. "I owe you a debt that can never be
aid."

"There are no debts between us now, Chandler," G[...]
Wolf insisted quietly.

As always, their gazes met and locked in sil[...]
understanding. It was an understanding devoid of t[...]
enmity that had filled their hearts these past seven yea[...]
The bond they had once shared could never [...]
completely forged again, and yet neither could it [...]
completely broken.

Ben rode homeward with Jessie held lovingly agai[...]
him. The Apaches would provide an escort as far as t[...]
town's outer boundaries, then would head back to t[...]
mountains where they would be safe, at least for a tim[...]
from the vengeance of those who would see them de[...]

"What about the children?" Jessie asked, her emer[...]
gaze clouding with renewed worriment when she recall[...]
the fear on her students' faces. "Are they—"

"They're all safe," Ben assured her. "They'll [...]
relieved to hear you're all right. James and Hannah we[...]
convinced you'd find a way to escape," he added with[...]
faint smile of irony.

"Oh, Ben, they were so terribly frightened wh[...]
Hagan burst in and took me away!"

"I know. But it's over with now, Jessamyn. Hagan w[...]
never torment anyone again."

"Is the danger truly past? I mean, what about t[...]
company and its—"

"You need have no further worries on that score," [...]
told her grimly. "The troops will arrive tomorrow. A[...]
now that we've got these men to testify how they we[...]
paid to terrorize the settlers, there won't be any mo[...]
outbreaks of violence. No, Jessamyn," he concluded, h[...]
deep blue eyes glowing with all the love in his heart, "y[...]
don't have to concern yourself with the company a[...]
longer. Nothing will ever part us again, wildcat."

Jessie felt tears gathering in her eyes at the sound [...]
his endearment, and she knew his promise to be tru[...]

Twenty-One

ne year later . . .

"Jessamyn?" whispered Ben. His handsome head ppeared around the edge of the door as he peered into e sun-filled warmth of the room.

"You may come in, dearest husband and father," ssie granted with a soft laugh. She cradled the tiny undle of humanity in her arms and shifted farther pward against the pillows. "Your new son happens to be eeping at the moment, but I suspect he will be awake nd demanding his dinner very shortly."

"Have I told you lately, Mrs. Chandler, how beautiful ou are?" Ben remarked in a low, splendidly resonant ne. He paused beside the big brass bed, his eyes irtually devouring the sight of his radiant young wife.

Her luxuriant golden curls tumbled down about her ace and shoulders, her eyes were shining softly, and here was a becoming color to her cheeks. Only hours arlier, she had endured the pain of childbirth, and et the memory of it was already beginning to fade in the ght of the joy that filled her heart.

"Oh, Ben, I—I never thought I could know such appiness!" she sighed, her gaze shifting from his be-

441

loved face to that of their son's. "I can already tell he i
a true Chandler. There is a look of determination an
stubbornness about him," she teased affectionately
"Heaven help the woman who tries to tame him!"

"Or any man who attempts to do the same to th
Chandler women."

"I haven't the faintest notion what you mean. Why
Hannah and I are sweet, biddable creatures who—"

"Sweet, yes. Biddable, never." He cast her a tenderly
crooked smile that made her grow warm all over. "S
then, wildcat, you've decided you won't mind not going
back to the school after all?"

"I'll have more than enough to keep me occupied at
home," she allowed, her eyes sparkling up at him. "And
besides, I count myself fortunate that I was able to
complete the year. Lissa will be the perfect replacement—
at least until she and Curly have a child of their own."

"I think Horace and the other members of the board
finally realized the advantages of having a teacher who's
from around here."

"Well, I am certainly glad they did not realize it
sooner," she proclaimed, heaving another sigh of
contentment. "Otherwise, I never would have left St.
Louis."

A knock sounded at the door Ben had just closed
behind him. He went to answer it, his mouth curling into
another smile when he saw that it was James and Hannah
who stood nearly bursting with excitement in the
hallway.

"Can we come in now, Papa?" pleaded Hannah.

"Aunt Martha said it might be all right, so long as we
don't get too close to the baby!" James hastened to point
out, his own lively blue eyes brimming with an appeal.
"And Uncle William wants us to tell him who the baby
looks like!"

Ben opened the door wider and cautioned them not to

442

too loud. They entered the room with their gazes
de and full of childish awe for the miracle that had
fted them with a new brother.

"Hello, my loves," Jessie greeted them warmly. "You
ay come closer. He's sleeping right now, but I'm sure he
ouldn't mind if you wanted to have a good look at him."

"Gosh!" breathed James. "He's awfully little, isn't
?"

"Babies are supposed to be little," Hannah informed
m quite solemnly.

"When will he be big enough to play?" was one of
mes's first concerns.

"Not for a long time yet, I'm afraid," replied Jessie.
But he'll need lots of attention, and I'm counting on the
vo of you to lend me a hand."

"Do you—do you think it's all right if we call you
other now?" Hannah asked unexpectedly. "After all,
at's what *he's* going to call you, and I don't think he'd
ke it if we called you something different."

Jessie's eyes flew to Ben. His blue eyes twinkled down
her, and her own eyes filled with sudden tears. She
oked back to the twins, giving silent heartfelt thanks
r the fact that her happiness was now complete.

"I would like that very much, Hannah," she answered
ther tremulously, then told her, "You and James will
ave to help us choose a name for your new brother, you
ow. Indeed, he cannot continue dwelling upon this
rth while being referred to as simply *the baby!*"

"Why don't we name him after Papa?" the little girl
ggested.

"Why, that's an excellent idea!" She turned to the
her twin, who was staring at the baby in rapt attention.
What do you think, James?"

"He doesn't look much like a *Ben* to me."

"He does so!" argued Hannah. "That is *precisely* what
e looks like!"

443

"Well, *I* think he looks like a—a—" his voice trail
away as he became lost deep in thought. His fa
brightened moments later, and he declared triumphant!
"A *Curly!*"

That precipitated another good-natured argume
between the twins, which Ben finally put a stop to l
announcing it was time they were running along. The
each gave Jessie a quick kiss, then hurried from the roo
to tell their Aunt Martha and her new husband what the
had learned about little *Ben* or *Curly.*

"I know whom I should like to name him after," Jess
remarked once she and her husband were alone with th
baby once more, "but it would hardly be appropriate.

"Who?" asked Ben, taking a seat on the edge of th
bed.

"Gray Wolf," she answered. "If not for him, I woul
not be here now."

"True." A wry smile played about his lips when h
added, "But somehow I can't imagine my son being calle
Gray Wolf the remainder of his life."

"Neither can I." Her silken brow creased into a sligh
troubled frown. "I wonder if he and his people will ge
the land they were promised."

"Time will tell," responded Ben, though the tone o
his voice was not hopeful. He purposefully turned the
subject back to happier circumstances. "It's been a yea
full of surprises, Jessamyn."

"Are you by any chance referring to the baby?" she
demanded with mock severity. "Because if you are, Ben
Chandler, I don't see how you can possibly claim him to
be a surprise!"

"I guess we did tempt fate a bit, didn't we?" he
drawled, his gaze alight with devilish amusement.

"Is that what you call it?" she retorted saucily.

"Call it whatever you like," he told her, his hand
gently smoothing a wayward curl from her forehead.

444

But rest assured, my angel-faced temptress, that I tend to keep on doing it every chance I get."

"Can I hold you to that promise?" whispered Jessie, her green eyes reflecting all the love in her heart.

"You can." To seal the bargain, he leaned forward and brushed her cheek with his warm lips. "I love you, Jessamyn."

"And I you, my dearest husband." She gave him a smile of incredible sweetness. "And I you."

SURRENDER YOUR HEART
TO CONSTANCE O'BANYON!

MOONTIDE EMBRACE (2182, $3
When Liberty Boudreaux's sister framed Judah Slaughter for r
der, the notorious privateer swore revenge. But when he abdu
the unsuspecting Liberty from a New Orleans masquerade ball,
brazen pirate had no idea he'd kidnapped the wrong Boudreau
unaware who it really was writhing beneath him, first in pro
then in ecstasy.

GOLDEN PARADISE (2007, $3
Beautiful Valentina Barrett knew she could never trust wea
Marquis Vincente as a husband. But in the guise of "Jordanna
veiled dancer at San Francisco's notorious Crystal Palace, Va
tina couldn't resist making the handsome Marquis her lover!

SAVAGE SUMMER (1922, $3.
When Morgan Prescott saw Sky Dancer standing out on a balco
his first thought was to climb up and carry the sultry vixen to
bed. But even as her violet eyes flashed defiance, repulsing
every advance, Morgan knew that nothing would stop him fr
branding the high-spirited beauty as his own!

SEPTEMBER MOON (1838;, $3.
Petite Cameron Madrid would never consent to allow arroga
Hunter Kingston to share her ranch's water supply. But the har
some landowner had decided to get his way through Camero
weakness for romance — winning her with searing kisses and slo
caresses, until she willingly gave in to anything Hunter wanted.

SAVAGE SPRING (1715, $3.9
Being pursued for a murder she did not commit, Alexandria di
guised herself as a boy, convincing handsome Taggert James
help her escape to Philadelphia. But even with danger doggi
their every step, the young woman could not ignore the raging d
sire that her virile Indian protector ignited in her blood!

*Available wherever paperbacks are sold, or order direct from tl
Publisher. Send cover price plus 50¢ per copy for mailing and ha
dling to Zebra Books, Dept. 2595, 475 Park Avenue South, Ne
York, N.Y. 10016. Residents of New York, New Jersey and Penr
sylvania must include sales tax. DO NOT SEND CASH.*